I0764523

CRYSTAL GATE

KARISA DELAY

Crystal Gate

Published by *Vendera Publishing*

Send all questions and comments to us via the contact page at:
www.venderapublishing.com

ISBN: 978-1-936307-34-0 (Hardcover)

Cover Art by: Silent Shudder | www.silentshudderphoto.com

Cover Formatting and Interior Layout by Scribe Freelance | www.scribefreelance.com

Published in the United States of America

This is dedicated to my loving husband and supportive family.

And a special thanks to my friends Sherry, Jenny, and Wanda, who believed in me along this journey.

PROLOGUE

GEORGE SAT AT A booth near the front entrance of the nearly empty diner. He peered over his shoulder as the waitress cleared tips from a table. The illuminated sign for lottery tickets blinked across the left side of his face as he watched her brush a strand of straw-colored hair away from her face.

You think she's pretty?

George pushed his plate to the middle of the table. The waitress looked up with a bright smile and approached.

"Did you want some dessert tonight, handsome?"

She called you handsome? She's never said that to you before.

George smelled cheap perfume and the lingering scent of cigarettes. He glanced up for a moment, took in her thick eyeliner and apricot cheeks, and quickly looked down, avoiding eye contact. "I'd like pecan pie, please."

"Anything else, sweetie?"

She called you sweetie.

"No."

She's flirting with you. You should talk to her—privately.

The waitress leaned in to pick up the plate, exposing her cleavage and a small unicorn tattoo on her right breast. As she reached for the plate, George grabbed her arm.

Her skin feels nice in your hands.

"I would like some milk with that, Sarah."

She jerked her arm back, and the plate crashed to the floor. A loud voice called out from the kitchen window.

"Everything is fine," Sarah said, but there was a quiver in her voice. "Just a broken plate."

As she put the broken pieces on a tray, George saw that her hands were trembling.

Don't feel guilty. You wanted to touch her body.

George was flushed and sweating, and his pulse raced. He felt the muscles in his neck begin to tighten as Sarah backed through the swinging door into the kitchen. A moment later, a tall bald man peered out through the window that looked into the kitchen and stared at George.

Get up, George.

George stood up, left some bills on the table, and hurried outside. He strode quickly toward the rows of parked semitrailers, away from the lights of the diner. His chest tightened as he inhaled the cool night air. He stepped behind a large trailer parked behind a blue semi truck and stopped to catch his breath. He peered around the corner of the trailer and saw the bald man from the diner standing at the front door scanning the lot. A moment later, he flipped the door sign to "Closed" and locked the door.

Talk to her. Take her back to your place.

George closed his eyes and listened to the sound of his own breathing.

Her vehicle is parked behind the diner, and the doors are unlocked.

George began to walk.

There it is, George. Get in, George.

George lay on the floor in the back of Sarah's car, his breathing ragged again. His body trembled, and his vision was beginning to blur. He would just talk to her, that's all. No one would get hurt, right?

George heard footsteps approaching.

The crystal, George, find out where she hid the crystal.

CHAPTER ONE

ALEXIS ZEN WAS BORED. The gray walls of the classroom held more interest for her than the repetitious poem her English teacher was reading. Alexis blocked out the sound and stared out the window. The windowpanes were dirty and cloudy with age, and the day outside was as monochromatic as the inside. Alexis sighed and glanced around the room.

A dark-haired boy sitting in the front row was staring intently at the book on his desk, contemplating the redundancy of a raven tapping, tapping. *He is definitely going for 4.0 GPA*, Alexis thought.

Sitting behind the scholar was a skinny, freckle-faced boy sleeping with his eyes open. *Probably doesn't even know what GPA stands for*.

A pretty blonde was checking her compact to see if her makeup looked as good as it had five minutes earlier, and a brown-haired plain Jane was longing to be half as popular. In the back row, a couple of guys were mocking the facial expressions of the English teacher, Miss Sharla, as she read the macabre words of the dead poet.

Her classmates were all so different, but all trying to find their place in the world. All trying to survive.

Alexis tried to pretend to be interested in the poem, but her thoughts wandered. It was a new day, at a new school, with kids she had never met before. So far, the day was a success, and a new memory was beginning to replace the old.

"What do you feel as you hear this poem?"

The question was directed to Alexis, putting an end to her daydreaming. "I feel the lingering shadows of loss hiding as the raven knocks at the door."

"Do you not like this poem?"

"No."

"Why not, Alexis?"

"This isn't the first use of a talking raven in literature, but I find this version to create the precedent for the supernatural messengers of death."

"Do you fear death?"

"No."

"What do you fear?"

This gave Alexis pause. Her mind wouldn't register the question.

"Alexis?"

She felt her heart beating in her chest, and the voice was ringing in her ear.

"Alexis?"

What am I afraid of?

"Alexis?"

No one can hurt me here.

"... 3 ... 2 ... 1 ... Alexis?"

Alexis opened her eyes. She was in Dr. Asael's office, undergoing a session of hypnosis. She took a moment to synchronize her thoughts with her body before she sat up. It felt as if she'd been out for only seconds, but the leather chaise felt warm where she had lain on it.

"What did I talk about today?"

"You went back twelve years again. You can't seem to get past that time in your life. What are you blocking, Alexis?"

Alexis was coming to him for answers, and so she found the question odd. "I don't know. Twelve years ago was when my mom divorced the second loser she married and we moved here."

The psychiatrist looked down at his notes. "You've dealt with the horrible things he did to you. There's something else buried deep inside that vault of yours. We need to focus on unlocking it. I would like to see you back here next week."

"I'll check my work schedule to see when I can come in."

"Talk to Mary to schedule it."

Alexis waited for him to look at her, but his eyes never wavered from his notepad. "Do you ever have weekend appointments?" she asked.

He glanced up, the hint of a smile tugging at his mouth. "I'll stay late or come in early if you need me to, just let Mary know your availability." He went back to his yellow legal pad.

Alexis stopped at the front desk and peeked down at her phone to check the time. "Oh, Mary, I'm late for dinner with friends, can I call you in the morning with my schedule to make next week's appointment?"

The receptionist smiled and said, "Sure thing, sweetie." Her Southern drawl sounded like a soft violin. "You have yourself a good night."

Night had fallen, and the parking lot was much darker than when Alexis had arrived an hour earlier. The only lighted pole fixture was more than thirty yards away, and Alexis hurried to find her car keys. She didn't fear the dark, but the thought that she might not be alone in the dark filled her with terror.

Alexis darted toward a sleek black sports car, pushing the button for her automatic starter as she went. She was eager to get inside the car, but she paused for a split second to admire it. It had taken a long time to attain such an expensive vehicle. It was a reward for her efforts to overcome her underprivileged past and gain her independence. She got in and took a deep breath, enjoying the smell of the ivory leather.

Doors locked. Headlights on. Alexis exhaled as she started to adjust her rearview mirror. She began to check her makeup but noticed that the parking lot was empty. She looked back and noticed Dr. Asael's office lights were off.

That was quick, I didn't even see them leave. Alexis shrugged off the thought. Her session had run late, and they might have been ready to leave. Their cars were probably parked behind the building.

"Okay, time for dinner with *friends*," Alexis said with a wry smile. She thought about the shortage of names in her social address book, but she wanted to get to Baba and Dzidzi's house before dinner was over and dessert all gone. She put it in drive and pulled out of the lot.

CHAPTER
TWO

IT WAS A twenty-minute drive out of the city to Alexis's grandparents' house, and she always took this time to reflect on the day, making sure she hadn't done something embarrassing or said anything offensive.

She took her right hand off the wheel and rummaged through her purse for her cell phone. She found it and pressed speed dial number four. She heard the sound of the phone ringing and then the recorded greeting, *You've reached the Zen residence*.

Alexis ended the call, pressed the five on her keypad, and waited for it to connect. She heard another recorded message. *Hello, you have reached Marcia. Leave me a message and I will return your call. If you would like to leave a call back number ...*

"Hi, Mom, it's Alexis, just calling to see what you were doing. I'm on my way to Baba's house, and I may not have service until I get off the top of the hill. Call me whenever. Talk to you later, Mom."

Alexis had already tried the rest of the people on her speed dial list, but no one had picked up. Apparently, everyone was busy. She gazed at the starlit sky and began to swerve.

Alexis focused on the road and turned on the CD player. The same disc had been in the player for months. She sang along with the words and hummed the soprano saxophone parts as her car slowly made it up the gravel hill toward her grandparents' house. Their home sat about three hundred yards from the road at the end of a long gravel driveway lined with faded plastic pink flamingos. The flamingos began as a joke between Alexis's grandmother and Aunt Nina, and they had became a Christmas gift ever since. As she pulled toward the house, her headlights caught the reflection of several taillights. She wondered who would be there so late.

She tried to recall the date, wondering how close it was to her birthday, but that was over a month away. Her family would have had to prepare long and hard to throw a surprise party not on the actual date, especially since Alexis was naturally suspicious and keenly attuned to odd questions or unexpected changes in plans. Most of her family thought she was borderline paranoid. She recognized most of the cars as belonging to aunts and uncles and saw her dad's truck parked near the back of the garden. She could hardly believe they had pulled off a surprise party without her discovering their plans.

Alexis stepped out into the humid air of the summer night and headed up the cobblestone path to the dimly lit backdoor. She walked up the steps to the back porch and glanced through the dining room windows. She didn't see anyone. They must know she'd see their cars. Would they really jump out from hiding and yell "Surprise"? Perhaps she'd top them by faking astonishment and pretending to pass out from the shock. She could practically hear them laughing at her antics.

Alexis opened the door and stepped into the narrow hallway of the mudroom, which led to the kitchen. She could hear someone talking and thought maybe they hadn't heard her pull into the driveway. When she turned left out of the kitchen toward her grandmother's sitting room, she could see everyone gathered. They didn't yell "Surprise" or even notice she was standing there. They were hugging or standing around with their focus on the elderly couple sitting on blue crushed velvet chairs along the back wall. Alexis realized that everyone in the room had been crying.

"Why is everyone sad?"

A few heads turned toward her. Her aunt Jo rose from the sofa and approached. "I'm sorry, honey, but we've had some bad news. About Aunt Sarah. She ... They found her in her car this morning, way off the road. Someone ... Alexis, someone killed her." Aunt Jo dabbed at her eyes and then gave Alexis a hug.

Alexis felt tears streaming down her face. She looked around for her mother, but Marcia wasn't in the room. A few moments later, the door to the back guest bathroom opened, and her mother, a beautiful middle-aged woman, came out. They made eye contact and walked quickly toward one another.

By the time the long night began to turn into day, only a few people remained at the house. The small group stood in the corner of the kitchen near the dishwasher, sharing stories. Soon after, everyone but Alexis and her mother had left to go home.

Alexis finished cleaning up the kitchen and grabbed a terrycloth towel to dry her hands before putting the dishes away. She closed the glass front of the cabinet and caught a glimpse of her own sorrow. The long champagne strands of her blonde hair couldn't hide the red around her eyes.

Her mother appeared in the glass. "How are you doing? Did you have a session tonight?"

Alexis turned toward her, trying to hold back her tears, trying to stay composed in front of her mother, who was trying to hold her own tears in check. It wasn't often that the two spoke, and Alexis welcomed any time they could share together.

"I'm doing well, thanks. I actually came here from Dr. Asael's office. You do understand that these sessions are merely a bureaucratic requirement for my job?"

"Yes, but you need it for other reasons."

Alexis cringed. She knew her mother was referring to a bad time in her life, when she began to fear the things lurking in the dark. She tried to stay matter-of-fact. "We haven't really delved into the past. He's doing the standard question-and-answer sessions. He seems to think we're making progress to get the clearance I need for my promotion."

For the first time since high school, Alexis had lied to her mother. Her sessions were neither typical nor standard. And she had no idea what her psychiatrist thought of her progress. He would typically say only, *You did well today* or *Let's pick this up more next week*. If he hadn't been the key to her next promotion, Alexis would have spoken her mind freely about his lack of personal skills and found someone else.

"I hope you decide to stick with it this time."

"I kind of have to, Mom, my job requires it. Besides, can you blame me for the last time? I was twelve, adults were acting weirdly sympathetic toward me, and the shrink was asking me where my mind went. Plus, my own mother blamed me."

They stood there for a moment staring at each other.

Alexis looked away and thought about why they were there so late. She decided to change the subject before her mother had a chance to explain her actions twelve years ago. "Do the police have any clues about what happened to Aunt Sarah?"

Her mother could no longer hold back the tears. "No, nothing. Not yet."

"When did it happen?" Alexis asked.

Marcia wiped away a tear. "The detective told us it was either late last night or early this morning. Sarah must have been on her way home from work from the truck stop. She's been working late and sometimes wouldn't get out of there until after 4 a.m. if she closed the restaurant."

"Do they think someone followed her from work?"

"They don't know. Hopefully, they'll know more tomorrow."

"Why didn't anyone call me?" Alexis had checked the most recent missed calls on her phone and discovered that no one had called since the morning before.

"I don't know, Alexis, I'm sure someone tried to call you."

"Please keep me updated."

"I will." Marcia pointed to the clock on the stove that was flashing *12:00*. "I wonder what time it is."

A meek voice came from the sitting room next to the kitchen. "It's three o'clock in the morning, ladies."

Alexis turned to see her grandmother sitting in a floral print armchair in the dimly lit dining area.

"Hey, Baba." Alexis walked to her and bent over to hug her. "I'm going to head home, but I'll come back first thing in the morning to help you with anything."

"Thank you, Alexis, that would be nice."

Her grandmother looked down at a small black journal in her lap. Alexis could see the worn pages filled entries her grandmother cherished. Alexis knew it had been a long day for her family, and tomorrow they would need strength. She headed home with much on her mind.

CHAPTER THREE

IT HAD BEEN three days since Alexis heard the news of her aunt's death. She still had several vacation days remaining and decided it was a good week to take them. Because of there being an autopsy, there was no viewing for Aunt Sarah. Instead, a beautiful memorial had been held the previous evening in the church gymnasium, and the gravesite service was for immediate family only. There were so many flowers, so many people, so many tears, and still so many unanswered questions.

Alexis needed the day to recover. She lay in bed, following the labyrinthine pattern stippled on the ceiling. A shaft of morning sunlight streamed in through the narrow gap between the closed curtains and warmed the tail of a silver-coated puppy lying at Alexis's feet.

Her cell phone rang and startled both of them.

"Hello."

"Good morning, Miss Zen, this is Mary from Dr. Asael's office. Just wanted to remind you that you never rescheduled your appointment."

"I'm sorry, Mary, I forgot. There was a death in my family."

"I'm so sorry to hear that, dear. Why don't I call you back?"

"That's all right. If you can hold, I'll look at my schedule right now." Alexis rummaged around her bedroom looking for her daily planner. She usually kept things where she could easily find them, but she had been so preoccupied with other matters that it took her a few moments. She finally found it and got back on the line with Mary.

"I only have tonight and tomorrow free until next week, so we might have to skip it since it hasn't been a full week yet."

"He can see you tonight," Mary replied.

"All right, what time?" Alexis listened for the latest available slot. "I'll take the last one and see you this evening. Thanks again, Mary."

Alexis got out of bed, threw on a robe, and moved into the kitchen. She was hungry. She opened the lid of her laptop to let it warm up and decided to scramble two egg whites. She got the eggs out of the refrigerator, dropped two pieces of potato bread into the toaster, and poured a bowl of puppy kibbles into a white porcelain bowl, which she set on the floor.

Alexis had eleven unread messages, including one from her bank with an alert. She logged onto her online banking. Her mind raced from the right side of her brain to the left, trying to recall all of her recent purchases and bills that had been paid. The page wouldn't load, so she dialed the bank's 24-hour customer service line.

As she listened to an endless series of recorded options, she thought about the person who had created the automated system and wondered if he had any idea what the words *customer service* actually meant.

Alexis began pushing buttons that were not on the main menu, listening to the little beeps, wondering what combination might confuse the mainframe and bring the entire system crashing down.

"Hi, this is Brad," a voice said from the other end. "May I have your account number, please?"

"Yes, hi, Brad. My account number is 4638595638."

"How can I help you, Ms. Zen?" Brad asked.

Alexis explained how she kept a tight budget and couldn't see how she could be overdrawn. "I tried viewing my online statement, but it wouldn't log me in, and after the third try it locked me out. I have direct deposit, and I was paid a few days ago."

Brad went away to check on the situation, and Alexis listened to what seemed like twenty minutes of silence. Brad finally came back on the line. "I think I found the problem, Ms. Zen. Our records show that funds were moved into your savings account."

"Savings account? I didn't know I had one. Well, can you move it back for me?" Alexis asked.

"No, I'm sorry, I can't. It looks like you set up a safe account with no cards or checks. Ms. Zen, you'll have to take care of it online or go to your local branch of the bank. This could have been a system error, so I do apologize."

"I can't take care of it online because I can't log in, remember? Can you reset my password?"

There was another long pause before he answered, "Okay, what would you like it to be?"

Alexis wasn't prepared to change her password, so she looked around the room for something she could remember. She spied a hardback book with worn edges lying on her desk with the words *Voynich Manuscript* on the spine. "Make it VOYNICH."

Alexis had to spell it three times before Brad understood it was a V and not a B or a D.

Alexis hung up and realized the day was already passing by fast and her "to do" list wasn't getting any shorter. She sighed and hoped the rest of the day would be better.

CHAPTER
FOUR

MARY HEARD YELLING and pounding on the window between the reception area and the waiting room, and she glanced up to see who was there. Before she could slide open the glass, one of the two young men standing there had shoved it open.

"Is the doc in, Mary?" one of them asked.

Mary was about to buzz Dr. Asael, when his voice came over the speaker.

"Mary, please send the two gentlemen back. Notify me if anyone cancels for the day or calls for me."

Mary rolled her eyes. No one ever called for Dr. Asael. Most of the incoming calls were from Mary's sister or mother wanting to gossip. The doctor rarely got personal calls, and most of his patients saw him only to have their mental stability approved so they could start or keep a job. As far as she knew, the doctor wasn't married and his relatives lived overseas.

She looked at the patient schedule. She had an hour before the next one was due to arrive, and she was starving. She retrieved a bag of microwave popcorn from a desk drawer and got up to put it in the microwave for two minutes and twenty seconds. The smell of popcorn filled the air as she waited. The microwave finally beeped, and she took out her treat.

Mary took her cell phone out of her purse and headed toward the front door. She usually used the back employee door, but whenever the doctor had nonscheduled visitors, Mary would go out the front so Dr. Asael wouldn't think she was eavesdropping. Plus, she wasn't allowed to leave the front area unattended.

Mary took a small index card she had scribbled her weekly lottery numbers on, folded it over twice, and placed it between the lock and the door leading to the reception area and Dr. Asael's office, which had to be electronically unlocked to allow entry from the waiting room. The facility was practically soundproof, and the one time she had forgotten to set the door, she yelled for an hour before Dr. Asael, who had been holed up in his office, heard her and let her in.

Mary stepped outside into the fresh air and squinted against the bright sun. She sat down on the small bench to the left of the front door, close to the alley. The bench had been put there so patients could smoke while they waited. Mary occasionally relaxed there to get a break from the beige walls and the oversized watercolor painting that stared at her all day from the waiting room.

She heard a car engine idling and looked around, but there were no idling vehicles in sight. She got up to peer down the long alley, which ran between Dr. Asael's office and Hamilton's Dry Cleaner, and saw a vehicle about two-thirds the way down the alley. The engine was running, and someone was sitting in the driver's seat. Mary frowned and returned to the bench.

Her curiosity trumped her better judgment, and she poked her head around the corner again. The car was small and platinum-colored, but it was too far away for Mary to see any numbers on the license plate.

Perhaps the driver was waiting for someone who was dropping off or picking up some drying cleaning. If not ... Mary went back inside to call the Hamiltons and satisfy her curiosity. No one answered, so she left a message on the Hamiltons' answering machine. When she hung up, she noticed that the patient lobby area was looking cluttered, and her own desk was littered with papers.

Mary headed out to the waiting area. She threw away an empty paper cup someone had left on the side table and tidied up the magazines that were scattered about. Two had fallen between the wall and a chair in the back corner, but Mary was too short to reach them. She wedged her pear-shaped body between the ficus tree and the chair and stretched her arm toward the magazines. As she grabbed one, she lost her balance and fell behind the chair. Mary felt her cheeks burning as she tried to extricate herself.

Someone touched her right shoulder, and Mary looked up to see Dr. Asael looking down at her, concern in his eyes.

"Mary, are you okay?" the doctor asked.

"Yes, I ... I mean, no, I ..." She started to focus and look around, and suddenly she felt her insides turn to ice water. "Why am I at my desk?"

"You fell asleep."

Her eyes widened and her mind raced. "No, I ... I was outside. I ...

"Mary if you need to go home ..."

"No, no, I'll be fine. I must have dozed off when I was staring at that crazy picture across from me." She smiled and tried to make a joke. "Self-hypnosis, I guess, huh?"

The doctor smiled, and Mary shuffled some papers, set them down neatly, and then opened a folder on her computer. She wanted to look busy so the doctor wouldn't think she needed a session with him.

"I need some time away from these fluorescent lights or something," she muttered. She pulled open a desk drawer and grabbed a chocolate caramel candy bar.

"Hey, Mary."

Mary jumped when she heard her name. She had been so preoccupied that she hadn't noticed Alexis come in.

"Oops, sorry, didn't mean to startle you," Alexis said. "I wanted to sign in, but I didn't see a log sheet anywhere."

Mary sighed and then gave Alexis a smile. "Ah, sweetie, it's okay. I just need to hit the restart button on this day." Mary looked through the clutter on her desk and found the clipboard with the sign-in sheet. "Here you go, just sign and confirm nothing has changed."

Alexis took the clipboard, signed her name, and handed it back to Mary. "Always know that if you survive today's trials you will find them to be tomorrow's laughs."

"No doubt, but I fell asleep on the job, so I'm a little frazzled right now," Mary said.

"I have something that will help unfrazzle you." Alexis pulled out her smart phone and went to the picture icon. "Look at my new baby boy."

"What? I didn't know you had a"—Mary took the cell phone and looked at the picture on the display—"oh, it's not a 'baby' baby. He's adorable. What kind of dog is he?"

"Weimaraner. I saw him at the pet store a few weeks ago, and it was love at first sight." Alexis glanced down at the image. "I'm glad he's not as hyper as the breed typically tends to be, but the tradeoff is that he barks at everything."

Mary's phone flashed and she raised her index finger and said, "Hold on a sec, Alexis."

"Sure thing."

Mary picked up the receiver. "Yes, she is. I'll send her back. No, no, I'm fine now, thanks." She hung up and looked at Alexis. "He's ready for you."

"Okay, thanks," Alexis said.

"Hey, by the way, what did you name your doggie?" Mary asked.

"His name is Oslonic, but I call him Oslo." Alexis put her phone back in her purse and went toward the door.

Mary pressed a button to buzz it open. "Where'd you pull that name from?"

Alexis stepped through the entrance but held the door open so she could answer. "It's the Polish word for protector."

CHAPTER FIVE

ALEXIS OPENED THE DOOR to Dr. Asael's office and stepped inside. "Good evening, Doctor Asael."

"Evening, Miss Zen. Are you ready to begin?"

"Sure. What's on for tonight? Hypnosis? Shock therapy? Water boarding?" Alexis smiled at her attempt at humor but got no response from the doctor. "Seriously, though, what are we doing?"

"Is there something you wanted to do tonight?"

Alexis resisted the urge to roll her eyes. Answering a question with another question, it was so typical of the man. "I want to do whatever it takes to get this clearance approved. I want to move forward with my promotion. The projects on my current level are complete, and I can't move forward without clearance. I do trust your judgment, so please do whatever you think will get me there."

"I sent a recommendation to the commander last week, so now it's up to him to grant more security clearance," the doctor replied, an unreadable expression on his face.

She felt her body sink. "No one from the base has called me."

"I tried to call you to let you know I was sending it through, but they said you had taken some personal days. Is everything okay?"

"I'm fine. I had a death in the family. I took time off to help out."

"Were you close to this relative?"

"Kind of, she was my—hey, wait a minute, you already sent the papers, and yet your office called today to set up an appointment. And I haven't heard from the commander. That means you must have ... Okay, fine, someone else can follow my project plans, no big deal. I can run samples the rest of my life."

"You won't be running samples for the rest of your life, Miss Zen. I have recommended you for the clearance, but you and I both know there is a lot in your mind that we need to uncover, which brings me to the reason you're here tonight."

Alexis was feeling a mixture of relief and confusion. "Please go on."

"I want to understand how you are blocking the dark parts of your life. This is the reason I want you to see me once a week instead of once a month, as required by the government."

Alexis, who had been standing during the conversation, walked to the large chocolate-brown leather chaise and sat down. She kicked off her shoes, crossed her legs, and leaned forward, elbows on her knees. "Let me see if I understand this—I'm a study subject *because* I have control of the past? I thought gaining control was the point."

The doctor got up from his usual seat and moved toward the desk in the back corner of the room, the first time he had done that in the three months Alexis had been seeing him, giving her a whole new perspective on the man. In the past, the doctor's thick black-rimmed glasses always seemed to obscure his face, and the room's dim lighting cast odd shadows and created a slightly eerie atmosphere, making it hard for Alexis to see who she was sharing her secrets with. Nor did she like waking up from hypnosis to all those shadows on the wall. Tonight, however, Alexis got a good look at the man who had been peering into her mind. She realized for the first time that he was good-looking, with wavy blond hair that blended to light brown at the hairline, a strong jaw, and smooth skin.

"I'm interested in knowing more about the life story of Alexis and how you reacted to things that happened in your past," the doctor said. "Typical shrink stuff."

Alexis was still fascinated by this new perspective on Dr. Asael. She couldn't help noticing his perfect posture and fit-looking physique as he stood in front of the large cherry desk. The doctor turned and reached over the desk to grab a pen and notepad from the top drawer and then headed back to his chair.

"As a matter of fact, this is purely a personal study," Dr. Asael said. "This won't affect your job."

"Personal study? I don't understand."

The doctor gave her a slight smile. "Don't worry, I won't be sending you a bill."

Alexis wasn't sure if she was shocked more by the smile, which she had never seen from him before, or his little jest, which was equally out of character.

"I guess this would be my pro-bono case for the quarter," he added.

"Can we find a better way than *personal study* to describe me? It sounds as though I'm a white rat in a cage with a number tag."

"Let's just say this is part of my personal investigation of a unique mind."

"Where do we begin?"

Dr. Asael was sitting with his leg crossed at a ninety-degree angle and his notepad ready. "I'd like to begin with your earliest childhood memories and work our way to where we are today. Not all tonight, of course. So, Alexis, tell me about your home life growing up."

For the next fifty-two minutes, Alexis described her Polish grandparents and how they were like second parents to her. She spoke of the amazing sense of peace that always filled their home when she was younger.

"You have told me that your father left when you were very young, but where was your mother during this time?" the doctor asked.

"I'm not sure if she was working a lot, or what really kept her from being around. I just remember my grandparents, mostly."

"These are your maternal grandparents, correct?"

"Yes."

"Have you asked your mother about those days?"

"No."

They talked more about the good days that Alexis remembered and ended the session on her positive recollections.

"That was a fine start," Dr. Asael said. "Let's remember to reschedule this time."

She saw a vague smile tugging at the corners of his mouth and realized he was making another mild joke. She decided she could get used to this version of the doctor.

She smiled and stood up. "I promise to do that before I leave."

The doctor stood. "Let me walk out with you."

Alexis made her appointment for the following Friday and left the office. She drove to the doggy-day-care kennel to pick up Oslo and then headed home, a ten-minute drive from the kennel. She pulled into the dimly lit parking space behind her apartment and switched off the engine. She was thinking about how long she'd sat at the bank that morning, all the running she had done for her grandmother, plus her own errands. It had been a long day, and she was glad to be home.

Her loft apartment was located above a vintage clothing store in a small suburb near Dayton, Ohio. A set of narrow wooden stairs at the back of the building led up to the apartment's only entrance.

Alexis counted the steps in her head while Oslo's long legs skipped a few to keep pace. She unlocked the door and stepped inside, and Oslo took off running. Alexis grinned. It wasn't unusual for him to run around crazy after a day at the kennel. She headed left toward the kitchen, realizing that she had eaten only once that day. Her single life didn't require gourmet meals or a lot of groceries, and most of her options were ready in less than five minutes in the microwave. She opened the refrigerator, expecting Oslo to come running back through the apartment.

"Oslo, here, boy," she called. "Oslo, where did you go?"

Alexis heard her cell phone vibrating from the counter where her purse and keys sat. She pulled the thin white cell phone from her purse and saw that the call was from her mother.

"Hey, mom, how are you?" Alexis leaned against the cold gold-flecked granite counter.

"I'm fine. I thought I would let you know they have a suspect." Marcia sounded relieved, but Alexis knew she still bore a heavy burden of sadness.

"Who is it?"

"The last person your Aunt Sarah waited on that night."

Alexis wondered why her grandma hadn't mentioned anything about it earlier that morning. "When did they catch the guy?"

"Yesterday. Today was his arraignment, but I couldn't bring myself to go. That's where Baba had to be all day, didn't she tell you?"

"No, but she has a lot going on right now. Do they think he followed her from work?"

"Can we talk about the details some other time, Alexis? I've had a long day. I just wanted to make sure you knew."

"Okay, sure."

Marcia sniffed and took a second before she continued. "Did you get all of Baba's bills taken care of today?"

"Yes. I just got home, but I need to go. I've got to find Oslo." Alexis was getting nervous that he wasn't barking.

"There aren't too many places he could go in that tiny apartment," Marcia pointed out.

"I know. He's probably got himself stuck in my bathroom. Thanks for calling, maybe we can talk more tomorrow."

Alexis was thankful that the police had found the person responsible for her aunt's death, and she hoped it would give her grandparents a sense of closure. It came as no surprise to Alexis that she was one of the last to hear the update on her aunt's assailant. It weighed on her mind, but she needed to focus on finding Oslo before she over-thought her level of importance to her mother.

The only bedroom in the apartment was located at the back, and the full bathroom was on the left side of the bedroom. Alexis called out to Oslo again as she walked out of the kitchen but didn't hear anything. She noticed that the bedroom light was on and the bathroom door was still standing open from when she left that morning.

"Oslo," she said, with less volume than before. Alexis was concerned that her puppy was stuck somewhere and couldn't bark. She closed her eyes and listened for any sound of movement.

All the lights went out. A chill ran down her spine as she felt for the light switch. She clicked it up and down, but there was no power. Her stomach tightened when she saw the large mercury light glaring in through the window of her bedroom. Only the lights in her apartment were out. Alexis tried to think—could she have blown all the fuses?

She continued toward the bedroom, but then every muscle fiber stiffened inside her body, and she felt the hair on her neck stand up. Something or someone was near. She smelled the odor of stale cherry cigars laced with vodka, heard the sound of a faint exhalation. Her heart was pounding and she was frozen with fear. She began to pray. *Please, please let me live.* Alexis heard the floor behind her creak. *If there is a God, please help me.*

CHAPTER SIX

SOMEWHERE ON THE edge of town, behind a remote strip mall, stood two slender men in dark suits. Cars rarely drove through the downscale neighborhood that surrounded the strip, so the lighting was poorly maintained. The two stood there as though they were waiting for someone. Neither spoke a word to the other.

From the east side of the building, near an alley, another man emerged from the shadows. He was taller and dressed more casually than the other two. He cleared his throat, drawing their attention. One of the two looked nervously at the other as they moved out of the dim light and approached the alley.

The tall man addressed them. "What is so urgent that you needed to see me right now?"

"We are certain of being seen ... tonight," one of them said.

His companion added, "In all these years, no one has seen us unless we wanted them to see us. How is this possible?"

"Perhaps someone only seemed to look in your direction but was really looking at something behind you," The tall man said. "You have a tendency to overreact, Azure."

"No, someone saw me," the man called Azure replied.

"And who do you think it was?"

Before they could answer, the tall man's phone rang. He retrieved it from a pocket and said to the other two, "Stay here while I take this call."

He turned and stepped away a few paces and picked up the call. The other two stood there mute, not daring to move.

"Do you need me there?" the tall man said into the phone. "All right, I think that's best. If you change your mind, I can be there in a few minutes." He ended the call and turned back to the two men in suits.

"Sir, we did not know it was possible for her to see us," Azure said. "Nothing about tonight was different."

The tall man turned to Azure's companion. "Cezar, how long has it been since this happened?"

"We came here at once, so approximately ten minutes," Cezar replied.

"Continue as planned. We will come back to this matter later. For now, since you may have been seen, it's best if you not stop to see me here or anywhere else for a while. This goes for everyone. See that this information filters through the ranks."

Azure and Cezar nodded and melted back into the night, leaving the taller man alone in the alley with his thoughts.

CHAPTER SEVEN

1:11 a.m. ALEXIS sat shivering in the corner of her bedroom.

3:16 a.m. *Do I call the police? Who would believe me? I need to forget.*

4:07 a.m. *Please help me forget.*

5:59 a.m. *I need to put this behind me.*

At 7:35 a.m., Alexis pulled into the far left lane at the light in front of Gate A of Wright-Patterson Air Force Base. Her head was spinning with thoughts of the previous night, and at times she wondered if she had imagined everything.

She caught some movement out of the corner of her eye and looked to her right. No more than fifteen yards away, twenty people were holding banners and signs and shouting at the cars that drove inside the gate.

"GOD IS IN CHURCH, NOT A LAB!"

Alexis smiled to herself. The protesters were at the wrong entrance. No one in this area would have a clue what they were protesting about.

Hoping a fresh start at work would clear her mind, Alexis turned left into the base and made a slight right before the guard shack. She parked in front of a small brown building. There were only ten other cars in the parking lot. Alexis figured no one in this area of the base would recognize her and hoped to avoid small talk with the people inside. After a deep breath and a slow exhalation, she checked her makeup and got out of the car.

Alexis stepped inside and saw several people in the waiting area. She looked around for a device to take a number and saw three computers to her right. A sign with bold red letters read "Sign In

Here." Alexis made her way to an available desktop. She sat down and moved the mouse to bring up the start screen.

Civilian ... Employee ... Area B. Alexis entered her information slowly and carefully. Typing fast was not one of her skills, and her job had never required it. She checked the screen one last time and hit Submit. Her name was called almost immediately.

Alexis walked to the counter and looked around, figuring she couldn't be next in line. "I'm sorry, did I enter something wrong?"

A female airman behind the counter smiled. "May I see your current ID, please?" The airman pulled a thin computer-like pad to the counter. "I also need you to place your hand here and hold it for five seconds, please."

Alexis showed her badge and driver's license and then put her hand on the scanner.

"Thank you," the airman said. "Please wait here."

This was new to Alexis. When she first got the job, she'd been escorted to a different building to fill out paperwork, provide fingerprints, and get her ID card. But a two-day-old message on her voicemail had instructed her to stop into Guest Services before heading to the lab. Alexis assumed that since her clearance level was changing, a supervisor would be meeting her, but it seemed as if she was on her own.

The airman returned with a small sealed envelope. As Alexis looked up from the envelope, she noticed the young female's nametag. "Thanks, Airman Wherry, hope you have a great day."

The petite airman nodded. "Thank you, ma'am, same to you."

Alexis turned and headed out the door. She hit the remote starter button and unlocked her car. She got in and sat for a minute, looking at the package in her lap. She pulled apart the seal and slid out a new ID, a parking pass, and a dosimeter—a radiation badge.

Alexis clipped the parking pass to her mirror and checked her eye makeup. She gave a start and a little gasp. For a split second, she thought she saw a dark figure in her backseat. But there was nothing there except her volleyball net and tennis rackets.

Alexis sat there a few minutes with her eyes closed, waiting for her heart to slow down. She pulled out of the parking lot and headed toward Area B, a quarter mile away on the other side of the base. She turned right into the secured checkpoint. This area was a bit different from most of the others. There were not only several armed guards but also three highly trained dogs standing watch. Each dog was trained to sniff out different hazardous materials, including radioactive and bomb-making materials. The dogs were also trained to attack on command.

The guard took her ID, scanned it, and handed it back with a nod.

After three right turns and a left, Alexis felt as if she must be circling back to the front gate. After ten minutes, she finally pulled into a parking area with a sign for the AFRL Wing, the Air Force Research Laboratory. The complex comprised eight large buildings, including two that resembled aircraft hangers left over from World War II. Five were long and rectangular, with huge bay doors on each side, but the main building was white and boasted a modern glass entrance. The front was marked Office for Scientific Research.

Alexis parked and checked her rearview mirror, hoping not to see what she thought she had seen earlier. With a sigh of relief, she grabbed her purse and badges and went forth to start the day. She headed inside and checked her personal items in with the airman assigned the front area. Once again, Alexis was required to show her ID badge.

"Miss Zen, you are to report to J. Mitchell in the lab on Level 6," the airman told her. He pointed down at the floor. "Level 6 is a sublevel."

"Yes, thank you," Alexis said, hoping she sounded as if she already knew who J. Mitchell was. She turned toward the elevator and pushed the faded red down button next to the eggshell-colored doors.

The elevator doors opened, and Alexis stepped in and joined a male passenger. She pressed the button for Level 6. Nothing happened. She tried again, with the same result.

"We're required to scan our ID badge over the sensor right there," the other passenger said, gesturing toward a scanner just above the buttons.

Alexis scanned her badge, and Level 6 lit up. The doors slid closed. "Thank you," she said, barely making eye contact.

"You must be Alexis, the Level 6 newbie. Welcome aboard, Alexis."

This time Alexis made eye contact. "I'm sorry, how would you know my name?"

"For starters, Level 6 is the only lab that requires ID scans, and since you didn't know that, I figured you were new."

He stepped toward the scanner and waved his badge past it. She caught a faint scent of cedar, aftershave maybe, or perhaps shampoo. He looked at Alexis and smiled. "I'm also assigned to that floor. As for knowing your name, I saw it on your ID."

"Oh. Yeah." Alexis felt like an idiot. She always looked at nametags, so it should have been her first assumption.

The man stepped to the back of the car. "My name is James, by the way."

James was a tall man, about her age, with dark brown hair. He flashed a friendly smile, which reminded Alexis not to stare at the perfect symmetry of his face.

"I guess I never knew there were so many floors."

"I'm pretty sure there are several things we don't know about this base."

Alexis wondered if he was referring to the rumored conspiracies supposedly connected to Hanger 18.

Alexis returned her thoughts to getting a higher clearance level. This meant having access to more information and possibly more equipment. She had asked for a specific environment for her work but hadn't realized that meant changing floors and going several levels below ground.

As the elevator slowed, Alexis apologized to her elevator mate. "Sorry if I sounded rude, I wasn't expecting ..."

He interrupted her before the elevator doors opened. "Don't worry, I didn't think twice about it. You'll have to scan your ID again as well as your hand at the big metal door." The elevator door opened and James pointed to a huge vault door to the left of the elevator.

Alexis stepped out and the door began to close. She stopped the door with her hand. "Are you not getting off here?"

"No, actually I was going up to the top level to get a new lab coat when you got on. I wanted to make sure you made it down. I'll see you soon. You're in Section 11."

Alexis continued toward the vault door and scanned her hand and ID badge. She heard the sharp click of a door unlocking and opened it. Cool air wafted out, but it left a sterile taste in her throat. Alexis crossed the threshold and glanced around. A vast space loomed before her. She stepped onto a metal catwalk and stared over the edge. The catwalk, at least forty feet high, wrapped the entire perimeter, with stairs every sixty feet, and the place was divided into about twenty different rooms. Most of them were small transparent spaces with different pieces of equipment, and a few were just doors along the side wall. Two rooms at the far end seemed to be as grand as one of the aircraft hangers outside. A square space sat alone beneath the catwalk. Alexis saw that there were two spaces within the one, each with its own door.

Alexis was eager to discover which part of this elaborate mousetrap was Room 11, but from where she stood she couldn't read anything on the door panels. Alexis was accustomed to working in windowless offices, but she didn't want to think about how far underground she was at that moment.

She heard the large door opening above and figured the morning rush was about to descend. She scrambled down the stairs to find her space. She began with the smaller spaces along the wall, but they were marked by letters instead of numbers. As Alexis had noticed from the catwalk, there were two doors to the mysterious solid room. They both were marked with the number 11.

After several of her new co-workers passed by, she spotted James, the man on the elevator. He was carrying a white lab coat and a thin black laptop. She flashed a smile. “Finally a familiar face. Can you please direct me to J. Mitchell. I’m supposed to report to him.”

“That would be me,” he said. “I didn’t want to make you nervous during our initial contact by telling you I was your boss, plus I wanted you to freely explore the facility while I grabbed your lab coat and orientation paperwork. Welcome to Level 6, Alexis.”

CHAPTER EIGHT

In the alley behind a vintage clothing store, two buildings down from where Alexis lived, a local police officer was putting up yellow caution tape while three other officers kept the curious away from the crime scene. Alongside the Dumpster behind an old furniture store were several empty boxes, a lot of outdated store flyers, and a body. The dead man's eyes were open and fully dilated, and his skin was pale, as if he were carved from slab of marble.

"You think he was an albino?" Detective Alan Carter asked his partner, Detective Stuart Lindsay.

"I don't know, but he does look a little overdressed for this time of year."

Detective Carter put on a pair of latex gloves. "I wonder if he was in the process of robbing someone. Why else would he wear long pants and a hoodie in the middle of summer? And where's his other shoe?"

Detective Lindsay waved over a uniformed officer who had been standing by one of the patrol cars. "Officer Adkins, I need you to begin a canvass of the area. Look for any of his personal effects, or possibly stolen items. Check the neighboring stores and try to find witnesses who may have seen or heard something."

"And try to find the vic's other shoe." Detective Carter was still combing the area near the body.

"Yes, sir." The officer turned to walk away.

"Hey, Adkins. Radio Dispatch to see if there were any calls about break-ins in this area."

The patrol officer nodded and headed to his car.

Lindsay laughed. "Poor guy. I'll be surprised if he remembers all that."

"Yeah." Carter was looking down at his cell phone, moving it around to block it from the sun. "Just got a text. Apparently the coroner has a lot of dead people to pick up. He said it's going to be an hour before he can get here."

"Let's go talk to the furniture store owners," Lindsay said.

As the detectives moved away from the body, two young patrol officers unfolded a stiff blue tarp and laid it over the area where the body was found. Detectives Carter and Lindsay stepped toward the small group of people who were behind the caution tape. Among them were several local store owners, all looking unhappy, a few people who happened to be walking by with their dogs, and a couple of men watching for no apparent reason other than morbid curiosity.

"Are you the Fuchellies?" Carter asked the couple who were standing to the left rear of the building.

The two nodded, disbelief written on their faces.

"I'm Detective Carter, and this is my partner, Detective Lindsay. Who found the body?"

Mr. Fuchellie cleared his throat. "I did."

"How did you happen to find him?"

"Well, my wife has a brother, Charlie, who works for the city, and he always gives us a shout from the back door on pickup days. When I realized we hadn't heard from him all day, I came out to see if he had picked up the trash without us hearing anything. That's when I saw the body."

"Have you ever seen this man?" Detective Lindsay asked.

"No, not that we can recall. I didn't really stare at his face. It was strange enough finding him. Right after I saw him lying here, I went back inside, and my wife called you guys."

Detective Carter nodded. "We'll call you if we have any more questions, and we may stop around once we have a better picture of his face to see if you recognize him."

"I'll give you one of our cards," Mr. Fuchellie said. "It has the store number and our cell numbers on it."

Detective Carter exchanged the card for one of his own. "If you think of anything, please call me."

Mr. Fuchellie turned with his wife and walked toward the front of their store. The detectives went in the opposite direction and questioned the other people standing around, but no one had any information.

Detective Carter looked down at his phone. "It's after five."

"Yeah?"

"I received that text from the coroner about quarter till four. He said an hour."

Detective Lindsay was flipping through his notes. "I guess that means we wait."

The crime scene was overflowing with forensic specialists taking samples and snapping pictures of the area near the Dumpster. The two detectives fanned out, looking for anything that could help make sense of what led to the death of the guy lying under the tarp.

One of the young investigators called out in the direction of the detectives. "Hey, Lindsay, take a look at this."

Lindsay and Carter walked over to the victim. "What you got there, Dominic?" Lindsay said.

"Your victim has a couple of battle scars," Dominic said as he pointed to scratch marks on the underside of the dead man's jaw. "Watch where you step, he's lying in a puddle of something."

Detective Lindsay wrinkled his nose and sniffed the air. "It's probably where he ..."

The tech shook his head. "It's not human waste. I think it's water."

"Something probably spilled out of the Dumpster." Detective Carter crouched down closer to the body.

Dominic gestured toward the area around the body. "At first I thought it might be a spilled bottle of water, but there's no sign of originated bottle."

"Maybe the downspout leaked," Lindsay suggested.

"Good theory, but it hasn't rained for weeks. It's probably nothing. I only mentioned it so you wouldn't step in it." Dominic turned and began cataloging items near the body.

Detective Carter patted Dominic on the back. "Keep me posted."

"Sure thing."

CHAPTER NINE

"Hi, Mom. Just calling to tell you about my day," Alexis said into the cell phone. "Especially since today is one of the few I'll ever be able to talk about. Anyway, call me later after you get this message."

Alexis ended the call, set the phone in one of the cup holders in the center console, and focused on the road ahead. She was relieved to have survived her first day, which had been filled with signing her name to confirm that she agreed to all security guidelines, walking what must have been miles to become familiar with the restricted areas, and meeting new coworkers. The activity had made it easier for Alexis to block unwanted emotions from the front of her mind, but with those distractions gone, her thoughts turned to the events of the night before. That's when she realized she didn't want to spend the coming night alone.

Alexis picked up the phone and hit 9 on her speed dialing, praying that Adrianna would pick up.

"Hey, Alexis, what's going on, girl?" a chipper voice squealed through the phone.

"Not much," Alexis said. "What about you, are you busy tonight?"

"Nope, I have no plans."

"Where's Audie?"

"Kentucky, on business. What about you?"

"I want to get Chinese and watch that movie you mentioned last week. Are you in?" Alexis heard the eagerness in her voice and tried to dial it back. "I understand if this is too last-minute."

"Not at all, it sounds perfect. Besides, Oslo probably misses me. I'll bring my PJs. Just in case we stay up late."

Alexis laughed, partly because she knew it was all but inevitable that they'd stay up late, mostly out of relief that she wouldn't be in her apartment alone.

She pulled into the side street perpendicular to her alley and gave a little gasp. Police vehicles lined both sides of the street, and a small group of people blocked the entrance to the alley. Alexis had to drive two blocks down and come in from the other side. She pulled into her parking space behind the clothing store, switched off her engine, and got out. She got Oslo out of the backseat and headed for the stairs leading up to her apartment, trying to keep anyone from behind the caution tape from noticing her.

She entered her apartment and locked the door. As Oslo made a break from his leash, Alexis began walking through the apartment, turning on every light and checking that all the windows were locked.

There was a knock at the door, startling Alexis. It was too early for Adrianna. Her heart pounding, she walked out of her bedroom and into the kitchen, staying out of the line of sight from the door, whose top half was glass. Scolding herself for not getting around to buying curtains for it, she picked up her purse from the counter and found her keys, which had a small canister of mace attached.

Still standing to the side of the door, Alexis called out, "Can I help you?"

"Fairborn Police Department. We'd like to ask you a few questions."

Alexis took a cautious step toward the door and saw a tall man with blond hair cut in a military style. He was wearing a gray suit. A dark-haired man in a navy suit, not as tall, stood just behind him. Alexis thought about the police cars in the alley and felt her muscles tighten. She knew she hadn't called the police the night before. At least she thought she knew.

"Ma'am?"

"Can I see your IDs?"

After the two detectives placed their badges against the window, Alexis released her grip on the mace, unlocked the door, and let them inside.

The blond detective introduced himself as Detective Carter and his partner as Detective Lindsay. Lindsay's chiseled, masculine features were a sharp contrast to Carter's soft, boyish face.

Detective Lindsay glanced around the kitchen and spotted the mace on the counter. "Everything all right, ma'am?"

"I don't often have unannounced guests, so when two men dressed in suits come knocking at my door near dark ... well you can understand my lack of excitement, Detective."

The men followed Alexis into the kitchen, where dishes were beginning to pile up and mail was carelessly scattered on the table. With her aunt's funeral keeping her busy most of the week, Alexis hadn't had time to worry about domestic details.

"What can I help you with?" Alexis asked, still trying to calm her nerves.

"Not sure if you noticed the commotion down at the end of the block, but a body was found by the Dumpster this afternoon," Detective Carter explained.

"Oh, no. I hope it wasn't anyone from the neighborhood."

Detective Lindsay pulled up a picture of the victim's face on his phone and handed it to Alexis, watching her closely as she looked. "Recognize him?"

Alexis felt a crawling sensation rise up the back of her neck. It was like reliving last night all over again, and she struggled to keep her emotions in check. "He doesn't look familiar."

"Sorry about the lousy image quality," Lindsay said. "I know there's a glare."

Alexis nodded. "It makes his skin look hypo-pigmented."

"If that's the same as albino, it isn't from the glare," Carter said. "That's how he looks."

Alexis couldn't stop thinking about the previous night. "Do you know what happened? I mean how he died?"

"That's for the medical examiner to figure out," Carter said. "There were no visible signs of foul play other than a couple of scratches." He seemed to be watching Alexis. "And they couldn't get an accurate liver temp since he was frozen."

Alexis frowned. "Frozen? In this heat?"

"We figure he was dumped there," Lindsay said. "Did you hear or see anything last night or this morning?"

Alexis wrinkled her brow and tried to appear thoughtful. "No, it was a pretty quiet night. Even Oslo was quiet."

Carter raised an eyebrow. "Your roommate?"

"My puppy." Alexis pointed to the wicker basket in the living room with a small silver-coated puppy nestled inside under a fluffy blue blanket. The detective went to the dog and reached out to pet him. Oslo let out a low growl.

"I wouldn't do that," Alexis said. "He only likes girls."

Detective Carter withdrew his hand, and Oslo resumed his nap.

An unpleasant thought occurred to Alexis. "Do you think he was there all night, and I drove right past him today?"

"It's highly unlikely he was there all day," Carter said.

There was a knock on the door.

"Expecting company?" Lindsay asked.

Alexis nodded and went to open the door.

Adrianna swept in theatrically but stopped short when she spotted the two men. She shot Alexis a big grin. "You left out the part about having guys over." She gave the detectives an approving look. "And they know how to dress. Just kidding, boys, I'm already taken." She raised her left hand to show off her one-carat yellow diamond engagement ring.

"Adrianna, these are Detectives Carter and Lindsay," Alexis said, trying to keep a straight face. "Detectives, this is my best friend, Adrianna Marshall."

The detectives nodded and then moved toward the door. "We'll be off, then," Detective Carter said to Alexis. "Thank you for your time."

Detective Lindsay drew a card from his jacket pocket and handed it to Alexis. "If you think of anything, please call me, any time. The card has my cell number, too."

Alexis took the card and ushered them to the door. She shut it behind them and locked it. She tossed the detective's card on the table and then walked into the living room toward Adrianna. She was relieved that the man who had attacked her the night before was dead, but her mind was reeling.

"What's up with the detectives?" Adrianna asked.

"Let's order some Crab Rangoon," Alexis suggested. "And then I'll tell you all about it." Even as she said it, she knew she wouldn't be telling Adrianna everything.

"I'm so glad you called me tonight," Adrianna said.

"Me too."

From a dark corner of the room, the shadow of a figure watched.

CHAPTER TEN

DETECTIVES CARTER AND Lindsay sat at their desks, going over photos and witness statements.

"I can't believe no one saw or heard anything," Carter muttered.

"I can't believe Forensics didn't find anything at the scene," Lindsay replied.

"Let's go see where Eric is on the clean-up of those security tapes."

Lindsay flipped over another photo. "If he found anything, we would have heard from him."

"We need a break."

Lindsay nodded. "Let's do it. These pictures are making me crossed-eyed."

As they stood up, a young female detective burst into the room from the hallway and hurried toward them.

Carter gave her an amused look. "Whoa, slow down, Hodge, where's the fire?"

Detective Hodge, a tall, full-figured woman with a strong voice, took a moment to catch her breath. "Stupid elevator is still broken," she rasped.

"Yeah, we know," Lindsay said. "So what's up?"

"Coroner wants you guys to head over there ASAP. You weren't picking up the phone."

"So you ran up six flights to tell us," Carter said. "You're a trouper, Hodge."

"Thank you," Hodge replied. "Maybe I'll just sit down here for a minute."

Montgomery Morgue was ten miles from the precinct station, an unremarkable 10-story building with a grey stone facade. The two detectives entered the building and showed their badges to a security guard. They had to show them two more times before they were allowed to enter the autopsy room, where Dr. Timothy Harris was looking down at a corpse on top of a stainless steel autopsy table. They entered quietly and breathed in the sterile aroma of antiseptic cleansers.

"All right, Dr. H, this better be something amazing," Carter said.

Dr. Harris, a lean man with curly chestnut hair and a thick mustache, glanced up and gestured for them to approach the table. They did and saw the John Doe who was found in the alley behind the furniture store.

"What do you two know about the process of freezing to death?" the doctor asked in a booming baritone that belied his scrawny build.

Carter shrugged. "It's been twenty years since high school anatomy class, but if I remember correctly it has something to do with ice forming and stabbing you."

Lindsay smiled and raised an eyebrow.

"What?" Carter said, frowning at his partner.

"Twenty years?"

"I'm only fifteen years older than you," Carter reminded his partner.

"I graduated ten years ago."

"Close enough."

The coroner interrupted the banter. "Normally people die from hypothermia because of their core temperature dropping. When you freeze to death, there's a lot of organ damage from the ice that you mentioned."

"Because the human body is mostly made of water, right, Doc?" Lindsay said.

The coroner nodded and pointed a finger at the body. The detectives moved closer to the table to see what Dr. Harris was trying to show them.

"But this guy was frozen from the outside," the coroner said. "There's no ice in his blood, which means his internal organs are probably perfect. It's almost as if he was frozen cryogenically. Once we cut him open we'll know more."

"Will this change the time of death estimate?" Carter asked.

"Yes. Your window will be twenty-four hours from when I picked him up, and I know this guy wasn't anywhere near Japan in that time frame."

"Japan?" Lindsay asked. "What's Japan got to do with it?"

"A Japanese scientist figured out how to preserve food without ruining the flavor or doing any molecular damage. He has a system that uses a magnetic field to cool the water in the foods and keep them from forming ice crystals during the freezing process."

"And you know this why?" Carter asked.

"Because the technique is used for organ transplants."

"Are you saying someone froze this guy like a package of Japanese fish cakes?" Carter asked.

"Your guy here was alive seconds before he froze, didn't even have time to close his eyes or exhale. If someone put him in a CAS freezer, like the one in Japan, they would have had to sedate him or restrain him, but his toxin screen was clean for paralytic drugs, and there are no abrasion or ligature marks showing signs of his being tied up. Besides, they would have needed a large freezer, not the type they use for organs."

"Did you get any of his fingerprints?" Lindsay asked.

"I was able to get a few."

"What about the scratches on his neck?" asked Carter.

"A couple of days old. They were already starting to scab over."

"Anything else, Doc?" Lindsay asked.

"That's it."

Lindsay nodded. “Thanks, Doc.”

Detective Carter turned to his partner as they began to walk away from the body. “Where do we even begin with this?”

CHAPTER ELEVEN

A DOZEN MEN IN well-tailored black suits stood in a group inside a large warehouse on the east side of town. They were gathered close together and whispering to each other.

"I don't think he realizes things are changing," one of the men said.

"He has never handled things this way," said another.

The man called Azure spoke next. "What makes this one different?"

"I thought we were not allowed to kill a human," said another.

The one called Cezar, who stood in the center of the group with Azure, spoke next. "Since he doesn't want us to be seen near him, how do we handle this? Who do we report to now?"

A voice called out of the shadows, a voice familiar to each of them, a voice they feared, a voice that silenced them all. "That would be me," the voice said, and a pair of eyes shined through the darkness like fire in the night.

"Master, we are unsure how to understand these recent events and your interactions with humans," Cezar said.

"I'm surprised you thought that here, or anywhere, would be a place of solace. Do you know who I am, Cezar?"

Cezar was brought forward to stand face to face with his master. "Master, we did not know why you didn't ask of us to take care of that filthy human. We wonder, Master, why you cared to rid him of his soul."

The Master moved closer to Cezar. "You and I know of the foretold fate ahead for our kind. But even things written in stone can be broken. But there are certain guidelines, as you all should know, that you can never cross. I never took anyone's life, I merely pushed his soul into the outer realm, where no flesh can survive."

"What happens next with the woman?" Cezar asked.

"To get things back on course, I will take over the search for the map."

Azure, standing among the group, took a step forward. "If you're going after the map, what are we supposed to do?"

"You have been following these human women. You failed to keep the first one alive, and now this one saw you. Opportunities have been given, and you have failed and failed again. I will not let you go back to create more disorder. Be thankful you are still here."

"But why her?" a voice from the group called out. "I thought the map was broken into twelve pieces, and the pieces scattered across this planet?"

"Why find twelve pieces when there is one that contains all? There is one that was forged by Eve after being cast out."

"How do you know this?" Cezar asked.

"I was there. I told her to eat the fruit. I watched her take something with her from the garden."

"Are you certain it will lead us to Eden?" another voice asked. "How do we know this human possesses it?"

There was silence then and no more questions. Finally, the man clothed in shadows addressed the group again. "For those of you who have joined these two in their voyage across dangerous waters, know that before long you will drown without me."

His voice rose, and the walls began to vibrate. "Do what you were brought here to do, and worry no more about my doings. Leave this place and do my will."

The group vanished into the dark, all except Azure and Cezar. Quiet fell, and all was stillness. The Master moved toward the two remaining there.

“I don’t want to see you again unless I call you. Stay away from Alexis Zen. You will not complicate this.” His tone was lower, but still intense. It stirred the dust from beneath their feet.

Cezar and Azure disappeared, leaving their Master standing in the warehouse alone. His mission was clear. He looked down at his diamond-encrusted watch, brushed a speck of lint from his custom-made pale-blue shirt, and headed outside. A sky filled with stars and a quarter moon lighted his way. He opened the door to his platinum Rapide Coupe and paused to look back at the warehouse. Then he looked up into the sky. “If only their eyes could have seen ...”

CHAPTER TWELVE

"HEY, LINDSAY!" DETECTIVE CARTER called out. "Come take a look at this."

Detective Lindsay left the main detectives' room and crossed the mint-green hallway to a ten-by-eight room to the left of the chief's office.

"Yeah, what is it?"

Detective Carter sat at a desk with two large computer screens. One of the police station's tech analysts, a man named Eric Bloor, was peering over his shoulder.

"Play it for him, Eric," Carter said, and then he motioned for Lindsay to come closer. "He found our guy on a couple of security cameras."

"Awesome."

They watched the screen as Detective Carter narrated. "Here's our John Doe walking down Main Street, ten blocks from where we found him. Notice the time stamp at the bottom, 10:07 p.m. Now check this out."

Lindsay squinted at the lower right corner of the screen. "This guy had to be a psych patient somewhere."

"Why would you think that?" Carter asked. "I figured the guy was on drugs or drunk."

"His toxin screening was clean for drugs. He's acting more paranoid than stoned."

"The screen doesn't test for all the homemade drugs."

"You're right."

Carter looked at Eric. "Bring up the furniture store's camera feed."

The analyst clicked his mouse, and the screen changed viewpoints to show the video from the alley where the body was found.

"Whoa, how did he get there so fast?" Lindsay asked.

"That isn't even the craziest part," Eric said. "Check out the time stamp."

Detective Lindsay's jaw dropped, and his eyes went wide. "How ... are you ..."

"I had him test it to make sure it wasn't faked or tampered with," Carter said. "It's real."

Detective Lindsay pulled a chair up to the desk and sat down. "Let me see that again, but slower."

The three of them sat very still and watched the monitor closely. For the first few seconds they watched the motionless dark alley with two-thirds of the Dumpster visible in the lower left corner of the screen. Then a white mist, like fog, appeared on the ground, and what looked like ice started to form. Ice crystals covered the side of the Dumpster and the back walls of the furniture store and quickly spread over the security camera lens.

"Can you take it one frame at a time?" Lindsay asked Eric, his eyes still on the monitor.

As each frame passed, the ice started to dissipate, and the mist began to clear. When the fog lifted, they saw their John Doe lying on the ground. Detective Lindsay looked at the time stamp again—it read 10:08 p.m.

"I figure first thing tomorrow morning we take Eric here to the furniture store and have him check out the security system to make sure its timing isn't set wrong," Carter said. "Before we go too crazy with wild-ass speculations, you know? Then let's see if anyone has invested in one of the freezers Dr. H was going on about."

"Yeah, okay, that's what we'll do," Lindsay murmured, still staring at the computer screen.

"There has to be an explanation," Carter said.

"May I offer a suggestion?" Eric asked.

"Shoot," Carter said.

"If we stop by a few of the other businesses, maybe we can get a better angle on the scene. And also see who dumped him there."

"Sounds good," said Carter. He and Lindsay left and crossed the hallway back to the main detectives' room.

"Hey, Carter, I left those fingerprint results on your desk," yelled a detective sitting a few desks away.

"I submitted these four days ago," Carter grumbled as he went to get the file. "What took so long?"

The other detective shrugged. "The lab guy said that they weren't the best fingerprint samples."

"Of course they're not. Why would anything on this case make sense or be easy?" Carter muttered.

He sat down, opened the folder, and began to scan the pages. He glanced up a few moments later and looked at Lindsay. "Says here our John Doe was a truck driver out on bail. His name is George Pliate, and his family lives in Fairborn."

"Guess we'll be bringing them the bad news about George," Lindsay said.

"Right. We'll notify them, maybe they can give us some answers. And let's keep the details of this case to ourselves for now."

Lindsay nodded, and the two headed down the hallway to the elevators.

"Finally these are working," Carter said as they stepped into the empty elevator car.

"Got any plans for the holiday weekend?" Lindsay asked.

"Me and the wife are heading to Lake Cumberland with her family. How about you, going anywhere?"

"No definite plans yet, but I'm sure I'll end up at my sister's, watching fireworks and eating way too much food."

"And you wonder why you're single."

"I just haven't found the right girl."

"Gotta look before you find," Carter said as the elevator opened to the lower level. Dr. Harris was standing there.

"Hey, Dr. H, what brings you this way?" Carter asked.

"You two. I couldn't get either one of you on the phone again, and I don't like to leave sensitive information on a voice mail. I was heading up to find you." Dr. Harris sounded worried.

"You want to ride over to the crime scene with us?" Carter asked. "We have to stop and notify the family first."

"No, no, that's okay. I have someplace to be."

Carter looked at the envelope in the coroner's hand. "What do you have for us?"

"Let it be answers, please," Lindsay said. "No more weird stuff."

"Sorry to disappoint you, Detective Lindsay." The coroner opened the envelope he was holding and pulled out a handful of photos. "This is a picture of what normal skin looks like under magnification."

"That's disgusting," Carter said.

The three stepped away from the elevator as a group of patrol officers approached, and Dr. Harris gestured toward a corner of the lobby. "Let's go sit on that bench. Away from traffic."

The three of them squeezed onto the wooden bench engraved with *America Forward*, and Dr. Harris explained the photos as he drew each one out of the envelope. "This is the magnification of the skin from a person with albinism, or an albino. Now look at our victim's skin, his muscles, and his organs. Everything is white, his liver, his heart, everything. This guy is white all the way through. It's as though the essence was leached from his body."

Lindsay stared at the image of an ash-white lung. "So much for answers."

CHAPTER THIRTEEN

ALEXIS DROVE UP the gravel hill toward her grandparents' house. The world outside her car was illuminated brightly by the glare of the sun, and its rays bounced in and out of her car as she drove past the tall red maple trees, creating a kaleidoscope of colors on her dash. Alexis had a feeling of peace and simplicity, until the car came to the top of the hill. The tree line abruptly ended, replaced by a sprawl of modular homes and lots spread with grass seed. A cloud sailed across the sun, and the vibrant colors faded.

Alexis turned left into the first driveway. A stream of memories played in her head like a series of flashes going off one by one. They were from the night her aunt died. The emotions unleashed by the memorial service flooded into her mind. She continued up the drive and parked about twenty feet from the house. She took deep breaths, fighting back tears.

Alexis saw her grandmother standing on the back porch and waving to her to come inside. Alexis turned off the engine, grabbed her purse, and stepped out onto the gravel driveway. The air whispered through her hair as she walked up to the back door.

Alexis grabbed the handle of the glass storm door and opened it, but she jumped quickly and then glanced around. With her heart racing and her mind reeling, she stood there looking for something that wasn't there.

Someone touched her arm, and she let out a screech.

"I'm sorry, Alexis, I didn't mean to scare you," her grandmother said. "Are you okay, dear, you looked frightened?"

Alexis let out a breath and forced a smile. "Yeah, yeah, I'm fine, I just thought I heard something out there, that's all."

"Let's go inside. I made your favorites. And your DziDzi has got the Scrabble board ready." Baba spoke with a strong Polish accent.

Alexis walked in and around the corner to the kitchen. She could see her grandfather sitting in the living room in his overstuffed recliner pretending to be asleep. She went over to him and softly kissed his cheek, then yelled to her grandmother in the kitchen. "I'll eat DziDzi's pierogis since he's napping."

The old man sat up. "Nie, Nie."

Alexis giggled. "Okay, now that you're awake, Polish, Hebrew, or English tonight?"

"Let's do English for tonight." The little man grabbed a handful of cashews from a jar on the kitchen counter.

The evening was soon taken over by pierogis, kielbasa, and triple words. After an hour, Alexis's grandfather tossed his last two lettered squares onto the board and slid his chair away from the table.

"Dobranoc! I'm going to bed. Alexis is cheating, so I can't even begin to win."

Baba and Alexis held in the laughter as the silver-haired man walked around the dining table to kiss his wife. He waved before heading to the bedroom at the back of the house.

"Your grandfather has always been a sore loser," Baba said.

"It's great to see your smile, Baba. Are you doing okay?" Alexis hesitated to ask. Burying a child couldn't have been easy.

"I have my moments. But I trust she is in a better place. Since they caught the person responsible, it makes sleep come easier."

Her grandmother looked frail, but Alexis knew she was strong in her faith. Alexis smiled, but she wasn't so sure a better place really existed.

"So, my child. Do you have anyone special in your life? Last week you were talking about that young man you work with. What was his name? Jimmy?"

Alexis blushed. "James. And no, he's my supervisor."

"Yes, but you mentioned he was cute."

Alexis had to laugh. "Baba, I did say he's nice to look at and smells good."

"Speaking of work, how is that going? I know you can't give me details, but I'd like to hear about what you can tell me."

"I've already told you about the promotion, and my new lab. It's wonderful to finally be able to test my theories, and their potential impact." Alexis winked.

Her grandmother had been there the day a couple of men in government vehicles showed up at the door looking for Alexis. Alexis had been in ninth grade when she wrote an essay showing a clear understanding of quantum physics and presenting a few of her own ideas to push the science community further toward an explanation of the universe. An anonymous person had forwarded the essay to the National Science Foundation, and someone had taken notice. At the time, Alexis's mother was struggling to put food on the table, and a college education for Alexis was out of the question. But the government didn't want to waste her potential, so it agreed to fund all her post-secondary education, including doctoral degrees and beyond. At age thirteen, Alexis was put under contract to work for the government once she finished college.

"I miss the days of reading over your book reports," Baba said. "I only pretended to understand what you were writing about."

"You did a good job of fooling me. I was impressed with the facts you taught me."

"Ah, you mean the fact snacks?"

"Exactly. Making a five-year-old recite the locations of countries across the globe to get a snack is torture."

"I always knew you were special, Alexis, and that your brain absorbed everything. I thought it would help you later in life."

"It did, thank you." Alexis turned serious. "But what about those stories about mythological beings."

Baba peered at her over the top of her wire-rimmed glasses."I don't know what you mean."

"You were so persistent in making sure I knew childish fables about Eve."

"Oh, those stories." Baba rubbed Alexis's hand. "You need not worry yourself."

"I'm not. But do you really believe Eve wrote down the secrets of Eden somewhere?"

"There are many different tales about how the world began. For most people, it's confusing. But someone kept a record of the truth, someone who knew the secrets of our existence." Baba smiled. "Who better than a woman?"

"Okay, but first you have to believe that a deity placed two humans on the planet in the beginning."

"Alexis, good and evil are present even if you don't believe in God. And the idea of God putting man on this planet is no more ridiculous than people spontaneously changing from a monkey."

"Very true. I would like to hear those stories again sometime."

Baba glanced at the bookshelf standing along one wall and then back at Alexis. "Someday I will share everything."

"Okay." Alexis heard the ticking wood clock behind her on the wall. "I'm going to head home, Baba, I have a full day tomorrow, and my brain functions better with at least four hours of sleep. If I leave now I might even get six."

"I'm glad you came over."

Alexis stood and walked over to her grandmother. She bent over and wrapped her arms around her small body and kissed her cheek. "I love you. I will see you soon."

"Okay, but next time bring that James fella over."

Alexis smiled. "Baba."

"What? You need a man, Alexis."

"No, I don't."

"I tell you what, you try to find a guy for the Fourth of July picnic, and I will stop mentioning it. Okay?"

"All right, that gives me about a week to save some money, then I can hire a date."

Her grandmother shook her head.

It was dark when Alexis stepped outside. She pushed the button on the remote starter for her Mustang, and the parking lights flashed on. It was a five-second walk to the car. She kept her eyes forward as she went. Once inside the car, she locked the doors and put the key in the ignition. She turned the radio on and tuned in a popular hit station. The moon, blanketed by a thin sheet of clouds, occasionally peeked through the branches of the trees as she drove down the gravel driveway.

Alexis thought about who she might take to her family's picnic. It would have to be someone who wasn't looking for a committed relationship. Unpleasant images from her past thrust themselves into her mind. The last thing she needed was a man in her life.

When she reached her apartment, Alexis pulled into her parking space, turned the car off, and exhaled. She grabbed her purse and some leftovers from her grandparents' house, got out, and held her breath as she headed up the stairs. Alexis had placed timers on most of the lights in her place and set them to turn on every night around six o'clock. It was a good feeling to come home and not walk into the dark.

Alexis entered her apartment, put Oslo on his leash, and took him outside for a walk. The usually calm alley seemed threatening and unreal. The darkness was changing shape. But no, it was just her imagination. There was no one standing there.

She tugged on Oslo's leash, and they returned to the apartment. Alexis locked the door and headed straight to her bedroom.

"Oslo, let's get in bed, boy."

Her puppy, almost the size of an average dog, jumped up onto her bed and curled up next to Alexis's legs. She set the timer on her TV for sixty minutes and then turned the lights out.

"Wonder if Baba would count you as my man, Oslo." His ears perked up as soon as she mentioned his name. "Probably not."

Alexis checked the alarm on her phone and then slid down into her covers. She prayed to be able to fall asleep. Five o'clock would come around fast, and she needed the next six hours to be restful.

Alexis fell asleep ...

... and he watched.

CHAPTER FOURTEEN

ALEXIS ROLLED OVER and brushed Oslo's coat with her hand. He nestled his wet nose near her forearm before letting out a sigh. "Come on, boy, you have to get up too."

Alexis wasn't scheduled to be at work until 8 a.m. But after walking Oslo for nearly a half hour, showering, eating breakfast, and obsessing over what to wear under her lab coat, she had only twenty minutes to get to the research building and down to her lab. Alexis liked to start her workday before most of her coworkers arrived, to avoid questions about her personal life.

When she was ready to go, Alexis attached Oslo's thick blue leash to his collar and walked him toward the door. "Let's go, Oslo, doggy daycare again today with all your girlfriends."

She tried to lead him down the steps, but he pulled against the leash.

"Oslo, they're just stairs, you have no issues going up them."

Alexis hurried across town to doggy daycare, dropped off Oslo, and tried to make up lost time by driving faster than usual. She arrived at the gate at 7:49, but traffic was moving slow. After five minutes of flipping through radio stations and checking her text messages, she got through the gate and drove to the research building.

It was 7:57 when she got out of her car and began speed-walking to the entrance. Inside the lobby, a large group of people was waiting at the elevators, and they were boarding four at a time.

She glanced around at the crowd, did a quick calculation, and said, "If we go five at a time, we could cut down the total number of elevator trips by two."

A few people chuckled as the elevator door closed.

"Alexis?" Someone was calling out to her from the front of the group.

She pretended not to hear. The last thing she wanted was to engage in mindless small talk. Then she saw a dark-haired man heading her way through the crowd, and she recognized the blue eyes, smooth skin, and full lips. *Okay, I have time for this.*

"I thought that was your voice." James said. "I'm surprised you're not here already. I thought you were an early bird."

"My morning walk put me behind schedule." *Don't say something stupid.*

"Technically you're still not late."

She gestured toward the crowd. "You can see why I try to be early."

"I'll ride down with you," James said.

Alexis could feel the deep cedar smell of James's cologne relaxing her mind, the subtle hint of spice making it slightly intoxicating.

"How was your weekend?"

"I went to my grandparents' house last night, but stayed home with my dog most of the weekend."

The elevator opened and three people standing in front got on and held the door for James or Alexis.

James waved them off and turned back to Alexis. "Grandparents and dog, huh? Sounds like a wild weekend."

"Are you making fun me?"

James grinned. "Uh huh."

"Thanks."

"It's just that I figured you for someone with a lively social life."

The elevator opened and they stepped inside and scanned their IDs.

"Why?" Alexis asked.

"Most lab geeks down here don't wear pink lip gloss or even bother to brush their hair every day. I just figured you always had some place to be after work since you always look so good."

Alexis felt her cheeks coloring slightly. She made no response.

Alexis and James headed through the checkpoints, and then she turned left and headed to her lab. She scanned her ID, and the lab door clicked open. When the door didn't shut behind her, she felt the hairs on her body tingle. Alexis could feel she wasn't alone. The memory from the night she was attacked in her apartment came rushing into her head. She tried to shake it off and get hold of herself.

"I'm hoping you'll show me around your space now that you've settled in some," James said as he shut the door.

Alexis let out a breath and turned around. "I didn't realize you were following me."

"I wanted to see inside this secret place."

"You've not been in here before?"

"No, it was still under construction when I was transferred to this department. I received a basic outline on what every researcher is supposed to be doing, and that was about it." James looked around the pristine lab. "This is bigger than my office."

Alexis walked him through the space, showing him the different tools and pieces of equipment required to operate her projects. Then she took him into an area attached to the main room, four white walls, no windows, and completely empty.

"I don't even need this room yet, I just come in here to clear my head."

"I noticed when I came in the other door the sound changed, so I'm guessing both rooms are soundproof?"

"Yeah, I need a controlled environment, especially for sound," Alexis replied.

"Controlled environment," James murmured as he looked around.

Alexis pretended not to hear him. "As you know, my job is to find ways of understanding the natural manipulations of the elements and possible form shifting. And no, that does not mean weather conditions, if that's what you're thinking."

"More like atmospheric manipulation, right?"

"Exactly."

"I wonder why they want you to find a natural way of doing that when we have machines to do that now. Seems counterproductive."

"Yes, but our machines are destroying habitats and air quality."

"You're not a Luddite, are you?"

"Of course not. But maybe we can learn something from ancient cultures. Think about the Egyptian pyramids and the Mesoamerican pyramids and the ziggurats of Mesopotamia. Some date back more than four thousand years and include details we would have trouble doing today with our largest equipment. Some of those megaliths weighed more than ten tons and had to be cut, moved, and stacked. And I'm talking about clean cuts."

"Okay, you've convinced me. I'm booking the next flight to Giza."

"Send me a postcard."

"I will. But seriously, Alexis, you are building a piece of machinery, are you not?"

"I am, but no fossil fuels will power it." Alexis thought about his Luddite comment and said, "You're not an anti-environmentalist, are you?"

"Ouch. No. Just a modernist."

Alexis smiled. "The ancients also had knowledge of the elements that enabled them to heal the sick without X-rays, CAT scans, or laser surgery."

"They didn't have aspirin, either, Alexis, and unless you've never had a headache, you have to admit that we're better off with aspirin."

"On that point I'll yield."

"I read that you named your machine Lazarus. Does that mean you're trying to raise the dead, too?"

"No. Lazarus was a character in a short story I wrote during my freshman year. He traveled through time to learn about the different civilizations, and ... well, here I am, trying to show the capabilities of human comprehension and the universe that holds us, from a different perspective, with a touch of science. But you won't find me chanting or burning incense or performing human sacrifice in here, so don't worry."

"I'm glad to hear it. You're not one of those religious scientists, you know, always looking to find God under a microscope?"

Alexis shook her head, but she was annoyed. She hated anyone trying to pin a label on her. "I'm not looking for God or divine answers through scientific methods."

James put both hands into the pockets of his lab coat and then looked around the room, as if he were looking for something to shift the conversation. "What are all these clear boxes used for?"

Alexis walked over to where several acrylic boxes sat on top of a high table. "You know how a tuning fork works, vibrating only to a companion tuning fork?"

James nodded. "Yeah, I know at least that much."

"Right, basic physics. Using this idea, I've placed several different slivers of metal in separate boxes."

"You're going to vibrate the metal slivers?"

Alexis opened the top of a box labeled "SAMPLE 143" and then fetched two pairs of glasses from a desk drawer. She handed a pair to James. "Put these on so you can see for yourself what happens."

James put on the blue-tinted glasses, and Alexis turned off the lights. He looked at the boxes. In the center of each box was a single piece of metal no longer than an inch and no wider than a strand of hair. With the lights out, each bit of metal glowed a cobalt blue.

Alexis covered one of the acrylic boxes with a lid that had a small metal contraption attached to the underside. "Now watch. This has only been achievable in a vacuum environment—until now." Alexis sealed the lid with two locks.

The metal fragment in the box disappeared. "Where did it go?" James asked.

Alexis smiled inside, knowing she'd just exploded James's preconceived ideas about who she was. "The *where* part is still an unanswered question."

"But you said you were doing things naturally. This is a remarkable achievement, but can you make it disappear without your magic box?"

Alexis removed the lid, and the sliver of metal reappeared.

"I had to know what type of elements I could manipulate most easily and then work up to larger pieces. And the box isn't magic." Alexis turned over the lid to show James the metal contraption.

"Is that a homemade battery?"

"Not exactly, but that would have been my first guess. Everything I'm using has been available since the dawn of time, except the box. The device I've attached to the lid simulates seismic activity. Of course, I have to control the environment to know what is or isn't working."

"This is extraordinary."

Alexis moved toward a large table in the back of the room. "My ideas aren't new."

"Explain."

"We know that everything has a counterpart. Matter and antimatter, yin and yang, good and evil. But we haven't explored the potential of this kind of knowledge. We may be able to cure problems versus suppressing them. We may be able to visit our ancestors and discover all sorts of answers."

"Time travel?"

Alexis paused for a beat before she began to laugh. "I was kidding, James. At least about the time traveling part."

James folded his arms and squinted at her. "I'm not sure you were. Anyway, what's that over there?"

Alexis went to a large white table strewn with sketches and picked up a metal device about the size and shape of a small gift box with three short rods protruding from one end. "This is what I do all day. Those boxes are the counterpart to this piece of equipment.

Where the boxes create a manipulated field of elements, this is a detector of those unique areas."

Alexis glanced at James and saw him frowning.

"But it's a machine; not quite a natural approach."

"It's a machine, but it's also a step toward understanding the things we can't see. It isn't some worthless EMF detector you can buy on the Internet from some paranormal huckster. This is designed to find breaks or weak spots in the natural environment before there would be activity."

"Are you ghost hunting for the government?"

Alexis wasn't sure how James would perceive all of this, but he didn't control her research approvals, so it didn't matter. There was a reason they allowed Alexis to work alone. Most scientists would have considered her research an unimportant waste of funds.

"I'm looking for facts to help strengthen the real world, not provide hype to all those fanatics chasing shadows."

"I take it you're not a spiritual person?"

Alexis decided to ignore the question and try a different approach. "Have you ever thought about the Bermuda Triangle and the strange electromagnetic anomalies going on there?"

James nodded. "Who hasn't?"

"There are places like that all over the world that we want to understand, and this device is like a thermal detector for electromagnetic waves. Basically, I'm going to find holes in our world and maybe one day the lining of the universe."

"That's really kind of out there," James said.

"No more than, say, string theory or exobiology."

James grinned. "This may surprise you, but one of my degrees is in exobiology, so you can understand my fascination with anything out of this universe. Except I'm looking for UFOs and possible evidence of aliens, not environmental sustainability."

Alexis smiled. "We might actually get along."

James looked at his watch. "I'm going to make my rounds with the other researchers, and I still have a project of my own I need to focus on. Keep me posted on your progress." He turned and headed out the door.

Alexis set down the device, turned to her sketches, and focused on getting through the day.

CHAPTER FIFTEEN

THE CLOCK STRETCHED its arms toward four, and Alexis began to shut down the equipment in her lab. She organized the papers on her table and then headed for the door, turning off the lights as she went. She stopped at the front desk to pick up her belongings and then walked to her car.

As she backed out of her space in the far corner of the parking lot, she saw James coming out of the building. He was walking fast, headed to a small silver vehicle. Alexis, used to seeing him in his lab coat, couldn't help but notice how his expensive dress shirt and pants fit his sculpted frame. She wondered what kind of car he owned, but other cars backing out of spaces and heading for the exit blocked her view.

Alexis drove out of the parking area and headed toward Dr. Asael's office, only five minutes away. The government required the scientists to undergo regular evaluations by an approved psychiatrist within the military network, and most of their offices were near the base. The powers that be wanted to make sure that employees working on secret projects, including some involving dangerous chemicals, had their heads on straight.

Alexis pulled in to Dr. Asael's parking lot and cut the engine. Her appointment wasn't until 4:45, but she didn't want to kill time by driving around and wasting fuel. The air was fresh as she stepped out of the car and went inside.

"Evening, Mary," Alexis said as she walked up to the counter.

Mary seemed not to hear.

Alexis signed her name and tried to make small talk. "I never liked my handwriting. I feel like I need to retake that part of kindergarten."

Mary didn't look up, but she grinned. "Sweetie, my signature is always lopsided, so I'm sure yours looks way better than mine. Have a seat. Dr. Asael is finishing up with someone."

Alexis sat in the chair in the corner of the room. She shuffled through the magazines sitting on the glass table, quickly passing over the parents' magazines and the golf and fishing publications. She came to a copy of *Weird Science* and opened it. The cover story dealt with solar flares and end-of-times prophecies that were wildly miscalculated. After two paragraphs, she put the magazine back on the table. She didn't need any more reasons to be paranoid.

As she reached into her purse to grab her phone so she could check her emails, she spotted a small red sedan pull into the parking lot, a woman in white-rimmed sunglasses behind the wheel. The woman sat with the engine running and the window cracked, obviously waiting for someone. The license plate read "LAB MOM." Alexis wondered who among her colleagues might still live with their mother.

The door to Dr. Asael's office opened, and she had her answer.

"Hello, Alexis."

"Hey there, Frederick."

Frederick Lucas, the youngest guy at the research facility and still fighting a losing battle against teenage acne, had a huge crush on Alexis. He had never had the nerve to actually ask her out, but he tried to hang out with her every chance he could, often sitting across from her in the cafeteria or next to her during department meetings. Alexis was always polite but made sure never to say or do anything that might encourage his amorous fantasies.

"I didn't know you came to Dr. Asael's," Frederick said. "You should stop over to my area sometime, I'd love to show you how my project is coming along."

"Actually, Freddie, I'm not on your floor anymore. But I'll try to stop by one of these days." Alexis knew his project was focused on sound manipulation of cancer cells, and she dreaded anything involving rats or animal testing.

"I thought you were still on leave for your family stuff. I hope everything is all right. If you want, I could stop over sometime to talk."

"Everything's fine, Freddie, but thanks for your concern."

Frederick turned to the window to wave at his mother and signal that he'd be out shortly, then he turned back to Alexis. "What are you working on?"

Alexis just smiled.

"Right, classified. I better go before my mother starts honking. She gets in a hurry for happy hour. We like to share the appetizer specials at Pablo's Restaurant."

"Awesome," Alexis said. Freddie was the only person with whom she used that term.

"It was nice to see you, Alexis. Don't forget to stop by to check out my project." Frederick waved and headed for the door, bouncing on the balls of his feet on his way out.

"Miss Zen, the doctor is ready for you now," Mary said.

On her way down the hall, Alexis noticed a familiar smell. It was the same deep cedar she had detected coming from James, but this was mixed with the scent of fresh rain. The scent intensified as she neared the door. She opened it and entered the office. Dr. Asael was standing just inside.

"Good evening, Alexis. I was just coming to see if you were on your way back."

"Hello, Dr. Asael."

"Come in and have a seat."

"I hope you have three hours blocked out for me today," Alexis said as she headed toward the leather chaise.

Dr. Asael closed the door and took his usual chair near the chaise. "Do you have a lot on your mind?"

"I had a situation the night I was here last. And I don't know what's been going on. I've been trying to push it out of my mind." Alexis sat down, considering how she might explain the situation without sounding like someone who should be committed.

The doctor put his pad and pen down and leaned forward. "What kind of situation?"

Alexis told him how a man had been waiting in her apartment that night. She said that every day since, she had pretended to be normal. "I haven't told anyone else because I'm not sure what was real."

"I suggest we try hypnosis again. It may help you recall the details from that night—if you're prepared to relive them."

"I don't want my job to be jeopardized."

"As I explained, these sessions have nothing to do with your job. This about you."

Alexis nodded and lay back against the cool leather of the chaise, focusing on Dr. Asael's voice, letting the sound wrap around her head and slow her thoughts. She lay down flat and stretched out, her body extended along the length of the chaise. As she listened to the doctor's soothing voice, she was aware of her surroundings, but it was like a lucid dream.

"Alexis, take me back to the last night you were here. What day of the week was that?"

"It was a Monday."

"Where did you go after you left this office?"

"I went home. Oslo came in the door with me, but then he ran off and disappeared somewhere in the apartment."

"What did you do?"

"I'm calling out to him. There's a light coming down the hallway from my bedroom."

"Alexis, I want you to walk me down the hallway to your bedroom. What do you see?"

"I can't see anything."

"Why?"

"The lights just shut off ... everything is dark ... Wait, there's light coming from my bedroom ... no it's coming from outside."

"Do you hear anything?"

"I hear footsteps ... there's breathing coming from behind me. My heart is getting louder ... my chest is pounding. It feels like I'm spinning."

"Focus on what you can hear."

"I hear ... Oslo? It's very faint, but I know he's in the apartment somewhere. The breathing behind me is getting closer. I don't know what to do." Her voice rose in pitch, and her fists began to clench.

"Alexis, can you tell me more about the breathing? How close is it to you?"

"It's right next to my ear," she whispered. "I can feel the heat on my neck."

"Can you see anything?"

"He has his arm around my chest. I can't breathe."

"Who has you, can you see him?"

"I can't see his face. I'm being taken into my room. What is he ...? Please let me live."

"What can you see Alexis?"

"My eyes are shut. I can't see what he's doing. No, this can't happen again. He's on top of me. Everything is so dark. I can't feel anything."

"Can you see anything?"

"No, everything is ... no, wait, I see some sort of a light."

"Where is the light coming from?"

"It's right in front of me."

"Alexis, what's happening?"

"My body is being forced down onto the bed, but I can see everything in my room. I'm standing in the corner and somehow watching everything happen. I don't understand."

"What do you see?"

Alexis shivered. "We are not alone in the room."

"Who else is there?"

"I can't see their faces, they're are not facing me."

"Can you describe the other people you see?"

"Two men wearing suits, black suits. I can't see their faces. One has sandy blonde hair, and he's standing near the bed, bent over by my body. It's like he's watching. The other one has light hair, almost white, and he's standing at the top of my bed. I am so scared. Hey!" Alexis jolted as she screamed.

"What happened?"

"They're looking at me. Their eyes ... so dark."

"Don't be frightened, they can't hurt you. What is happening now, Alexis?"

"I ... they ... they just disappeared."

"Who disappeared?"

"I don't see them. They just vanished. And the man who grabbed me, he's getting up and walking away. He's stumbling. He didn't ..." A tear slowly made its way down the side of Alexis's face.

"Didn't what, Alexis?"

"My clothes, they're still on, I'm still alive. But that man just stopped ... and those two men ..."

"Did you see the man who attacked you?"

"Yes, but he looked different. The photos were different."

"What photos, Alexis?"

Alexis described how on the night of the attack, the assailant appeared to be badly sunburned. But he looked pale and almost translucent in the photos the police had shown her.

"Why did the police have his picture?"

"His body was found in the alley behind my apartment."

The doctor hesitated. "Alexis, did you kill the man who attacked you?"

"I don't remember."

Dr. Asael encouraged Alexis to continue, but she couldn't remember anything after that point.

Dr. Asael brought her out of hypnosis. She took a deep breath and sat up, wiping away a tear. "I was crying."

"How do you feel?"

"It's strange, but I feel good. Not as anxious as when I got here."

"Alexis, you have experienced several traumatic and emotional trials in your life. I think your mind is responding by blacking out and then seeing things that aren't there, perhaps to help you block a deeper pain." He paused for a moment as he looked at his notepad. "How do you deal with issues during the week?"

"Since I can't share details of my job with anyone, it makes it hard to talk through anything that comes up. I try to deal with personal issues myself, until I see you, of course."

"Describe what you do when you're with friends. Let me rephrase the question. Describe your social life."

Alexis nearly laughed out loud. "I don't get out much. My guy friends only hang out at my house whenever they want to see the big game on my TV during football season. I have one female friend who's absorbed with wedding plans. I work out by walking my dog. For fun, I read blogs by other scientists or play Scrabble in foreign languages."

"Not dating anyone?

Alexis shook her head. "My family nags me about finding a boyfriend. Just the other day, my Baba demanded that I bring a date to the family's Fourth of July shindig."

"Is that a problem?"

Alexis considered the question. Depending on how she took it, she could answer either way. Instead she said, "I don't do Internet dating or speed dating. Anyway, that's about it for my social life, such as it is."

"Interesting."

"I know, endless fun, right?" Alexis looked down at her purse and reached for her phone, which was vibrating.

"Six missed call from work. Something must be up."

"Do you need some privacy?"

"No, I should be going anyway. We're way over the scheduled time. I appreciate your staying this late for me."

"You were the last appointment for the evening, so it's not a problem," Dr. Asael said.

Alexis stood up from the chaise and moved toward the door. "Thanks, doc."

The doctor stood up and followed behind Alexis. "This might be crossing the line, but if you are unable to find yourself a plus-one for your family gathering, I would volunteer—as a friend, of course."

That stopped Alexis short. She had to think fast. "Wow, really?" Although it had come out of the blue, his offer was worth considering. "I may have to take you up on that. Thanks."

Dr. Asael handed her a small business card. There was a number printed beneath a faded Celtic symbol of the trinity. "This has my personal cell phone number on it."

Alexis brushed her thumb over the card, feeling the smooth finish. "I've never seen a business card with no name."

"I was afraid that if one of my friends ever misplaced one, I'd risk having a random stranger get my personal line. This way only my friends have the number."

Alexis smiled and headed out the door. Once again she was leaving in the dark.

CHAPTER
SIXTEEN

"I DIDN'T REALIZE ANYONE would be at the lab this late," Alexis said to the guard as she checked in her personal belongings.

"Twenty-four hours, ma'am," the guard replied with a nod. "Although we rarely see anybody here this late, so tonight is getting interesting."

That piqued her interest. "How many other people have been here tonight?"

"Only one other civilian," the man replied cryptically.

Alexis was about to say something when the elevator chimed and the door opened. She thanked the airman and got into the elevator car, going through the usual protocol at each checkpoint. The door opened on the sixth sublevel, and Alexis stepped out onto the catwalk. She leaned over the railing and was startled to see thirty men and women in military uniforms, including the base commander, Colonel Logan, and other high-ranking officers, standing in front of her laboratory door. One man in a white coat stood in their midst. It was James. Alexis felt a knot forming in her stomach, but she headed down the stairs toward them, trying to figure out what she might have done wrong. James spotted her and approached.

"What's going on?" she asked.

James took a deep breath before answering. "You've uncovered something, Alexis, and we don't know how you did it or what to do about it."

"I don't understand."

"I can't explain it. You'll have to see it with your own eyes."

James took her arm and guided her through the murmuring crowd to her lab's door. He stopped and turned to her. "This is a huge step for you and the science community. But you'll need time to process what I'm about to show you."

Alexis felt her body began to tremble. She swiped her ID badge, and the lock clicked. She pushed the door, but James let her open it only wide enough for them to step inside.

The lights were off, but Alexis noticed something was different. The intense chill in the room sent a shiver down her spine, and she drew her arms in close. Everything in the room appeared to be covered in ice crystals. A faintly glowing blue orb with a dark center hovered in the air about twenty feet from her. She moved toward it to see how it was being suspended. Then she gasped.

She turned toward James. "Please tell me this is some kind of prank initiation to Level Six."

James stepped closer and wrapped a lab coat around her trembling body. "I'm afraid not."

"How did you find this? My lab is sealed."

"We have a failsafe to make sure we don't blow up half the northern hemisphere. When I was shutting down the main lab, I saw there was an abnormal temperature reading coming from your lab. It was extremely low, and I wanted to make sure no chemicals had spilled, so I came down here myself. This is what I found."

James took Alexis's arm and drew her closer to the orb. "You need to see this close up."

"Wait, I want to get some readings. I have a special camera in the trunk of my car. May I bring it down here?"

"I'll have Colonel Logan phone the guard to approve it," James said.

Ten minutes later, Alexis brought a large camera bag down to Level 6, where James was talking to Colonel Logan and some general, whose chest was overflowing with ribbons. She unzipped the camera bag and pulled out a large black camera. "This isn't a normal camera," she explained. "It used to be a typical full-spectrum camera, but now it can detect infrared and other invisible wavelengths. I've also tweaked it to capture atmospheric disruptions and changes in the electromagnetic field."

"It sounds like the device you're building for us," Colonel Logan said.

"It's a test version of what I'm building for you, sir, but much less complicated."

The general, who was clearly superior to anyone Alexis had ever seen or met on the base, looked at her and said, "My dear, after tonight's events you will be funded to build whatever you need."

"I'll get some readings and shots from inside the lab," Alexis said.

"I'll take sound readings and monitor the differences in temperature throughout the room," James added.

"This could take a while," Alexis said to Colonel Logan as she changed the lens on her camera.

"Carry on, then," Colonel Logan said. "Call if you find anything more, Mitchell," Then he and the general headed for the stairs that led back up to the catwalk.

James glanced at Alexis as she scanned her badge. She looked back and noticed his eyes, clear blue and as intense as she remembered. "Thanks for staying and helping me with this, James."

They stepped into the lab.

"I wouldn't miss being a part of ... well, I guess we don't know what this is that we're a part of, but you're welcome."

James placed a small digital recorder on the ground, inches from the glowing area, Alexis began to take pictures. After several shots she stopped to review them.

"James, look at what the camera just caught—tell me what you see."

SEVENTEEN

FIFTEEN MINUTES OUTSIDE of town, in a densely wooded area, stood Azure and Cezar. The moon was their only source of light, and a dirt road their only connecting point.

"Why are we here?" Cezar asked.

"I was about to ask you the same thing," Azure replied.

In the distance, they saw headlights coming slowly up the dirt road. Cezar glared at Azure. "Who told you I was meeting you here?"

From behind them came a familiar voice. "I had you come out here."

The two men turned toward the voice, and a short red-haired man stepped from the shadows.

"You should move away from the road before the driver sees you," the man said, and the three of them moved farther into the tree line as the car drove past.

Azure shot the newcomer a harsh look. "Samuel, why would you have us meet here when he told us not to be seen together."

Samuel's dark eyes glittered in the moonlight as he made his response. "Look around. He's not here. He's preoccupied with his new mission." Samuel shook his head, disgust written on his face. "We have a bigger problem. A gate is beginning to open."

"Who has that kind of power?" Cezar asked.

"No human, that is for certain," Samuel replied.

"Samuel, where is it opening?" Azure asked.

"Over the ridge, on the base."

Cezar gave a glare. "Is the filthy human woman to blame?"

"I thought no human ...," Azure began but stopped when he saw the expressions on his companions' faces. "What do we do?"

"Close it," Cezar said.

"We can't do that, none of us have that kind of power," Azure pointed out.

"It is possible if more than one of us bond together," Cezar replied.

"But if we used that kind of power without the Master ..."

"The others know," Samuel said. "And before you say anything stupid, Azure, we are doing this quietly. So don't screw up again. We are worthy of this power, and it's time we take it."

Samuel strode off, disappearing deeper into the woods.

Cezar turned to his companion. "Azure, why are we messing with this?"

"Let's just get this over with."

"We could eliminate the problem by getting rid of her."

"Don't be a fool. Remember what happened when you did that before. And how would you explain it to him after he told you to leave her alone?"

"She will probably be at the base," Cezar said.

"Which means he will be close by," said Azure. "He's going to see us."

"Yes, and as you said, we answer to him, not Samuel."

"Do you think he already knows about all of this?" Azure asked.

"Our meeting with Samuel?"

"No, do you think he knows that she has opened a portal? I didn't think the human mind had advanced that far," Azure said as he stared in the direction of the base.

"I still don't have a clear understanding of what his abilities are, even after all this time," Cezar said. "And if I had such understanding, that would be his weakness, so he will never share that with anyone."

"What if this gate opens to the outer realm?"

"Then none of us are safe."

CHAPTER EIGHTEEN

"I THINK WE SHOULD call them, James," Alexis said. "It's 7 a.m., and we keep getting the same results."

James shook his head. "We'll keep them in the dark a little longer to give us time to consider all possible explanations and hypotheses."

"The orb is gone. There's nothing more to test."

"I don't want something this big to go through a hundred hypotheses and make it look as if we're guessing. It would reflect badly."

Alexis was feeling a heaviness in her mind from lack of rest. "All right. We'll hold back for a while, but you have to be the one to tell them why we're stalling." After a long yawn, Alexis began to gather her equipment.

"I'll tell them we're going to sort through this with clear minds tonight."

"I'm going home to get some sleep. I'll come back and print those pictures so we don't have to keeping staring at screens. And I'll prove that my first and only hypothesis is correct."

"When will you be back?"

Alexis rubbed her brow and tried to think. "Around three. Right now, I need to get home to Oslo. He's probably upset that I didn't come home last night." She shot James a quizzical look. "You don't even look tired."

"I drank a lot of caffeine."

James headed out the door while she finished putting her equipment in their cases. She could hear James talking to someone as she finished zipping and snapping.

"What are you guys doing here?" she heard him saying.

When she pushed the lab door open to leave, she saw two military guards with James.

As she slipped past them, James said, "I'll see you later on today, Alexis. Sleep well."

Alexis nodded and continued walking toward the stairs. "Thanks, you too." She paused to let her vision adjust.

"Is everything all right?" James asked.

"Just my autopilot malfunctioning. My eyes are having trouble adjusting to the light."

Alexis headed up the stairs and crossed the catwalk. As she went, she glanced down, trying to see the two men James was talking to, but their faces were blocked by beams that ran the width of the ceiling. Alexis frowned and continued toward the large metal door.

When the elevator opened at the main lobby, Alexis saw the usual crush of people waiting to start their day. She zigzagged through the crowd and made her way to the front desk.

As she waited her turn, a woman from Level Six said, "Did we forget to change out of our pajamas, newbie?" A group of female researchers standing nearby chuckled.

Alexis looked down at the yoga pants and tight T-shirt she had changed into before her appointment with Dr. Asael the day before.

"I didn't make it home last night," Alexis said with a sheepish grin.

"Out partying, eh?"

"Actually, Paige, I was here all night working with James. He called me on short notice, and I didn't have time to change."

The laughter stopped. Alexis knew that the mere mention of James would draw the attention of any woman in the department. She had seen plenty of her female colleagues, including some in the group she was talking to now, gawk whenever he passed by them. Alexis smiled innocently, put on her rhinestone sunglasses, and walked outside.

Her usual quick drive home turned into a stop-and-go ordeal of red lights and school buses. When she finally pulled in, she glanced at the Dumpster behind the furniture store.

As she headed up the stairway, she heard another car pull in, and she reached in her purse for her mace. The vehicle came to a stop and the passenger side door opened.

"Miss Zen, do you have time to talk?"

Alexis dropped the mace into her purse when she saw one of the detectives she had spoken to earlier in the week. She walked down the steps toward their car. The other detective got out, and the two met her at the front of their vehicle.

"You told us you're a research scientist, right?" Detective Carter asked.

"Yes, I'm a physicist."

"We think you might be able to help us understand something about this case," Detective Lindsay said. "We wanted your input before we have to hand it over to the FBI, and I told my partner we should ask you for your thoughts."

"I'd be happy to, but can I do it later? I pulled an all-nighter at work, and I'm beat."

"Sure, you could stop by the station, or I could come here when it's convenient and show you what we found," Lindsay said.

"I have to go back to the lab later for a few hours, so I'll stop by the station on my way home."

Alexis excused herself and headed up the stairs. She was back in the fresh air with Oslo a few minutes later, and she took him for a long walk. Once inside the apartment again, she locked the door and put down fresh food and water for her puppy.

Alexis changed into a different pair of yoga pants and a fresh T-shirt and climbed into bed. It wasn't long before her body was feeling light and her mind was dropping into a deep sleep.

Oslo jumped onto the bed, rested his head on her leg, and followed her lead.

CHAPTER NINETEEN

Alexis stands in the middle of a jade-colored meadow, feeling a cool breeze and the warmth of a brilliant sun. The lush green grass of the meadow is speckled with dandelion seed heads swaying in the breeze. As she walks through them, they parachute into the clouds. Alexis turns and sees the top of a hill close behind her. She turns toward it, hoping to see an endless field of daisies. As she nears the top of the hill, she closes her eyes and takes in a slow breath. Her body feels weightless, and she hears music in the distance. Alexis ignores the sound and keeps moving closer to the top. She slowly exhales and begins to open her eyes. They fill with tears as she's overcome by darkness—and evil.

"Oh, no!" Alexis shouted.

Oslo jumped off the bed as Alexis sat up and looked around frantically. She finally realized she was in her bedroom, but her hands were trembling and her heart pounding. "It was just a dream," she murmured before searching for her phone to check the time. It was 1:30 p.m.

Alexis lay back down to try to get a few more hours of rest, but her mind was fully alert, and she couldn't close her eyes without seeing the perdition and feeling the despair that had awakened her. She threw off the covers and sat on the side of the bed.

Alexis rubbed the top of Oslo's head. "Shall we restart the day, boy? Want to go for a walk?"

Alexis grabbed Oslo's leash and hooked it onto his collar, and they headed toward the door. There was a soft knock. Alexis peeked out the kitchen window that overlooked the back parking area and saw her mother's car. She opened the door, and Marcia stepped inside.

"Sorry, Mom, I didn't know you'd be stopping over. Hold on, why did you stop by, I'm normally at work at this hour?"

Marcia took a moment to look around and then handed Alexis a small plastic shopping bag that bore the logo of a local boutique. "I was going to drop this off on your porch, but I saw your car and figured you must be home."

"Thank you."

"Why aren't you at work?"

"I was there all night, so I came home to sleep for a while. I'm going back later."

"Aren't you going to open the bag?" Marcia asked.

Alexis opened it and pulled out a floral-pattern blouse with pearlized buttons. She tried to hide her distaste as she held it up to see if it would fit.

Marcia was opening the refrigerator. "It doesn't fit me, but I thought you might wear it," she said.

Alexis folded the shirt neatly and placed it on her kitchen table. "How are you, Mom? Anything new?"

Marcia closed the refrigerator door and headed back toward Alexis's bedroom. "I'm good. Are you going out to your grandmother's house this weekend?"

"Oh, right, the Fourth is this weekend."

Alexis looked down at Oslo. "Remind me to make a call, your mama needs a date."

"Who are you bringing?"

Alexis followed her mother into her bedroom. "Mom, what are you doing?"

"Snooping."

"I'm a little too old for room inspections, Mother."

"I figured you'd have stuff strewn everywhere."

"What, did I all of a sudden become some closet hoarder?"

Marcia left the bedroom and walked back to the kitchen. She stared at the sink. "Something wrong with your dishwasher?"

"No, why?"

"Your dishes are piling up."

Alexis glanced over and saw two breakfast plates and three glasses in the sink. "I'll take care of those later."

"You need to, they're starting to smell and ..."

"What are you looking for? Why do you always do a scan of my place? Do you think I'm hiding something?"

"I just stopped by to give you that shirt, not get harassed, so you're welcome." Marcia turned to leave.

"Mom, I'm sorry. It's just weird, that's all. I don't go through your underwear drawer or tell you to clean up."

"I'm your mother, and it's none of your business what's in my underwear drawer. Besides, my house is always clean."

"Mom, I hate to break it to you, but it's no longer your business to know everything I'm doing," Alexis said evenly. "But I appreciate your concern."

"Fine, I'll see you this weekend," Marcia said with a hint of aggravation in her voice.

"Okay, mom."

"Your grandma wanted to know if you were bringing anyone, so I'll let her know it's none of her business."

"I never said that. And maybe I am bringing someone," Alexis said.

Marcia shook her head slowly as she opened the door. "Bye, Alexis."

When her mother closed the door, Alexis waved at it.

"That's it, Oslo, where's my purse. I think I stuck his card in there."

Alexis dug through old receipts, gum wrappers, and random scraps of paper until she found the white card with the faint grey writing. She went back into her bedroom and dialed the number. Dr. Asael picked up after one ring.

"Hello, Alexis."

"Hey, Doctor Asael. So I'm calling to see if you were still interested in being my plus-one for my family Fourth of July party. But I understand if you ..."

"I would enjoy it."

"Okay, great. It's this Saturday at noonish. Shall I pick you up or ..."

"I will come to your place if that's all right with you."

"Yes, fine. I'll text you my address. It's a picnic, nothing fancy."

"I'll forgo the tux. Any other requirements?"

"No, sorry, I just wanted you to be prepared. So I'll see you in a couple days."

"Have a nice day, Alexis."

Alexis clicked her phone off and looked at Oslo with a big smile. "I got a date for this weekend. Okay, so it's not a date, but close enough, right?"

Oslo gave a happy little bark. She grabbed his leash, and they headed out the door for a walk.

CHAPTER
TWENTY

MARY TRIED NOT to be obvious as she listened to the doctor's phone conversation. She began organizing the files on her desk and scribbling unimportant notes while she turned away from where the doctor was standing.

"Mary, I need your thoughts," Dr. Asael said after he ended the call. He was leaning on the counter that overlooked her work space.

Mary furrowed her brow. "About a patient, sir?"

"Yes, actually."

She gestured toward her computer. "Doctor, unless it's about entering information into the database, I don't think I'm qualified to give an opinion."

The doctor smiled. "That's not the type of input I need. I'm going out this Saturday afternoon with Alexis Zen, and I need to know what to wear to a family picnic."

"I didn't think dating a patient was ethical," Mary blurted, immediately regretting it. "But, of course, that's none of my business. Anyway, if it's a picnic, go casual."

"I'm not dating her, Mary. She needed someone to help get her family off her back about her social life, so it's a faux date. Although just between you and me, I'm glad for the opportunity to see her in an environment where she can be herself, and I will be assessing her while I'm there."

"Does she know that?"

"No, and she doesn't need to."

"Wear something you normally relax in, or when you hang out with friends."

"Mary, I don't hang out. My associates are not the casual family type."

"Then shorts and a short-sleeved shirt, sneakers or sandals, no tie, no shiny shoes. Here, let me find you an example." Mary grabbed the latest edition of *People Fashion* from her desk and flipped through the pages. She found what she was looking for and handed the magazine to the doctor. "Like this."

He glanced at a page depicting a scrawny teen wearing rugged cargo pants and a short-sleeved plaid shirt.

The front door opened, and an older gentleman walked up to the counter to sign in. Mary looked down at the appointment schedule. "Mr. Accord is here, sir."

The men went back to the doctor's office, and Mary went back to her work. By the time she was finished with the last file folder on her desk, an hour and forty-five minutes had passed. It was past time for her to go.

Mary closed out the patient entry page and the solitaire game on her computer screen, dropped a pile of manila folders into the file cabinet behind her desk, and locked it. She glanced down the hall. She hated to leave without saying goodbye, but it was late, and she wanted to go home.

Mary turned off the lights in her area, locked the front door, and grabbed her things before heading down the hallway to the employee exit. When she walked by Dr. Asael's office door, she heard low voices. She looked straight ahead and continued out the exit.

Mary pushed the door open and stepped from the air-conditioned cool of the building into a warm and slightly humid early evening. Sitting in the usually empty alley that ran between the two buildings was a familiar car. Mary had seen it before, but at the time she thought it was a dream. This time she knew it was real. The engine wasn't running, and there was no one inside. Her curiosity trumped her better judgment, and she began to walk over to get a better look. The vehicle didn't belong to anyone from the dry cleaner, the doctor always parked in the back close to the security lights, and his patient had been dropped off in a van. The vehicle was a mystery.

Mary approached the car but stopped when she heard voices coming from the front of the building. Quickly she moved backwards and slouched down near the Dumpster, feeling like an idiot.

She peeked around the edge of the Dumpster and saw a couple walking their Siberian husky in front of the building. She let her heart slow down and then stood up and walked toward the car. She looked around, saw no one, and placed her hand on the door handle. She took a deep breath and lifted it. The door was unlocked.

She opened the door and looked inside. The interior smelled like the back woods of her parents' house, and the soft leather upholstery felt like silk on her hand.

"Excuse me."

Mary jumped even as she felt the blood drain from her face. She turned around and found herself staring at a tall, well-dressed, well-built man. His dark hair was styled perfectly, and his intoxicating blue eyes seemed to put her mind in a trance.

"I'm so sorry," she murmured, her voice quavering.

"You seemed to be looking for something."

"No, no. I was ... I was trying to see who owned the car. I wasn't sure if someone was stranded or if something strange had happened. I work right here and didn't know who would have their car in the alley this time of day. I am truly sorry."

He tilted his head to listen as she made her explanation. She felt heat prickling at the back of her neck.

He fixed her with an intense gaze. "In future, stay away from my vehicle."

"I said I was sorry," she told him, but it came out in a quivery whisper. All she wanted to do was get away, but she was flushed and flustered and unable to move.

The man brushed past her, got in his car, and drove away.

CHAPTER TWENTY-ONE

THE PRECINCT STATION was quiet as Detectives Carter and Lindsay sat at their desks going over the paperwork for a recent robbery/homicide they had solved.

"I still can't believe that guy thought he could outrun you," Carter said as he looked up at his partner.

"Not the sharpest knife in the drawer," Lindsay replied.

Carter cleared his throat loudly. Lindsay looked up and saw his partner gazing past him and gesturing with a slight thrust of his chin. He turned around and saw a patrol officer ushering a tall young blonde in their direction.

"Afternoon, Miss Zen," Carter said. "Thanks for coming."

Lindsay stood up. "I'll get you a chair."

"Why don't we take her down to the tech room?" Carter said.

Lindsay nodded, and the three stepped from the detectives' room into the hallway, followed by the appreciative gazes of the other detectives.

"So, Alexis, what kind of things do you like to do for fun?" Lindsay asked.

"Besides work, I love an occasional chess match or word games with my grandfather," she replied.

"Awesome," Lindsay said.

Alexis laughed. "I wasn't always such a drudge. Back in high school, I liked riding horses, star gazing, and rock climbing."

"I have a friend who has horses if you ever want to go riding again," Lindsay said.

Detective Carter opened a door, and they entered a small room. A young man was sitting at a desk, gazing at a computer monitor. "Hey, Eric, this is Miss Zen. Miss Zen, this is our tech genius, Eric Bloor."

"Nice to meet you," Alexis said after Eric waved to her.

"Will you bring up the Ice Man footage for us, please," Carter said as the three approached Eric's desk.

Alexis raised an eyebrow. "Ice Man?"

"Watch first, then we'll explain," Lindsay said. He dragged a guest chair from the corner, set it down next to Eric, and motioned for Alexis to sit.

"This first video is across town from where the John Doe was found," Eric said. "Note the time stamp on both vids, because the second is from where we found him, near your place."

Alexis peered at the screen and watched a man frantically stumbling around and talking to himself. As soon as the man disappeared from view, Eric clicked his mouse to bring up the next video.

Alexis's mouth fell open as she noticed the time stamp. When she saw the edges of a circular glow in the lower right side of the screen, her eyes went wide. She tried to compose herself. "Let me guess. The body was frozen, thus the nickname?"

"Yes, but how would you know that?" Detective Carter asked.

"He wasn't frozen in the normal way," said Lindsay.

"He was frozen from the outside in, right?" Alexis said.

The two detectives glanced at one another and then looked at Alexis. "Seriously, Miss Zen, how would you know that?" Detective Carter asked.

"I think I might know what happened to your Ice Man, but it will sound crazy."

"Try us," Carter said.

"Were ice formations found?"

Carter motioned to Eric. "Start the video again."

Alexis watched ice crystals form across the security camera lens.

Lindsay leaned over her shoulder. "The coroner mentioned magnetic freezing."

"That explains the freezing, but not how he managed to teleport across town," Alexis said. "I need to get back to the base."

"If you know something that could help us solve this, please share," Lindsay said as Alexis stood up to leave.

"I have incomplete answers that will just create more questions," Alexis said. "I really can't help you. I have to go." She turned and left.

"She obviously knows something," Carter said after Alexis had gone. "Eric, go over those again and see if you can see Miss Zen's apartment. I want to know where she was that night."

CHAPTER TWENTY-TWO

Detective Carter entered Alexis Zen's information into the search task bar and began searching. A few moments later, he gave a low whistle.

"What did you find?" Lindsay asked. He got up from his desk and came around to take a look.

"She's not dumb, that's for sure," Carter said, staring at the screen.

"No kidding," Lindsay replied. "She's a physicist. Most physicists have higher IQs than you and me combined."

Carter looked from the screen to his partner. "Which hasn't stopped you from flirting with her."

"No way."

"Never mind. Check out all the awards she got in high school for academic science achievements. The Naval Science Award, The U.S. National Physics Olympiad Award, there must be five or six in just physics, and the list goes on."

"Wonder why she's working on a military base?" Lindsay went back to his desk and began a search of his own.

Carter laughed. "Dude, she's way out of your league."

"Why, because she's smart and pretty?"

"Check out the newspaper article about all her scholarships."

Lindsay looked up the article on his computer. He frowned and grabbed a file from the stack sitting on his desk. "This is odd. I'm not seeing Cornell on here, or MIT. I know she graduated from both of them."

"I don't remember her telling us that," Carter said.

"I saw pictures on her wall of her and friends in caps and gowns. And it's listed on her sheet." Lindsay started typing.

"Why do we have a printout of her record?" Carter asked.

"I thought it would be good to know more about her, you know, make sure she didn't have any priors," Lindsay said as he continued to type. "I can't find anything on her parents having a military connection. You saw her apartment; it's not huge or elaborate."

"That car had to be expensive," Carter noted.

"Why wouldn't she go somewhere that offered her a lot of money instead of government pay?"

"I don't know, Stuart, but it's not relevant to this case. But she knows something that is relevant, and I think you should ask her about it."

"Why me?"

"Why not, you were checking into her anyway."

There was a noise from the hall and both men turned to look. Two men dressed in military camouflage and two men in suits came down the hall and went into the office marked "Steven Jenkins, Chief of Police." A moment later, Chief Jenkins came out and led the four visitors to the tech room. After several minutes, the group emerged from the room, and the four visitors headed back toward the elevator. The chief, an older balding man, came into the detectives' room and approached Carter and Lindsay.

Carter looked up and said, "Hey, Chief, what was that ..."

"So, who's going to the festival this week?" Chief Jenkins asked in a loud voice, giving Carter a look that put an end to any more questions.

"Yeah, we'll be there," Carter said.

"The wife is trying to get me to enter the lip sync contest," the chief said.

Eric Bloor stuck his head into the detectives' room.

"What is it, Eric?" Carter asked.

Eric stepped into the room and approached. "I found something," he said in a low voice. He handed a flash drive to Detective Lindsay. "I expanded my screen view and started watching the furniture store video again. Except I played it in reverse this time."

"I thought they wiped all those files from your system and took the hard copy," Chief Jenkins said.

"They did," Eric replied. "But when this case turned weird, I made a few more copies of the files. I figured someone from ... someone else might take over."

"Smart kid," Carter said. He inserted the flash drive and started the video.

Eric took over and found the place on the video he wanted. "This shows George Pliate leaving in a hurry from Miss Zen's apartment. Now let me back it up more. Right here she's pulling in."

"When did Pliate get there, though?" Lindsay asked. "I mean, he leaves within ten minutes of her getting home."

Eric slid back the cursor on the "Play" icon. "It could take me a minute to find it."

The chief stood up. "Okay, gentlemen, fill me in later. And talk to Miss Zen again." He headed back to his office and shut the door behind him.

Eric found what he was looking for and resumed the video. "That's him right there."

"Who's he talking to?" Carter asked. "I don't see anyone else."

"I looked at the other camera angles from the other side of the alley, and there is no one else," Eric said.

Carter glanced at Lindsay. "Let's go check on your girlfriend, Stuart." He stood up and pulled open the right top drawer of his desk. He took out a Glock 17 and put it in his holster.

"She's headed to work, so we won't be able to talk with her right now," Lindsay said as he clipped his badge to the left side of his belt.

"Yes, but now the crime scene has expanded to her front door."

CHAPTER TWENTY-THREE

A FEW STARS WINKED in the night sky, and a cloud slowly crossed the face of the moon. Crickets chirped in time to the flashes from thousands of lightning bugs waltzing through the high grass surrounding the research facility of the Air Force base.

Three black SUVs pulled into the facility, parked, and shut off their headlights, but only the lead SUV's doors opened. Four men emerged, two wearing camouflage, and two in dark suits. The suits followed the other two men as they headed into the building.

"I need to see your ID, please," the airman behind the counter said after the four men entered the main lobby.

Before anyone could respond, the elevator chimed and opened, and James Mitchell stepped from the car. "They don't need passes," James said to the airman as he approached the group. "They're not going any further."

James turned to the two in suits. "How are you gentlemen tonight?"

"Cut the crap, Mitchell, you know this was pushing it," one of the suits replied.

"Did you get it?"

"Yes, but I think the tech has another copy. He gave everything up way too easily."

"Per our agreement, we have a copy as well," the other suit added. He took a flash drive from his pocket and handed it to James. "This makes us even."

James took the red flash drive but made no response. The four visitors left. When they were gone, James turned to the airman at the counter. "Never trust the CIA." Then he went to the elevator and scanned his ID. He stepped into the elevator and headed down to Level Six.

Alexis was pacing in front of her lab, looking up every time the large metal door opened. A few of the female researchers were leaving for the day and saw Alexis standing there. She smiled, hoping they'd reciprocate.

"Night, Alexis," Paige said. "Looks like a pretty lonely night for you."

The metal door opened, and James appeared. "Good night, ladies, see you all tomorrow," he said from the catwalk.

Paige and the other women shot quick glances at one another and then headed for the elevator.

"Your lab," James said to Alexis as he came down the stairs.

They headed to the door, and Alexis scanned her badge before they stepped inside. The past thirty-six hours and the last few weeks were playing in her head. Her life was spinning out of control, and she couldn't stop it.

James handed her the flash drive. "This took quite a few strings being pulled and favors cashed in, so it better be worth it."

"It's worth it for the scientific aspect, but we may have some disgruntled detectives on our hands."

"Explain to me again why you couldn't just tell me what this is?"

"Words don't do it justice. You have to see it to believe it. And even then you might not believe it."

She sat down at her desk and put the red flash drive into a USB port on her laptop, then pointed to a 42-inch monitor on a stand to the left of the desk. "I'll play it on both screens. The first feed was taken across town from where the second video feed was recorded. Note the time stamps on both."

James rolled a chair to the large screen and sat down.

Alexis played the video numerous times, pointing out the similarities of the crime scene footage and what they had witnessed in her lab. "See the white orb forming in the bottom right corner of the video screen?"

James shrugged his shoulders. "It has some common aspects, I will give you that much. However, I don't see anything other than a tampering with the time stamp and probably someone's high beams reflecting in the fog."

"Then how do you explain the screen crystallizing, not to mention that the man was frozen?"

"Food truck would be my guess," James suggested.

"It would have to be a magnetic food truck."

"There's a CAS portable freezer here."

Alexis frowned. "What would we need that for?"

"Let's just say they like to keep certain things on ice without causing tissue or cell damage during transport."

"The victim here was not an alien on ice, these are not headlights from a vehicle, and the police verified the time stamps from both locations. You know what you witnessed in this very space less than twenty hours ago. Are you really going to dismiss this as headlights in the fog?"

James made no reply.

"Something is creating these anomalies, these openings, and I think there's a way to re-create them." Alexis turned back to the monitor to go over the footage again.

James stood up. "I'm going to go check on some other stuff. I'll be back later."

Alexis slid her chair to the left and grabbed her camera bag from a large white work table. She pulled out the memory stick and waited as the computer downloaded the images. There were more than a hundred pictures, mostly shots of Oslo and few random landscapes. She stared at one of the landscape images, admiring the white petal-like bracts of a dogwood tree and the tri-pinnate leaves of Queen Anne's lace. Suddenly, her eyes went wide. She picked up phone on her desk, dialed extension 224, and waited for James to pick up.

The lab door chimed, and James stepped inside.

Alexis hung up the phone. "I was just calling you."

"About what?"

"More evidence for my hypothesis that the orb is a type of portal."

"I didn't mean to offend you earlier," James said. "I'm a skeptic about almost everything."

"You study aliens and you're a skeptic? Highly illogical, Captain."

"Thank you, Mr. Spock, but I have other reasons for my exobiology degree."

"Have a look at these pictures," Alexis said, and she moved a chair to the right, making space for James to sit next to her.

James sat on a chair next to hers and looked at the screen. "Where did you take these?"

"About a mile from the base. I was testing the camera."

James pointed at a photo on the screen. "That looks like the center of the orb that was here."

Alexis nodded and brought up a grid of photos taken in the lab. James pointed to one. "Can you bring that one up and put them side by side?"

"That's what I've been doing." Alexis moved her finger in a circle over the center of the picture. "There are a couple of differences between the two."

"The lab's orb has a black center, and this one doesn't," James said. He gave her a puzzled look. "You never said anything about the other orb."

"I had no idea it was on my camera. It wasn't visible in daylight."

"We should do some night shots in that location," James said.

"Yes. We should also test the area's electromagnetic levels with my new equipment."

"Doing anything special for the Fourth?"

"My family is having a get together."

"Is Oslo going?"

"Probably not. He's not much for crowds."

"Boyfriend's an introvert, huh?"

Alexis chuckled. "Oslo is my dog, not my boyfriend. But he does think he's the man in my life."

James got up and headed for the door. "I have something I need to check on. I'll be back."

Alexis continued to scan through the pictures, hoping for more insight into these strange events. The next time she checked the clock, it was 3 a.m., and her eyelids were heavy. She shut down the computers and was putting her camera away when James came back.

"Hey, after your family thing, do you have plans?" James asked.

"I'm not sure," Alexis said. "I have a friend going with me, and, well, I guess it depends. Why?"

"I have a boat on the lake, and I usually take it out to watch the fireworks. If your family event finishes up in time, you and your friend could join me, if you like."

Alexis realized that he must have thought her friend was a woman. She decided not to correct him. "Thanks. I'll definitely consider it."

CHAPTER TWENTY-FOUR

AZURE STOOD IN THE dark with Cezar near a loading dock behind the strip mall. They were waiting for Samuel. At length, Samuel stepped around the corner of the building.

"Why this urgent meeting?" Cezar asked.

"Do you two find pleasure in being pawns in his cause?"

"What do you mean, pawns?" Azure asked.

"Do you two enjoy your limits, or would you rather have the freedom to dominate this world?" Samuel asked, his face impassive.

Azure and Cezar looked at each other. In their world it was not wise to test the ways of their master. "We all know that's not an option," Azure replied. "You know we have inviolable boundaries."

"Boundaries, not walls," Samuel said. "Since we are blamed for this world's evil, some of us think it's time to show these humans what we are capable of."

"There are those who already do that, whose purpose it is in the balance of things," Cezar said. "Your desire to emulate them is hubris." Cezar began to turn away.

"The ones you speak of still fall under his dominion. We will take over the lives of those who won't listen. We will force people to put their thoughts into action. We will show him how things should have been done when we agreed to join him so long ago."

"That is not why we are here," Azure said.

"Was not his offer to make these humans know the difference between good and evil?" Samuel asked, pacing impatiently.

A familiar voice came from the shadows. "Samuel, why do you persist in your defiance?"

Azure and Cezar moved away from Samuel as he began to tremble.

"Master, we just want to take our place in this world," Samuel said.

The Master stepped out of the shadows and looked at Samuel with pity, knowing his desires. "You have been in rebellion for many years. You have recruited many. For that I commend you."

Azure and Cezar glanced quickly at one another, confused by what the Master had said. Samuel, also confused, dropped to his knees.

The Master's gaze took in the other two as well as Samuel. "You all knew the rules when you chose to stay here with me."

"Please give me another chance," Samuel said. "I will follow. I will restore the other dissenters to your side. I will deal with the human woman."

"Enough!" The Master's voice was like a clap of thunder, and it echoed against the building. Azure and Cezar approached the Master and stood next to him, one on either side, like loyal retainers.

The Master looked at Samuel as a man might look at an insect. "It is not my place to forgive."

"What will you do to me?"

The Master gestured for Samuel to approach. He did, still on his knees. The Master leaned down and whispered into Samuel's ear. When he stood up straight again, his eyes were filled with an indescribable blackness.

The sound of static crackling through nearby electrical towers disturbed the quiet of the night. Sleeping birds rose into the sky and scattered, and the buzz and click of a million insects rose to a crescendo. The strip mall's security lights flickered and dimmed, and a gust of frigid air pushed Cesar and Azure away from where Samuel was kneeling. An eerie chill descended as the night returned to stillness.

A blue sphere of light appeared overhead and began to descend. The light brightened, and ice crystals began spreading across the ground. The orb came close and hovered, as if it were waiting.

Samuel stood up and tried to back away, but the Master grasped his shoulder in an iron grip. When he let go, the illuminated ball changed shape. A black center formed, and the sphere expanded. In the next instant, Samuel and the orb were gone.

The Master looked at Azure and Cezar. "I have kept you here to witness the price of thwarting my purpose."

"We understand," Cezar said. "But why have you not got rid of the human woman?"

Azure turned to his companion. "It doesn't matter. We have others matters to attend to."

As the two disappeared into the dark field behind the strip mall, the Master stood watching. He stared into the darkness, listening to the faint sound of a cricket chirping and the call of a whippoorwill from somewhere in the distance. A breeze blew across his face as the blackness melted from his eyes. He turned and disappeared back into the shadows.

CHAPTER TWENTY-FIVE

ALEXIS CRAWLED INTO bed at 3:45 a.m. Oslo jumped up next to her and snuggled close. She stroked his head and thought about her family's Fourth of July celebration, only hours away.

For her, it was one of the longest days of the year, the day her extended family gathered together in one place, aunts, uncles, cousins, spouses, boyfriends, girlfriends, all surrounded by the chaos of a small army of children set free on five acres. Everyone would catch up on news and gossip, tolerating each other's differences in the name of family harmony. The men would debate politics, the women would discuss the latest rumors and scandals, and Alexis would be questioned repeatedly about her lack of a social life and her top-secret job, including the usual jokes about the legendary Hanger 18. Alexis enjoyed seeing everyone but wished she had more to share.

She put the coming day out of her mind and focused on Oslo. "Night boy, and I promise I'll get us back on a normal schedule soon." Alexis petted his head and rubbed behind his ears. Before long they were both asleep.

She dreamed of a beautiful valley full of wildflowers and streaming sunlight and cool breezes. A stand of soaring red maples loomed in the distance, beckoning her, but she couldn't move. She was rooted to the hillside, and when she tried to pull away, the atmosphere began to change. Alexis felt the wind pick up, saw clouds gather and darken and begin to run swiftly, like ghosts fleeing from—what?

The air turned chill, and it began to rain. In the distance, the maple trees were receding, but still Alexis couldn't move.

She peered around and saw that she was close to the top of the hill, the one place she didn't want to be. Memories of an unknown despair clutched at her soul. She closed her eyes and took in a deep breath of cold air.

When she opened her eyes, she was surrounded by darkness. A feeling of sorrow and pain burned inside her, and she felt as if she couldn't breathe. The darkness shifted, and faces began to emerge from it. Alexis heard music, and the sound was getting louder.

Alexis opened her eyes and felt Oslo lying against her chest. She sighed with relief and then reached over to grab the phone and shut off the alarm.

Oslo waited on the bed as she showered, dried her hair, put on makeup, and then waded through the plenitude of clothing in her closet, trying to find the perfect outfit. She didn't want to be too casual and make Dr. Asael feel out of place, but she didn't want to overanalyze the situation. She turned toward Oslo and held up an outfit. "What do you think, boy?"

Oslo had no opinion.

Alexis turned back to the closet and found a pair of tan Capris and a black tank top with a crocheted embellishment on the neckline. She figured that once Dr. Asael arrived, she could see what he was wearing and accessorize accordingly.

At 11:15, as she waited for her iron to heat up, there was a knock on her front door. Alexis jumped and nearly burned a finger. With butterflies taking flight in her stomach, Alexis opened the door. Detectives Carter and Lindsay were standing there.

"Oh. Hello, detectives."

"Expecting someone else, Ms. Zen?" Detective Carter asked.

"Yes, a friend." She motioned for the two detectives to step inside. "I need to apologize for the other day. I didn't realize they would be so aggressive in getting a copy of that file."

"Don't worry about it," Detective Lindsay said.

Detective Carter leaned against the counter, his arms crossed. "Did you watch the whole video?"

"No, just the parts you showed me with the frozen man."

"What made that part so interesting?" Carter asked.

"I had a similar effect in a recent research project."

"You have a project on frozen people?" Carter asked.

"No."

"What kind of research?" Lindsay asked.

"Sorry, it's classified."

Carter frowned. "Did you know there are gashes on the outside of your door and door frame?"

"I know."

"It looks like someone tried to break in. Funny you didn't report it. Or did your dog do that?"

Alexis let out a long breath. She had swallowed enough secrets in her life. This time she'd come clean. "Someone was in my apartment, but I didn't know him or why he was here."

There was a light rap on the door.

"Excuse me, detectives." Alexis went to the door and opened it. For a split second, she didn't recognize Dr. Asael. He looked as if he'd just stepped off a movie set. He wore muted tan cargo shorts, a black polo, and leather flip flops. His arms and legs were perfectly proportioned, the muscles well defined. Obviously, Dr. Asael took very good care of himself.

"Hello, Alexis."

"Hi, come in, sorry for seeming a little spaced."

"You do seem just a bit distracted."

"It's just that I've never seen you in anything but a suit and tie. You look good. I mean you look normal, but in a good way. A good normal."

"Thanks. I think."

Alexis grimaced. "Why don't you come in before I say something stupid."

Alexis introduced Dr. Asael to the detectives and then excused herself to get ready.

The three men stood awkwardly for moment until Detective Lindsay broke the silence. "What type of medicine do you practice?"

"Psychiatry" Dr. Asael said.

The awkward silence resumed.

Alexis returned to the kitchen in a black tank top and denim Bahama shorts. Not wanting to match Dr. Asael, she had rejected the Capris and added a soft green rhinestone belt, jade bracelet, and matching earrings. Her hair was loosely pulled to the side, with her bangs sweeping across her forehead.

All eyes were fixed on her as she entered the room.

"You look great, Alexis," the doctor said. "I hope I'm not underdressed."

"No, you're perfect," Alexis said.

Detective Carter cleared his throat. "We know you need to get out of here, so we'll keep this brief." He glanced at Dr. Asael. "Perhaps the doctor would like to wait outside."

"I've already told Dr. Asael everything I could remember about that night," Alexis said. "We can speak about it in front of him."

"Was Mr. Pliate already in your home when you got here that night?" Carter asked.

"He was here when I got home, waiting somewhere in the dark. He grabbed me from behind and tried to ... um ..." Alexis began to feel her emotions spinning. "Sorry, it's hard to describe exactly what happened."

"Perhaps I can help," Dr. Asael said. "He attacked her from behind and tried to force himself on her but failed. He was spooked by something and left abruptly. She didn't mention this in your original interview because she wasn't sure it was the same man."

"I'm sorry for not explaining this earlier," Alexis said.

"Its fine, Ms. Zen, we'll be in touch if we have any more questions," Carter said. The two detectives walked to the door and left.

Alexis turned to Dr. Asael, who was leaning against the island in the center of the kitchen. "Thanks for rescuing me from my inability to translate that night, doc."

"You're welcome. And it's Ben."

"Benjamin is my favorite name from biblical history."

"Why is that?" he asked.

"Second chances."

"How do you mean?"

"After Rachel thought her firstborn son, Joseph, was dead, she was given a second chance to give Jacob another son. His name was Benjamin. I believe everyone deserves a second chance in life."

"Interesting thought. You do realize she died shortly after giving birth to him?"

"Irony, right?"

"Right. And in some cultures my name is thought to mean 'son of my pain.' Others revere the name as 'the righteous son.' "

"Which are you?"

Ben smiled and said, "I haven't decided." He walked to the door and opened it. "Let's get out of here before we miss the hot dogs."

"Yes, I don't want to be late."

"I've gathered that your mother is a stickler for punctuality, and I want this to be a positive day for you."

Alexis excused herself and took Oslo to her bedroom. She adjusted the blinds and tuned in the television to Animal Planet. "See you soon, boy."

Back in the kitchen, she grabbed a medium-sized dish from the refrigerator, a cooler filled with purified water, and her purse. She headed toward the door, which Ben was holding open.

"I can take those," he said, reaching for the containers.

"Thanks, I'll just set this alarm before we go." She pressed a four-digit code on the keypad on the wall, and they headed down the steps.

"Smart investment," Ben said.

"I also have a couple of cameras." She pointed to the small state-of-the-art security camera by her door. "I asked one of my old colleagues to hook the system up. I can access the feed from my phone. See, there's Oslo watching *Animal Cops*."

"Why didn't you bring him?"

"Too many kids, and I'm not sure today is the day to test his tolerance level." Alexis started rummaging through her purse.

"We can take my car," Ben said.

Alexis looked down at the car parked next to hers. "Are you kidding me? You have an Aston?"

"Sorry if it seems pretentious."

"It's my dream car. If my family sees you pulling in with this ..."

Ben grinned and held out the keys. "Then I guess you'll have to drive."

"What?"

"This way I won't have to keep asking for directions."

"Since you insist." Alexis took the key and got behind the wheel, her brain racing along the Autostrada in Italy. She started the engine and listened to it purr. Then she released the emergency brake, toed the accelerator, and headed out.

CHAPTER TWENTY-SIX

THE PROLLOFSKY HOME was full of energetic harmony. DziDzi and a few of his grandsons carried brown metal folding chairs up the hill from the garage and set them out in the backyard, and his three sons were setting up the last two long rectangular tables near the clothesline. Grandchildren over the age of ten goofed off near the edge of the woods, while the younger children made a shambles inside. Daughters and daughters-in-law were packed inside the small kitchen helping to prepare two large bowls of salad and three pitchers of lemonade, slice two seedless watermelons, shuck corn, and season forty pieces of chicken and twenty steak burgers for grilling. The aromas of Texas sheet cake, fresh cinnamon apple pies, and baked beans wafted from the kitchen to the outside, where a group of young adults was putting up a badminton net and the poles for ladder ball.

Marcia Zen looked up from the ears of corn she was rinsing and asked no one in particular, "Has anyone heard from Alexis?"

Alexis's younger sister, Rebecca, who was carrying an armful of patriotic table coverings, nodded vigorously. "I texted her fifteen minutes ago, and she said she was on her way."

"Does Alexis have a boyfriend yet?" asked Marcia's oldest sister, Naomi, who sat at the table drinking iced tea.

"No," Marcia replied.

"Hard to believe a beautiful girl like Alexis is still unattached."

Marcia shrugged. "She works all the time, and spends her weekend nights with Baba and DziDzi."

"Looks like you'll have to wait a while for grandkids," Naomi said.

"Don't start," Marcia replied.

"I told her to invite that James fellow she works with," Baba said. "Alexis is always mentioning his name."

"That'll be the day," Marcia said.

"No, she's bringing a guy," Rebecca said.

The other eight women stopped talking and stared at Rebecca.

"Who is it, Becca?" Aunt Janis asked.

"She didn't tell me," Rebecca said. "She just said it was someone she met through her job."

CHAPTER TWENTY-SEVEN

MATTHEW ZEN WAS standing with five other men next to a large built-in stone grill, scraping the racks. The conversation was focused on sprint car racing, fishing trips, and the type of fireworks each man had brought.

"I brought aerial shell fireworks, some fountain types, and sparklers for the kids," Matthew said.

The heard the sound of a car engine, and everyone turned to look down the hill. Jack, who had come with Alexis's cousin Adeline, gave a low whistle and said, "Now that's something you only see in the magazines."

Matthew squinted at the car coming up the gravel drive. "Dang, that's my daughter behind the wheel."

"What did you say she did for a living?"

"She's a physicist."

"Sign me up," Jack said.

"I seriously doubt that's her car," Matthew replied.

"Too bad," said Jack. "That's a new V-12. We're talking over a hundred grand. It probably belongs to her mystery guy."

Matthew frowned. "What mystery guy?"

Alexis pulled the car slowly up into the driveway, trying not to throw too many stones. She saw her stepfather and some other men setting up, and they were looking in her direction.

"This should be interesting," Alexis said. "I've only ever brought my girlfriends around my family."

"I feel honored."

Alexis glanced at Ben and noted how his thick lashes outlined the mystery in his eyes. It sent a strange tingle down her spine. "They're going to eat you alive."

"I think I can handle it."

Alexis chuckled. "If not, you'll have to turn in your shrink's license. Speaking of which, let's not divulge that you're my shrink. It might seem a little creepy, no offense." She stopped and car and turned off the engine.

"I can't, even if they ask. It's against professional ethics."

"Perfect."

"Have you dreamed up a cover story?"

"We're friends who met through work. And most of what either of us do is classified or confidential, so we won't have to answer a lot of questions about work."

"I like it," Ben said. "By the way, everyone seems to be staring at us."

CHAPTER TWENTY-EIGHT

JAMES HEADED INTO the research building flanked by two men. They stopped at the desk, and James showed his ID to the airman on duty.

"Airman Bennet, these gentlemen have been cleared for Level 6 as visitors and should be on the list," James said.

"Names and identification, please."

The two men showed their IDs and visitor badges.

Airman Bennet keyed something into the computer system. "Yes, sir, the commander approved them."

After signing a document stating that he would stay with the visitors at all times while they were on base, James took them down to Level 6, where he entered a five-digit code into the keypad on the panel next to the large metal door. James placed a palm on the scanner and told the other two to do the same. "It'll read your palm prints into the system," he said, and then they made their way through the large door and onto the catwalk.

"You said the staff was away for the weekend, but what about the woman?" one of the visitors asked. "You mentioned we would need her."

"She had plans," James said. "I'm capable of doing this part without Alexis Zen."

They walked to a small white door with a large yellow-and-black hazard sign.

"Please, no comments or questions until I explain everything," James said.

He opened the door and switched on the overhead lights. The room was small and cluttered with large pieces of equipment. In the middle of the room was a long white table similar to the one in Alexis's lab. Most of it was covered with small stacks of paper, but in the center was an area covered with a black cloth. The men stepped closer to get a better look.

"Throughout history we have been told stories of how we all came into existence," James said. "We have questioned our purpose and searched for ways to be like gods. I think I found something that will answer those questions."

He flipped a switch that turned the table's light on and removed the cloth, revealing a velvet-lined box containing a small, strangely shaped object. "Does this look familiar?"

"It looks like a smooth gemstone, maybe a type of crystal," one of the visitors said.

"Look closer," James said. "It isn't smooth."

One of the men pointed at the object. "Are those letters or symbols?"

James pressed a button, and a white metal arm with a large glass magnifier descended slowly from the ceiling.

"Look at it through the glass, and I think you'll understand why you were brought here."

One of the men picked up the object and examined it under the magnifying glass. "This is an old gemstone with some old inscription. We've found objects like this before."

"No, not like this," James said. "I didn't bring you here to look at a lousy piece of quartz."

The man holding the crystal set it down. "We were told you found something. You show us a crystal that's no different from any of the others. How does this change anything?"

James picked up the crystal and held it to the light, where it cast prisms of color everywhere. "This crystal came out of the orb, the one that appeared in Alexis Zen's lab."

The shorter of the two men took the crystal from James and gazed at it. "You think this is some kind of relic that came through a wormhole?"

"I'm certain of it," James said as he reached over and took the crystal. "I'm also sure this is one part of a rare collection. We've been searching for a long time."

"What will you do with it?"

James walked to the end of the table where a square box with wires coming out of the back was sitting. "I've programmed this to read the inscriptions on the sides of the crystal—the code."

James placed the crystal between two small prongs, adjusted the prongs to secure the crystal, and then sealed the lid.

"This will take several hours to process. I'll escort you out and let you know what I find."

James rotated a red knob near the bottom of the box until it clicked. Several beams of blue light streamed across the crystal.

"How does it work?" one of the men asked.

"It will scan all the inscriptions and cross-reference them with languages from every possible database to translate those symbols. It will find any common variables in ancient religious or mythological glyphs or any type of written record. It will also analyze the minerals and microscopic particles to pinpoint its previous environment."

The three exited the lab, and James escorted the two men up the stairs to the large metal door. One of the men turned to him. "If you like, we could take it off site."

"Not possible."

James had them press their palms onto the scanner. "Scan your badges in the elevator and press the 'ML' button, and then sign out at the front desk."

James turned and headed back down the catwalk.

CHAPTER TWENTY-NINE

ALEXIS AND BEN had barely made it to the garage before they were stopped by the first wave of introductions.

"Ben, I would like to introduce you to my dad, Matthew Zen, and my Uncle Brock." Alexis smiled as her father and uncle shook hands with Ben.

"Better let your mom know you're here," Matthew said.

"Okay."

Matthew looked Ben over and then glanced at the expensive luxury coupe in the driveway. "Ben, I'll catch up with you later, but for now I'm in charge of getting these ready." Matthew began laying steaks on the bottom rack of the grill and hot dogs on the top rack.

Alexis motioned for Ben to follow her to the backyard. They passed several of Alexis's relatives on the way, and she made the introductions. She saw her mother and Rebecca walking around tables in the back corner of the yard. She grabbed Ben's hand to lead him through the crowd.

She suddenly felt lightheaded. She stopped to take a few deep breaths and regain her balance.

Ben let go of her hand and looked into her blue-green eyes. "Alexis, are you okay?"

"I think so. I just had a weird hot flash or something. I'll be fine once I eat."

"Do you want me to find you something?"

"No, let's head over to my mom before she has an excuse to be irritated with me."

They made their way through the aisles of tables covered with red vinyl cloths and baskets of white daisies for centerpieces.

"Wow, how many tables do we need, Mom?" Alexis joked, trying to gauge her mother's mood.

Marcia turned and feigned surprise. "Alexis, you made it. This must be the James I keeping hearing about."

"Mom, this is Benjamin, Benjamin, my mother, Marcia Zen."

Alexis and her mother glared at each other through forced smiles.

"That's a lovely ring you have, Mrs. Zen," Ben said, flashing a thousand-watt smile.

Marcia held up her right hand and gazed at the antique gold ring on her ring finger. It had an intricate lace pattern and a perfectly cut two-carat diamond in the center.

"Thank you. This has been handed down for generations, and eventually will be given to Alexis." Marcia paused for a beat and added, "But the handing down will probably stop with her, since she's never going to have children."

Alexis rolled her eyes. "Mom, really?"

"Hi, I'm Alexis's younger sister, Rebecca, and if you two don't work out, you can call me." Rebecca flipped her long dark hair around her bare shoulders.

"Seriously, you two. Come on Ben, let's go find my grandparents."

"It was only a joke, Alexis, lighten up," her mother yelled as Alexis and Ben made their way to the porch.

They passed more relatives, and Alexis made more introductions. They finally made it to the kitchen, which was packed with people, some carrying bowls of food and trays of dessert while others gathered utensils and plates. Everyone greeted Alexis with cheerful hellos as she wended through the crowd to find her grandmother.

"Baba." Alexis got her grandmother's attention and then walked up to her and gave her a hug.

"Oh my, there you are. Alexis, sweetie, hold on a second while I get this out of here," said the tiny woman, who was in the middle of the kitchen, directing traffic.

"Colin, take this out to your Uncle Matt and tell him to put cheese on these ones."

She refocused on Alexis and Ben. "And you must be James. It's nice to finally meet you."

Ben took her hand. "Thank you, Mrs. Prollofsky, but ..."

"Baba, this is Ben," Alexis said with a smile.

"Oh, so sorry, young man, I should not have assumed," Baba said.

Ben gave her a big smile. "No need to apologize."

"What can we do to help?" Alexis asked.

"Did you bring the chicken salad?" Baba asked.

"Yes, but I left it in the car. I'll go get it."

Alexis and Ben walked together down the long driveway to the car. "I'm sorry if this is awkward for you," Alexis said. "I know my family can be a bit overwhelming."

"No need to apologize," Ben said for the second time in as many minutes. "Although I do seem to be having an identity crisis."

She grinned, relieved that he was dealing so well with her crazy family.

"I do have a question, though. "Is James the same James who's your supervisor?"

"Yeah, he is. I happened to mention him to my Baba one time, saying he was nice-looking, and she's been obsessing over what he looks like ever since and trying to get me to ask him out."

"Why didn't you invite him?"

"I'm not in the habit of asking out my direct superiors. Besides, we only ever talk about our—well, my—research, and even then he can be a bit overbearing. Nice guy, and very nice looking, but I wouldn't have been comfortable with him."

Ben unlocked the car and grabbed the cooler and a white plastic container from the back seat. "What's in this one?" Ben asked as he handed the container to Alexis.

"Chicken salad. My grandmother loves it, and she usually sneaks a bunch of it before dinner even starts."

"I'll make it a point to try some."

The day proceeded. Food was consumed, a dozen conversations took place at the same time, bandages were tenderly applied to children's scrapes and scratches. As the sun approached the western treetops, Alexis and Ben helped gather empty food trays while listening to her family tell embarrassing stories about each other.

"Thanks for helping, you could have relaxed with the rest of the guys over by the fire ring," Alexis said.

"I like to help," Ben replied. "Besides, I'm not much for small talk."

After the dishes were put away, and the last of the leftovers rationed out, Alexis let out a sigh.

"Do you have plans for tonight?" Ben asked.

"No."

"Would you like to go into town and watch the fireworks?"

"Only if we can stop and get a jumbo bag of spun sugar."

"Cotton candy? Really?"

Alexis nodded.

Ben gave a shrug. "Okay, deal."

"Let me say some quick goodbyes, and then we can get out of here," Alexis said.

Alexis led Ben through the goodbye gauntlet and found her parents on the back porch with a few of the other adults.

"Night, everyone," Alexis said before hugging her father and sister.

"You guys leaving already?" someone asked.

"Yeah, we're going in town to the festival," Alexis said as she bent down to hug her mother. "Night, Mom."

Her mother barely hugged her back.

"Nice to meet you, Ben," Marcia said. "Sorry she's making you leave before the fireworks,"

"Actually, Mrs. Zen, I have a huge craving for deep fried Oreos, and we figured we'd catch the fireworks in town."

"Oh. Okay," Marcia said.

Before they left, Matthew Zen gave Alexis a sheet of paper with balloons printed on it and a heading that read *Zen Family Reunion*.

"It's in three weeks, at that roller coaster theme park near Cincinnati."

"Thanks, Dad, I'll try to make it." Alexis hugged him again and kissed his cheek.

"I hope you can, and bring your friend." Matt gave an approving eye toward Ben.

"I'll try."

Ben drove, and as they headed toward town, he said, "If I hadn't already known, I would never have guessed you were Matt's stepdaughter."

Alexis gave a short laugh. "I know, you probably would have assumed Marcia was the evil stepmother."

"I think she has your best interests at heart. Forgiveness is never easy."

"I wish it were."

CHAPTER THIRTY

DOWNTOWN DAYTON WAS crowded with slow-moving cars and throngs of pedestrians as Ben looked for a place to park. Alexis let out a long breath.

"What is it?" Ben asked.

"It's embarrassing, but this crowd is making me slightly lightheaded."

Ben found a spot in a grocery store parking lot and pulled in. A river of people was streaming toward carnival rides, games, and a two-mile stretch of gooey treats.

"I see a cotton candy truck," Ben said. "I'll go and grab us a bag."

As Alexis watched Ben make his way through the crowded street, she shivered. She felt cold. Cold and afraid. She pressed the lock button, and heard the locks click. She gazed at the crowd, looking for Ben, and saw something out of the corner of her eye.

A dark form made its way across the parking lot.

I've been watching you Alexis.

She squeezed her eyes closed. It had to be her imagination. There was nothing there.

Your body is trembling like the night we first met.

Who are you?

You fear us most when you close your eyes.

What are you?

A profound silence descended. Alexis waited for a response to her question. The stillness lasted forever in her head but only minutes on the clock.

Click.

The doors unlocked, and she cringed as the driver-side door opened.

"Sorry, it seems everyone in Dayton wants cotton candy," Ben said as he got into the car. He looked at Alexis, and his smile vanished. "Alexis, you're pale. What happened?"

"You startled me when you opened the door."

"Didn't you see me coming?"

"No."

"Are you sure you're okay?"

"No. But I don't want to sound like a mental case."

"You're not. Tell me what happened."

"I'd swear that I saw one of the men who were in my apartment. I closed my eyes to block it out, and that's when you opened the door."

"Let's head to my office, and ..."

"I knew it. You think I'm crazy."

"Actually I was going to say let's head to my office to watch the fireworks. There's an open field at the end of the parking lot where we can see them perfectly, without contending with this crowd. You'll be able to relax."

"I would like that. And Ben, thank you for such a great day."

"I should thank you for sharing your day and your family with me."

Ben started the car and began to pull away from the festival.

Somewhere in the crowd, Cezar smiled as he watched them drive away.

CHAPTER THIRTY-ONE

ALEXIS SAT AT her desk, staring at the computer screen, fully absorbed. When she heard someone shout her name, she blinked and took off her headphones. She turned from the screen and saw James standing there.

"Hello, James. You can stop shouting now."

"You were really engrossed. What were you listening to?"

"Sound bytes."

"Care to share?"

"Not really."

James raised an eyebrow. "That isn't very collegial."

"Neither is your constant skepticism."

"Healthy skepticism has a purpose. A challenged idea will be a better idea—assuming it's a good idea to begin with."

"Fair enough, which is why I challenge my own ideas. Meanwhile, I'll wait for concrete evidence before I share."

Alexis picked up her headphones.

"I'll listen with an open mind," James said. "I promise."

"I'll hold you to it," Alexis said before plugging a second set of headphones into the splitter on the side of her laptop. She unraveled the cord and handed the headset to James. "Listen for two minutes, and then tell me what you hear after it plays all the way through."

A white noise of soft static played for the first ten seconds, and then a faint humming began. It slowly changed to a crackle and then back to the hum. The humming and crackling sounds alternated for almost the full two minutes until the white noise returned.

"Can you clean that up?" James asked after they removed their headphones.

"I was trying to filter the sound when you came in," she replied. "What did you hear?"

"I can't tell if it's words or radio disruption, or possibly both. Why would you be listening to frequencies?"

"It isn't a radio transmission, it's the sound feed from the ball of light. The entire audio file is filled with white noise except for these two minutes."

She noticed James about to say something and had an idea where he would take it.

"Before you ask, this was recorded during the time I went to my car and no one was in the lab. I left the digital recorder in here. And these rooms are soundproof."

"Make me a copy of this," James said.

"What will you do with it?"

"Run it on my computer against other known sounds. The work will go faster with both of us on it."

James pulled two flash drives from a pocket and handed one to Alexis. She took it, copied the audio files onto it, and handed it back to James.

"The code to open the encryption files is OSLO. Don't let anyone else see these files."

James took the flash drive. "What do you mean, files?"

"I also put the audio file from the alley where they found that frozen guy. The sound is the same."

James looked at the rectangular drive and then headed for the exit.

Alexis turned to her desktop computer and began typing commands to filter the sound bytes, hoping to enhance the small sections of noise. A fleeting thought came to her, and she tried to ignore it. But it wouldn't go away. Alexis picked up the phone and dialed the extension for Paige Schmitt.

Paige was the researcher who purposefully snubbed Alexis except to make inappropriate comments to her. But she was conducting experiments on communication between marine life forms, which meant that Paige's group had access to state-of-the-art sound-enhancing equipment.

Alexis gritted her teeth and listened to the phone ring. When there was no answer, she hung up without leaving a message. She decided to review some of the other files of data from the day they found the orb in her lab.

To protect her equipment, Alexis had set up hidden audio recording devices throughout her lab for the times she wasn't there. She had placed a digital recorder in each corner of both rooms to cover all possible angles. Alexis sometimes allowed her paranoia to make decisions, and this was one of those times.

She started pulling up the audio files on her laptop. All interruptions or sound fluctuations would be shown in red by date and time. On the screen was a long list of daily recordings, including three red-flagged files. The first flagged file was dated the night James had entered her lab to find the mysterious ball of light. The file size was a few seconds shy of being five minutes long. Alexis highlighted it and pressed play.

She listened to four minutes and thirty-two seconds of silence before she could hear James entering the room. Puzzled by the silence, she replayed the first thirty seconds six times, hoping to catch whatever sound had triggered a red flag. Alexis sat for a moment, staring at her screen.

She replayed the file, but this time she started thirty seconds before the red flagged area. This time she heard the sound of something hitting the floor.

Alexis opened a program that would analyze the sound. It would measure the sound waves and evaluate the frequency of its given vibration. This would also give Alexis approximate dimensions of the object, its precise mass, and a list of potential items that might match. As Alexis waited for the file to download, she looked around the room, trying to find something that could have made the sound, but everything seemed to be in its place.

Alexis grabbed the flash drive next to her laptop and rolled her chair to the desktop computer, which was connected to a large LED screen.

She picked up the phone and tried Paige's extension again. There was no answer. She scrolled the cursor to the start menu, and for the next two hours Alexis filtered the background noise to amp the clarification of the humming and crackling sounds from the two-minute section she had shared with James. Alexis knew the process would take a while, and the program on her laptop was still running a comparison algorithm for the other audio file.

She looked at the clock on the wall. It was 3:45 p.m.

Alexis decided to take a break and find James, hoping he might have found something. She was walking toward the door when a *ping* echoed from her laptop. She went back and looked at the screen.

Quartz?

Alexis gazed at a wooden box sitting on a shelf of a tall bookcase. She walked to the bookcase, picked up the eight-by-eight box, and placed it on the table. It was carved with a detailed landscape and a Hebrew inscription—*A World of Messengers*. Alexis could smell the smokiness of the unique wood as she lifted the dome-shaped lid, but then she heard the lab door opening. She turned around and saw the base's commander standing there.

"Commander. What brings you here, sir?"

"Miss Zen, we need to ask a favor of you ... again."

"What favor is that, sir?"

"We need you to finish that piece of equipment that detects weak spots in the magnetic field, and ..."

"It's already finished. It just needs to be tested in different environments, particularly near other areas with known disruptions. I've already tested it here."

The commander looked relieved. "Let us know where you need to go, and we'll provide travel and accommodations anywhere on the planet."

"I'll develop an itinerary," Alexis said.

"When can you begin testing?"

Alexis thought about what she had to do to rearrange her schedule, which wasn't much, besides arranging boarding for Oslo. "I can do a few more readings in this area this week and arrange a travel schedule for next week. Can I take another researcher with me?"

"James Mitchell, I assume?"

"It would be good to have another scientist to brainstorm with and help input the data—and carry the equipment."

"I'll let you know by tomorrow. Come to my office first thing in the morning with a list of the places you want to go besides Belize."

"You know me too well."

The commander smiled and headed out the door.

Alexis turned back to the box and lifted the lid. Something was missing. She frowned and began searching, wondering how a piece of quartz could have fallen out of the box.

CHAPTER THIRTY-TWO

"DID YOU AND Alexis have a nice time, Dr. Asael?" Mary asked.

"Yes, we did, Mary, thanks for asking," Ben replied in a tone meant to imply that any more questions would be highly inappropriate.

Mary was about to ask another question anyway when the front door opened. She looked and saw a man wearing sunglasses, an orange and brown baseball cap, a pair of faded blue jeans, and a black Lycra shirt with a small insignia on the left breast. Mary had never seen him before and assumed he was a new patient. She got up and handed him a clipboard through the glass window that connected her area to the waiting room.

"Just sign in here, sir, and then fill out these forms. Dr. Asael will be with you shortly."

The man didn't say anything, but he took the clipboard and sat in the chair by the painting.

Mary slid the window shut, grabbed the file she had assembled earlier, and handed it to Dr. Asael. "Your last patient of the day is new. I put the letter of request he faxed over with his appointment information."

As Dr. Asael glanced at the letter and then looked up. "Mary, this gentleman already has his clearance evaluations from another psychiatrist. Who requested that I see him?"

"He called in and made the appointment himself," she said in a low voice. "He said he needed a new perspective and wanted you to do a few sessions. He works in the research area of the base and has a pretty high clearance level."

"He told you all this over the phone?"

"No, he just made his appointment over the phone. The clearance information was in the fax he sent." Mary started to input the insurance information from that day's prior patients.

The doctor looked down at the fax. "Mary, these pages are confidential. Even though you have to read and record this information, it doesn't give you permission to talk about it freely."

"I know, and I won't tell anyone," Mary replied.

The doctor's cell phone vibrated in his pocket. He answered and headed back toward his office as he spoke. Mary couldn't make out what he was saying until he started back toward the waiting room door. That's when Mary could hear enough to know that he was talking to Alexis Zen.

The doctor placed the faxed information inside the patient file and opened the door to the waiting room. "Good evening, I'm Dr. Asael," he said, and they shook hands.

"Nice to meet you."

"Follow me, Mr. Mitchell, and we can get started." Dr. Asael held open the door that led back to his office.

"You can call me James," the other man said. He took off his sunglasses and looked at Dr. Asael before going through the door.

Mary couldn't get a good look at his face, but she watched the two make eye contact. If she hadn't known better, she would have sworn they'd met before.

Mary glanced at her pink kitten watch and then returned to her work. She finished the day's tasks and got things ready for the next day. When she next looked at her watch, she saw that it was time to go.

Mary headed to the waiting room to lock the front door and close the blinds. She looked outside for a moment to catch the sun before it was gone for the day, but something in the parking lot caught her attention. A familiar car sat in front of the building. Mary stood staring out the window as she thought about the last time she had seen that car, the day she got caught trying to snoop inside. She remembered how rude and intolerant the man who owned that car had been and how embarrassed she'd felt. The pieces of a puzzle snapped into place, and Mary gasped. The owner of the car was the new patient. No wonder he'd ignored her. But if he was a new patient, why had he been parking in the alley? And how did he know Dr. Asael?

Nothing made sense. Mary grabbed her purse and headed toward the employee exit. She heard the new patient's voice and became nervous, hoping he wouldn't tell Dr. Asael that she'd been snooping in his car. With that weighing on her mind, she bolted out the door.

CHAPTER THIRTY-THREE

AZURE MOTIONED TO Cezar as they sat in the corner of a crowded restaurant. "There is a way to follow her."

"Explain."

"Alexis Zen is leaving this week."

"And?"

Azure glanced around, even though no one could see him. "We can have someone get close to her. I think she is smarter than we thought, and we need to keep her from finding out who we are."

"There is no way she could know what is really happening unless he shows her."

"Or if she dies."

"If she dies, the crystal is lost." Cezar leaned back in his seat. "And he won't tell her."

"Are you sure? You know he hasn't been following a normal pattern. Killing that human in the alley, showing himself in public more, what he did to Samuel."

Cezar glared at him. "We need not talk about that, what's done is done. There is a reason for his actions."

"Since when did you become so annoyingly complacent about this?" Azure asked.

"Since our last encounter, when I saw what happens to those who rebel."

Azure wasn't sure if he should share his concerns with Cezar. The lines of loyalty were always shady with his kind, and Azure could see they both had insecurities about how they should carry on.

"Cezar, what's our next course of action? I don't know who we can trust. He has us questioning our actions. He's instilling a fear that we're not following him for the right reasons. We can't trust a single one us, and that is what he wanted to achieve."

"What do you expect after all this time? We exist to persuade people that their choices are wrong, even if it isn't true. It's only natural that we feel that same confusion and doubt. And everything that has happened with Alexis Zen will create paranoia in some of us, perhaps all of us."

"We agreed to be a part of this, just like everyone else," Azure said. "I enjoy this world, and I'm not ready for it to end. Alexis Zen is too close."

Cezar nodded. "Don't worry about Alexis Zen. I think she's about to have a nervous breakdown."

"You know this how?" Azure asked.

"I saw her alone in the car at the festival the other night, and I stood close enough to let her see me."

"Did anyone else see you?" Azure asked.

"No, but I'm not worried about her. I can take care of it."

"You and I were both told to stay clear of her, that's why I think we can ask one of the others to take care of it when she leaves. Unless there is something you are willing to sacrifice yourself for that I should know about?"

Cezar grinned.

"Never mind, I'd rather not know. Besides, we may have a different issue."

"Other than the human woman?"

"Yes. The crystal."

"Was her aunt lying?"

"No, Alexis has it, but it's on the base."

"Are we sure it's the right one?"

"They said it had all the markings of the Bereishit Crystal, but of course it will take some effort to get it out of the building," Azure whispered.

"Does Alexis Zen know about it?"

"I don't know. I have steered clear of her, which you should do as well."

"What did he say about it?"

"I don't know. I'm not on his 'go to' list right now."

"I will find out what Alexis Zen knows," Cezar said.

"I don't want to know what she knows."

"If it's the real crystal, it would be better if she were gone. I have a feeling she plays a bigger part in all this."

"I know."

CHAPTER THIRTY-FOUR

ALEXIS HURRIED THROUGHOUT her apartment, putting things in their place and spraying the scent of eucalyptus onto couch cushions, pillows, and throws, trying to mask the aroma of an indoor pet. Oslo followed close behind, sneezing vigorously.

She stood back, looked around her living room, and made a few final swipes with a dust cloth. Alexis wanted her space to appear clean before her guest arrived. The clock in her bedroom displayed 5:59 p.m. She checked her eye makeup and gargled a small cup of spearmint mouthwash.

Then Alexis sat down and waited. At 6:15, she checked her phone for missed calls and text messages. She organized the mail that was piled up on her counter, tossing most of it. At 6:20 her phone rang. It was Ben.

"I'm just now leaving the office," he told her. "My last patient ran longer than expected."

"Okay."

"I'll be there in five minutes. I'm sorry."

"Don't worry. I'll see you when you get here."

They ended the call, and Alexis glanced down at Oslo, who was sitting near her feet, waiting his turn for attention.

"Where's your rope, boy?"

Oslo ran to the computer desk and retrieved the rope lying under it. He ran back and dropped it at Alexis's feet. She picked up one end, and they tugged back and forth. Alexis was glad Oslo had come into her life. Friends were hard to keep when your job required the majority of your time. Alexis had only one true friend who had stayed with her throughout all her trials and tribulations, but now Adrianna was engaged and planning a new future. So a little over a month ago,

Alexis decided to adopt a pet. One look into his sweet puppy eyes was all it took to melt her heart.

There was a knock on the door. Alexis stopped playing and went to open it. She flipped on the light to make sure she could see who was knocking. It was Ben.

"That was faster than five minutes."

Ben came in, accompanied by the smell of fresh rain and clean cotton. "It's the car."

"You smell amazing."

"You look amazing, as usual."

Alexis had put on an off-the-shoulder white knit top with a soft pink tank peeking through and a pair of black leggings.

"Thanks." Alexis looked at her clothes, pretending to forget what she was wearing.

"How are you?" Ben asked.

"Good. Oslo and I just started a game of tug-of-war." Alexis looked around for the dog. "He must have run to my room. He's not much for guests."

Alexis moved into the living room and turned on the antique floor lamp behind the sofa. She looked down the hallway toward her bedroom. "Oslo, come here, boy."

She turned to Ben, who was still in the kitchen. "What about you, did you have a good day?"

He shrugged. "Typical day. The sun came up in the east and is setting in the west."

Alexis shot him an odd look and saw the grin on his face. "You're funny, but strange."

"I wanted to see if you were paying attention."

"Trust me, you have my attention." Alexis immediately regretted saying it. She didn't want to seem too eager. She needed to remind her hormones they were only friends.

"It was a fine day, but unfortunately I didn't get to finish everything, so I have to go back later."

"If you need to cancel tonight ..."

"Paperwork can wait. Besides, I've looked forward to seeing you all day."

Oslo finally came down the hall, looking tired. Ben knelt down and stuck out his hand in front of Oslo's nose.

Alexis warned, "He might growl, so don't ..."

Oslo sat down in front of Ben and began licking his hand. Ben started petting him.

"That's a first" Alexis said. "What are we going to do tonight?"

"I saw the way you looked at the stars the other night, before the fireworks started. If you like, I know a place where we can see them even better."

"That would be perfect. When I was younger, I would climb on top of our roof, mostly to hide from my degenerate stepdad, but that's when I fell in love with space, and stars, and physics, and ... did you eat yet?"

"No, I haven't. I thought maybe we could grab something first and then head out for some stargazing," Ben said.

"Sounds good. What kind of food do you like?"

"I overheard you tell your grandmother about a place in north Dayton that has good pierogis."

"Amber Rose, it's my favorite restaurant. I'll bring the menu up on my phone, and we can order on the way."

She reached down and rubbed behind Oslo's ears. "Night, boy, be home later."

As Ben drove toward the restaurant, Alexis called to place their order. Alexis recognized the voice of the waitress who answered.

"Yes, Lila, can I preorder for dine in? You have one for 7:15? Wonderful, can I have two Warsaw dinners? The reservation is under Asael tonight."

Alexis looked at Ben as the fading sunlight highlighted the amber flecks in his eyes, reflecting the sense of warmth and comfort she felt every time she was with him. "Thanks for hanging out with me tonight, Ben."

"Don't thank me too soon, the night's not over yet. Besides, why do you assume you're the one needing something to do? I don't have a plethora of friends in my speed dial."

As Ben drove, Alexis thought about work and all that was going on. She couldn't understand how a piece of quartz had fallen out of a box in her lab or where it went after it fell. Meanwhile, she was devising a plan to recreate the lighted orb using different energy waves. She was also worrying about traveling around the world with James. On the positive side, getting away would give her a chance to forget a lot of the things on the home front.

"Are you okay, Alexis?" Ben asked as they pulled into the restaurant parking lot. "You look like the weight of the world is on your shoulders."

"I'm okay. It's just that I can't make heads or tails of some of the things going on at work, and the things that do make sense I have to put on hold until I get back. But never mind all that, we're here, and I'm starving."

They went inside and waited for their table, sitting on a plush bench near the hostess station.

"You know, it's kind of hard to have certain conversations with each other," Ben said.

"Why do you say that?"

"Between your classified research and my patient confidentiality rules, we really only have ourselves to talk about."

"I know, makes for either good conversation or boring company."

"Asael, party of two" the hostess announced.

Alexis stood up and instantly became lightheaded.

"Are you okay?" Ben asked as he took her arm to keep her from falling.

"Yeah, sorry, I must have stood up too fast."

The hostess showed them to their table, and five minutes later their food arrived. Alexis didn't say much as she ate her cabbage roll and potato onion pierogis. When they were finished eating, Alexis and Ben talked until she noticed there was only a handful of people left in the place. She checked her cell phone for the time. It was after nine o'clock.

"Did you have some place to be?" Ben asked.

"No, but I don't want to keep you out all night since you still need to finish up at the office."

"My office is on the way. If you don't mind, we can stop in, and I can finish what I need to do. It'll take about fifteen minutes."

"That's fine with me." Alexis meant it. She was beginning to enjoy spending time with Ben—as her friend.

Their waitress, a tall brunette named Lila, handed the bill to Ben. "This is just the receipt," she said. "A man stopped at the front counter and paid for your meals. He said to give this to you."

"That's odd," Alexis said, glancing around. "Any message on the receipt?"

Ben nodded. "It was an acquaintance of mine who didn't want to bother us, but wanted me to know he had seen me."

"Wish I had friends like that," Alexis remarked.

They stepped outside into a pleasantly cool evening. Alexis saw another couple walking close to each other and envied what they had. Wherever love was waiting, she hoped to find it someday soon.

They drove to Ben's office and entered the building through the side employee door.

"I have to admit this place is kind of creepy at night, especially with no one else here," Alexis said as Ben turned on some lights.

Ben grabbed a file from the counter and then turned on Mary's desktop computer. "Feel free to surf the Internet while I finish up."

Ben headed back to his office and shut the door. Alexis sat down at the computer and logged in to check her social networking page and personal email. That took five minutes. She unlocked her phone and clicked on a chess app that allowed her to play against a few long-distance friends. While she waited for updates to load, she took a visual tour of Mary's desk.

It was obvious that Mary really liked frogs. There were ceramic frog tchotchkes sitting everywhere. Mary even doodled frogs on the appointment book. Alexis thought about her own strange collection of books and colorful crystals and laughed.

And then she saw it. The last appointment of the day, the patient that had caused Ben to run late, was James Mitchell. Alexis pushed the appointment book aside and turned off the computer, wondering why James would be coming to Ben.

Ben came out of his office.

"You ready to get out of here?"

"Definitely."

Although she hadn't been snooping, Alexis felt guilty about seeing James's name, and she didn't want to tell Ben.

They got back in the car and headed east. Ben had been driving for a while when Alexis realized that she didn't recognize the area. The road was densely lined with trees and thick brush, and there were no houses around.

"Where are we going again?" Alexis asked.

Ben pointed. "Up there."

Alexis saw porch lights on the side of a hill about three hundred yards from the road. As they got closer, she could see more clearly through the trees. A huge house, almost a mansion, stood by itself.

"Tell me that's not your place," Alexis said.

"That's my place. I thought you might not want to come if I told you where we were going."

"I thought we were going stargazing."

"We are."

As they climbed the steep paved driveway, the house came into better view, and Alexis tried to take it all in.

"Ben, this is amazing. Wait, do you still live with your parents?"

Ben laughed. "No, it's just me."

He parked, and they took a path that led to the entrance, a beautiful, intricately carved oak door. Below them, the lights of the city sparkled and sprawled.

The interior of the house featured simple modern furniture and bamboo decor. To Alexis, it looked like a photo spread from an eco-friendly lifestyle magazine.

"Everything is on this level, the kitchen, the study, and the living space," Ben said. "Well, almost everything. What I want show you is up here." Ben pointed toward a large spiral stairway.

Alexis felt uncomfortable following Ben up the stairs. She wasn't the type to go home with a guy, let alone up to his bedroom. The stairway twisted upward until it came to a big open room with floor-to-ceiling windows and moonlight pouring in. It was obviously not a bedroom. It looked more like a ballroom. Alexis followed Ben across the room's black marble floor to a glass door that opened to a large balcony.

"You need a grand piano in here," she said before stepping onto the balcony. She looked around and heard herself gasp when she spotted the large telescope sitting off to one side. "Is that a Mead 16-inch?"

"It's the 20-inch," Ben replied.

"Thirty-four grand," she murmured, shaking her head. "Are you a drug dealer on the side?"

Ben laughed. "No, I have old money that's come down through the generations, building interest, and I enjoy spending it. Why don't you have a look?"

Alexis looked over the telescope's controls and started adjusting the settings. Minutes later she was peering through the lens at the night sky.

"I knew you'd figure out how it works," Ben said.

They looked at the sky for hours, sitting in cushioned wicker chairs, sipping Courvoisier from large snifters, pointing out constellations, watching the moons of Jupiter circle the giant planet. Alexis shared stories about her college days while Ben listened. Finally, it was time for Alexis to go.

"This has been wonderful," she said.

"Let's do it again, soon," said Ben.

"Actually, I'll be traveling for a while, so I'll have to take a rain check."

"Vacation?"

"No, a coworker and I will be testing a piece of equipment I built in various places."

"Lucky coworker," Ben said.

"Which brings me to the confession portion of our program," Alexis said, hoping her attempt at mild humor might mitigate the potential consequences.

"Confession?"

Alexis nodded. "Please don't be angry, but when I was in Mary's chair I accidentally saw the name of your last patient. He's also my travel companion."

"What?"

"I swear I didn't look on purpose, I was noticing all the frogs on …"

"I believe you, and I trust you. But are you saying you're traveling with James Mitchell?"

"Yes. He's the only one who knows all my work, and no one else really talks to me other than some of the weird male researchers who have major social issues when it comes to co-existing with female scientists who don't look like the missing link, and … and … wait—do you think James is a bad person?" Alexis realized she was rambling. "I'm sorry, I know you can't say anything."

"That's true," Ben said. "But you can. Anything you might tell me about your work would be under the patient confidentiality clause."

Alexis took a breath. "We're leaving at the end of next week and heading to the coast of Japan, the southern coast of Mexico near the

Mayan ruins, and then Bermuda." Alexis could see that something bothered Ben about James, but she knew he wouldn't tell her.

"Sounds fascinating," Ben said. "Good for you. But it's getting pretty late, and I know you're tired. Why don't I take you home? Maybe we can get together this week before you leave."

"I'd really like that."

As they got in the car, Alexis looked at Ben. His eyes looked sad.

"Are you sure you're not upset that I saw the appointment book?" she asked.

Ben gave her a warm smile. "Alexis, you didn't do anything to upset me. I know it wasn't intentional."

His warm hand touched her face, and he pressed his lips to her cheek. Alexis felt a strange but intoxicating sensation run through her body that washed her cares from her mind.

CHAPTER THIRTY-FIVE

AZURE PACED AS HE waited for Cezar in front of a turret-shaped stone structure in the middle of a wooded field. The night sky was clear, the moon and stars visible.

The song of the crickets stopped. The breeze died away, and the air was still.

"What a crazy night," came a familiar voice out of the darkness. "Are you waiting for someone, Azure?"

Azure felt a strong energy weighing him down and knew he couldn't lie. "Yes."

"Cezar?"

"Yes."

"Where is he?"

"I'm not sure," Azure said. "Cezar doesn't keep a tight schedule."

"Do you know what he has been working on lately? Or perhaps I should ask who he has been working on?"

Azure begin to pace. "I don't keep tabs."

"You didn't know he was following Miss Zen? Is there anything you need to share before he gets here?"

Azure remembered how his own presence on this planet was only possible because this man gave him a way, but the cost was eternal loyalty to him and only him, which Azure had gladly agreed to. The rebellious knew they'd be severely punished, and Azure feared the worst for Cezar.

"He mentioned seeing her at a local festival but said nothing about following her." Azure wasn't lying, but he wasn't being completely honest. He knew Cezar was planning something.

"What do you know?" the other asked.

Azure hesitated, but only for a moment. He knew it wasn't wise to make the man wait. "I did find out about the crystal being found, and I didn't know if the rumors were true."

"And what are the rumors?"

"The Bereishit. I have heard it said that it was found."

The man didn't respond. Azure knew he wanted further explanation.

"Everyone's afraid that if Alexis Zen figures out its purpose and a way to decode or read the inscription, she will know too much. Especially about us, possibly how to control or destroy us."

"Azure, she doesn't know that you are even a possible explanation. Like most humans, her brain is rationalizing what she has seen as fear. And she doesn't know about the importance of the crystal—yet."

"What happens when she does find out?"

"If it is the Bereishit, which I will know soon enough, then there is no database or reference book that would have all languages recorded. And as soon as there is a way to get the crystal away from the base ..."

"Can we destroy it?"

"It cannot be destroyed by our hands, Azure, but do not doubt my plan to use it for our benefit. You have seen these worlds come and go. You have seen beings be tempted and choose their path."

"But this is the first time we have ever been forbidden to leave."

"I don't think Cezar is coming tonight."

"I'll go then," Azure said.

"When you see Cezar, tell him to leave Miss Zen to me. I will deal with her and the Bereishit Crystal."

"I will."

Azure knew then that things were changing. If he didn't do something, their very existence would be in jeopardy.

CHAPTER THIRTY-SIX

ALEXIS COULDN'T SLEEP. Her thoughts kept returning to the expression on Ben's face after she mentioned that she'd be traveling with James. He didn't seem to like the idea, yet he couldn't disclose why. But if Ben had doubts about James, then perhaps she should as well.

She went into the kitchen and opened the refrigerator. After three slices of Amish Swiss, a handful of pretzels, and an organic fruit rope, Alexis finished her late-night binge with a banana split cupcake her grandmother had made for her. Alexis turned off the lights in the kitchen and browsed through the limited selection of DVDs in her living, looking for something boring that might put her to sleep, but they were all comedies or suspense.

Her mind was wandering, and her feet seemed to be following. She browsed books on organic chemistry, pagan religions, and evolution but found nothing mind-numbing, at least not for her.

Oslo came running into the living room. He was alert and sniffing the air. She crouched down and rubbed beneath his collar. "Sorry, boy, I didn't mean to wake you."

He looked at her and surveyed the rest of the room before going back to the bedroom. Alexis followed him down the hall. A light came from the small window where the street lamps outside cast a soft amber glow onto the bedroom wall. She could make out the outline of her bed, and the outline of Oslo lying at the bottom.

Following Oslo's lead, she crawled into bed. She pulled up the burgundy satin sheets and ivory duvet and closed her eyes. Her breathing slowed, and she finally drifted off to sleep.

From the shadows of her bedroom, Cezar watched. He approached the bed where Alexis lay so tranquilly, with Oslo curled around her legs, and touched her face.

Alexis. I will show you darkness.

A vibrating sound came from Alexis's night stand, and Cezar melted back into the shadows.

Alexis awoke confused and disoriented when the vibrating changed to loud music. She felt around for the object that had disrupted her hour of sleep.

She finally found her phone on the edge of her night stand and picked up the call. "Hello," she said with a dry voice.

"Hey, sweetie, it's Dad."

"Dad. What time is it?"

"Alexis, there has been an accident with Amanda. You need to come to University Hospital right away."

Alexis was now fully awake. "I'm on my way."

She found most of her family already at the hospital, in the fourth floor visitor lounge. Most had red eyes, and all wore melancholy expressions. She saw her father and sister standing near the vending machines and went to them. As she passed by the multitude of familiar faces, she could hear them sharing stories of Amanda.

Alexis hugged her father and sister and asked them what happened.

"We were having a cookout," her father said. "Uncle Willis and Aunt Leah and their kids, your grandparents, your Uncle Brock and Aunt Elaine, our friends from down the road, and the Bethels came. There were a lot of people there and ..."

Alexis could hear the strain in her father's voice as he tried to be strong for Rebecca, who was now sitting on the floor against the wall.

"Everyone was old enough to know how to swim, so we weren't really paying attention. But your cousin Amanda must have jumped in and hit her head on something. We didn't realize it at first, and when we first saw her we thought she was pretending."

Matthew swallowed back a sob, and Alexis put her arms around him. "You can tell me later, Dad."

"No, I can do this. We got her out as fast as we could and called 911. We were so afraid to move her, but it took the squad forever. But once they got there they were able to get a pulse."

"That's a good sign," Alexis said.

"That's what we thought, but when we got here to the hospital ... they said ... the lack of oxygen ..." He couldn't suppress his tears or say any more.

Alexis felt her own tears flowing. Her cousin Amanda was brain dead. "When did this happen?" she finally managed to ask.

"Around 5:30," Rebecca said.

"Why didn't you call me earlier?"

"Your mother said you were probably working, and there were others we needed to tell first. I'm sorry, I didn't realize."

Marcia Zen entered the lounge and made her way to the middle of the group, wiping tears from her eyes. Matthew went to her and took her hand.

"Everyone will have a chance to go up and see Amanda," Marcia said.

A glimmer of hope spread across everyone's face, until Marcia began to weep. That's when it hit Alexis. They were pulling the plug on her cousin.

"This decision was difficult for Willis and Leah, but there is no way Amanda will ever regain consciousness," Marcia said. "There has been no brain activity since we arrived." She waited a moment. "They said we can go in groups of three."

Everyone began going up in small groups to see Amanda and say their goodbyes. Alexis wanted to wait until the end. She tried to call James but kept getting his voicemail. She finally left a message explaining that there had been a family tragedy and she wouldn't in that day.

Alexis sat and waited, her eyes gradually becoming heavier. She propped her head up with her right hand and rested her elbow on the arm of the chair. She watched everyone walk past her down the hall.

The shift changed, bringing in a flood of nurses and technicians. As she drifted, Alexis thought she saw several men wearing black suits standing in the midst of her family, but she was exhausted and couldn't keep her eyes open. When she did finally open her eyes, the men were gone.

Alexis felt a tap on her shoulder and the soft voice of her grandmother whispering in her ear. "Alexis, Alexis, sweetheart."

Alexis took a deep breath and stretched. She looked up at her Baba's sweet face and smiled.

"Hey, Baba. Why don't you let everyone else go first. I can go last."

"Everyone has gone up already," her grandmother said.

Alexis sat up. "What time is it?"

"Around 7:30."

"I've been asleep for three hours?"

"You needed it. Now, come on, I will go up to the room with you."

"Thanks, Baba, but I would like to go alone."

Her grandmother nodded and kissed Alexis's cheek.

Alexis dreaded this moment. She knew her cousin wouldn't be able to hear anything, and Alexis was only saying goodbye to her body. She headed down the long hallway toward the elevator and passed a half dozen nurses standing at their station. They were talking to a man wearing a pale blue dress shirt and slacks. It was Ben.

"Alexis?"

"Ben. Why are you at the hospital?"

"To keep my privileges here I do psychiatric rounds every couple of months," Ben said as stepped away from the nurses. "Is everything okay? Why are you here?"

"Can we talk later? I need to see my cousin Amanda."

"Sure, I have one more patient to see. I can come by your place in an hour or so, if that's okay," Ben offered.

"That would be perfect."

The elevator door opened and Alexis stepped inside. The doors closed, and she let her tears come.

CHAPTER THIRTY-SEVEN

CEZAR WALKED TO A booth in the corner of a nearly empty restaurant where Azure was waiting and sat down across from him.

"He will be joining us soon," Azure said.

Cezar looked around. "Why would you have me meet you here if you knew this?"

"What are you afraid of, Cezar?"

"You know what."

"You shouldn't be following Alexis Zen."

"What harm is done if she thinks she is going crazy? If she starts ranting about men in the shadows and a magical crystal, no one will believe her."

"You're getting careless, and he knows you have been following her."

Cezar rolled his eyes and began to slide to the outside of the booth.

"Going somewhere, Cezar?" asked the tall man standing next to him.

Cezar slid back into the booth.

"Azure and I missed you last night."

"Look, I need to fix this. I know we screwed up, but ..."

"How? By letting her see you or because you've been watching her? Or was it because you pushed a human too far and Sarah Prollofsky was killed prematurely."

"You have taken a life. How is that any different?"

"Do you not understand? I killed that man to counterbalance your mistake. Every person has a time, and if we shift the balance it will bring war before we are prepared. And we have yet to find Eden. The crystal can take us there."

"Why do we still need Alexis Zen if we know where the crystal is?"

"I need her to translate the crystal. I need to know if this crystal is one of the original twelve or if it's the Bereishit. I cannot destroy her until we find the garden, so stay clear. Your actions have been third-rate skullduggery, Cezar, not the work of a dark mediator."

Cezar paled at the insult but didn't let it stop his questions. "How will we get her to translate the inscription? How do we know it will take us to Eden?"

"I remember the look in Eve's eyes. Whatever she hid on that crystal is valuable to our side. You need not worry."

"How will we get the crystal off base?"

"The solution to that problem is already in motion." He stood and disappeared before Cezar could respond.

Cezar looked at Azure. "Do you think his power is growing?"

"I think it's changing," Azure replied.

CHAPTER THIRTY-EIGHT

ALEXIS PULLED HER CAR into the alley behind the antique store. She was exhausted and knew she needed rest before going through another emotional night of mourning. She would be seeing her family again at her grandparents' house, where everyone would be gathering for dinner that night. Alexis was going to help sort through pictures of Amanda to make a photo memory board.

She saw a silver sports car sitting in the employee parking area near the north wall of the connected business. It wasn't Ben's car. She tried to see the license plate.

Alexis slowly pulled in as far as she could and waited a moment to see who was sitting in the other car. The tinted window on the passenger side started to go down, and Alexis rolled down her own window.

She saw James's blue eyes peeking over black sunglasses. "James. Hi."

"Sorry to show up unannounced."

They got out of their cars and stood together.

"How did you know where I lived?" Alexis asked.

"I have access to personnel files, remember."

Alexis was well aware he could see her certifications and employment files, but all personal information, like psych evaluations, addresses, and phone numbers, required special permission to access, and requests were not automatically approved.

"So, why did you stop by?" she asked.

"You sounded upset on the voice message you left, and I wanted to check to see if you were okay. I guess I should have called first."

Alexis told James about her cousin's death. By the time she was finished, she was in tears.

James stepped in closer and put his arms around her. "Your cousin is with others who have passed on, and I'm sure she's in a better place now."

"If you believe that."

"I do."

Alexis wanted to let out everything that was causing her emotional stress but didn't feel comfortable with James. She didn't want to seem standoffish, so she lightly put her arms on his waist. She took in a deep breath and with it the scent of cedar and fresh rain.

"You always smell amazing," she said softly.

"That was very random." He looked at her and brushed a strand of hair from her face. "But thank you."

Alexis let go and stepped back. "Sorry, it was the first thing that came to mind. It helped take my mind off my cousin." She laughed for the first time in hours.

There was a sound of crunching gravel as a car drove up the alley. Alexis smiled when she saw Ben behind the wheel. "There's someone I want you to meet," she said to James as she approached the car.

"I'm glad you're here," Alexis said to Ben after he parked and got out of the car.

"I'll be here as long as you need me. I had Mary reschedule my appointments."

She led him back to where James was standing.

"Hey, doc, I didn't know you were friends with Alexis," James said as he leaned against his car.

Alexis knew James was one of Ben's patients, but she didn't let on. "You know Ben?"

"I know him as Dr. Asael. Just had my first appointment with him yesterday. My old shrink was falling asleep during our sessions, so I thought I'd try a new one."

"You picked the best of the best," Alexis said.

"You see him as well?"

Before Alexis could answer Ben said, “No, she’s no longer an active patient of mine. Since we became friends and started spending more time with each other, it wouldn’t be kosher to see her as a patient. Especially considering the sensitive nature of your jobs. The Board might frown on that.”

Alexis looked to Ben, aware of how heavy her eyelids felt. “Can we head up to my apartment?”

“Guess I’ll head back to the base,” James said. “I’ll call you later, and don’t worry about the flight arrangements, I can move things around as needed. I’ll check on your lab, too, so no worries.”

“Just move the flight forward one day,” Alexis said.

“You sure that ‘s enough time?”

“I’m sure. And don’t worry about my lab. I locked everything down the last time I was there, so if you go in without my ID card or an override, it will set off an alarm.”

“Oh. Okay.”

Ben put an arm around her shoulder and nudged her toward the stairs. “Let’s get you upstairs so you can rest.”

“Yes, please. Things are beginning to blur together.”

James gave them a quick wave and then got in his car and drove off.

Alexis looked at Ben. “I find it really strange that he stopped by.”

“Why do you say that? Maybe he was truly concerned.”

“It might be sleep deprivation causing my paranoia to flare, but it felt like he was here for other reasons. You did say I should be more careful around him.”

“I know, and I wasn’t supposed to tell you that. Just be alert around him. After all, he’s an attractive guy, and you’re a very beautiful woman.”

When they stepped inside the apartment, Oslo came running through the kitchen and jumped up onto Alexis.

"Hey, boy!" She bent down and rubbed him until he ran off to find his tug toy. Alexis got up from the floor and washed her hands. "Would you like something to eat or drink?"

"No, I'm fine."

Alexis sat on the sofa. "Hey, Ben ..."

"Yes?"

"I know this is a strange request, and I want you to say no if it's too much to ask or you don't want to, but while I sleep ..." She took a breath and exhaled before continuing. "I've been having some really odd dreams, and I would be more relaxed knowing ..."

Ben sat down next to her. "I promise I'll be here when you wake up."

Alexis let out a long sigh. "Thank you. I didn't want to sound weird or immature."

"I know your cousin's death is extremely upsetting, but I have a feeling there's more going on with you right now. I'd like to help, if you'll let me."

Alexis grabbed a pillow from a basket next to the couch and positioned it behind her. "There's a lot going on at work, a million things stuck inside my head, but I can't share it with anyone except my coworkers. That's more stressful than the work itself."

"I thought that was part of James's job description. Don't you share things with him?"

"He made a great first impression, and his background is in the weird sciences, but it doesn't feel like a mutual interest when I talk with him."

"How do you mean?"

"James doesn't get excited when I show him things, and he expresses skepticism about my theories. Then he apologizes for being rude and becomes a complete gentleman. It's like being on a roller coaster and makes it impossible to create a bond. I wish I could tell you everything."

"Actually, you can. Under my privileges you can tell me whatever you want. I just can't ask."

"Even classified info?"

"A lot of high-ranking officials have been given access to classified information on my approval, so I have pretty high clearance as well. But let's talk about these dreams you mentioned."

"Lately when I go to sleep, it's like I'm not all the way asleep. Sometimes I think I'm dreaming of watching myself sleep. And I keep having this recurring dream that I'm standing in the most amazing field. I want to stay, but something keeps pulling me toward the top of a hill. I've seen what's on the other side, and I try to run back down the hill, away from it, but I keep getting closer to the top."

"What do you fear on the other side?"

Alexis put a hand over her mouth as she yawned. She could barely keep her eyes open. "It's pure evil. And I get this urge to scream for help when I ... when I see ... so many of them ..."

Alexis fell asleep in mid-sentence. Ben found a soft throw on the armchair next to the couch and covered her with it. He lifted her legs to the couch and adjusted the pillow behind her head. Then he closed the blinds.

He went to Alexis's bookcase to look for something to read. On the bottom shelf he spotted a small booklet that was held together with staples.

It was titled *From the Beginning, by Alexis Zen, Grade 9*. On the bottom of the cover page was typed *English Lit., Mrs. Hale*. Ben smiled and sat down to read it.

From the beginning, we have been connected by some unseen force. Our minds are confused by the perception of our existence. Even if the earth was alone in this vast complex system, it couldn't happen by chance or natural selection. The task of knowing cannot come through faith alone, but in the truth of what lies in front of us.

Our ignorance has allowed history to repeat and not progress much further than our own pride, but opening the eyes of this world will take us one step closer to God....

CHAPTER THIRTY-NINE

THE ELEVATOR DOOR opened on Level 6, and James stepped out. A group of researchers and assistants on their way to lunch was waiting there for an elevator. James politely declined their invitation to join them and proceeded to the main floor. The level was quiet during the lunch hour, so James knew he wouldn't be disturbed.

After walking almost a mile, he came to a door marked with the symbol for hazardous chemicals. He looked around before scanning his badge. The door clicked, and James stepped inside.

A table in the center of the room was covered with several sheets of paper. James picked one up and scanned it.

Origin: UNKNOWN, Data Incomplete. Language: UNKNOWN, Data Incomplete. Material: Quartz

"Tell me something I don't already know," he muttered to himself, dropping the page on top of the table. He folded his arms and stared at the printouts, trying to think of a way to gain access to Alexis's lab. It wouldn't have been a problem if she were there.

James opened a box that was sitting on the table and pulled out the crystal. It sparkled and flashed hues of green and purple across the room.

"This might go faster if she knew about you," James said, holding the oddly shaped crystal up to the light.

James perked up and reached for the phone. Underneath an old lab coat was the outdated phone base and receiver. He punched in a four-digit extension and waited for someone to pick up.

"This is Commander Spacey."

"Good afternoon, Commander."

"What can I do for you, Mitchell?"

"I need your permission to take something off the base."

"You can't take anything, you know that."

"Yes, I know. But this is not a part of any projects or classified data."

"What is it?"

"A crystal I found. I need Miss Zen's expertise."

"Why do you need to take it off site?"

"She's at home, sir. There was a death in her family."

"Is this government property?"

"No, I just found it lying on the ground. I brought it to my lab to test, but didn't get anywhere. And I can't take it with me without your override."

"Give me an hour to alert security. Is Miss Zen's trip still on?"

"Yes, we're leaving in a couple of days. And thanks again, sir."

James put the crystal back into the box, closed the lid, and secured it with a coded lock. He turned off the overhead lights and left the room, shutting the door behind him.

CHAPTER FORTY

ALEXIS WOKE UP REFRESHED and invigorated. No bad dreams had haunted her sleep, and she had slumbered peacefully for hours.

Alexis heard the muffled sounds of Ben talking to someone on the porch. She got up from the couch and stretched. She walked to the kitchen and looked at the clock on the microwave. She figured she had slept for five hours. And Ben had stayed the entire time.

The front door wasn't closed all the way, and Ben was holding the doorknob. Alexis gently pushed it opened the rest of the way to see who else was there. It was James.

"James, what brings you back?"

"Well, Sleeping Beauty, I need you to look at something."

"I'm not going to the lab tonight, so it'll have to wait."

"No need, I was given permission to take it off base and bring it to you."

Alexis frowned. "Unless it's a cheeseburger from the vending machine, it's classified and you can't take it off base."

Ben cleared his throat. "Why don't I take Oslo for a walk while you two discuss this ... cheeseburger."

Alexis grabbed Oslo's leash, called Oslo, and snapped the leash to his collar.

"Don't let him walk you, and be careful near flowers, he likes to eat the tops. "

"Got it. Be back in thirty."

As Ben and Oslo passed James on their way out, Oslo began to growl. Ben nudged the pup and continued out the door.

James stepped into the kitchen carrying a locked, silver-colored container, no bigger than a child's shoebox.

"Let's see what's in you secret box," Alexis said.

James set the box on the table. "The reason this was easy to get off base was because it was never catalogued as being there."

James turned the rotating dials to a five-digit code and then pushed the center latch to pop it open.

"I found this the day I discovered your lab had been turned into a deep freeze with an oscillating orb floating in the middle of it."

"Do you have a piece of quartz crystal in there?" Alexis asked.

James's jaw dropped. "How in the universe did you know that?"

"I have highly sensitive ears all over my lab. The system hears everything within those walls, and it picked up the sound of the quartz dropping minutes before you came in. I never pegged you as a klepto."

"I didn't steal anything. I just ... kept it from you.

James handed her the box. Inside was a piece of quartz cradled in a soft black spongy material. Alexis picked up the crystal and sat down at the kitchen table.

"I have a very interesting quartz collection in my office, and no one knew about it, until now. When I ran the sound identification program, it came up with quartz. So I checked my collection. This one was missing—the Poczatek crystal."

"Is that Polish?" he asked.

Alexis nodded.

"Where did you find it? And who secretly collects quartz?"

"It's a family heirloom. It's been foretold that it will give knowledge to those who seek with true intent."

"Nice."

Alexis laughed. "I always thought the stories about it were old folklore or crazy talk, and it really only had sentimental value to me. On the other hand, my other pieces of crystal are worth a little more to certain collectors."

"What does *Poczatek* mean exactly?" James asked.

"*In the beginning*. Why?"

"That's what I thought. Will you elaborate more on those stories that were told about this crystal?"

"Sure. My grandmother says this crystal was handed down through every generation since the beginning of time on this Earth. But it has only been given to the oldest daughter with direct blood ties. It's also believed to have all the information of creation stored within it, including the placement of the first set of humans. One of Baba's sisters even tried to say it was the fruit that Eve ate, from the Garden of Eden. These markings are supposed to be the original language that existed before the biblical story of Babel."

"So your mother gave you this?"

"No, my grandmother gave it to me years ago."

"Why didn't she pass it to her oldest daughter?"

"My grandmother's oldest daughter, my Aunt Sarah, couldn't have children, so it went to the next in line, my mother. Since I'm her firstborn daughter, my grandmother skipped the usual inheritance tradition."

James stared at the crystal in Alexis's hand. "Do you think this is tied with the orb phenomenon?"

"Maybe. I have a few theories worked out in my head. I just need to test them. If not this week, it will have to wait until we get back. Not that you'd be interested in my findings."

"Don't be too sure about that."

"I'm sure enough. You call yourself a skeptic, James, but you're really a cynic, and a pessimist. I'm an optimist. I invite possibilities. You've been knocking me down with your negativity and restrictive mindset."

"I always check to see what you've found."

"I showed you that crime scene footage. It matched up with the lab phenomenon, and you said that the time codes were tampered with and it was probably a food truck. The pictures I showed you, you blew them off at first. I'm stuck in my lab with these crazy unexplainable things happening around us, and I'm buried in classified red tape. It would be nice to have someone to share this with, a friend to understand me and not someone who mocks my thought process."

James sighed. "I didn't realize you felt that way. Alexis, you don't understand how you intimidate everyone. You're beautiful and a brilliant physicist, a rare combination. I guess I was becoming a part of the crowd, feeling inferior. Regardless of what your master's degree is in, I know you could step into anyone's lab and help them solve their problems."

James stood up and headed toward the door.

"Wait," Alexis said. "I honestly didn't realize any of this. I always try to make others my equal, and they probably see it as a challenge to their own abilities. I'm sorry."

"I'm sorry, too," James said. "I promise to be more open-minded. I hope you'll share your theories with me."

Alexis smiled and stood up. "Okay, but you need to figure out your part before the end of the week, because there's no way I'm traveling anywhere with a boring pacifist biologist."

"Deal."

James made his way to the door and Alexis followed.

"Are you and Ben an item now?" he asked.

Alexis had been wondering about that same question. "We're just friends."

"Well, maybe you and I could get together outside the lab sometime. You could tell me more about your crystal collection."

"James, you and I will be spending way too much time together starting Friday. Let's see if we're still speaking to each other after we get back."

"Got it."

"Thanks for stopping by and bringing back what you stole. I'll look into these markings."

"Good night, Alexis, see you soon."

Alexis closed the door behind her and went back to the table. She sat down and examined the crystal under her jeweler's loupe and saw hundreds of flawless inscriptions. There were no noticeable tool markings, and the lines appeared perfectly cut into the crystal.

"This would be impossible," she murmured.

"Quartz? I'm pretty sure it's not impossible."

She looked up and saw Ben. She hadn't heard him come in. "I wasn't referring to the quartz itself. This is a unique piece, actually. James was just returning it."

"Ah."

She put the crystal down. "How was Oslo during the walk?"

"He ate the tops off a couple of purple daisies."

"Oh, no, Mrs. Hawk. She yells at me every time I walk past her place."

Ben sat down at the table with Alexis and looked at the crystal inside the small metal case. "What's so special about this particular piece?"

"This crystal has belonged to my family for generations, but somehow it's become something more."

"Go on."

"Supposedly, there are twelve other crystals that were placed throughout history by God or maybe the gods, but they were scattered because of human pride. I need to ask my grandmother to tell me the stories again."

"Is that where you developed the ideas for your English paper?"

Alexis frowned.

"Sorry. I read it while you were sleeping. I thought it might help pass the time, and I wasn't expecting a high school research paper to be so deep."

"That's why this crystal has sentimental value for me. I've taken it everywhere, and it's inspired my theories about several historical mysteries. I incorporated natural physics, time travel, and adaptation, but of course, I've tweaked those freshman high school theories since then. But for the most part, I think I was right about what we were in the beginning and what we've come to be."

"It's an amazing twist on creation and evolution, without using the typical Big Bang excuse or Neanderthal's in evolution," Ben said.

"Thank you."

"By the way, I'm starving, how about you?"

Alexis laughed and nodded. She closed and locked the metal box and put it on the shelf near her desk, then sat down at the table across from Ben. "Ben, I think it's time you share a little of who you are with me. You know so much about me, and I know so little about you."

"Ask me anything," Ben replied.

Alexis thought about all the things she wanted to know about him. She had figured most of his family had passed and that was how he'd inherited the old money he had mentioned. Based on the credentials hanging on the wall in his office, she knew where he had spent his college days. There weren't many interesting topics left. "What kinds of things interest you?" she asked. "Chess? Macramé?"

Ben shrugged. "I don't do much outside the office. I do like a good game of chess, though."

"That could hamper one's love life," she said, hoping for a clue about his intentions concerning her.

"I've never had the time, or really the desire, to have a love life," he said. "No, I'm not gay. I just don't think I was meant for anyone."

Alexis was taken aback. She'd thought the same about herself. "You've never had a girlfriend?"

"No. Not that I haven't been around women. It's just that none were ever a priority to get to know."

"Yet you're getting to know me. What makes me special?"

Before Ben could respond, there was a knock at the door. "Taco Pizza."

As Ben got up and went to the door, Alexis sighed. He was everything any woman needed to stay happy for an eternity, but the

Ben she had begun to enjoy and wanted to know more about was slipping out of her reach. She didn't know what her next move would be, but whatever it was, it needed to happen soon.

CHAPTER FORTY-ONE

DETECTIVE STUART LINDSAY was ready to call it a day when he noticed a manila envelope sticking out from the slotted organizer marked **Open Case Files**. He pulled it out and saw that it had come from Montgomery Forensics almost three weeks before, sent to the attention of "Detective Lindsay and Detective Carter."

Lindsay swore under his breath and hoped that whatever was in the envelope wasn't urgent. He opened it and slid out the contents. It was a collection of crime scene photos. Lindsay didn't remember ordering them.

He dialed the tech room, but Eric Bloor had left for the day.

Lindsay sent a text message to Carter. *Found new Ice Man evidence left on desk. Stills from vid feed. Did u order these?*

While Lindsay waited for a reply, he sorted through the pictures. All but three were in focus.

He called the tech room again. "I know Eric left, but can I have his cell number?"

Lindsay wrote down the number and dialed. "Eric, it's Detective Lindsay."

"What can I do for you, Detective?"

"Did you happen to order still shots of the Ice Man surveillance video?"

"Yes, but that was a while ago. Are you just now looking at them?"

"Yeah, three of them are out of focus."

"The focus is fine, that's mist or fog we were seeing. Look closer, because there's a face."

"A what?"

"A face, maybe the killers, but I really don't know."

Lindsay frowned at the pictures. "I'll look at them again and have Tonya scan them."

After he hung up, he walked over to the tech room. Tonya, a twenty-two-year-old part-time technician with pale skin and red hair, was running a fingerprint program.

"Tonya, I need a favor. These have been cropped and enhanced, but Eric says that's a face behind the fog. Can you run this against facial recognition?"

Tonya flashed a coffee-stained smile and gestured toward a spare chair. "Sure thing, Detective, sit right here."

The detective pulled the chair up to the monitor, and watched as Tonya scanned the three images. "Work your magic, Tonya."

Tonya grinned. "The process of facial recognition isn't magic. The program uses algorithms categorized into appearance-based and model-based schemes. For appearance-based methods, three linear subspace analysis schemes are presented, and several non-linear manifold analysis approaches for face recognition are briefly described."

Lindsay, who understood not a word, nodded. "You're a tech goddess, Tonya."

"Thanks, Detective."

"How long does this usually take?"

"It can take a while, even with good-quality images. These will take a lot longer. Don't be upset if it comes up with no matches."

"Can you scan all three?"

"Sure, I'll call you when I'm finished."

"Thanks, Tonya, you're the best. I'll write down my cell number. I'll be at home."

The detective left, and Tonya turned to the two screens. The computer application scanned thousands of images from the database comparing size and shape of the eyes, cheeks, jaw, and nose, trying to verify the person in the video frame. Points were racing all over the screen.

"Oh, hey, Tonya."

"Eric?"

"I decided to come in tonight and run a different program on these video feeds."

"I'm already running all of them."

"Yeah, but I have a 3D program, and this is a perfect case to test it." He continued to enter commands onto the keyboard.

"Oh, okay. Let me know if I can help."

"Will do."

"I'm gonna head outside for a smoke then." Tonya grabbed a lab coat and headed toward the elevator.

CHAPTER FORTY-TWO

THE WEEK HAD PASSED quickly for Alexis, and now she was staring at three red canvas suitcases lying open on the bed. The first suitcase held solid-color T-shirts, black yoga pants, Bahama shorts, two sundresses, and one nice outfit suitable for evening, along with running shoes, brown leather sandals, and black two-inch heels.

A smaller suitcase contained notepads, ten recording devices, two different types of cameras, and a plastic container filled with new SD cards. Her carry-on bag had a complete change of clothing, her smart tablet, a couple of paperback thrillers, and a handful of glossy magazines.

Oslo watched as she closed the suitcases and started getting dressed for her cousin Amanda's memorial service. After the service, most of her family would go out to dinner. Early tomorrow morning, Alexis would leave for Japan.

There was a knock at the front door.

Alexis walked out of her bedroom and opened the door expecting to see Ben. Instead she saw Detectives Lindsay and Carter.

"Detectives, I haven't seen you in a while. Let me guess—you've solved the Ice Man case."

The two men stepped inside.

Detective Carter wasted no time. "Our tech systems guy, Eric, who you met the day your band of military men showed up, was going over the video feed from the alley and thinks he may have found ..."

Another knock interrupted him.

"Hold that thought," Alexis said.

She opened the door to find Ben standing there. Ben came inside and raised an eyebrow when he saw the two detectives standing in the center of the kitchen. "Hello, detectives."

"Evening," Detective Lindsay said. "Dr. Asael, right?"

"That's right. Are you still investigating the frozen gentleman?"

"Yes, we were just telling Miss Zen that our tech guy thinks he found a face in the video from the security cameras," Detective Carter said.

Lindsay nodded and turned to Alexis. "We're hoping you can stop by the precinct station and look at some of the pictures our system came up with, see if any look familiar."

"I would, but my cousin's memorial service is tonight, and I'm leaving the country tomorrow morning at four o'clock. I'll be away for two weeks. Besides, I didn't know the guy who attacked me, so it's highly unlikely that I would know who is responsible for killing him. I may not be much help."

Detective Carter nodded. "If it's not too much of a bother, please stop in when you get back."

"I will," she said. "I promise."

Alexis knew the detectives were unhappy, but it was out of her hands. As the detectives turned to leave, Alexis had a thought. "Detective Lindsay, can you email the recognition files to me?"

"Not sure, but I'll ask Eric," he replied.

Alexis wrote down an email address on a slip of paper and handed it to Lindsay. "Here's my email at the base, which I can open while I'm away."

Lindsay took it, and the two detectives left.

Alexis walked to where Ben was standing. He was wearing a soft platinum-colored dress shirt, a black satin tie with a faint diagonal pattern, and tailored charcoal slacks. His arms were crossed, and she could see the contours of his biceps through his shirt.

"You look very suave, Ben." She felt a tingle as she moved closer to him. "It means a lot to me that you're coming with me tonight."

"I'm glad you and I have gotten to know each other."

"Speaking of that, I haven't been able to figure out if our relationship is purely academic or if there's actually something between us. But just so you know, I'm a better person when you're close to me, so thank you."

Before Ben could reply, Alexis stepped away. "I need to grab my other shoes and finish my mascara. I'll be ready to go in thirty seconds."

Alexis decided to find out that night where she stood with Ben. She wasn't in love with him, but she was feeling something. It was unexpected and a little confusing, and she needed to know Ben's perspective. Alexis had been hurt by men throughout her life, which Ben knew because of their sessions. She hoped this was different and that he'd be honest with her.

Alexis insisted that they take her car, because she had to take Oslo to the home of Debbie Wilson, who owned the dog kennel where Oslo sometimes boarded. Debbie had offered to keep him at her place with her own dogs, who Oslo liked to play with. While Alexis was working, Oslo would be on vacation.

The church where the family was having the service was thirty minutes from where Alexis lived. She tried to break the silence during the drive.

"How's Mary?"

"Good, I guess," Ben replied. "She's been on vacation this past week, hanging out with her sister, catching up on gossip and going to bingo. She asked about you the other day. I apologize that I forgot to tell you."

"I'll have to call and say hi one of these days when I'm not doing anything." Alexis laughed at the idea of free time.

They pulled into the crowded church parking lot. Alexis recognized most of the cars as she drove around looking for a space. She finally found one between two SUVs and parked.

"Have you had to go to a lot of funerals?" she asked Ben.

"I've been to several over the years. They don't really bother me."

"It's not the loss of a person that makes me cry, it's the sadness I see on everyone's face," Alexis said. "They realize they'll never see their loved one again. Lately though, losing people close to me, it's been harder."

"What's different besides knowing them?"

"I think it's the uncertainty of truly knowing if they're in a better place. I don't know what to believe anymore."

Alexis switched off the engine and looked in the mirror to check her makeup.

"Appropriate weather for something like this, don't you think?" Ben said, pointing to the dark, cloud-covered sky.

"Yeah." Alexis opened her door. "Let's go."

As they walked up to the church, Alexis took Ben's arm. The chapel facade was brown brick with a plain white steeple. Ben opened the door, and they stepped inside.

CHAPTER FORTY-THREE

A BALDING MAN WITH a thick waist conducted the service. He spoke about our purpose and the privilege of having a body. After a lengthy prayer, the family showed a slide show set to music that highlighted Amanda's life. People came from several hours away to pay their respects, and the chapel was full.

Alexis and Ben sat quietly in the back, watching everyone give their condolences before they left. Alexis found herself checking her cell phone every five minutes.

"Are you finished packing?" Ben whispered to her.

"Yes, I just need to go over my list one more time."

"Sounds like you're in good shape."

"Not really. I don't think I have time to go out to eat with my family."

"Just tell them. I'm sure they'll understand."

"You don't know my mother. The fact that I have to get up at four and I'm already tired won't cut it with her."

"Then don't tell your mom."

"Come with me," she said to Ben.

Alexis began hugging her family and saying her goodbyes. Marcia Zen was standing inches from Alexis. "Are you not going with us to eat?"

"I wish I could, but I still have so much to do before morning."

"What do you have to do tomorrow?"

"I'm leaving for Japan."

Marcia looked at Ben. "Oh. Well, have a great time."

"It's for work. Good night, Mom."

Alexis and Ben made their way out to the parking lot.

"Did you feel a weight lift once you left the building?" Ben asked as they walked to the car.

"I never like going to church."

"Because of the establishment itself?"

"I'm not sure. It's like I know there's something out there, but I don't believe a church has the answers I'm looking for."

"What are you looking for?"

"Ben, are you shrinking me right now?"

"Habit, sorry."

They got in the car, and Alexis pulled out of the lot. Thirty minutes later, she was home.

Alexis put her hand on Ben's arm before he opened the car door. "Will you walk me inside?"

"If you want me to."

Alexis unlocked her front door, and an uncomfortable feeling swept over her when Oslo didn't greet her. Then she remembered he was at Debbie Wilson's.

Alexis threw her purse on the table.

"Now that we're alone, and I've had time to think, I would like to open the relationship topic," Ben said.

Alexis felt a knot developing in her stomach. Now that the discussion was at hand, she wasn't sure if she wanted to know. But she took a deep breath and nodded.

"Since I've known you, as your doctor and now as your friend, I've come to realize one thing for sure," Ben began. "You're a compassionate person who wants to please everyone by taking on too much or doing things to create a utopia for others and not necessarily yourself. You go out of your way to make situations work. You've been subjected to drug-addicted babysitters, been molested and almost raped, left to fend for yourself on countless occasions, and your biological father called you a mistake. Yet somehow you function and try to do what's right."

Alexis didn't like hearing a reminder of her past. "What does all of this have to do with us?"

"I think that when you found out that I had never had a girlfriend, it was a trigger in your mind that you needed to help, and the solution was for us to start a relationship."

Alexis scowled. "What? You're going to use that psycho crap to tell me you don't want to be in a relationship with me?" Alexis walked to the kitchen sink. Her mind was trying comprehend what Ben was saying and not get offended.

"Alexis, we could never date."

"Let's see, we're about the same age, we both love astronomy and good food, and we have a great time together. I guess we're not compatible."

Ben joined her by the sink. "As I said before, I'm not meant for anyone. And I've kind of gotten used to the idea."

Alexis wasn't buying it. Her friendship with Ben was terrific, and she wasn't imagining the tingle she felt whenever she was near him. He had to feel something. "We could at least try," she murmured.

"I know you need to get up early, so I'll head out so you can rest. Please be careful with James, I think his intentions with you may be off course. And call me if you need to. I still want us to be friends."

Alexis knew their friendship would never be the same. "Okay, one thing before you leave, and if there's nothing between us after that, then so be it."

"What?"

"I want to try one thing first before you close the door on the idea of us." Alexis turned around to face him. For first time Alexis could see confusion in his eyes.

"What are we going to try?"

"This is about trust," she said.

"On your part or mine?"

"Kiss me," she calmly instructed.

"What?"

"Trust me, it will let me know if I really like you or if I'm feeling sorry for you." Alexis noticed the confusion switch to concern, but she wasn't letting him talk his way out of it. "Ben, close your eyes and follow my lead."

"I know how to do it, I was just never ..."

Alexis stopped him from saying anything else by pressing her lips to his. His were soft and smooth, which instantly caused her body to surge with an inexplicable energy. She was starting to feel the warmth of Ben's hand as he traced her jaw line up and back toward the nape of her neck. He leaned his body in closer, and her heart began to pound. Their movements were in perfect sync, but Alexis's mind was spinning, and she could no longer concentrate. The air was calm, and she felt so relaxed.

The alarm penetrated Alexis's consciousness, and she opened her eyes. It was 3 a.m., and she was alone. But she felt surprisingly well rested.

CHAPTER FORTY-FOUR

HE STOOD IN THE predawn darkness thinking about everything that was in his reach, but unsure how to obtain it. The pieces to the puzzle were not fitting together as he had planned. He wasn't used to obstacles with humans, and for the first time ever he didn't have complete confidence.

"Sir, did you get the crystal?" Azure asked as he came out of the shadows.

"No, but it's off the base. We need her to translate the markings before we can use it."

"So, it is the Bereishit?"

"Yes, but the name was different, *Poczatek*. It's no wonder it has been hard to find. Since they passed it through the bloodline of Eve's daughters, the crystal married into many families and many languages."

"I see."

"It won't take her long to put it all together for us," the tall man said.

The two of them stood inside a vacant warehouse outside of town. The floor was covered with dirt and scatterings of gravel. A piece of the tin roof was missing in the back corner, allowing in a shaft of moonlight.

Azure became nervous as the tall man began to pace. He saw a change in the man's eyes—they were the opposite of darkness. "I know this isn't any of my business, but how will you get her to translate it?"

"I have the next two weeks to figure that part out." He turned away from Azure, who was staring at his eyes.

"Is everything all right? You asked me here, but you seem distracted."

Instantly the darkness was back, and Azure saw the coldness returning to his eyes.

"Everything is fine. And you can extend that thought of yours no further. We both have places to be right now, so you're dismissed."

Azure stepped away slowly and began to fade into the shadows, but not before he saw the man they called their leader, the one they all feared as the master of evil, the one who controlled their existence, drop to his knees.

CHAPTER FORTY-FIVE

"WHERE IS SHE?" James muttered as he paced the waiting area of the Cincinnati Airport. The clock showed 5:43.

The flight attendant at the desk called for first-class passengers on Flight 364 to Los Angeles to begin boarding the plane. Alexis strode down the hall with her handbag and carry-on suitcase and turned into the waiting area. She seemed perfectly calm, calmer than James.

"I thought you might have overslept," James said.

"It took a while for all my equipment to be checked in. I had to make sure they put the right tags on it."

James eyed her. He thought there was a new glow surrounding her. "Did you have a good night with the doc?"

She nodded noncommittally. She couldn't remember, but she wasn't about to tell that to James.

They boarded and took their seats in first class. Once the airplane was in the air, Alexis pulled out her smart tablet and headphones. "I think I'll close my eyes for a bit."

"Must have been a rough night."

"Kind of. It was an emotional and kind of exhausting memorial service. There were so many people, but I didn't stay too late. Is something bothering you, James?"

"No, I'm fine. I have a lot on my mind this morning, which is nothing new." He changed his focus back to Alexis. "Sorry, I was listening. What happened, did your boyfriend keep you up late last night?"

"He's not my boyfriend, trust me, he said he wasn't interested. But I'm not sure what time he left." Alexis plugged in a pair of high definition red headphones into her tablet.

"Really? I knew there was something odd about him. So Dr. Ben is no longer in the picture and you're still smiling?"

"Smiles only count if you find them on the inside," she whispered.

Slightly taken aback, James furrowed his brow and thought about what she had just said. "Let me know if you need someone to talk to."

Alexis didn't reply. She put her headphones on over her ears and pressed *Play* on her Bamboo Radio app. She reclined her seat as far as it would go and then closed the window shade.

She usually enjoyed the sounds of her favorite male contemporary jazz singer, but today she couldn't get past the voice in her head.

I'm not sympathetic to his lack of girlfriends. How did I get to bed?

Alexis tried to replay the previous night. She was certain that she kissed Ben, the energy still lingered on her skin, but she couldn't recall anything after that.

I'll text him during the layover.

The flight to Los Angeles was a little under four hours, but with the time zone change they would land at 7:03 a.m. Pacific time, and the flight to Japan didn't leave for another four hours. Alexis wasn't about to venture into the morning rush hour traffic of L.A., and she didn't want to wait in line again for security. She looked around and didn't see anything that grabbed her appetite or attention.

"How do you want to spend this huge gap in your day?" James asked.

"I'm going to head to our next gate and people watch. Plus, I need to let my mother know I landed. Go ahead and do what you want."

"I need to finish a few reports on my laptop, so I'll probably stay around there also. Okay with you if I tag along?"

"It's fine," Alexis said, but she hoped the trip would allow her some time by herself.

The next four hours lasted longer than the four-hour flight to California. Alexis looked out the window and watched baggage crews carelessly throw luggage onto planes. She wanted to talk to Ben but didn't know what to say, or even how to start.

The voice of a male attendant came over the intercom. "We will be boarding passengers for Flight 142, nonstop to Tokyo, Japan, at Gate 11A in ten minutes. If you're on standby, please come to the counter."

Alexis decided to text Ben.

Sorry if I was too forward last night, and I understand if you don't want to maintain our friendship. My flight to Japan takes off in 10 min., and I wanted you to know that I don't feel sorry for you.

Alexis went to where James was sitting. He was staring at his laptop screen and quickly closed the lid when she sat down.

"There are a lot of business types on this flight," she said, peering around at all the people wearing suits.

"What makes you say that?"

"Half the people are dressed for Wall Street, which you'd think would be uncomfortable on such a long flight." Alexis was staring at one particular gentleman sitting across from her.

James sat up straight and glanced around. "Alexis, I see only one person in a suit, over there."

Alexis's concentration was broken.

"What?" She looked and saw a man in a grey suit sitting behind them. When she turned back she didn't see the others, and the one who had been across from her was gone.

"Where did you see those people?"

Alexis shook her head. "Must be side effects from fatigue. Sorry."

Alexis stared at the empty seat where a man in a black suit had been sitting moments ago. She had seen two men in dark suits in her bedroom the night she was attacked and had seen men in dark suits a number of times since, always at random. Alexis wished Ben was with her, to help sort her thoughts and remind her she wasn't crazy.

She wondered who they were and why she saw them only at certain times. She wondered if she was losing her mind.

She glimpsed down at her phone. There were no new texts.

"Time to board, Alexis."

James and Alexis sat on the left side of the aisle in business class. The airplane was wider than the previous one and packed full. Alexis became nervous and tried to control her breathing, inhaling slowly through the nose and exhaling through the mouth. As she watched the plane load, her mind calmed and her breathing returned to normal.

Her phone vibrated from inside her purse just as the flight attendant announced that all cell phones and electronic devices should be turned off. She ducked down and grabbed her phone. She had one missed call, from her mother, and one missed text, from Ben.

I know that now. Call me when you land.

Alexis shut off her phone and sat back in her seat, smiling inside.

When the flight attendant came to them, Alexis asked for a blanket and pillow and a glass of ginger ale. James took a glass of Chardonnay.

"I hope you like movies or have something to read," James said. "The flight's twelve hours."

"I might research the crystal and start looking into those markings," Alexis said.

"Good luck. I couldn't find anything."

"What will you do to pass the time?"

"I'm going to read up on the Dragon's Triangle. I figured I might as well do some research of my own while I play mule and haul your equipment around."

"I told the commander I needed a jackass," she said with a wink.

CHAPTER FORTY-SIX

HALF A WORLD AWAY, in the Fairborn police headquarters, phones were ringing, people were talking, doors were opening and closing as uniformed officers and detectives went about their work, answering calls, shuffling through files, striding purposefully through rooms and corridors. No one noticed a man wearing a dark suit enter the tech room. No one asked for his credentials. No one asked who he wanted to see.

Cezar sat next to Eric and began typing in an access code. Eric continued to face his computer screen, oblivious to the large man sitting next to him.

Cezar whispered into Eric's ear, then got up and headed down the hall to the desks of Detectives Carter and Lindsay. Both men were working on a report from a recent case they'd solved, entering data into the computer. Cezar lifted out three of the case files sitting in Detective Lindsay's divider and took three slips of paper from one of files.

The fire alarm sounded. People got up from their desks, frowning and muttering about unannounced fire drills, and stepped into the corridor. Four people locked in the detention area started yelling to be let out.

Carter and Lindsay stepped into the hallway and saw Eric standing by the alarm.

"Who pulled the alarm?" Carter asked.

Eric looked lost as he stood staring at it. "I think I did."

"You okay?" Lindsay asked.

"I don't know," Eric replied.

"Don't worry about it, man, we'll tell the chief it was an accident," Lindsay said.

Cezar faded into the shadows.

After things settled down, Lindsay returned to his desk. His computer monitor displayed his report on the Ice Man case. He was certain that report hadn't been there when he left.

CHAPTER FORTY-SEVEN

DESPITE AIR TURBULENCE and the squalling of an infant from the back of the airplane, Alexis fell asleep and dreamed.

She's standing amid the ruins of a city street, surrounded by emptiness and destruction. She looks up and sees dark grey shadows devouring the clouds as the sun disappears behind the shell of a building. She gazes into the distance at a field that lies just outside the gates of the city. It's darker there. Something is swallowing the light, but a hill stands above the gloom, reflecting a pale light on the devouring darkness below it. Bright green grass covers the hill, waving like living brushstrokes.

Alexis knows the hill. She knows faces are embedded in a vast field of darkness on the other side. She knows the faces stand between her and the only illumination left in the world.

She turns her gaze back to the ruined city, spots a tall brick building with boarded windows to her left and a crumbling granite skyscraper to her right. She goes left and climbs cement steps, only to be stopped by a locked door.

*She hears a whisper in her mind—*Refuge. *She softly speaks to the door, asking for refuge, puts her hand on the knob ...*

"Alexis, we're here."

"Where's here?"

"We just landed in Tokyo," James said.

Alexis opened her eyes to the brightness of the sun streaming in through the airplane's windows and tried to collect her thoughts. She grabbed her tablet and headphones and put them back in her purse.

"That must have been an intense dream you were having," James said.

"Sorry, I didn't plan on falling asleep."

As soon as they were allowed to stand, she reached up and took her small bag from the overhead compartment. She pulled out her phone and powered it up. It was 3:15 p.m., Tokyo time.

"It's quarter past two in the morning back in Ohio," she announced.

"Personally, I don't want to think about Ohio, at least for a while, "James said as he stepped into the crowded aisle.

Alexis followed James into the aisle. "I wanted to let people know I landed safely."

"I'm sure your mom is waiting up to hear from you."

Alexis knew her mother would be fast asleep, but her mother wasn't who Alexis had in mind.

As the two walked through the expanse of Narita International Airport looking for baggage claim, Alexis admired the Tokyo skyline through the glass walls of the terminal building. It felt as though they were inside a piece of moving art and were a part of one of the multiple layers.

Alexis got the attention of a Japanese woman who was trying to scurry by. "*Sumimasen! Tetsudatte kuremasuka*?" Alexis said to her.

The two had a brief conversation, and then the Japanese woman pointed down the hall.

"*Arigatou*!" Alexis said as she bowed.

"I don't remember seeing Japanese on the list of languages in your file," James said.

"I started learning it this week," Alexis said. "I asked her for directions to the restroom."

"I know."

Alexis raised an eyebrow. "I didn't know you spoke Japanese."

"There's a lot you don't know about me, but I'm sure you'll be an expert by the time we land back in the States."

Alexis nodded and then headed to the restroom to change into a fresh set of undergarments, T-shirt, and yoga pants. The restroom was a modern design with everything set up for a hands-free environment. The sleek pendant lighting that dangled above each stall and wash basin created a museum feel.

She let out a huge sigh. Her mind and body weren't prepared for the dream she had just experienced, and she needed to find answers to help explain the Freudian meanings. She also needed Ben to help calm the colors of her aura. She took a deep breath and slowly exhaled.

Her phone began to vibrate. The caller was Ben. She hesitated. She wanted to talk to him but didn't know what to say. The phone vibrated again. Acting on impulse, Alexis picked up the call.

"Hey, Benjamin, why are you not asleep?"

"I stayed up because I wanted to talk to you when you landed, and I figured you'd be too considerate to call me."

"You know me too well."

"How were the flights?" Ben asked.

"The one to California was okay, and the one to Tokyo was fine until I fell asleep."

Alexis decided to not mention the dark-suited men she was hallucinating about in the airport earlier that morning, especially since Ben had already expressed an opinion about that. She didn't want to add to her already paranoid state by having him think twice about being friends.

"Was there a lot of turbulence?" he asked.

"I had a weird dream. Too many strange airplane noises, I guess."

"Alexis, did you have a dream like before?"

"It's really not a big deal."

"Were you in the meadow again?"

Alexis wasn't sure how much to reveal. To her it was real, but to others she knew it would only be a dream.

"Yes, but this time I didn't start out on the hill. I was in the middle of a city. It felt as though I was there." She looked to see if anyone was coming. "I know it wasn't real, because that's crazy. It's just strange that I haven't had one for days, and then wham."

"The anticipation of this trip has been especially stressful coming on top of your cousin's death, so you could be experiencing some anxiety. I'm fully aware that you're going to be busy, but if you need to video message me, I'll be available," Ben offered.

"Thanks. Hey, this is an odd question but how did I get into bed last night?" Alexis asked quietly.

"You don't remember?"

"Honestly, the last thing I remember is"—she looked around—"kissing you."

"Let's talk about that when we see each other next. Speaking of which, when will you be leaving Japan?"

"We're here for three days, then we depart for Belize. Depending on the data I get, we may be heading to Bermuda. I may just lie on the beach and not work while I'm there," she said with a laugh.

"I'll join you there," Ben said.

"Sounds good. See you in ten days in Bermuda."

"Just promise to be safe and keep your eyes open."

"I'll be fine. Talk to you soon, Ben, good night."

"Good night, Alexis."

Not far from the entrance to the women's restroom, stood two dark-haired men in dark suits. The people flowing past them on the way to their gates were oblivious to them. The man known as Ellory had soft features and sallow skin. The other, Zavdiel, had a military haircut and a bulging brow.

"Azure said we need to keep our distance as we keep an eye on him," Zavdiel said.

"I don't like it," Ellory said.

"Neither do I. This whole thing is going to get us caught by either one of them."

"I heard that she could ... that she could somehow see us," Ellory said. "Do you believe it's possible?"

Zavdiel watched as Alexis exited the restroom and joined James, who was standing there pretending to look down at a magazine while he eavesdropped on what he could hear of her conversation with Ben.

"Sorry to make you wait so long," Alexis said.

"I overheard you talking to someone. Did you get your mom?"

"No, it was Ben. He stayed up to talk with me." Alexis smiled and walked away.

Zavdiel motioned his head toward James. "We should see for ourselves, when she's not with him."

The two men disappeared into the shadows.

CHAPTER FORTY-EIGHT

ONE HUNDRED MILES southwest of Tokyo, in an area marked as a danger zone on most Japanese maps, a small a blue monohull charter boat dropped anchor three miles from shore. Alexis and James grabbed their gear and headed to the stern of the boat, where an inflatable motorized dinghy waited. The two crewmen that came with the charter yacht were talking to each other in Japanese, unaware that their passengers could understand them.

"Should we let them know?" James asked quietly.

"Not unless they mention robbing us or leaving us stranded," Alexis said.

"Right."

James came over to help her with her life jacket, and she got a whiff of his cologne, the same deep cedar that had intoxicated her mind the day they met. It left the same sensation now.

"Do we have everything?" she asked, trying to refocus.

James looked over the gear he had placed in the dinghy and then looked up at Alexis. "I don't see your small black bag."

"I must have left it in the cabin," she said. "I'll be right back."

Alexis walked back along the starboard side toward the hatch leading below. She descended the ladder and headed toward the stern, where there were three separate cabins. Alexis's was the furthest one from the galley. The yacht wasn't anything you would find in Miami Beach, but it had quite a bit of space, and sailing had been smooth. Alexis hoped the nights would be just as calm.

Her phone had service, so she tried her mother's cell, but it went straight to voicemail. "Hey, Mom, I know it's like 5 a.m. there, just thought I would try to call you again. I'll try again later."

Alexis had called her mother after landing in Los Angeles and Tokyo but hadn't spoken with her yet. She knew the time difference would be a factor, but her mother hadn't even returned her call from California, when the time was still reasonable. Alexis decided not to worry. Her mother's phone was probably in her purse where she couldn't hear it.

With her black bag in hand, she tossed her phone onto the bed and headed up to the main deck. Something was different. The air felt heavy and wet. She looked at James and pointed north. "Rain is coming. We need to get closer to those volcanoes and set the monitors out before it hits."

The two crewmen were standing on the port side, pointing to the dark clouds rolling toward them. Alexis got their attention, but they didn't seem to understand her English.

"*Watashi to issho ni kite kudasai*," Alexis said, insisting that they follow her.

"You speak Japanese?" the younger one asked in broken English.

"Yes, and I heard everything you said earlier about American women."

The men stood silent for a second.

"Sorry," the young one said. They hurried to follow behind her.

James was waiting at the stern. Alexis had the two men help her untie the dinghy and lower it into the water, and then she and James boarded it.

"*Mata atode aimashou!*" Alexis called back to the two men. "Don't leave."

"You know you're intimidating, right?" James said as he started the motor. He grabbed the motor's tiller handle and steered the dinghy toward a large three-rock formation. A few miles out he asked Alexis what the monitors were for.

Alexis motioned for him to kill the motor. "These are VEs, visual electromagnetic sensors. I'll be using them to detect energy fluctuations and take other environmental measurements. These record data from underwater and in the atmosphere above, to a 422-mile radius."

"And you chose the middle of the water?"

"We're sitting in one of the world's epicenters for scientific phenomena, everything from boat and aircraft disappearances to alien underground cities. This is the twin to the Bermuda Triangle here on the Devil's Sea."

"I've heard that before."

"I have a theory about that volcanic area right there," Alexis said, pointing to three uninhabited islands.

"What's your theory? And since when are you interested in aliens?"

"I think this area experiences volcanic activity and low seismic activity underwater. Somehow they weaken the atmosphere and disrupt polar magnetics. These devices are going to help me figure it all out."

Alexis dropped five dumbbell-shaped devices into the water, each of which had a solar cell on top and could be guided by remote control. The boat swayed as James moved closer to watch them float toward the rocks.

"Would you reach in my bag and get my tablet?" Alexis asked.

After he handed it to her, he looked over her shoulder to watch her input her password.

"To answer your other question, I'm not interested in aliens. There are scientists who think they've solved the mystery of these triangles, but I don't buy the hypotheses about methane bubbles or mud bubbles. These things exist all over the world, and these hypotheses are not new ideas. I'm not as interested in the lost ships and planes per se, it's the military that wants to know how it's happening, so they can recreate it," she explained.

"So why are we going to Belize? There's no triangle there."

"I convinced the commander to let me stop at one of the Mayan ruins before we head to Bermuda," Alexis said as she brought up the application for the VEs on her tablet. "I want to test another piece of equipment,"

The screen was divided into four separate readings. The top right showed waves of colors, the variations in lines representing the change in the spectrum. The top left and bottom right quadrants showed different number outputs but not labeling, just different units of measuring.

James pointed to the numbers. "What are these measuring?"

Alexis was still trying to guide the VEs closer to the volcanic islands.

"The one at the top monitors the magnetic field, and the bottom one displays the atmospheric pressure."

"Why is there nothing on this bottom one, here on the right?" James asked.

"I can't turn that one on until I have these in position, or it would be off the charts as I moved it around. Once it's in position, it will take a sample reading of the noise in the area for a baseline, and then it will record anything that breaks that sound frequency."

"Like the one you have in your lab?"

"Yes, but that was a prototype. I had to manually command and run the program every time. This one will run through an updated version of that program and then automatically cross-match it against known sounds. It also flags them so I can review them later. That's how I knew about the quartz."

Alexis watched as the devices she had put in the water slowly scattered to various positions around the volcanic islands. She began to type a series of number and letter combinations into a task bar at the top of the screen.

"Not to be nosey, but what are you telling it to do?" James asked.

"I just locked their positions. The currents will move them naturally, and the satellite will turn their motors back online to reposition them. As long as they stay within a mile of Ōnohara-jima, the data recording will work." Alexis closed her tablet and moved toward the center of the dinghy.

"Ready?" James asked.

Alexis could see the storm clouds coming in fast. "Yeah, let's hurry before we get caught in the rain."

They made it back to the boat before the clouds arrived overhead. Alexis went into her cabin, worried about being hit by lightning, but James stayed on deck on the port side while the dark clouds painted the skies. The two crewmen joined Alexis after a bolt of lightning struck three hundred yards away near the volcanoes.

"Sir, you come inside, not get hit by lightning," the short Japanese man yelled to James.

"I'll be fine," James said.

Alexis sat at the dining table, monitoring the storm readings from her laptop. She tilted it to keep the information private as the crewmen walked to the table.

"Did you guys need something?" she asked.

"What is wrong with your friend? He's crazy to be out in storm like this," the younger one asked.

Alexis laughed to herself and thought she would have some fun. "Oh, don't mind him, he's waiting for a spaceship."

The two men fell silent, waiting for Alexis to explain or admit she had made a joke. When she returned to entering numbers into her other laptop, they hurried to the back of the cabin and stayed there the rest of the night.

The storm lasted an hour, but the storm miles below them was just beginning.

The seabed extended out to the deep ocean floor, too deep for man to explore safely. An orchestral timpani sound, heard only underwater, rumbled across the sea bottom. Dust formed in the sand, and clouds of it rose up everywhere as vibrations began to ripple in all directions. The vibrating stopped after several minutes, and the floor became quiet as the dust settled. Soon, various slumbering crystals beneath the sand began to make their way to the top of the silica blanket. The crystals reflected the glow of bioluminescent fish as they swam by. A vast radius of a once-dark ocean floor that encompassed the Dragon's Triangle and the eastern shores of Japan, was now a glowing alabaster.

Above, the shimmer of city lights danced on the water's surface, concealing the radiance of what was happening below, keeping its secrets.

Standing on the rocky shoreline of Miyake-jima, Ellory and Zavdiel stared at the large charter boat ten miles to the west.

Things on the water began to change. The waves died, and the surface of the water became smooth. Only Zavdiel appeared agitated.

"Someone wants her to see this," Ellory said as he gazed at the calm sea.

"I know."

Ellory looked up at the glistening twilight. "You don't think they know about her?"

"Why do you think they keep coming here?"

CHAPTER FORTY-NINE

ALEXIS LAY ON THE thin mattress in her cabin, staring up at the faded wood ceiling. A mixed odor of wet canine and salty ocean air swept in through the small porthole. She didn't want to fall asleep, but she didn't want to watch the monitor of her smart tablet the whole time, either. Tired and bored, she grabbed her cell phone. It would be one o'clock in the afternoon in Ohio. Ben would probably be with a patient.

While Alexis typed a text to Ben, she heard James talking to someone out near the galley. She sent the text message and then peered out the door of her cabin to see who else was there. James was sitting at the booth-style table in the galley, but she didn't see or hear anyone else. Alexis was certain the two crewmen had retired hours ago. James must be on his phone. Intrigued, she moved slowly down the narrow hall, trying not to make any noise.

James was speaking softly. "Her eyes see only what her mind will allow."

Alexis stole forward another step. Her phone started ringing. James spun around to see Alexis in the shadows about a foot from where he sat.

Alexis answered the call. "Hello, Ben," she said.

"I got your text," said Ben. "Do you have time to talk?"

"I would love to, but ..."

"Is something wrong?"

"No, I don't think so." Alexis smiled as James watched her. "Something just came up, can I text you?"

"Yeah, if you get a chance call me later, and I'll talk you to sleep," Ben said with a laugh.

After Alexis ended the call, she turned away to send a short text Ben.

Sorry. Weird situation happened right before your call. Didn't want James to hear us. Will call later.

Ben responded. *Understood.*

Alexis headed into the galley to talk to James, but the booth was empty. She glanced back into his cabin and didn't find him there, either.

She climbed up to the main deck. The night sky was clear, and the northern hemisphere's constellations and the cluttered trail of the Milky Way sparkled. Alexis went to the starboard side of the yacht and saw James standing near the port bow staring into the water. He turned back as she came closer.

"I'm sorry I startled you before," Alexis said.

James gave a little smile. "That's okay. I was writing in my journal, and I tend to talk to myself."

"I couldn't help overhear you, so can I ask who you were referring to?"

He glanced at the sky and then looked at her with a serious expression. "Let me ask you something first. What do you think is out there beyond all that man has discovered?"

Alexis wasn't sure if this was a philosophical or spiritual question. She stepped closer and stared up into the infinite sky as Cassiopeia winked.

"I have been gazing up there since I can remember, and it has got me through of a lot of terrible situations. I have hope in something, that there is at least someone who knows the answer to that age-old question of where we came from. It's just hard to find strength in unseen things when you're surrounded by tangible scientific evidence daily. But at the same time, I grew up trusting that unseen voice in my head to be a spiritual navigator."

"You didn't answer the question."

Alexis walked to the rail. "We both know the answer to whether we're alone in the universe. We know extraterrestrial life exists. Why else would the base need a magnetic freezer?"

James nodded and smiled. "That doesn't answer what you believe to be out there. Even if I admitted that there was proof of alien life stored on base"—he peered intently at Alexis—"I'm not saying that, but if I was, that still wouldn't answer the question. It creates new ones. The idea of accidentally coming into existence would be less plausible, and to argue it happened to another planet is too convenient. Would you agree?"

Alexis nodded. "We could apply that notion to most origin hypotheses. Whether one believes we're a product of the Big Bang and evolution, or the offspring of aliens mating with a lesser species, or that a divine power created it all, each has to start with something. Even Scientology would need to rethink its foundation."

"So no one can be right?" he asked

"I didn't say that. I just know that everyone argues the one point—the one point no person can prove."

"You're right. And it's the one point that divides humans from each other. I believe that knowledge would solve everything that's wrong in this world."

He looked at Alexis, with her blonde hair blowing away from her face and the boat's lights highlighting the softness of her skin. "To answer your question, Alexis, I was referring to you earlier."

"What?"

At that moment, the young crewman appeared on deck shouting, "*Sumimasen! Sumimasen!*" He was dressed in his boxer shorts and a thin white shirt.

"What is it?"

"Miss Alexis, your flat computer keeps beeping, it woke me up."

She looked at James. "Can we talk about this later?"

"Sure," he said.

"It probably only needs to be charged," she said to the crewman.

Alexis was trying to figure out why James was suddenly a voluble conversationalist and the even bigger puzzle of why he'd been talking about her.

Inside the galley, she saw what was wrong with her tablet. "See here, the connector piece slipped out of the adapter part." She quickly reconnected the device, and the beeping stopped. "I'm sorry it woke you up."

"No problem."

James opened the galley door and sat at the table across from Alexis.

"I might as well transfer the data from the past several hours to the projector to see if it works before I send it back to the base." Alexis typed several commands and started compressing the data into a smaller format.

James gathered his papers, which were scattered on the tabletop, while Alexis entered the commands into her tablet to create a duplicate file for her personal security backup.

"Would it be impolite if I asked why the doc said he wasn't interested?" James asked.

"Okay, let's go with random questions tonight."

"Sorry, I was just curious."

Alexis didn't see the harm in sharing. "He seems to think he was meant to be alone."

"I can relate," James said.

"I don't buy that for a minute."

It was hard for her to fathom James not following through on his flirting with her along the way. Alexis had witnessed her female coworkers flock to him when he was around, and she saw how he enjoyed the attention.

"No, really, I've watched people who are in serious relationships, and I've watched some of the most supposedly perfect ones fall apart."

Alexis glanced at him. "What do you mean?"

"I wouldn't want to have that happen to me, that's all."

"So you don't want to chance a breakup because you've seen others who have had bad experiences?"

"Honestly, you want to hear my sob story?" James asked.

Alexis laughed. "Uh, yeah."

"All right. I have ... let's just say I'm the master of charming the ladies, but that's as far as I've gone. Plus, it's hard to meet anyone worth dating when you work underground in a research facility. Our options are limited. And you yourself have been irritated with me for my lack of empathy, so imagine me on a date."

"I guess you'd be the type to send mixed signals."

"I thought I was in love once, but it didn't work out. The girl married some guy while I was ... off on my studies."

"Wow, I assumed you were a regular Casanova. Especially with those alluring eyes. Oh, and by the way, there are plenty of woman in the lab who would love to go out with you. I can fix you up with one of them when we get back."

James raised an eyebrow. "Alluring eyes?"

"You look like the lost love child of Clark Kent."

James laughed. "Really? Superman? I can believe you're into superheroes. No wonder your have trouble sorting reality."

"It was a diversion during school when I had to wait for everyone else to finish their math assignments. I was lucky that most of my teachers were men who also appreciated comics. And I never said Superman. I referred to you as his geeky alter ego, the one who's an attractive bumbler."

James chuckled. "What does that make your blond-haired Ben? Peter Parker?"

"No, I haven't compared him to a superhero."

"I think Ben could be the perfect Professor X."

"Ben isn't old, bald, or in a wheelchair."

"I wasn't referring to physical characteristics, I was thinking of him sitting in a chair with mutant mind powers," James said, but Alexis had stopped listening.

She glanced back to her computer and scrolled through her email inbox. "Crap, this email didn't come with the attached file."

"What file?" James asked.

"One of those detectives sent me an email yesterday, and it had some mug shots for me to skim over. They found a face in one of the frames of the security video where they found a dead guy in the alley, and they want me to make sure none of the matches look familiar. I'll email them back later."

The two of them sat at the table working. Alexis finished the data transfer, and James read over his notes.

Suddenly, Alexis shouted, "It's done!"

"What's done?"

"You want to see the first test run of my H2E?"

"What does that one stand for?"

"Holographic Heaven and Earth," she replied excitedly.

Meanwhile, in the large cabin closest to the galley, the two crewmen listened to the two Americans talk. They whispered back and forth to each other, wondering why Alexis was monitoring the Dragon's Triangle and what she was recording on the devices still out in the water.

The U.S. government was paying them to man the ship, and it took a lot for them to agree to stay out in a boat overnight. Now, legend and superstition were starting to get the better of them.

Alexis and James cleared the table, and she placed a small circular device no bigger than dessert plate in the center of it.

"This is a three-dimensional look at what the VEs recorded in the past several hours," Alexis said.

From her smart tablet she pushed the start command. A violet-blue light shot straight up and out from the small device in a circular pattern. It showed a detailed view of the night sky as far up as orbiting satellites and all the way down to the bottom of the ocean floor.

"This will be a time-lapse version of the past seven hours," she said. "Let's hope it works."

"Is this the first time you've tested this?" James asked.

"This is the largest area I've tested." Alexis reached back and pressed the play button on her tablet to start the holographic feed.

The detail amazed them. They could see boats on the water, birds in the air, and fish swimming in the sea. The smallest waves were visible as the tide moved across the viewing area.

"That was us," she said, pointing to a small dinghy.

"You're a genius. We could go anywhere with this."

"That's the military's plan. This could save lives if I could get it to work as a live feed."

"When we get back I'll introduce you to a couple of friends of mine who could help you solve that problem."

"I can't share this with outsiders."

"They're not outsiders. In fact, they have more clearance than you do."

"Do I know them?"

"No, they kind of stay in the shadows. They work in the basement in a hanger by themselves."

"Thanks, James."

"Is that the holograph or the table moving?" he asked.

"It does look like its vibrating."

Alexis got up and touched the blue light emanating from the holograph with both hands. When she spread her hands apart, the display expanded.

"Push the display option on my tablet, please," she asked James. When he did, a task bar appeared above the hologram.

Alexis pushed the holographic play button, and they watched it from the beginning again. Right after the storms, the ocean floor began to vibrate and stir up dust.

"I think we caught a deep-sea earthquake."

The vibrating stopped, and a calm settled across the ocean floor.

"Are those diamonds coming out of the sand?" James asked.

Alexis stared in silence as the ocean bed glowed. She paused and widened the display again. "You would think that amount of diamonds would have been discovered by now, right? I have a new hypothesis about why things go missing."

"Let's hear it."

"It's not easy to explain."

"Try me."

"I'm going to go over the other data to make sure it makes complete sense in my own mind before I start rambling to you," she said.

"I can understand that, but if this is because you don't believe I'll be open-minded—I promise I'll listen and try to see your perspective."

"It is in a way, but I do need to make sure I can prove it before I start jumping to conclusions."

"Give me something to go on."

"I don't want to sound like an idiot."

"Alexis, you're far from that in my mind."

"Okay, imagine layers of worlds."

"Like realms?"

"Yes. And imagine the missing planes and boats are like the metal slivers I have back in my lab."

"The ones in the boxes?"

"Yes."

"So you think the earthquake has something to do with it?"

"And those diamonds."

"I see where you're going with this, and it fits with other phenomena in this area. But you're right about testing that before you share it with anyone else."

Alexis shut off the holographic display and put the device in her bag. “I’m going to head to bed, maybe I can sort it out by morning.”

“Goodnight, Alexis.”

“See you in the morning.”

Alexis walked toward her cabin. The two crewmen moved away from the door so Alexis wouldn’t see them. There was fear in their eyes as she walked past and shut the door.

CHAPTER FIFTY

BEN STOOD ON THE balcony of his hidden mansion in the woods, under a periwinkle-blue sky. His cell phone rang, and he pulled it from his pocket. It was Mary. Ben hesitated before answering.

"Hello, Mary."

"What am I supposed to tell everyone?" she asked. "When can I reschedule them? When are you coming back?"

"I'll only be gone for a couple weeks, so just cancel them for now and tell them to keep their follow-up appointment for next month. If it's an emergency, have them call Doctor Tenpenny."

"Did you want me to go into the office to answer the phones?"

"Mary, I sent you an email detailing everything, but you have to read the entire message."

"I read that you're leaving town."

"Yes, that was the first sentence. I need to take some time off, and this seemed like the best time. Please read the rest of the email. You'll also find out that you'll be paid in full during the time I'm off. Okay?"

"Okay, thanks. I didn't even think about that."

Ben knew better than that. Mary worried about money all the time. She spent most Friday nights playing bingo, and on Mondays she bought rolls of scratch-off lottery tickets hoping for the big win.

"I'll talk with you in a couple weeks, Mary."

Before she could ask anything else, he ended the call. As he put the phone back in his pocket, it started ringing again. It was Alexis.

"Hey, I thought maybe you weren't going to call," he said.

"I was on the phone with my mom, who finally answered. Plus, I was overdue on calling Baba. Sorry, but you were at the bottom of the list tonight."

"I'm fine being third in your life, for now. How's the top-secret expedition going?"

Alexis spoke quietly, almost in a whisper. "It's been really interesting and even somewhat exciting. I would share if I were alone."

"Are you still leaving in two days for Belize?"

"That's the plan. We have to go out further on the ocean in the morning, then we'll head back to shore tomorrow night."

"Is everything okay? Why are you talking so quietly?" he asked.

"I wanted to be sure no one was listening. I think the two guys on the boat with us have been listening to James and I as we go over the data. Anyway, what have you been doing today?"

"I took the afternoon off. I've kind of been lounging around listening to nature. It's a pleasant change from listening to people. It's been interesting. I can't remember the last time I did that."

"You should take off a whole week and meet me in Bermuda," she said with a little laugh.

"Yeah, you mentioned that last time, and I wish I could, but there is so much going on. Plus, it's hard to reschedule people on such short notice."

"I understand," she said. "Can we talk about the other night?"

"Yes, but can we discuss it when we see each other face to face? The phone is so impersonal."

"Okay, but will you least tell me how I got to bed?"

"You said you felt a little lightheaded and asked me to help you to your room. You climbed into bed, and you were out within seconds. I stayed for a while and made sure you were okay, but you seemed fine, so I left."

"I'm embarrassed."

"Don't be."

"You probably thought I was bored, but ..."

"Actually, the way you kissed me was quite the opposite, so I never thought for a moment that you were bored. But I do want to discuss this more when I see you next."

"Okay," Alexis said.

"Will you tell me about the James situation?"

"It was nothing, he was talking to himself as he wrote in his journal. I read more into it than I should have."

"Still, be cautious. I don't trust him yet."

The two talked for over an hour about nothing and everything.

A hundred yards from Ben's house, Azure stood with Cezar. They had observed Ben while he spoke with Alexis, seeing a man struggling with his emotions. Ben turned away from the silence that now lingered on the balcony and headed inside.

"Why are we watching him?" Cezar asked.

Azure stared up at the enormous house, its large windows reflecting the forest vista below.

"I haven't figured that out, but there is something going on between him and Alexis."

Cezar wanted to be somewhere else. "Did Ellory notice anything in Japan?"

"Ellory and Zavdiel couldn't follow them onto the water. But Ellory did say a faint vibration came from the ocean floor not long after Alexis put something in the water."

"What kind of vibration?"

"Zavdiel described it like someone was trying to pull out from underneath them, and then they heard some of the crew talking about mysterious lights under water," Azure said.

"That's not good. Has anyone reported humming on the water areas? Or any unusual lights or sounds on land?"

"No, but why does it matter? Those things are not unusual."

"Everything vibrates to a unique frequency, including us," Cezar explained.

"I know that, Cezar, but vibrations are normal underwater and on land."

"But if they felt anything from underwater, then it is strong enough to also vibrate upward into the atmosphere." Cezar was trying to watch Ben through the windows of the house but couldn't see where he went.

"Which means?"

"Which means it will also vibrate that same unique matching frequency across the planes, and that includes ..."

"I still don't see reason for concern. Those portals open every time."

"What if—" Cezar stopped.

The two disappeared for a moment as they saw Ben looking out of the first-floor window. When it was clear they came back into the light.

"I completely understand the process, but the earth experiences earthquakes and frequency manipulation all the time. That's how we got here, and that's how we travel, so why would this be any different?"

Cezar scowled at Azure. "How is it that you don't get this?"

Azure shrugged and waited for Cezar to explain. "Yes, these are normal to us, but imagine if she figures out how this works. We need to get rid of Alexis Zen, then we won't have to keep worrying about who she's with or what she knows."

"She needs to translate the crystal first. He's supposed to be working on getting her to do that."

"I think we should ..."

"Quiet, I hear something," Azure said, and both men disappeared into the trees.

Ben came down the stone steps at the front of the house carrying a duffel bag and a small suitcase. He scanned the tall trees that seemed to salute him from the front of his driveway. Everything was quiet and still as he tossed his bags into the trunk and slammed it shut. He got in the car and drove down the long, steep driveway and headed south, away from the city.

CHAPTER FIFTY-ONE

ALEXIS WOKE UP AFTER a refreshing night of sleep. She didn't remember dreaming, and she counted every night without dreams as a victory. She walked out of her cabin thinking about the previous night's discoveries. Alexis didn't hear anyone and figured they were above, trying to stay quiet while she slept. She made her way to the kitchen.

"Morning," she said to James, who was sitting quietly in the galley at the far side of the table.

James stood up and walked to the countertop. "Good morning. I got you some breakfast. I didn't take you for the cornflakes type, so I got some local treats."

"Wonderful, thanks, I'm starving."

Her tray was filled with rice, seaweed, tofu miso soup, a dipping bowl with soy sauce, and a small cup of something light green and chunky. "Where did you get miso soup and nori out here?" she said looking down at a neatly portioned plate.

"We're no longer out here anymore," James said with a frown.

"What? When did we leave? What time is it?"

"It's around eight. When I woke up, the crew was gone, and we were already docked. I looked around outside for a while, but I didn't find anyone, so I got us some food."

"Why did they bring us in? We were supposed to go out further tonight."

"Your snoring probably scared them."

"I don't snore," she said indignantly. "Do I?"

James grinned. "No. I honestly don't know why they brought us in."

"I'm glad you didn't get me fish," she said as she sat down across from him.

"Nobody had any fresh fish this morning, or I would have had some fried mackerel for myself. Everything was at least three days old."

"That's odd."

"I heard one of the locals mention that all the boats were coming back empty," James said as he finished his tsukemono.

Alexis shrugged it off as a side effect from the storm the night before and began to eat. She opened her tablet and read over some pages of notes.

"Trying to figure out those diamond anomalies underwater?" James asked as he watched her.

"Diamonds would be possible, especially considering the immense pressure so deep and the volcanic proximity. It would be a perfect breeding ground," Alexis said before taking a bite.

"But you're thinking something else is going on?"

"I thought about it all night, and, yes, I do think I'm right in my suspicions. And while we're docked, we can put a few VEs along the coastline, then come back and check the ones we placed last night, okay?"

"That's fine."

"Then I'll have a bigger picture of what's happening."

"What if someone grabs one of the VEs?"

"It's only valuable to the person who has my tablet and laptop, my specially designed program, my holographic disc, and my access codes." She peered over her laptop. "And they would have to know what it is they stole in the first place, and since it's a top-secret prototype, it's highly unlikely anyone will."

"In that case, I should find the port manager to give him the travel info from yesterday. Otherwise we won't be able to dock here. He wasn't there when I went out for breakfast."

"Okay, while you're out, I'll get ready," Alexis said.

James left to report to the port manager, and Alexis returned to her breakfast. When she was finished, she grabbed her tablet and miscellaneous gear and made her way topside. The day was bright, and she put on her rhinestone-accented sunglasses to block the sun. The docks were busy, and she had to make her way between angry fisherman, frustrated customers, and innocent bystanders. She proceeded to the place James said he would be and waited. After five minutes, she became anxious when he still hadn't shown up. Her pulse quickened when she heard a whisper in her right ear.

You appear to be lost.

Afraid to look, she pretended not to hear. Another whisper came.

You need to go back. There's nothing here but evil.

Alexis tried to relax and rationalize what she was hearing. She heard the whisper again in her left ear. Alexis was tired of being paranoid.

You need to ...

Alexis turned around to see two Asian men in suits standing close to her. They stood there as if Alexis couldn't see them, smirking.

"Do I know you?" Alexis asked, looking them up and down.

Ellory's and Zavdiel's expressions changed to shock and confusion. They looked at each other, hoping the other would know what to do.

Alexis felt a surge of adrenaline as she confronted the two men. "I asked you something and heard you loud and clear. I know you speak English."

They knew interaction was forbidden, but they also knew that no humans were supposed to be able to see them.

Alexis glanced to her right and saw James coming out of a small general store along the strip. When she looked back, the two men were gone.

Ellory and Zavdiel didn't go far. Staying at a safe distance, they followed Alexis and James as they headed down to the shoreline.

James carried the equipment over his right shoulder. "Who were you on the phone with back there?"

"Phone?" Alexis asked as they found the entrance to the coast.

"Yeah, it looked like you were highly irritated with someone."

"I wasn't." Alexis wondered if she had just experienced another hallucination. "I wasn't annoyed, I was trying to hear my grandma. The reception was bad."

Alexis glanced around, looking for Ellory and Zavdiel.

"How did she see us?" Zavdiel asked his companion.

Ellory was still in shock that she had seen them. "Azure said she saw them, and that is one of the reasons she is his new priority. And that is why Ad-neinu has put himself into her life."

"Do you believe all the rumors?" Zavdiel asked.

Ellory saw Alexis place probe-like tubes into the shallow sands of the shoreline. "If you had asked me that ten minutes ago, the answer would have been no, but now I don't know what to believe."

Zavdiel leaned against a vendor's stand. "If she is the one that has the bloodline to control us, why are we not trying to get her to like us?"

Ellory paused a moment then looked at Zavdiel as though a light had come on. As he spoke he looked back out at Alexis and James. "I think you are on to something. Let's go see Azure first, before we start anything."

And like the others of their kind, they vanished quickly, and no one noticed.

Down on the rocky shore of the small Japanese island of Miyake-jima, James carried a small bag of metal probes. Alexis buried a handful and then headed back up to the boardwalk of the small village.

"Let's go watch the data from the rest of last night. I want to see what else happened," she said.

James followed as Alexis strode past everyone. They had walked five or so miles down the shore placing land receptors for the H2E, and now James was trying to keep up with Alexis. The crowds seemed smaller as they made their way back to the dock.

James caught up to Alexis. "Why are you in such a hurry?"

"I'm sorry, I usually start power walking when I have things weighing on my mind," she said.

"Are you still working out your theories? Because I think they're solid."

Alexis couldn't tell him about the men she'd seen—or imagined. "Yeah, still trying to put it into words that everyone can understand."

They boarded the boat and went below, and Alexis set up the holographic imager on the table.

"You want to talk about it?" he asked.

"No, I just need to sort things out in my head, that's all." Alexis said.

"It helps to talk about things."

"Thanks, but I'm fine," she said as she powered up the small circular device sitting on the table.

"If you change your mind ..."

Alexis laughed. "I'm afraid you'll judge me or label me."

"I thought we moved past that."

The two watched the 3D holographic replay of the ocean and the sky. Even though it was in a time-lapse mode and going faster than real time, it was boring. Once or twice, James pretended to nod off.

"You don't have to stay," Alexis said. "If you want to go into the city, feel free."

James got up and stretched. "Good idea. I'll bring back some lunch. How long will you be working on this?"

"I still have to transfer the data, that way I can see everything on a linear graph. Give me an hour."

James grabbed a shoulder bag and started for the door. Alexis snickered as he walked past her.

"What?" he asked.

She was looking at his bag.

"It's for my notebooks and laptop, just in case I think of something important. Plus, I always have my camera."

"Ah, so it's not a European man bag?"

James rolled his eyes and went outside. Alexis went back to her work.

CHAPTER FIFTY-TWO

IN THE BACK OF the restaurant where the two usually met, Azure and Cezar sat back watching two customers argue with their waiter about the way their eggs were prepared. Another table was full of women bickering about another coworker who was running late, not knowing she was standing in line to be seated and could hear every word. The mood in the restaurant was tense, and Cezar was enjoying the show.

Azure felt a presence and looked around.

"Mind if we join you?" a man's voice asked.

Two men were standing at their table. "Why are you not in Japan?" Azure asked.

Zavdiel sat next to Azure, and Ellory slid into the booth next to Cezar.

"How can she see us?" Zavdiel asked.

"Did you not hear the question you were asked?" Cezar said. "Why are you here?"

"Because Alexis Zen talked to us," Ellory said.

"So let me ask you again, how is it possible that she can see us?" Zavdiel asked.

"We have no idea, it's not supposed to be possible without our will," Azure said. "The night she saw us was the same night we influenced that drunk to break into her apartment to steal the crystal. She astral-projected and somehow was able to see us standing there."

"None of the others who learn to astral project can see us. Why her?" Ellory asked.

"I am certain that she didn't know how to before that night," Cezar said.

"She wasn't projecting when she saw us," Zavdiel said. "She saw us in broad daylight with a lot of other people around."

"And I'm certain she heard me telling her to leave," Ellory added.

The four of them sat there staring blankly at each other. The restaurant was starting to get busy for the breakfast rush, and tables were filling up.

"Why do they not seat people here?" Ellory asked, finding it curious that Azure and Cezar would choose such a public place to relax.

Cezar laughed. "The servers have a superstition that this seat is bad luck, so they avoid it as much as possible."

"That's ridiculous."

"I know."

"We have a suggestion to help with your Alexis Zen problem," Zavdiel said. "You should open up to her."

Ellory and Zavdiel explained their thoughts to Azure and Cezar. After they were finished, all four left the booth and vanished into the shadows.

Not far from the restaurant, at the Fairborn Police Station, Detective Stuart Lindsay was standing near the water cooler talking with patrol officer Erin Shannon when his desk phone rang. He excused himself and went to answer it. "This is Lindsay."

"Hello, Detective."

"Oh, hey, Miss Zen."

"I've been busy and was just now able to open your email, but the file wasn't there when I tried to open it. Can you resend it in a different format?" she asked.

"Sure, let me find it."

Lindsay looked over the Ice Man data entries. "Why are you calling my desk? I thought I gave you my cell."

"I'm out of the country, and I left your card in my other purse."

"Where are you?" Lindsay asked.

"I'm in ..."

Before Alexis could answer, the detective interrupted. "That's odd, the file isn't there. Let me do a search." The screen search came up with NO FILE on the screen. He entered several key words, and each time found FILE LOCATION UNKNOWN.

"I can call you back later, just give me your cell number again," she suggested.

Detective Lindsay gave Alexis his number and told her to call back in thirty minutes. After he hung up, he went to talk to Eric, who was helping one of the new female detectives with her password setup.

"Hey, buddy, when you're finished I need your help locating something," Lindsay said.

Eric looked up. "The bathroom is down the hall, you need to find it yourself this time."

"Very funny," Lindsay said.

"I'll stop at your desk as soon as I'm finished here."

"Thanks," Lindsay said. "Say, what's the name of your old girlfriend?"

"What old girlfriend?"

"You know, the one who cross dresses?"

Eric finished with the password setup and went to Lindsay's desk. "What's up?"

"I need you to locate the facial recognition file for the Ice Man case," Lindsay said. "It wasn't in the data file under the case itself, and I couldn't find it with a search."

Eric rolled a chair from another desk, sat down in front of Lindsay's computer, and began a search. "What would you guys do without me?"

Ten minutes later, Eric gave up. "This is nuts. It isn't there." He looked at Lindsay, a look of confusion on his face. "This is the craziest case I've ever seen."

"You don't think the government did this?"

"Wouldn't surprise me."

"Can't we run it again?"

"Yeah, but I'm not finding that file at all. Where's the paper file? I'll just rescan it."

Lindsay searched through a stack of files in the "Open Cases" bin on his desk, becoming increasingly frustrated. "This is nuts," he said. "It should be near the top."

He finally found what he was looking for in the monthly "Solved Cases" stack. He looked through the pages but found only the crime scene shots of the body and the report from the morgue. The photos Eric had ordered for the facial recognition were gone.

Eric stood up. "Let's go over the video again."

The two spent the afternoon in the tech room reviewing the footage and trying to find the face in the misty fog, but they had no luck. They couldn't even play the whole video file without error codes popping up on the screen.

"I think someone is trying to sabotage this case," Eric said quietly. "Too many strange things for just one case."

Lindsay gazed out through the glass window that looked into the hallway and into the detectives' room across the way. "But who?"

CHAPTER FIFTY-THREE

THE SUN TURNED A dull red as it sank toward the sea. The last of its rays reflected from the boat's metal cleats and silver-plated rail onto Alexis's cheek, highlighting the dampness of her skin. Sitting in front of the forward hatch with her knees drawn in toward her chest, she tumbled the mysterious crystal around in her hands. It occasionally caught the fading light and reflected colors like a prism. Through tears gathering in the corners of her eyes, Alexis could see symbols sparkling on the crystal's surface.

The boat rocked, and she knew it must be James coming back, but she didn't bother to look. Instead, she wiped away her tears and focused on the millions of things running through her head.

"You brought that with you?" James asked as he joined her.

Alexis looked at the crystal and nodded. "I thought if I had any free time it might help distract me to research these symbols. Not that I thought I would actually have free time."

"You do now. It looks like we're stuck here until another boat arrives to take us back."

"What about going out further tonight?"

"No one is willing to take us out there tonight, or any night. I called and changed our flight to tomorrow morning instead of tomorrow night." James sat down next to Alexis and handed her a small brown paper bag.

"What's this?"

James just smiled.

She opened the bag and looked. "Edamame! And shrimp dumplings."

"I'm figuring out your food preferences," James said.

"Thank you," Alexis said before popping an edamame bean into her mouth.

"I take it there was nothing interesting from the data since last night?"

Alexis looked up and shook her head. James caught a hint of redness in her eyes. "Have you been crying?"

"I was lost in thought when a few unwanted memories found their way into my consciousness."

"You want to talk about it?" he asked.

She shook her head.

"All right, then what about this quartz? Any idea what those strange markings on the sides represent? I couldn't make head or tail of it."

"I thought at first that they didn't have a starting point, but I noticed that as it spirals around, the size of the inscriptions increases, possibly indicating a pattern to follow. I just need to figure out which end is the beginning."

"That's more than I found. The computer didn't even have matches to its origin or to any recognizable language or codes."

"I did notice that some of the languages looked familiar, but that each one is different. That would make it hard to create a key to translate the others." She was searching the crystal's surface, trying to find a few she recognized.

"Let's head below and look at it in there. I can't see the details very well."

"It's getting late. I probably need to call home first, since we're leaving so early in the morning. Which also means I need to set the VEs to satellite mode."

"I should pack my things up as well."

"I haven't seen you call home."

"My family is usually kind of hard to get hold of without planning a set time. They know I'm not home."

"I'm sorry to hear that."

"It's fine, they know I have a rather important job." James chuckled. "Other than right now, when I'm just an errand boy."

"You didn't have to agree to come along."

"Who would you have brought instead?"

"I'm going to get a shower."

After they went below, Alexis headed to her cabin and shut her door. James sat in the galley on a cushioned bench that ran along the port side. He leaned his head back against the wall and folded his arms as he looked up at the knots in the wood paneling. Everything was amplified below deck, and he heard the water quietly lapping along the sides of the boat. He heard Alexis leaving a voice message for someone.

"I'm too lazy to shower right now," Alexis said.

James sat up and almost hit his head on the shelf above him. "I didn't hear you come out."

Alexis sat at the galley table with her tablet. "James, do you know how to play chess?"

He moved from the bench to the table and sat across from her. "Don't tell anyone, but I have a chess set that has little green men for the pawns, and the rooks are spacecraft with beams shining down."

"Your secret is safe," she said with a laugh. "Only because it's not that great a piece of gossip when the only people I know to tell would probably have something similar in the bedroom of their mom's house."

"That's harsh, Zen."

"You want to play or not? It's only fair to tell you that I haven't lost since I was five."

"Confident, aren't we?"

Alexis had her tablet set up with a digital chess game and placed it between them on the table with white facing James.

"How's Ben holding up without you?" James asked after his first move.

"I haven't been able to get him since last night. I left him a voice mail that we were leaving earlier than expected, but with the time difference, I'm sure he's working." Alexis moved a bishop.

"Maybe."

They played silently as the night wore on. The sea was calm, and the air still.

Then Alexis looked up at James. "Did you feel that?"

"Yeah."

The floor of the boat began to vibrate. They jumped to their feet and made their way to the deck. The vibration sound intensified as they went to the bow. Alexis looked around and didn't see anyone or anything that might be responsible for the continuous rumble they heard from below. She ran back toward the hatch.

"Where are you going?" James yelled over the noise.

"I'm grabbing my camera," she said.

Seconds later, Alexis was back on deck with her gear. She put a special lens on the camera and started taking shots of the water and sky.

"Why are you shooting the sky when the sound is emanating from the water?"

As another strong vibration rumbled through, Alexis took shots of the water. "I figured something out today while I was wallowing in self ... reflection."

"And?"

"We're experiencing an earthquake right now, but it's so far below us that the intensity is mitigated by the water."

"Why are there no screaming people?"

"Just listen," Alexis said, turning her ear westward toward the village.

There was a faint sound of metal banging and glass clanking from the shops along the walkway twenty yards off shore.

Alexis pointed upward to a nearby hillside. "This area is dead at night because everyone lives further off the shore."

"This still doesn't explain the photo session."

Alexis leaned over the side of the boat when the vibrations began to die down. "James, look at these full-spectrum shots."

James looked at the camera display and noticed a starlike figure in the upper corner of the image. "What's the bright spot?"

Alexis flipped through the other shots, and the bright spot got bigger. "I'm not sure, I didn't see it when I was shooting. It's probably an airplane."

From out of nowhere a loud humming came from above the water, and then a cool breeze flowed past Alexis. The noise was overpowering. She covered her ears and looked around, trying to see where it was coming from, but it was emanating from all around. Alexis looked over the edge of the boat and noticed the surface of the water looked almost solid as the vibrating created a fine diamond pattern. The noise stopped, leaving Alexis with ringing ears. When she looked at James, he was staring up at the night sky.

"Alexis," he said in a hushed tone.

She followed his line of sight and saw a triangular object floating a few hundred yards above them. She raised her camera and began to snap off shots. The object wasn't moving, nor was it making any noise. There was an illuminated circle of lights shining from the center of a large black triangle. The lights intensified and lit up the area where Alexis and James stood.

"Is this really happening?" Alexis whispered.

The lights shifted and a narrow beam hit the bow of the boat and began moving. Alexis stood directly in its path.

"James?"

Alexis stepped back toward the stern to get a different angle, snapping a shot with every step. The deck was slippery on the port side, so she leaned away from the edge to steady herself. Once she made it to the stern, Alexis found her line of sight was still off. She needed to go back further to capture the entire object.

She climbed out onto the dock, stepping back about three or four feet to find the right angle. The object was as long as a football field and equally wide toward the back. It didn't look like anything she had ever seen at the base, but they were in Japan, so anything was possible with their technology.

The sky was dark, making it hard to see the details of the object hovering in the sky, but Alexis could make out something connected to the top.

She stopped taking photos when the lights from the object began to spotlight her area again. As before, she slowly stepped out of the light and into the darkness. The lights switched and began to shine on James and do a short series of blinks. Then it stopped and everything was dark again.

Alexis stood still, listening and waiting. Her head was no longer pounding, and she could see the boat by the docks. Still in shock, Alexis looked at James. "What was that?"

Ellory and Zavdiel came out of the shadows and watched from the distant shore. Alexis and James seemed quiet. They both stared into the sky.

"This can't be good," Ellory said.

"Which part? The one where an Apex ship just hovered unusually close, or that they probably know about her?"

"Both are a concern, but I was talking about the part where this was the third craft this week," Ellory said.

"Why does that concern you?"

"With everything going on with this human woman and the crystal, I think they are up to something."

"This is one of the main areas they can enter undetected. Not that I am sticking up for those disgusting creatures."

Ellory gazed upward. "I hope you're right."

"Trust me, I am not comfortable about this at all." Zavdiel watched James take a cell phone from his pocket and answer a call. "It's her we need to worry about. I hope he knows what he's doing."

CHAPTER FIFTY-FOUR

James and Alexis stood on the dock in the early morning darkness, waiting to board the large cargo ship that would take them back to the mainland days earlier than planned.

"I can't believe we have to leave," Alexis said.

"I know. But the commander insisted it was best to keep the peace with the locals."

"We didn't do anything." Alexis leaned closer and whispered, "It's not like we're the reason that UFO was here."

"I'm pretty sure it was you putting strange things in the water the night before that alarmed the locals. The UFO just confirmed their superstitions."

"I need more time," she insisted.

"We'll get back here, I promise."

"We have some amazing evidence. I can't wait to see those images on the big monitor back at the lab."

"I'm still in shock," James whispered as he waited for someone to take his bags. "I can't believe they came in so close."

Alexis glanced around at a few nearby people and then looked at James. "We need to stay quiet about this unless we're alone, agreed?"

"For once, I think we agree."

The two boarded the freight carrier that was to take them back to Tokyo. The captain gave them a room to relax for the next couple of hours. While James wrote in his journal, Alexis lay on one of the bunks trying to sleep. Once they made it to the docks, they'd have an hour's drive to Narita International Airport.

An old dented truck was waiting for them. The driver was a gray-haired man with deep wrinkles and drooping ear lobes. He knew very little English. "Uh, where you drop at?"

"Narita International, SkyLine Air terminal," James said.

"Oh, okay, okay."

When they reached the airport, Alexis hopped out of the truck and started unloading her bags. "I want to do curbside check-in."

James nodded. "Yeah, I don't feel like dragging that stuff through the airport."

The check-in attendant was standing behind a podium with a welcoming smile. "May I have your passport and flight information?"

Alexis handed him her passport and itinerary.

The curbside attendant waved his hand. "Your flight has changed, ma'am. You're not on SkyLine Air anymore. You are to report to the private flight area."

"What does that mean?"

"You will need to take the next to shuttle to Hanger 11, and your pilot will help load your personal luggage. I will have security take your marked cases directly over."

James put his passport on the counter. "Has my flight changed as well?"

The attendant typed in James's information. "Ah, yes, you both leave in seventy-eight minutes from Hanger 11."

Alexis turned to James. "Since when does the U.S. government splurge for a private plane?"

"When two of their scientists see something more than lights in the sky," James said as they walked to the area for shuttle departures.

Alexis stopped and began searching through her small carry-on bag. She pulled out her white smart tablet and a small plastic container. She opened the container and sorted through a dozen memory sticks. She took one and plugged it into the side of the tablet.

James saw that she wasn't behind him. He went back to help her with her luggage cart and saw the memory stick sticking out of the port on her tablet. "What's up?"

"I'm copying the photos from last night to email to myself before they get confiscated."

"You better encrypt them, Mata Hari," James said.

Before Alexis could respond, she saw the shuttle coming up the ramp. She put everything back into her bag and ran to catch up with James, who was standing by the curb with three American women who were also waiting for the shuttle.

"Did you send them?" he asked quietly.

"Yeah, I sent all the data I gathered from the past couple of days, and now it's wiping last night's data from my tablet's memory."

"You have serious trust issues."

The shuttle arrived. The driver, a little man whose foot barely reached the brake pedal, got out and opened the luggage hold in the back. Alexis and James rolled the luggage carts over, and they stowed their bags.

"What hotel or car rental you want to go?" the driver asked them after they and the three other passengers boarded.

"No hotel, sir, we need to go to Hanger 11," Alexis said.

"We take you first," the driver said as he closed the door.

There was some not-so-quiet muttering from the three women tourists, but Alexis ignored them and looked out the window, focusing on the world outside the bus. The shuttle went around the main building and headed past all the gates, and Alexis watched as several planes taxied to the runway and waited for their turn to take off. In the near distance she could see several private airplane hangars, all but one closed. The second from the end was marked by a numerical eleven, as well the kanji symbol for the word, on the top right of the building. The large bay door was open, exposing the elongated nose of a Challenger 850 jet.

There was murmuring from their three fellow passengers, and Alexis thought she heard one of them sniff about "rich snobs with a private jet."

Alexis didn't correct her, she just smiled and continued to look out the window.

James stood up and leaned over Alexis to look out her window. "I don't see any military escorts."

"There are probably men in black standing next to the plane to make sure we get on," she said.

The driver pulled the bus into the hangar and turned off the engine. "I help you get your stuff."

"That's okay, we can get it," Alexis said as she stood up to exit.

"What do you know, the princess isn't helpless," one of the women muttered.

Alexis rounded on her. "You need a personality transplant." She turned to James and said in a commanding voice, "Colonel Mitchell, when we get back to the Pentagon, I want full dossiers on these three on my desk within an hour. I think they may be spies."

"Will do, General, and I'll have Langley send some agents to follow up."

The woman who had insulted Alexis turned white. "Wait, I didn't mean ..."

But Alexis was already walking off the bus and didn't hear the rest.

Inside the hangar, James signed documents for the cargo as three men loaded the boxes onto the plane and two security officers watched.

"Where are the government agents or military escorts?" Alexis whispered.

"This plane isn't military or government," James replied.

"Then who's plane is it?"

James frowned at her. "He didn't mention this to you?"

"Who? Mention what?

"This is the doc's personal jet," James said.

"How do you know that?"

James handed Alexis six pages with items of their cargo listed. Each page listed the flight number, destination, pilot, and owner of plane. Alexis glanced over them and saw the name Benjamin P. Asael as the responsible party.

"Is he on board?" Alexis wondered aloud.

"No idea," James said.

Alexis headed to the plane, hoping to find Ben. She could hardly believe he owned it, and she wondered how he'd managed to get their flights changed.

For the hundredth time, she wondered about his feelings for her. Excitement was slowly rotating in the pit of her gut, and it was beginning to make her lightheaded. She tried to regulate her breathing as she climbed the steps to the open hatch of the airplane.

Alexis entered the plane and looked around. The walls were a soft white, and a faint blue glow from hidden lighting illuminated the ceiling. A plush cream-colored carpet invited her to step in further. She stepped toward the crescent-shaped leather couch that wrapped around on the right side and put a hand on the cool leather. On her left, two armchairs were turned inward to face an oval black granite table that held a small box wrapped with pink paper and topped by a simple white bow.

"I'm sorry I didn't tell you I was coming," Ben said from behind Alexis.

Her heart skipped and her eyes glistened when she turned around. "Oh, my gosh, why are you here? I mean this is wonderful, but why didn't you tell me?"

Ben smiled and moved closer. "Have you forgotten what today is?"

"Today is my birthday. But Ben, you could have just said something over the phone."

James came around the corner. "Why didn't you tell me your birthday was today."

"It's no big deal. Besides, we've been so busy I didn't think to mention it."

James made his way into the main cabin area and stood for a minute with Alexis and Ben. Ben handed her the pink box.

"Here, this is from Baba. She said you'd be able to figure it out."

Alexis took the box and looked it over for any clues indicating what might be inside. "I tried calling her and my parents, but no one answered," she said.

"It's my fault," said Ben. "I stopped at your grandparents one night and told her my plan to fly to see you for your birthday. Baba didn't want to slip up and tell you I was coming, so she avoided the calls. Same goes for your parents. They gave me this to give to you." Ben reached under the bar that ran along the side of the couch and pulled out a wrapped box twice the size of the pink one.

A pilot appeared at the door to the cockpit. "Dr. Asael, we're loaded and ready to depart," he said.

"Let's get comfortable before we take off, then you can open those," Ben said.

Ben and Alexis each sat in one of the armchairs divided by the granite table, while James sprawled onto the dark brown leather couch. Two male flight attendants secured the hatch door and then pushed a button. A panel slid shut, creating a cozier space.

"How were you able to make this happen?" James asked.

"I have found that money will get you almost anything in this world, and so I started handing it out to people with political influence. Being a psychiatrist provided me the keys to bigger connections, some of whom asked that I work for them as a government shrink. That allows me certain perks, including being friends with the commander."

James sat up. "But what we're doing is under a high-level clearance. The only way you could know where and when to find us and change our flights is if you had equal clearance."

"Or a higher one," Ben said.

Alexis knew Ben had top clearance but didn't realize how much more she could have shared with him. There was obviously a lot more to him than beautiful eyes and an innocent smile.

"I don't usually tell people because I want them to be natural at our sessions," Ben explained. "And when Alexis and I became ... well, when we started seeing each other outside the office, I didn't know how to tell her without coming across as officious and overbearing."

"Why don't you open your gifts, Zen," James said.

She picked up the one from her parents. It was wrapped in floral peach-colored paper and bore a simple happy birthday sticker in the center. Alexis opened it and found a book with a glossy cover.

"What book did you get?" James asked.

Alexis held it up. "It's *Spending Your Life Wisely*, written by some pastor my mother worships. I guess it's a Christian's guide to money sense. It appears to be used."

James laughed. "I guess that shows good money sense."

Alexis thumbed through the book quickly and saw there were highlighted paragraphs on several pages. "Maybe my mother went through and found the important parts for me."

Over the intercom one of the pilots announced, "Sir, we are ready for takeoff, and we will be arriving in Honolulu in approximately seven hours twenty-three minutes."

Alexis became flushed and tried to hide her nervousness. Ben extended his hand out on the table.

"Let me help you stay calm during takeoff."

"Is it that obvious?" Alexis's face had gone pale, and she could feel her heart pounding.

"A little."

"I don't have a fear of flying. It's the uncertainty of not landing where we're supposed to and ending up stranded on some island."

Alexis placed her clammy fingers into Ben's hand, and he closed his warm fingers around hers with a gentle squeeze. Alexis could feel her pulse slow, and her breathing become more steady. As she put her head back and closed her eyes, she let the hum of the plane's engines hypnotize her into a state of relaxation. It was as if she were weightless and floating on a cloud straight into the sun's warmth.

"Are you going to open the pink one?" James asked.

Alexis opened her eyes. They were airborne, and James was standing next to the couch eating cashews coated in sea salt and olive oil and holding a glass of wine. There was a fresh array of nuts, fruits, and cheeses on the bar, plus a bottle of Moscoto D'asti on ice near the large flat-panel television.

Ben was leaning against the bar, looking at Alexis. "I know you're hungry, so they're making you an omelet."

Alexis sat up. "You didn't have to do that." The wonderful aroma of the cooking omelet was making her mouth water. "But thank you."

"No trouble at all," Ben said as he joined her on the sofa. He leaned closer and added, "Do you think we can find some private time later to talk?"

Alexis had wanted to hear that since the moment she had awakened confused a few days earlier, but she didn't know how it would be possible with James around. She shrugged and nodded ever so slightly toward James.

"Maybe during the layover?"

"Speaking of that, how long will we be in Honolulu?"

Ben sat back and grinned. "Twenty-six hours."

Alexis beamed. *Hot shower and soft bed.* "I guess we'll find some time."

Alexis had been slowly working on untying the white ribbon decoratively tangled around the pink box and finally managed to unravel it and remove the wrapping paper. Alexis lifted the lid of the white cardboard box and pushed back the tissue paper. She took out a slip of paper that was lying on top of a worn, black, leather-bound notebook.

"What is with your family and books?" James asked.

Alexis was also puzzled by the small notebook. "I think this one is a journal of some kind."

"Maybe that note will explain," Ben suggested.

Alexis unfolded the piece of paper and began to read. The slanted lettering and subtle hint of lavender gave away that her grandmother had written it.

My sweet Alexis,

I sense that your birthday will be amazing and that you may be able to spend some time with your gentleman friend. We have really missed seeing you, but know that we also have been praying for the day things would change for you. This fellow must adore you to travel such a distance, so don't take your eyes off this one.

I am handing down this journal in hopes that it will become a part of the collection I have given you throughout the years and you will learn to cherish them for all your days. Inside you will find all the stories I promised to share and more. I have written my entry as those before, and you will do the same one day, finding the words to leave the next generation.

I caution you to stay clear of danger on your path around the world in search of truth, and we hope to see you when you make it home.

Love,
Baba
Revelations 20:2

A tear slipped out as she put the letter back into the box. The journal pages were discolored, and their edges were faded and beginning to crack, but they were smooth to the touch and bound together well, and they had a unique smell.

Alexis brought the journal closer and peered at the sheets. "These pages are ancient parchment."

James shrugged. "So?"

"They would have been made from the skin of a baby calf or baby goat. These pages are better than papyrus and a lot more expensive. I wonder why my grandma has this."

Ben watched her flip pages and pause on one not written in English."Is that in Polish?"

James moved in closer to get a better view. "She gave you a notebook written in Polish?"

"Not exactly. These pages are in Polish, but there are several different languages throughout the entire thing. Look here." Alexis set the journal on the table and pointed out different languages.

James pointed to one of the pages. "I'm sure that one is Egyptian."

Alexis nodded. "I recognize some languages, but there are a lot that I've never seen before."

One of the flight attendants opened the panel door and brought out a plate with an omelet and crisp fried potatoes. He sat the warm plate in front of Alexis and then filled her glass with cranberry juice.

"Thank you. Spinach Swiss omelet and home fries, my favorite breakfast when I'm not worried about calories." Alexis set the journal to the side and picked up a fork. Before she could ask, the attendant came back with a small bottle of ketchup.

"Can I get you anything else, ma'am?"

Alexis grinned. "I think I have everything, thank you. If I need anything else, I'm sure you'll read my mind again."

When she finished her breakfast, Alexis took the journal and started to examine the passages she could read.

CHAPTER FIFTY-FIVE

SUNLIGHT GLISTENED ON the clear blue water rolling toward the shore of the Hawaiian beach as two frigate birds soared overhead. Twenty yards out, waves crashed against a huge rock that loomed above the water like a obelisk, sending up a sparkling spray. A fine mist floated all the way to the shore, cooling Azure and the hundreds of men who stood there with him. There were no trees to cast shadows and offer cover from the sun. Each man had his eyes turned toward Azure, who was in the center, turning as he spoke to take in the assembled group.

"Alexis Zen is on her way here, and she is with him," Azure said. "Keep your distance."

A voice rose up from the crowd. "Why should we listen to you? All you and Cezar ever do is preach about your own personal fear of the end."

"Do you see Cezar standing with me?" Azure replied.

"He may not be with you, but we know what you have to say is not for our benefit."

"Just stay clear of the woman."

Another voice rose up. "Is it true that she interacted with the two in Japan?"

The group was silent as they waited for an answer. Azure knew the chaos the truth could unleash and chose his words carefully.

"Ellory and Zavdiel thought she spoke to them, but it was in the middle of the day, with other humans around, so they could have mistakenly assumed she was talking to them. It's nothing to get worked up about. You must keep your distance."

A man near the front glared at Azure. "Did you mistakenly assume she looked at you the night you were in her apartment?"

"No."

"I heard we are not the only ones watching her from a distance," another man called from the other side of the group, sparking a stir of whispers.

"I just wanted to warn you, as I did the others in Japan," Azure said pointedly, to remind them of their place in the order of things. "She is coming to Hawaii, and he is with her. It would be wise to control your curiosity."

"We got the message a month ago when you made your blunder," the man replied. "Besides, I'm sure there is something else you should be doing in your own area of the world."

Azure tried to ignore the blatant disrespect. He took in the crowd standing before him and understood the overwhelming power one must possess in order to control so many, not to mention the many unseen beings around the world.

Two by two the men disappeared into thin air, and before long all but one pair were gone. The man who had insulted him stood with another, staring at Azure.

Azure looked upon them with disgust. "Is there a problem?"

"Azure, remember your place. You do not speak for him. We need not listen to your ranting every time you think something is afoot."

"Chuave, I have seen what happens to those who go against him, and I wish it upon no one. It was my intention to keep you from that fate sooner than planned. If you dismiss my advice, then feel free to go your own way, but know that there is a hell far worse than the one you are living now. It's possible this human could help us."

"Impossible." Chuave raised his hand with his palm up, allowing a white butterfly to come to rest there and flutter its wings. "It was understood from the beginning what side we chose and where our fates would lie. There is no need to alert everyone when you feel something is amiss or when you think our leader is acting uncharacteristically."

He paused to watch the butterfly and then closed his fist around it.

"Death will happen to all of us, Azure." He opened his hand to reveal the lifeless insect. He raised his brow before disappearing.

Azure stood alone, looking around at the world he had come to know and love. The sun was in the west, and distant palm trees cast afternoon shadows on the hillside. He watched an airplane flying toward the airport on the other side of the island and knew he needed to leave before the jet carrying Alexis Zen arrived. Azure moved into the soft shadows of the distant tree line and disappeared.

CHAPTER FIFTY-SIX

IN THE RECORDS DIVISION of the Montgomery County Court, a quiet clerk was making his way through a stack of paperwork and correcting the information in the public record database. Normally Herman Cowley was ahead of schedule, and there was never a pile of papers unfinished. Often he would read mystery novels rather than work, but a recent computer system crash had put him behind schedule. Herman also worked three days a week as a clerk for the Fairborn Police Department, and a recent rise in crime had made his workload heavier there as well.

Herman finished entering births from the past six weeks and began to enter death certificates. He had been struck by a noticeable increase in male babies coming into the world and several baby girls named Samantha, and now he noted the recent deaths of a lot of middle-aged women. One name, *Sarah Hanover*, stood out. Her cause of death had been blunt force to the head.

The car accident involved in her death had been near his home. Out of curiosity, Herman called the police station downtown.

"Dayton Police Department," the female on the other end answered.

"Good afternoon, Officer Shultz, it's Herman Cowley, I work at the Fairborn precinct. We've spoken over the phone a few times before."

"What can I do for you?" she asked.

"I need to speak with a detective."

"One moment," she said, and he heard the click that let him know she'd transferred his call.

"Schaffer here," a deep voice answered.

"It's Herman Cowley from the Fairborn Police Department. Can I ask about an old case?"

"What's the case?"

"A woman named Sarah Hanover was in an accident by my house a month or so ago. Whatever happened with that case?"

"It was deemed a murder. Detective Webber was the lead."

"Murder?" Herman was sure the local papers hadn't mentioned foul play.

"Yeah, some guy followed her from work then ran her of the road. But she didn't die from the crash. This guy, George Pail or something, slammed her head against the dash. He left a single partial print on the dash or seatbelt or somewhere, Webber would have the details. Case took a funny turn, though."

"How so?" Herman asked.

"They caught the guy, but then someone paid his bail, and he never showed for trial."

"What did the guy look like?"

"I'll look up the arrest warrant and email it over to you," the detective offered.

Herman thanked the detective and gave him his personal email and cell phone number. He checked his phone every few minutes, but nothing came. The digital clock on the computer screen changed to four o'clock, and Herman had to rush to confirm the last four entries sitting on his desk. He had to leave soon to pick up his mother and get her to bingo by five. As he verified the last entry, his phone signaled an incoming alert.

He opened the email and looked at the image of a man in his late thirties. The name *Pliate* sounded familiar, and Herman wracked his memory for a clue.

And then he remembered exactly where he had seen that name and that face.

CHAPTER FIFTY-SEVEN

"Please watch your step, Miss Zen," the male flight attendant said as Alexis stepped into the bright Hawaiian sunlight.

The green-roofed buildings were untypical for an airport, as were the flat green grasses surrounding the landing strips, but it was the distant tree line that took Alexis's breath away—so many shades of green, with bursts of electrifying colors, welcoming visitors to the small island in the Pacific.

Alexis, Ben, and James exited the plane as a crew of men pulled up to unload its cargo. James tried to walk close to Alexis, trying to at least feel like he was a part of the conversation.

"Where are we headed from here, doc?" James asked.

Alexis was wondering the same thing. "I don't care as long as it has a hot shower and a place to take a nap."

"I figured you both were in need of some pampering," Ben said. "So I upgraded you from the boat style you've enjoyed this weekend."

"It wouldn't require much to upgrade from those fish-saturated accommodations, isn't that right Alexis?" James joked.

"Or the cracker mattresses, but I guess it could have been worse."

Ben glanced at James. "I hope this hotel will be more enjoyable."

Alexis leaned in toward Ben and whispered in his ear, "You're amazing. Thanks for this."

"You're welcome."

A black town car pulled up to the hanger and took the three on a short drive to their hotel. Alexis was able to enjoy a bit of scenery before it was taken over by the towering buildings along the beach. Among those, one stood out, shimmering with reflective glass all the way to the heavens and open to the ocean view. Alexis could only imagine what the inside would be like or how much it would cost for a night.

Ben looked at Alexis, who was sitting next to him, then back toward James. Both were staring out their windows.

"The room has three separate suites with their own privacy. Alexis you can have the suite with the king-size bed, while James and I will take suites with queen beds."

Alexis glanced out the window as they pulled into the hotel she had been admiring from miles away. Speechless, Alexis stepped out of the car and followed behind Ben. Two tall walnut doors opened into a bright lobby that offered breathtaking views of the ocean. Ivory-colored marble floors had a soothing effect, and perfectly placed leather furniture signaled comfort and high standards.

The concierge made his way to Ben before they were halfway through the lobby. "Mr. Asael, so nice to have you back, sir."

"Thank you, Carlos, will you have them bring our bags up?"

Ben and James walked straight toward the elevator.

Alexis paused to look around. She thought such a place could be found only in a forbidden city, and she had just been given access.

The ride up the elevator was the worst part for Alexis, only because she didn't enjoy rides with the potential of a free fall from a staggering height. Ben stepped closer and gently put a hand around Alexis's white knuckles. She closed her eyes and forgot her nerves.

The door opened to a pristine hallway with only four rooms. As soon as they were inside the large apartment-size room, James looked at Ben and Alexis. "Sorry to be rude, but I'm taking a shower and then a nap."

Alexis was smiling inside, knowing she could have some alone time with Ben, but she quickly realized that she needed a shower, too.

Ben pointed to the left to show James which room he would be staying in and then escorted Alexis to her private room. "If you're up to it after your shower, I'll meet you on the balcony."

Alexis smiled and headed into her room.

Six hours to the east, Detective Stuart Lindsay answered his phone. "This is Lindsay."

The voice on the other end spoke fast. "It's Herman, I found a tie to your case with the frozen guy, and I think I know ..."

"Whoa, slow down. I can barely understand you."

The voice on the other end began again. "Over a month ago, a woman was killed near my place. At first they thought she died from impact when she wrecked her car. I remember driving and seeing the twisted tire tracks. She was a waitress from the truck stop."

"Right, I remember that one from the papers."

"I just made a connection between her killer and one of your victims."

"Who?"

"George Pliate. Read the obituary of the woman I just emailed you, you'll see what I mean."

Lindsay shot a glance to Detective Carter, who was closing up a file. "Herman, will you send everything you have, please?"

"I'll forward you the file from the other detective."

"Thanks, buddy."

"What was that all about?" Detective Carter asked.

"That was the part-time clerk in Records, Herman something. He says our Ice Man was suspected in another crime a few nights before we found him dead."

"Is he sending over the case file? And where did he see this?"

"He's forwarding the file from the county where the guy supposedly killed some woman. But he said it's the obituary that will get our attention."

Lindsay opened Herman's email and downloaded the file he had sent.

"He didn't tell you what to look for?"

"I think there was a bingo game going on in the background," Lindsay said. "He still hangs out with his mom."

"You still hang out with yours," Carter said.

"No, I go to my sister's place."

"Your mom lives there, man."

Lindsay pulled up the page that listed the obituary and began reading it to Carter.

> *Hanover, Sarah Reese*
>
> *On the morning of Friday, June 8, Sarah Hanover, daughter and sister, passed away suddenly at the age of 36 years. Sarah will be forever remembered by her parents Ghetta and Ann Prollofsky, as well as by her three brothers and four sisters. Sarah will also be a beautiful inspiration to her numerous nieces, nephews and extended family and dear friends.*

It went on to describe her accomplishments with local service groups and her favorite things in life, along with information about a memorial service. At the bottom of the obituary was a family picture.

"I don't get it." Carter said. "What am I missing?"

They read the obit again, wondering why Herman thought it important. Then Detective Lindsay glanced at the photograph at the bottom of the page.

"I think this is a picture of her and some family members."

"She was a very attractive lady, but I don't recognize her. Tell Herman to leave detective work to the detectives." Carter put on his bifocals. "Wait a minute, is that who I think it is?" He pointed at a young woman standing near Sarah Hanover in the photograph.

Lindsay stared, and his eyes went wide. "That can't be a coincidence."

"I'm pretty sure this makes her a person of interest now," Carter said. "But let's connect the dots before we bring her in. We don't want another episode of vanishing evidence."

"We have to wait until she gets back in the country," Lindsay said. "I hope Alexis has a good explanation."

Carter leaned back in his chair. "Until then, print me a copy of that case he sent. I want to know more about how this lady died and how our guy ended up over here with her niece."

CHAPTER FIFTY-EIGHT

ALEXIS WASN'T FOCUSED on the warmth of the shower, or the massaging pressure as it rinsed days of dirt down the drain. Her mind was on Ben. She was running through a perfectly scripted night ending with harmless pillow talk. Alexis had a bad habit of playing out conversations before they happened, a way to not be caught off guard. Her heart raced as she rummaged through her suitcase, knowing she hadn't brought many things for an elegant night of lounging. She put on a little T-shirt and a pair of cotton pajama shorts and then slipped into a pair of flip flops.

As she searched for deodorant, her hand felt over the velvet bag in which she kept the quartz crystal. She was reminded of the day it pinged on the floor of her lab.

Did you create the orb? What is your purpose? Alexis tumbled the crystal around in her hand before putting it back.

She stepped out of her master suite into the large contemporary living room, its soft ivory and coral hues flowing across warm fabrics. She saw a silver pedestal tray of various fruits by the counter in the fully equipped kitchen. She walked over to grab a piece of fruit and saw a copy of the National News. Alexis piled a plate with strawberries and pineapple slices and then picked up the newspaper and a bottle of water and headed to the balcony, where Ben said he'd be waiting.

The hotel was wrapped with glass windows and festooned with wide balconies that seemed to float with the clouds. Alexis took in the spectacular view as she stepped onto the balcony. Ben was sitting on a wicker couch made for two.

"I bet you feel better after that shower." Ben wasn't wearing his glasses and Alexis had to remind herself to blink when she looked into the amber flecks in his eyes. He was wearing khaki cargo shorts and a tight black Lycra T-shirt that showed off his sculpted abs. Alexis suddenly felt underdressed.

She sat down and turned toward Ben. "You have no idea how grateful I am for all this—and how confused."

"I wanted you to have a birthday to remember."

"You do this for all your friends' birthdays?"

"Well, no."

"This is an extravagant gesture for someone who turned me down for a relationship. One would assume something was going on between you and me."

Ben looked out to the painted sky. "I've never felt a connection like the one I have with you and which I honestly don't know how to pursue. I'm better at listening to others talk about these situations and helping people avoid emotional roadblocks. I'm not so good at actually having to make a decision."

"You're not good with change, are you?" Alexis looked down at the newspaper as she grabbed a strawberry from the plate.

"Not exactly, I just like to be in complete control of things, and you made it difficult."

"All I did was ..."

"Alexis?"

She was holding the paper open to the third page, reading a small article titled "Full Moon Brings Out UFO Watchers."

Ben was looking over her shoulder. "Is crop failure in the west so interesting that we're changing the subject?"

"What? No, no, I'm sorry."

"We have plenty of time to figure us out. I want to know what grabbed your attention on that page."

Alexis pointed to the UFO article. "James and I witnessed something like this last night. And it appears we weren't the only ones."

"You saw a UFO?"

Alexis sat up straight and gazed at the sky. "UFO implies unidentified. What we saw was clearly identified as not from this planet."

"And James also saw this?"

"Yes. It was the most amazing thing I've ever experienced. Indescribable."

"I imagine it was."

"Do you want to see what we caught?"

Ben nodded and followed Alexis to her room. She closed the door and then got out her smart tablet and inserted a portable drive. She brought up the pictures from the night before and handed the tablet to Ben. Then she plugged in her laptop and set it on the desk.

Ben sat on the corner of the king-size bed and looked at the images. "Alexis, these are unbelievable shots. I'm amazed that camera of yours can get such detailed shots from such a distance."

"Ben, the object was no more than fifty yard from where I was standing."

"No one has ever caught something this detailed. I'm stunned."

"I'm looking for more descriptions from eyewitnesses," Alexis said as she stared at the screen of her laptop.

After reading several eyewitness accounts, Alexis found a pen and notepad in the drawer and drew a map of the world. Then she started plotting points. Most of the sightings were along the west coast of the Americas, with a high concentration near California.

Ben pointed to a picture with an audio symbol in the center of it. "What's this?"

Alexis stood up from the desk to stand next to Ben. "It was strange, but I swear it was giving off a weird low-pitched frequency. I recorded it with a piece of equipment I attached to my camera. I'll run it through a program back at the base."

As she spoke, Ben began to move in closer. "Why are you being so quiet?"

"I didn't tell James I recorded anything. That way he has deniability for my actions." Alexis couldn't help but be taken in my Ben's eyes. He leaned forward and put her tablet on the desk.

"What about my deniability?"

"I didn't think about that, sorry."

He caressed the side of her face and pushed a strand of hair out of the way. "I think we should talk about something else."

Alexis could feel her hands becoming sweaty and her head starting to spin. Ben moved in closer but wasn't touching her. His breath was on her cheek, and the sound of her heart was pounding in her ears.

He touched her hand softly. "Just relax and let your mind feel."

"It's not that easy without ..."

She didn't get to finish her thought before she felt the warmth of his hand move to the back of her arms. Her lips barely began to touch his when her mind lost concentration.

There was a knock on the door.

"Are you two hungry?" James called from the other side of the door.

Alexis snapped back into reality and went to open the door for James.

"I don't know about you two, but I'm starving," he said as he stepped into the room. "Since it's Alexis's birthday, I'm treating everyone to dinner tonight."

"Sounds good to me, but I need to change first," Alexis said as she motioned both Ben and James out the door.

Ben set down the tablet and got up from the bed.

"I'll be right out," Alexis said as she closed the door behind them.

She grabbed the sundress she had packed and the pair of thin-strapped sandals from her suitcase. The bathroom mirror was huge and grabbed the natural light from the windows that wrapped half the room. After she touched up her makeup and slipped into her dress, Alexis dusted her body with the scent of light lavender.

She took one last look in the mirror. When she walked past the desk she thought about the eyewitness accounts. Alexis picked up her tablet and started scrolling through the pictures from the previous night. She frowned and went to the laptop, logged back in, and scanned through the amateur photos and shaky videos that people had posted. Then she decided she'd have to go through everything carefully later.

She found Ben and James on the balcony. "Do you remember seeing the moon last night?" she asked James. "It would have been a full moon."

James thought for a moment. "I can't say for sure that I remember seeing it. Why?"

"I went through images and videos online, and none of them showed the moon."

"It would depend on the angle of the camera taking the shot." James said.

"I looked through more than fifty images and ten videos. There was no moon in any of them. So either these crafts only come in from a side where the moon is not visible or something bigger is blocking it."

Ben stood up from the wicker seat. "Let's have dinner and look at the other footage when we come back and figure this out together."

James and Alexis looked at Ben. "What other footage?" James asked.

"My properties have top-of-the-line security cameras that take 360 degrees of footage with a rooftop cam, and I can access them from anywhere."

"Alexis, that gives me an idea," James said. "You should review the VEs' recordings from Japan on your H2E. They're still recording, right?"

"Yes, good idea," Alexis replied.

Ben looked at Alexis. "We could call for room service, if you like. It's your birthday, so you get to choose."

"Or I can grab something and bring it back." James offered.

"If you guys don't mind."

"It's settled then, we're eating in." Ben reached for the phone.

"Hang on, Ben, why don't I go to the hotel restaurant and order our food? I have a couple calls to make while I'm waiting."

James wrote their orders on a slip of notepad paper and left.

"That reminds me, I have a package to grab at the front desk," Ben said.

"Okay," Alexis replied. "I'll make some calls to my family."

CHAPTER FIFTY-NINE

THE SUN CAST THE last of its rays through clouds floating on the horizon. Chuave and several others who wandered the earth in the shadows watched from the peak of Diamond Head Volcano as manmade lights winked on, and the tide began to rise. Their presence was as ghosts in the shadows to all those who stayed on the island, all except one. Now standing amongst them was the master of shadows.

"Why are you gathered together here?"

"We watch everything change up here, sir," Chuave said. "It's the only time of day where the dark and light are in perfect balance."

"Is there something you want to share?" their Master asked.

Chuave didn't hesitate. "Azure was here earlier."

"Spreading his joy or preaching his gloom?" The man looked across the faces of the silent men and waited for Chuave to respond.

"I am still uncertain of his motives, but he seemed concerned for you this time and wanted us to remember to stay clear of you and that human woman."

"But?"

"But we told him to leave. I explained that we knew we must keep our distance, especially after the Japan incident with the human."

"The human woman has a name, Chuave, have some respect. I don't call you malignant spirit." The man turned to a small man standing behind him. "Yosep, tell me your thoughts."

In a nervous tone, Yosep tried to answer. "I'm not worried about what Azure was saying. You would let us know if it's time, and the rumors about Alexis Zen being our possible redemption are crazy."

The man shot a look back to Chuave. "What is he talking about?"

Chuave swallowed before explaining. "Azure and a few others discussed revealing themselves and getting the human woman to be on our side once the crystal was translated. He didn't ask, but of course I would have told him we were waiting for your orders to change our position with this human."

"Chuave, your jealousy is showing. Her name is Alexis. Explain what else Azure wanted and why he is concerned for me." His eyes were stern and commanding as he spoke.

"He has said that you've acted differently around her and that you were losing focus."

"What do you think?"

A silence fell as he asked the question that none of them ever wanted to answer. Honesty could get them sent to a space of endless torment, especially if their Master disagreed. But dishonesty was never an option.

"I don't know what has brought on his suspicions, and I can't base an opinion on a mere perception of Azure's," Chuave said.

The man didn't respond immediately but looked out across the water as the waves crashed into the white, shimmering shoreline.

"Chuave, I have never lost my focus, and the mission has always been the same. I have interacted with these worlds since the beginning of their existence without the slightest doubt about my reasons. This is no different from any other time or planet."

Chuave found his courage. "Except this time you can't leave."

"Azure was right about one thing—you need to stay as far away from her as possible. She does have the ability to see you, just as you see her."

Everyone but Chuave disappeared without a sound. "Sir, how long are you going to keep her alive?"

The man made no reply. Chuave disappeared into the shadows and left him alone atop the volcano.

CHAPTER
SIXTY

DETECTIVES CARTER AND Lindsay walked out of the elevator and headed back to the robbery/homicide department. Some of the detectives were out on calls, and others had gone home for the night, leaving the place feeling desolate. Fluorescent lights buzzed overhead and cast a bluish hue onto the white walls.

"I can't believe no one put the pieces together until now," Detective Carter said as they entered the room. "Those people thought their daughter's assailant was still in jail awaiting a trial date."

Lindsay sat at his desk and began sorting through his case files. "I was just thinking about something Mrs. Pliate said the day we notified her of her son's death."

"What was that?"

"She said he used to be such a good guy. At the time it didn't mean anything, but now I wonder how much she knew about his wrongdoings." Lindsay pulled a file from the stack sitting on his desk and opened it. "It says here he didn't have a criminal record."

"So what makes a good guy turn bad?"

"And why was he targeting that family?"

"Do you think he would have continued if someone hadn't killed him?"

Lindsay glanced up from the file. "I'm thinking someone else knew, and that's why they killed him."

Carter grabbed his gun and badge and stood up. "Since we can't speak with Miss Zen, I say we visit the parents of the woman who died."

"I just wish something in this case made sense," Lindsay said as he picked up his own badge and gun.

CHAPTER SIXTY-ONE

ALEXIS WAS STRETCHED out on the wicker love seat, her head and back propped up with two pillows, flipping through the pages of the journal her grandmother had sent. Each entry was less than a page, some no more than a short paragraph. All were in different handwriting and languages. The leather vellum appeared well preserved, which made it hard for Alexis to estimate the age of the book.

Ben came back into the hotel room and joined her on the balcony. "Where's James?" he asked. "I didn't see him when I passed the restaurant. I thought he'd be here with the food."

Ben leaned against the rail and peered out as if he were looking for something.

"Are you okay?" Alexis asked. "You seem a little distracted."

"I'm fine, I'm just looking at the pool. We should go for a swim in the ocean later." He turned toward Alexis and pointed at the journal. "How many languages have you recognized?"

"Only a few." Alexis stood up and showed him some of the unfamiliar ones.

He moved closer. "Can I kiss you right now?"

That took Alexis by surprise.

Unable to speak, she slowly nodded her head and then moved in with her eyes closed. The sweetness of Ben's kisses sent an overload to Alexis's head, and she felt everything spinning. A numbing tingle rushed through her body, and she could no longer hear her heart beating. He hugged her in a warm embrace, and she began to move her hands to his face and back through his hair. She felt weightless.

"Alexis, can you hear me?" Ben said as he put his fingers on her carotid artery to check for a pulse.

"Should we start CPR?" James asked as he knelt down next to Ben.

Alexis was watching them from across the balcony as they tried to resuscitate her. She looked around for answers or a way to awaken but found nothing. She felt panic begin to rise.

A group of five people dressed in long white garments materialized in front of her. A male member of the group spoke to her. "You are not dead, but you are in danger of the darkness that is coming if you stay on this path."

"Who are you?"

"When I send you back you must finish what your family started and follow the path of truth." He pointed to the book lying next to Alexis's body.

"What are you talking about? What path?"

He looked at the black journal her grandmother had given her. "From the beginning."

The people in white disappeared. Alexis felt a surge of energy charge through her body, and everything was dark and cold.

There was a faint song in the distance, or maybe it was someone calling her name. She recognized the voice as Ben's, and she felt the warmth of his arm around her neck. "Alexis, can you hear me?"

"There's a pulse," James exclaimed.

Alexis felt as though she were waking from a winter hibernation, and she wanted to curl in toward the fragrant smells of cedar. Reality caught up to her subconscious, and she remembered what just happened.

She took in a deep breath. Adrenaline surged and blood rushed to her face as she stared into the familiar eyes of a dark-suited man and watched as he disappeared into the shadows.

Ben was on his knees beside her. "Alexis?"

She looked at him and saw a tear slip from the corner of his eye. She glanced at James, who was sitting to her left, tears flowing.

"Don't be so sad, I just passed out," Alexis rasped. Her mouth was dry and scratchy as she spoke.

James exhaled. "Alexis, you didn't just pass out."

She looked to Ben.

"You didn't have a pulse."

Alexis's memory flashed to the man in white. "I wasn't dead. He said I have to finish what I started." She looked at the journal lying on the floor of the balcony. "But how do I know what that is?"

Ben and James looked at each other. "What are you talking about?" Ben asked.

Alexis started to get up. "I need to look at something."

Ben and James helped her to a chair.

"You need a doctor first," James insisted.

"Ben is a doctor."

"You need a doctor who has his black bag with him and doesn't specialize in psychiatry," Ben said. "Let us take you to the E.R. and get some tests to make sure you're all right."

"Okay," Alexis said. "Can I freshen up first?"

They walked her to her suite, and she sat on the edge of the bed.

"I'll be just outside," Ben said. He and James left, closing the door behind them.

Alexis lay back and looked up at the ceiling, her mind a roiling sea of thoughts. She closed her eyes, recalling everything she had seen and heard on the balcony.

Finish what your family started ... You are in danger ... The path of truth ... Darkness that is coming.

The phrases spun through Alexis's head like a song that sticks in the mind. The words began to sound familiar. Then it hit her where she had heard them before. It was in the note her grandmother had included with the journal—the journal the man in white had been pointing to.

There was a knock on the door. "Alexis?" Ben called. "May I come in?"

"Give me a second." Alexis threw on a pair of yoga pants and a T-shirt and ran a brush through her hair. "You can come in now."

Ben walked in as she stepped out of the bathroom. "The island's concierge doctor is coming here to examine you. He won't be here for an hour, so I think you should rest."

Alexis was relieved and grateful. "I will. And thank you."

Ben came closer. "You really scared us. It might be wise for you not to fly for a couple of days. I'll stay with you."

"I feel fine, really," Alexis said. "Let me grab my tablet, and I'll relax on the couch. I promise."

"All right, I'll be out here waiting."

Ben turned and left the room. Alexis waited until she heard the latch click before she exhaled. She put one of her bags on the luggage rack and opened it. She unzipped an inside compartment and took out the gift box her grandmother had sent with Ben. She opened the lid, took out the folded letter, and reread it. The last sentence made Alexis rethink what had just happened.

"Stay clear of danger on your path across the world in search of truth, and we hope to see you when you make it home."

Alexis picked up her smart tablet from the desk. She snapped a picture of the letter and put it in a password-locked folder. She put the letter back in the box and headed to the living room, where James and Ben were waiting.

"Are you hungry?" James asked as he stood up. "I can warm up something."

Alexis grinned. "How cold can it be, it's only been fifteen minutes."

Ben got up from where he was sitting and walked over to the elevated bar connected to the counter.

"Alexis, James brought that food up forty minutes ago. You were out for almost fifteen minutes. We thought you weren't coming back."

Alexis opened the silver tray cover and touched one of the fries on James's plate. It was cold and hard. Her eyes welled with tears as her emotions caught up with theirs.

"I'm so sorry. I didn't realize. It only seemed like a few seconds before I was pulled back in. I'm really sorry. That's why you both were so upset, and I feel terrible."

"What do you mean pulled back in?" James asked.

Alexis realized the significance of the words she had just used to describe her experience. "It was like I was out of my body again."

James stared at her. "Again? Is this a normal thing for you?"

"You should rest," Ben said. "We can talk about what happened after the doctor checks you."

She headed to the couch, where Ben had arranged the pillows and laid out a cotton throw for her.

"No, James, this is not normal, but it has happened a couple other times."

Ben furrowed his brow. "Was there another time besides today and the time in June?"

"This happened last month?" James asked.

Alexis lay down on the sofa and put her head on a pillow. "Yes, but this time it was different."

"Do you want to tell us about it, or do you want to talk later?" Ben asked.

Alexis's eyes felt heavy, and she stifled a yawn. "I saw a man in white, and he said some weird stuff to me and then disappeared and …"

"What kind of weird stuff?" James demanded. "What did this guy look like?"

There was a knock at the door, and Alexis heard Ben welcoming the doctor.

"What did the guy in white say?" James pressed. "Did you talk to him?"

The doctor stepped into the room and sat near Alexis. He was a broad-built man with Polynesian features and a long ponytail. He wore a floral short-sleeve shirt and khaki shorts. Alexis could smell almonds as he walked past her.

"Alexis, I'm Dr. Kāohi, the local concierge doctor on the island." He looked toward Ben and James, who were sitting on the sofa. "Would you like your friends to step outside for more privacy?"

"No, they can stay."

Ben stood up. "Actually, I think I need some fresh air."

He kneeled beside Alexis as the doctor began to take her blood pressure. "Will you call me when he's finished?"

Alexis smiled and nodded, and then Ben leaned in to kiss her forehead. The blood pressure gauge plummeted, and the doctor frowned at it.

Alexis laughed. "Ben, you're making it spin out of control."

"No, it's dropping to where I can't get anything," Dr. Kāohi murmured.

James stood up. "I think I'll get some fresh air, too. Be back after while."

Ben and James stepped out into the hallway and took the elevator down to the lobby.

CHAPTER SIXTY-TWO

AZURE WATCHED AS James and Ben left the hotel. Ben headed toward the beach, and Azure followed, trying to stay in the shadows. It was easy to blend in as they walked past the strip of restaurants and specialty shops overflowing with people and noise, but when he got closer to the beach Azure concealed himself in the darkness. He watched Ben walk toward the shore.

Ben took off his sandals and walked barefoot through the sand. He sat down on one of the large broken rocks lining the beach and gazed up at the night sky and an infinite sea of stars. Waves crashed against the large rocks poking up from the shallows. After a long exhale Ben dropped his head into his hands.

Confused, Azure moved in closer, to the rock directly behind Ben.

Ben looked up, his face streaked with tears, and gazed out at the water. Everything was dark against the white sand, and the sounds of the street were muffled by the rolling waves. Ben stared toward the black horizon as Azure moved closer, only a few feet away.

"Why are you following me?" Ben asked, still gazing at the horizon.

As fast as a thought, Azure was standing beside Ben, looking in the same direction. "I was there when she died and ..."

Ben turned and looked at Azure. "Alexis is alive. Why did you follow me here?"

"I wanted to see where you were going and find out what she said after ... after she was back."

Frustration turned Ben's eyes to the darkness Azure was used to seeing. "Why did you follow me to Hawaii? Why were you and Cezar standing outside my house a couple of days ago. Why are you here now?"

Azure knew he was treading the line of his boundaries but also knew forthrightness was his only option. "Master, I have never seen you shed a tear or show so much interest in one person. I needed to know why."

Ben frowned. He seemed puzzled. "You were there tonight when she collapsed? Why? I didn't feel you there."

"Because I'm still the dark spirit you tasked to destroy the line of Eve, and I didn't show up freely."

"The only way you would be brought involuntarily is if …" Ben paused.

"If she had died." Azure watched the fear return to Ben's face. "I only knew for sure because I saw one of the spirits from the light talking to her."

"She said there was a man saying things to her, and then she was pulled back in. At first I thought she was having one of her strange dreams."

Azure said nothing as he watched an expression of uncertainty and confusion cloud the face of the sole leader of the Nefilim dark spirit world.

"If she died, why did they send her back?" Ben asked. "They have never sent anyone back, even if they were gone for only a minute."

"I don't know," Azure said, wondering if he should ask the question that was plaguing his mind. He decided he should. "Master, I know I am taking a risk by asking you this, but do you have feelings for Alexis?"

It was though everything stopped. The only thing Azure could hear was the pulse that came from deep beneath his feet, and he knew he was in danger of being cast into darkness.

Azure decided to interrupt his own question. "I chose to follow you because I believed in your plan, and I have been your servant this whole time. I want you to know I am in this with you until the end. I just need to know if this thing with Alexis Zen is different."

Ben was still staring out into the vast ocean, but the sounds of the waves and commotion from the street returned, and Azure felt a small sense of relief that he was still standing there.

"This was never my plan," Ben said. "I have been on this earth for too long, and I have interacted with many of these humans without the slightest concern for their fate or personal affairs. My desire has been revenge for what was taken from me, and we have found the line of Eve. With the crystal it will all change."

"What is the plan if not revenge?"

Ben stood up from the rock and walked toward the wet sand.

Azure thought he caught a glimpse of a tear falling. "What makes Alexis Zen different?"

"I thought she was dead and gone forever into the light, but I didn't see or feel the presence of you or anyone else. For the first time I didn't know what was happening."

"Why do think this is so? It's not as though you ..." Azure didn't finish his thought because Ben had spun around to face him.

"I have been trying to understand this for myself, and up until tonight I wasn't clear about what I was feeling or thinking in terms of Alexis Zen." Ben turned away and headed up the beach.

Azure's fears were becoming a reality. "Are you in love with her?"

Ben never looked back but Azure knew the answer. And he understood that everything would change.

CHAPTER SIXTY-THREE

"Ms. Zen, physically everything appears normal," Dr. Kāohi said. "I will take these blood samples to Queen's Hospital and have them run a full panel of lab tests. I will call you in about an hour with the results. Until then, take it easy." Dr. Kāohi headed toward the door.

Alexis got up and opened the door for him. "Thank you again for coming,"

Dr. Kāohi left, and Alexis felt the emptiness of the hotel room. The night was no longer young, and she felt exhausted from all that was going on in her life. She decided to lie down and wait for Ben and James to return.

Alexis climbed onto the bed and melted into the softness of the pillow. Her mind was on overload as she tried to make sense of the crazy event that had happened that evening. It was hard to focus, let alone try to relax, but she closed her eyes and began to concentrate on her breathing. Soon she found herself listening to the faint whisper coming from the air conditioning, which slowly lulled her into a state of suspended consciousness.

It didn't take long for her mind to take her to the field of jade and emerald where blue delphiniums kissed the copper poppies blowing in the wind, but this time she wasn't alone. Standing in front of the distant forest, the place she was never able to go, was the man in white. She glanced back to the top of the hill, remembering the desolate city past the sea of darkness. When she returned to look at the forest again, the man in white was standing in front of her.

"You have seen what lies on the path behind you," he intoned. "Do not trust what you see."

"I have tried to go the other way."

"The moment you look over the ledge, he will never let you go."

"Who will never let me go?"

"He that is respected by many yet loved by none, he that is known by all yet denied from the highest. He that walks in your life as your friend may be your enemy in the end." The man in white began to fade.

"Who is he?"

The man in white was moving his mouth, but Alexis couldn't hear the words. "I can't hear you. Who may be my enemy?"

The man took Alexis's hand and pressed something cold and smooth into her palm, and then he disappeared. She opened her hand and saw a piece of quartz. It was the same crystal her grandmother had given her, with the same interesting markings.

"Some puzzles are solved backwards," a female voice announced.

"Amanda? How ... Why are you here? Are you an angel?" Her cousin stood where the man had been only seconds before.

Amanda smiled. "Not an angel, at least not yet. When you solve this, you will have the knowledge, as did Eve, and be able to choose your path, but you must stay on the path of truth to live."

"I don't understand."

Amanda touched the crystal. "This was the forbidden fruit. You are smart, that's why this burden is yours to solve."

Alexis gazed at the small crystal. "This is from the tree of the knowledge of good and evil?" She looked up to find herself alone.

A storm was coming from behind, and Alexis needed to get to the forest for shelter. Charcoal clouds moved in from where Alexis had once seen the decayed city, and a wind blew up, bending the long grass and rattling leaves. She tried to run toward the tree line, but like all the times before, she could not. Instead, she found herself coming closer to the edge of the hill.

She wanted to awaken from this nightmare, but someone was calling her name. Alexis felt paralyzed as the voice came from the darkness. Someone was calling out to her from the other side of the hill.

"Alexis, I need you," the voice called out.

She closed eyes and turned an ear to the sound in the wind and took a few cautious steps toward the top of the hill. The wind howled in her ear. Alexis didn't want to be here, she desperately wanted to wake up. Suddenly it went quiet, and the air was still. A warm brightness emanated from her hand, and she slowly opened it to find the quartz glowing. The inscriptions were a shade of amber against the spiraling illuminated crystal.

"Alexis, I need you!" the voice called again.

The voice sounded familiar, but she felt disoriented as it called to her.

"Alexis, I need ..."

"What do you need from me?" she called back, finally finding her voice. She opened her eyes and saw Ben, felt his hand on her shoulder.

"Alexis, I needed you to wake up." He was sitting next to her on the bed.

"Oh, sorry. I didn't plan on getting lost in my dream." She sat up and moved closer to Ben. "Thank you for waking me up."

"Dr. Kāohi called and said you should contact him when you woke up, unless it was late," Ben explained. "That's why I woke you."

Alexis looked at the clock beside the bed. "It's 7 a.m. I slept all night?"

"I stayed on the floor in here in case something happened."

Alexis blushed at the idea that someone would care enough to lose sleep for her. "Thank you. I'm sorry to worry you."

"Alexis, I don't know if this is the right time to say this, but after what happened last night, I want you to know my heart," Ben said.

"All right."

"You have changed a part of me that I didn't realize existed, and you have shown me what I've been missing. I won't make this weird and tell you things we're not ready for, but I will say that you have become my only desire."

Alexis began to process what he'd said and thought about how much had changed in her life. "I'm speechless," she replied. "Speechless but ecstatic. I'm happy to know we can move forward together."

He stood up and held out his hand. "Will you take a walk on the beach with me?"

Alexis slid off the bed and stood up. "I would love to go anywhere with you."

He leaned in and started to kiss her but noticed the energy that was created when he touched her, so he backed off. "How about I order you some breakfast before we head out?"

"Okay, but I probably should send my reports to the base and check a few things."

Ben nodded. "I'll let you change and get everything done, then I'll meet you in the main restaurant."

After Ben left the room, Alexis grabbed her cell phone and dialed Dr. Kāohi's number. She went into the bathroom where she kept her luggage and pulled out the piece of quartz crystal. It was wrapped inside a black velvet bag that she normally used for necklaces.

She sat down on the white marble floor in the bathroom and waited for the receptionist to put the call through. "Dr. Kāohi, it's Alexis Zen."

"Aloha, Alexis, I hope you had a good night of rest."

"I didn't even realize I had slept so long, so it must have been good." Alexis was rotating the crystal in her hand, feeling the inscriptions with the tips of her fingers.

"All your tests came back negative. I did notice your blood pressure was on the low side, which can sometimes cause dizziness if you're not drinking enough fluids. Just take it easy the next few days. I'll be available if you have any questions."

"Thanks so much, doctor."

They ended the call, and she focused on the crystal, thinking about the pattern on it. In Japan she had noticed the size of the markings increased as it spiraled around, but after her recent dream something started to repeat in her head.

Some puzzles are solved backwards. The forbidden fruit. Finish what your family started.

Alexis walked to the desk and opened her tablet. The "Send Report" reminder notice she had set up appeared on the screen. She set down the crystal and checked through the data her devices had been recording in Japan. She was so anxious to get back to solving the mystery of the crystal and the journal that she missed a significant change in the underwater temperature. After the data downloaded, she sent it to the base.

She plugged her camera into the side port of her smart tablet and began taking pictures. One at a time, following the spiral pattern, Alexis took pictures of the markings and saved them to a separate folder.

Azure watched from the unlit corner of the room. But this time he wanted her to see him.

CHAPTER SIXTY-FOUR

THE HOTEL RESTAURANT was bustling. The busy wait staff moved as if they'd been choreographed, servers and bussers taking orders, delivering meals and drinks, and clearing tables with well-practiced movements. Ben had been waiting in the foyer for nearly an hour, and he was beginning to wonder if Alexis was coming down.

James came around the corner and saw Ben watching people come down the hall. "Hey, can I join you? Where's Alexis?"

"Still upstairs." Ben skipped the part about James joining him because he wanted to be alone with Alexis.

James sat down next to Ben. "She's probably caught up with her data. She hardly ever joined us for lunch, she was so consumed by work."

"She mentioned she needed to forward the data to Wright Patterson, but that was an hour ago." Ben continued to watch as another group of people came out of the elevator.

James started to stand up. "I can check on her so you don't lose your table."

"That's all right, I'll check on her. Besides, I'm taking her somewhere else once she gets here."

"Oh. Okay. Have a nice breakfast."

Ben got up. "I'll see you later, then."

The hostess walked up to James. "Sir, will you be eating alone or are you meeting with a group?"

"Just me," he replied.

Alexis had just finished creating a panoramic layout of the markings she photographed of the crystal when a tingling sensation danced across her body. It was as though the air had changed, leaving her cold, and she sensed that someone nearby was watching her. With the recent out of body experiences, vivid dreams, and bizarre UFO sightings, she was no longer afraid of unexplained sensations. Her curiosity was trumping her usual overreaction and paranoia. She rotated in the desk chair and saw Azure standing six feet away.

He hadn't expected her to turn around.

"Please don't scream. I don't have time to tell you everything, but I want to help you find answers."

Alexis saw him start to fade and knew he wasn't an ordinary intruder. "Who are you?"

He looked toward the door. "Tell no one I was here. I will return to answer that question when you are alone."

Alexis frowned. She *was* alone. What did he mean? She thought she must be dreaming again and hoped someone would wake her up soon.

The lights flickered and dimmed, and Azure stepped back until he vanished. Alexis sat watching in amazement, and within seconds there was a knock on the door.

"May I come in?" Ben asked.

She jumped up and opened the door. "I'm sorry, Ben, I got distracted. I'm ready now."

"Are you feeling okay? You seem a little jumpy."

She grabbed her purse, and they headed out of the bedroom. Ben scanned the room, but Alexis closed the door behind her to block his view. "I'm fine, just trying to keep up with all the boring tasks of this job."

Azure waited until Ben and Alexis were away from the hotel before he went back into her room. Alexis had left her smart tablet on the desk with the crystal beside it. Azure stood next to the desk and drew his hand across the tablet, prompting it to show a password box. He entered the password he had seen her input earlier and found the linear layout of the crystal's inscriptions still pulled up on the screen. The markings were all different. One had simple lines, while others looked more complex. Azure pondered the meaning and hoped to gain the forbidden knowledge when it was unlocked. He glanced to his right and saw the piece of quartz lying on the table. He fell into the chair, longing to touch it but knowing his fate if he tried.

Chuave stepped out of the shadows. "You were right to warn us, and I apologize for our ignorance."

Azure continued to stare at the crystal. "Why this change in your heart?"

"We have watched the way he looks at her, and we know there is a change in him."

"What are your plans?" Azure asked, knowing their powers depended solely upon the leader.

"Chaos is always a source of distraction, and it is within our purview. We will do what is within us to do."

"He will find out. He always knows what we are doing before we do it. Why is the connection not the same?"

"Because we don't know him like he knows each of us, and he will never let anyone know his real darkness."

Azure turned around in alarm, but Chuave had already disappeared.

CHAPTER SIXTY-FIVE

BEN AND ALEXIS SAT in the hotel restaurant eating freshly sliced pineapple and eggs Benedict. Outside the windows, the beach glowed under a bright morning sun.

"I've never had this made with Spam," Alexis said. "It's really not bad."

"Spam is a staple food here," Ben said. "Ever since World War II."

"This place is beautiful, but I don't think I'd want to live here forever."

"Why do you say that? Most say the opposite."

Alexis gazed out at the white sand and followed the coastline. "I wouldn't want my highest vantage point to be a volcano."

Ben smiled. "No worries, the plane leaves in six hours. The doctor cleared you to go ahead with your trip, and I'm sure you're excited about doing more tests with your equipment."

"I'm going to miss this vacation vibe," she said as she picked up a glass still half-filled with a creamy mango drink.

Ben gazed out the window at the beautiful white-sand beach and the waves lapping the shoreline. "Me, too,"

"I'm really happy you decided to come with us to San Ignacio."

"I've never known anyone in this world who was worth following until I met you. I will go wherever you want me to go. I would also like to spend some time alone with you at some point since we have a long flight with our plus one."

Alexis looked into his amber eyes. "What did you have in mind?"

"I know you have to pack up your stuff, and we can't go far, so maybe just take time to be together? Unless you wanted to do something."

"I would love to lie around with just you." Alexis stood up and pushed in her chair. "Shall we?"

Six hours east of Hawaii, the day was not ready to begin. The sun had not made its way to the horizon as Cezar waited in the booth of the restaurant in Fairborn, Ohio. At this quiet hour darkness could give solace, but today was different.

"I think we are going to have an issue with Chuave," Azure said as he slid into the booth opposite Cezar.

"I heard," Cezar replied. "I think it's about time we make some adjustments to the order. Power is strengthened by numbers."

"Your strength is his, not the other way around."

"And without him we can be free."

"That's not how it works."

Cezar didn't want Azure to oppose him. "All will be better. Join with us."

Azure could see his side would not be easily accepted. "You were given an opportunity long before this day to choose the other side, and your stubbornness is what drove you to him."

"I didn't want to be on either side, but his was the only one that ensured my fate without physical suffering," Cezar said, but there was frustration in his voice.

"Our physical pain was traded for one greater, especially if you deny him. One will taste it sooner."

"I will not be on standby for our destruction while he plays with these filthy humans. I am with Chuave on this," Cezar said.

"There is no place to go. You are bound here until the end, just like the rest of us."

Cezar turned his body inward to look at Azure with his dark eyes. "I didn't say I was leaving. We are meeting within the circle."

"Which circle?"

"Oh, brother of mine, how thoughtless you think I may be." Cezar stood up from the table. "I can't have you telling him."

"He will know."

Cezar shook his head and then laughed. "He seems distracted lately."

"You know he will cast you out along with whomever else, so why are you doing this?"

"We cannot change our destiny on this path, and I am tired of waiting."

"What if she could help us?"

Cezar laughed as though the idea was unthinkable.

"I spoke with her this morning," Azure whispered.

Cezar stopped laughing, and a look of fear crossed his face. "No."

"If I help her solve the crystal ..."

"Azure, I have decided to take a chance and hasten my fate, but you have ensured yours will be early. You will face more than his wrath."

"With the crystal we can know our other options."

"That crystal doesn't just provide the fundamentals of good and evil. It is a full knowledge of all good and all evil, which means even those things we fear will be brought to pass, and all the evil forces will be at hand for war."

Azure felt the same fear that he saw on Cezar's face, yet he persisted. "I know, but she ..."

"She is nothing, did you hear what I said? All evil forces, which means they will be coming back."

Cezar slid out of the booth and slipped away as Azure pondered the things to come. The world that had been his home for thousands of years was now on a path toward the end of a long war to keep the balance of good and evil. But the end of that war would begin a new one, a war that would end the current reign and fulfill all that had been foretold. Azure knew he would need Alexis to solve the crystal if he wanted to survive.

CHAPTER SIXTY-SIX

ALEXIS STARED AT her cell phone as it chimed. "That's strange."

"What's strange?" Ben said, looking over her shoulder as they cuddled face-to-face on the couch.

"I keep getting missed text messages and voicemails." She sat up and began checking them.

"Is everything okay?"

"I should check my voicemails. I'll be right back."

"I'll wait on the balcony." Ben headed outside, where the sun blazed in a clear blue sky.

Alexis had thirteen voice messages, mostly from her family. Two were from Adrianna, who wanted to talk about her wedding plans, and three were from Detective Lindsay. Alexis called her family first. After she spoke with her sister and grandmother, she called Adrianna and left a message apologizing and explaining that she was out of the country and her phone hadn't been delivering her messages.

Alexis searched through her contacts for the Fairfield Police Department's number. She placed the call and was connected to Detective Lindsay.

"Hello, Detective, this is Alexis Zen." She heard a yawn from the other end of the line. "I'm sorry if it's a bad time."

"It's okay. Fairfield apparently decided it needed a crime spree, so we're all here late."

"It's hard to imagine a crime spree in Fairfield."

"We've had more than thirty reported break-ins, two homicides, and at least ten arsons. One woman claimed the devil visited her and told her to mutilate the neighbor's cat. But that wasn't why I called you last night."

"Why did you call?"

"The man who tried to attack you in your apartment was out on bail that night after being arrested for another crime."

"Really?"

"Yes. And you're sure you'd never seen him or heard of him before that night?"

"No, why?" Alexis had moved past that night and didn't care to reflect on the aftermath in her alley.

"He was the same man who was charged with murdering your aunt."

Alexis's mind started spinning, and she had to hold back tears. "I don't understand. How would this be connected?"

"I was hoping you could help with that piece of the puzzle."

"I'm at a loss. I thought the guy who killed my aunt Sarah was still awaiting trial."

"So did your grandparents," the detective said. "When we told them, they were shocked that he was out on bail the same night he was caught."

"My grandmother didn't mention anything."

"We didn't tell them about the attack at your place."

"I wish I could help you," Alexis said before ending the call.

The feeling that someone was watching her returned. She looked around and saw Azure standing against a wall, staring at her with dark eyes. Alexis crossed her arms and glared at him.

"Why do you follow me?"

"Don't you want to know who I am?"

"I asked you a question. Why do you follow me?"

"I was assigned to follow you, and now I am here to help you solve this riddle." Azure pointed to the crystal that lay on the desk.

"You're too late. I've already figured it out. But I haven't had time to test my hypothesis."

"You figured out what the crystal says? No one has been able to read that, and we have been here for ..." Azure stopped.

"Let me guess, you've been here since the beginning, right?" Alexis unfolded her arms and reached for the piece of quartz. "And this is a key piece to something important, and that's why you're so eager to know how this translates, right?"

Azure frowned. "Why are you not afraid of me?"

"I have seen you several times in my life," she said.

"You've seen us more than once?"

"Yes, and recently you've been haunting my dreams. I have made my mind aware of the strange possibility that you're some kind of subconscious persona I created for when I'm experiencing trauma or conflict. Now I have escalated into making you a visual person that I can hold a conversation with to motivate me to do ancient translations."

"You are wrong."

"How do you expect me to believe otherwise?" Alexis asked. She couldn't believe she was arguing with her own hallucination.

"Alexis, I am real, and I will show you the truth soon. But now I must go before I am seen. Know that everything has an opposite and a path."

And then Azure was gone.

Alexis exhaled. She heard James come in the main door of the suite yelling something. She opened the door to see Ben sitting on the chair closest to her room and James standing by the couch.

She looked at James, who was flushed. "Why are you yelling?"

"We need to get our stuff and leave. A really bad storm is developing off the southwest coast."

Ben pulled his cell phone out of his pocket and looked to Alexis. "I'll call the pilot. You two get your things ready, and we'll head out."

James walked to Alexis's room. "How are you feeling?"

"Fine. I feel like I fell asleep, had a strange dream, and then woke up."

Ben came into the room and stood next to James. "A car will pick us up in ten minutes, and the pilot will be ready to take off in thirty."

"I'll get my things together," James said before heading to his room.

"Did you contact everyone who left you messages?" Ben asked Alexis.

Alexis nodded but avoided his eyes. She wasn't ready to expound any further.

Ben touched her shoulder. "Know that you can always talk to me, about anything."

Alexis nodded. She would tell him the rest later, in Brazil, when they could find time alone.

At the vantage point of an eagle, around the world, men were gathered at a specific point that stayed within the boundaries of a peculiar path.

CHAPTER SIXTY-SEVEN

FROM THE GROUND ONE can only take in what is in the line of sight, but in the air one can erase those lines to create an endless path of vision. Alexis moved toward a new perspective by peering through the window of the plane as it flew into Belize. She saw the Cahal Pech ruins from a god's-eye view, and something clicked in her mind.

The man in white said everything had a path, and the letter from Baba mentioned a path. Alexis thought about all the things her grandmother had taught her growing up. It was all coming together as a single thought.

"I can't believe I'm doing this," she murmured.

"Doing what?" James asked.

He and Ben were sitting on the sofa that ran lengthwise along the inner wall of the cabin, across the aisle from where Alexis sat.

Alexis hadn't realized she'd spoken out loud. "This crystal, I've put off translating it."

Ben looked at her. "Go on."

"It may not be anything, but I think I may have figured out some of the nagging things in my head." Alexis opened her purse and pulled out her smart tablet.

James and Ben made room on the sofa, and Alexis got up from her seat and sat between them. She opened her tablet to her photo application and selected the panoramic view of the crystal. Alexis scrolled by each inscription one at a time.

"What are you looking for?" James asked.

Still gazing at the screen, she voiced the thoughts running through her head. "Everything has an opposite and a path."

Ben seemed uneasy after he heard those words, but he just watched and listened.

"Some puzzles are solved backwards," Alexis said. "Start at the beginning."

"Are you into riddles now?" James asked.

Alexis looked away from the screen and turned to the two men watching her. "It's a long story, but I think I know what these mean. Or at least how to find what they mean."

"We have time before we land, so tell us this long story," Ben urged.

"I didn't realize until recently that this whole thing started when I was little. Baba would tell me what I took to be old folklore, but now I wonder how much of it was true."

"So what's the connection?" James asked.

"A lot of what she said is coming to me in my dreams and …"

Alexis hesitated, unwilling to mention the conversation with her alter ego in a dark suit. "I guess I've been remembering these phrases and stories lately."

Ben pointed to the crystal inscriptions on her tablet's screen. "How does that help with solving this?"

"Everything has a path, meaning this has a path I need to follow. Some puzzles are solved backwards might refer to the direction of the path, meaning that instead of solving this from smallest to largest, I should do the opposite."

Another clue came to Alexis, but this one was from her own mind, not from the voices in her head. "This is a really off-the-wall thought, but these markings are all different."

"I know that," James said.

"But not like the letters of our alphabet are different. It's changing in its style and size. What if this is a graduated line of language?"

"I'm confused," James said.

"This might be why your program couldn't find the language. There's more than one."

The pilot interrupted the conversation. "Please prepare to land, we will touch down in five minutes. The weather in San Ignacio, Belize, is reported to be unusually cool today."

"Let's discuss this more on the way into San Ignacio," Ben said as they rose from the sofa and took individual seats.

The plane began its descent, breaking through heavy cloud cover before landing. The afternoon was gloomy, and a gust of cold air hit Alexis as she exited the airplane.

The flight crew retrieved their luggage and took it to the ground transportation pickup/drop-off area and set it on the ground.

James looked around and frowned. "Where is everyone?"

Ben looked at his watch. "The car should have been here to pick us up. Wait here while I make a call."

Ben walked to the south side of the hanger, where a large door was open, waiting for Ben's plane. As he spoke into his phone, Alexis could tell from his body language that he was not happy about what he was hearing.

"Hey," James said. "What kind of stories did Baba tell you about the crystal?"

"It's hard to separate what's fact and what's embellishment, but supposedly this came into my family from Eve. And I bet solving it will give unlimited knowledge. But that's a guess."

"You told me about this that night in your kitchen," James reminded her.

"It was just a story then," Alexis said. "Now it's a possibility."

"Did your Baba tell you where Eve got it?"

Alexis thought for a moment. "The tree, that's what she meant."

"Tree?" James asked. "And what who meant?"

Alexis shook her head. "Something my cousin said to me once."

"Where are you going?" James asked as she started toward Ben.

"I'm going to see what's going on with our transportation. I'm hoping to set up at the Cahal Pech before nightfall." Alexis walked off and left James by the bags.

"Wait. We're doing this at night?"

Alexis turned back and smiled. "Are you afraid of the dark?"

"No, only the things that come out when it's dark."

As Alexis approached Ben, she thought she could still hear him talking on the phone.

"Did you find anything out?" she asked.

Ben turned quickly toward her. "We have a taxi coming. The car service is stuck in traffic, so I just had them send an airport taxi instead."

"You looked upset earlier," Alexis said as she moved closer to him. "I haven't seen you like that, are you okay? I don't mind riding in a cab."

"I'm not upset about that. I was talking with someone else about some personal issues."

"Anything you want to talk about? You always listen to my problems, I never ask you if everything is okay with you. I feel slightly selfish."

"Thanks for your concern, but it's nothing I can't handle. However, because of this issue I'm going to head to the hotel while you and James are at the temple ruins." Ben brushed his right hand across her cheek and leaned in to kiss her forehead.

Alexis swayed a little and then smiled. "Even that sends a rush right through my body."

Ben frowned. "What do you mean?"

She smiled and shrugged. "I get an awesome tingle every time we touch, and it even happened when you kissed my forehead just now."

An emptiness come over Ben's face. "Every time?"

"I think so. Don't you feel anything?"

"Yes, but I thought it was just me."

James joined them. "Have we found any civilization?"

"Taxi is on its way," Ben said. He pointed to a building in the center of the airport on the other side of the runway. "The control tower is running off the generator, so they're only letting in flights that are already close. The rest have been cancelled or rerouted. That's why it's so empty."

"It's downright spooky," James said. "I hope the rest of the area has electricity."

Alexis turned to James. "Let's get everything ready."

CHAPTER SIXTY-EIGHT

THE TAXI DRIVER STOPPED in front of the hotel, and Ben got out. Alexis told the driver to wait, and she got out to say goodbye to Ben.

"I'm already missing your face," Ben said. He started to kiss Alexis's cheek. She turned, and her lips grabbed his. There was a jolt like electricity. "I'll see you in the morning."

"Can't wait."

Ben touched her hand. "Please be careful."

"Always."

Alexis got in the cab again, and the driver headed east to Cahal Pech. The countryside was filled with fruit-bearing trees covered with various shades of vibrant green foliage, a view that reminded Alexis of her dream. Except here she would be able to get close enough to touch everything.

The cab pulled up to a small white visitors building with a bright blue roof as dusk was falling. Alexis had already found the trails marked for the ruins, but she needed to alert their guide that they had arrived.

"I'll be right back," she told James before heading up the worn steps.

James got the bags from the trunk as Alexis headed inside the building. She emerged a few minutes later with a dark-haired man wearing a yellow polo and knee-length denim shorts. His English was good but occasionally peppered with a few words of Creole. He pointed James and Alexis in the direction of the temple of Cahal Pech.

"You're not coming with us?" James asked.

"Not at night," the man replied.

James eyed him. "What is it? Wild animals? Snakes?"

The guide shook his head. "Animals and snakes do not frighten me. I can see them."

"What then?" James asked.

"Things I hear but cannot see."

"We have night-vision goggles," James said. "We'll see just fine."

The man gave James a vague smile. "There are some things your fancy equipment can't see."

"What exactly are you talking about?" James asked.

The guide turned to Alexis and handed her a map. He pointed to a spot in the middle. "This is where you should set up your camp."

"Thank you, Oscar," Alexis said, and she turned and headed toward the marked trail.

James frowned at Oscar and then ran to catch up with Alexis. "What was he talking about? Things he hears but can't see?"

"Ghosts, James, ghosts." Alexis kept walking.

James stopped. "Are you serious?"

"James, you're a scientist. Act like one."

"So says the gal who's starting to believe the myths about her mysterious crystal," James said as he jogged to catch up with her again.

"We look at the facts, remember, and I have yet to see proof of anything after death." *Other than my dreams.*

"What about what we saw in Japan?"

"That just proves there's life out there, not life lingering here." The trail turned, and she began walking down a shallow slope.

"I thought you believed in a creator?"

"I believe in something more than spontaneous complexity, but I rely on facts, not faith and the hope of an eternal life. Until I see something with my own eyes."

"How do you explain the orb in your lab?"

"I don't. It's an unexplained energy ball."

"But you showed me ..."

Alexis stopped walking and spun around. "I showed you pictures, and the orb appeared to have something on the other side. It could have been a reflection."

James was silent as Alexis looked around at the forest of tall trees. After a moment, she turned back to him. "James, to be honest I'm split in my thinking. The science side says stick to the facts, but the abstract thinking side that got me to where I am says there is more out there. This is causing me to believe in the possibility of the paranormal. If I told people the things circling through my mind, they would lock me up. It has taken me a long time to control what I say, so yes, I believe in the possibility of ghosts, but I won't announce that until I see something for myself."

"According to the crazy guy back there you might get your opportunity tonight," James said.

Alexis smiled. "Why do you think I requested this place as one of my test sites?"

"Right, and next you're going to tell me you planned out Japan to see a flying saucer."

"No, the Dragon Triangle and Bermuda Triangle were to be for the magnetic readings and the atmospheric monitoring. The UFO was an unexpected bonus."

Alexis turned back to the trail and headed down into the center of the Mayan temple site.

Alexis and James entered the tall stone structure and stood there listening to the strange silence that echoed through the ancient courtyard. Thick vines scaled the walls, covering a good portion of them. Narrow corridors connected rooms with windows that looked out to where the two of them stood.

James gazed around at gray walls that ascended more than thirty feet into the air, like oversized bleachers. "I feel like we're being watched."

Alexis handed him four small black boxes and four tripods. "Come on, let's set up base camp."

James stared at the equipment and then gave Alexis a quizzical look.

"Right, set one at each of the four corners on the perimeter of the structure. I'll lock them in range."

"Motion sensors."

"Not just any motion sensors," Alexis said.

"Let me guess—you upgraded them?"

Alexis nodded. "These will detect anything within fifty feet, which will trigger a warning signal. If something happens to cross the barrier between the four points, it sets off a loud siren. Plus, it takes high-resolution video with a complete spherical view the whole time, instead of just one still vantage point."

"Okay," James said, staring at the devices. "I'm amazed that something so small could be so complex."

"Press the white button once you have it set in place."

James started back up the trail with a map and the four sensor tripods.

"You have an hour or so before sunset, so don't dawdle," Alexis yelled after him.

He turned back toward the western skyline and picked up his pace.

Alexis put up a tent made from a unique net material. It was translucent from the inside out and metallic silver on the outside. The space was large enough to sleep six comfortably. Night would fall soon, and Alexis went about setting her land VEs at various points around the temple. As she did, she had a vague feeling that someone was watching her.

The trees were silent, and the air was still, but it sounded as if someone was whispering.

Stay close to her. She can't see us.

Alexis spun around and looked, but no one was there.

CHAPTER SIXTY-NINE

SOMEWHERE ACROSS THE globe, where clouds looked like stepping-stones across a pale blue sky, men in dark suits gathered in the center of a stone circle placed atop a grassy hill covered with wildflowers. Chuave stood near the center of the group, all of them looking at the sky.

Chuave turned his focus to the multitude and began to speak. "Brothers, we have come here together to claim our rightful place and partake of the power we deserve. Our master has told us that he is the only one able to bear this power, but I say he lies."

The crowd chanted its agreement.

"Tonight, we will call upon Eta Tauri to hear our plea for change. It's time we take this world for our own."

"Stop!" someone from outside the stone circle yelled. "You have no idea what you are doing."

Every dark eye turned to glare at Azure, the one who had spoken. Chuave moved from the center and made his way to the outer edge.

"Azure, my fellow brother, why would you stop this? Is this not what you desire, ultimate power over these blind humans?"

"This is not my power to hold, it is only mine to sustain," Azure said.

"The power was given only to one for a reason. Power was meant for all, and you know that. You were there when our fates were decided because of him."

"Yes, but you came here of free will to follow him."

"That you still stand by his side shows your weakness," Chuave said. "You have always been weak. That is why he chose you as his pet."

Chuave was sneering, but his face paled when another voice rose up from within the circle.

"I chose him for his loyalty," Ben said. "That is not a sign of weakness. It's jealousy that shows weakness and eventually destroys you."

Chuave bristled at the implied insult. "You flatter yourself. Our actions are not out of jealousy. We seek only that which we deserve, equal power on this earth. If you had kept your ego in check in the beginning, this would still be the paradisiacal planet it was meant to be."

"And you believe that? I did what I always would with every planet thus far established, but this was the one world where everything changed. And now I too am stuck here until they return."

"You don't seem to mind it. In fact, you are the only one of us that can interact tangibly with the humans on this planet, and you expect me to compare our situations? None of us have touched their skin or felt their warmth."

"You had full knowledge of what would happen, and you had a choice. You chose my side."

"That was because—"

"I'm done with this conversation. It can end only one way."

Chuave shook his head. "It always ends your way. We have no choice, no freedom, and no power. And no human toy."

A breeze rose up, blowing debris into the circle as it funneled through the men standing there. The breeze swelled into a powerful wind that howled between the thick stone pillars arrayed in a circle. Azure watched from outside the circle as the skies darkened.

Ben stared at Chuave with jet-black eyes. "The power you deserve was lost the moment you chose to follow me."

Ben looked around as the men shifted uncomfortably. "Did you really think you were capable of bringing forth any dark energy successfully?"

No one dared answer.

"Did you really think I wouldn't know?"

Ben returned his baleful gaze to Chuave.

"You haven't been ... yourself," Chuave murmured.

"I have been myself more than you know."

The gray darkness that had sailed in from the east now filled the skies, obliterating the white clouds in its path. The men looked uneasy and were turning to Chuave.

"You are a coward if you destroy us all," Chuave called out against the screaming wind.

Azure watched silently as a faint orb appeared next to Chuave. The black orb increased in size and changed shape as the wind continued to whistle through the stone columns. The orb changed from a rotating black hole to a dark entrance with a bluish band of light glowing around the circumference. Azure could see through to the other side, could hear the sounds of despair from within its realm.

Ben stepped closer to Chuave. "You are right for once, Chuave. I would be a coward if I destroyed all of you. That is why this is meant as a mere reminder to those I spare."

The portal opened and began pulling Chuave in, but before it could take him, he looked at Ben with what appeared to be sadness. "I hope she destroys you."

In an instant, Chuave and the strange opening were gone. The wind died down and whispered away, and the sky brightened, scattered puffs of cotton drifting across its brilliant blue field.

Ben, whose eyes were now back to glistening amber, looked at the ones he had chosen not to send with Chuave.

"It is not in my nature to forgive, so don't consider this to be an act of kindness, but rather an assurance of your loyalty henceforth. You will go out and tell the others that nothing has changed."

No one spoke a word. Each bowed his head in respect before disappearing.

After everyone else was gone, Azure approached Ben and stood before him. "Others of them will try again."

"Yes, I am sure of it," Ben said as he turned away from the stone monument.

Azure didn't know if it was the right time to ask a personal question, but he decided to risk it. "Sir, do you regret your decision to go against the Intelligences?"

Ben glared at Azure. "I don't regret my decision, but I do find it disturbing when I have to remind others of their free will and have to take such harsh measures to prove my power."

"Reminders can often hurt us."

Ben looked toward the circle. "If they only knew what that power would do to them."

"What do you mean?"

"Azure, maybe next time." Ben stepped back and disappeared into the daylight.

Azure was curious about Ben's last comment, so he stepped into the circle where the men had been standing. He gasped when he felt the lingering energy from the opening of the portal. He closed his eyes to take in everything around him, listening to the echo of souls across the English countryside in search of peace, the sound of a cool breeze weaving through the hills, the strange quietness that emanated from where he stood.

It wasn't unusual that he could hear the prayers of the vain and selfish, for this opened the doors to let Azure and his kind into the human subconscious. Like the others, Azure could also hear the complaints of the suffering, the sadness and pain of those who had chosen the wrong path. Normally he was able to sense emotions, knowing the difference between sorrow and contentment. These sensitivities allowed him to wreak chaos in a person's life, but at that moment an unfamiliar feeling came upon him, as if those sad human feelings were coursing through his body. Azure moved away from the center of the ancient stone monument, and those feelings dissipated. Confused and intrigued by what he had just experienced, Azure found himself feeling sadness for his kind.

CHAPTER SEVENTY

We need to help her ...
... but how?

ALEXIS POPPED UP from where she was sleeping when she heard the voice of a female coming from outside the tent. "James, did you hear that?"

She looked to the other side of the tent, where James was sprawled on top of his sleeping bag. Alexis lay back down, thinking it must have been her imagination. She tried to go back to sleep but found herself listening to every rustle of leaves outside the tent walls. The trees swayed, and the wind ruffled the feathers of the hooting crested owl. The smell of the tent's nylon material triggered memories of her childhood.

Alexis remembered camping with her mother and her first stepfather, Rusty Wilkins. Every summer they would travel to an old family farm hours outside the city and meet up with another family. Alexis dreaded the nights her mother would get drunk by the campfire and pass out until morning, leaving her alone with Rusty. Flashes of him on top of her boosted her pulse rate and clouded her mind. She reminded herself that it was all in the past, that he could no longer hurt her.

Alexis rolled her body away from the tent wall and pulled her blanket close to her nose. The fresh cotton smell helped her relax, and she listened to the faint melody of the crickets. She forgot about whatever had awakened her and suppressed the memories that still haunted her.

Where do we start?

We need to open her eyes.

Alexis heard whispering again, but she couldn't determine what direction it was coming from.

"James," she whispered, hoping he would hear, but he didn't budge.

Alexis crawled to where he was lying and nudged his arm. "James, wake up."

James finally stirred and opened his eyes. "What time is it?"

"It's 2 a.m. I hear someone talking."

James sat up, fully awake. "Who would be out here this late?"

"It sounds like there's more than one person," she whispered. "I think they're speaking English."

James and Alexis sat motionless, listening to the whispers and trying to make sense of who it might be. The voices were faint and sounded feminine.

Guide her to the temple ...

"Why didn't the motion sensors activate?" James asked.

Alexis had no answer.

James called out, "Identify yourself!"

There was no response. The whispering continued.

James made to call out again, but Alexis grabbed his arm. "What are you doing?"

"Trying to scare them off." He called out again, "Hey, who's out there?"

The whispers continued, but neither Alexis nor James could make out any complete sentences.

"We can hear you!" Alexis called.

The whispering stopped. So did every other sound.

James looked at Alexis. Despite the blanket wrapped around her, she was shivering.

"James, are you cold?"

James shook his head. "It must be a hundred degrees."

"Feel the air around me," she said.

James came close and felt a chill shoot through him. He was about to say something when Alexis grabbed his hand.

"James, look."

He turned to stare at the tent flap. "What am I looking for?"

"I see people standing in front of us, inside the tent." Alexis's hands were trembling.

"How many do you see?"

"Two," she said quietly.

"I think I can see them, too."

Still staring toward the front of the tent, Alexis reached behind her and felt around for her full-spectrum camera. James moved closer to Alexis's position, hoping to get a better view of whatever they were seeing.

"What are you looking for?" James whispered.

"Camera. I want to get a shot of this."

He found her camera case at the back of the tent, got out the camera, and handed it to her.

Two soft white apparitions were inside the tent, staring back at James and Alexis. Alexis turned on the camera, aimed the lens at them, and squeezed the shutter. The apparitions vanished.

Alexis jumped up and unzipped the tent flap."Come on."

"What are you doing?"

"Let's check the sensors you placed and make sure there isn't anything to cause a strange reflection or noises," she said.

"Like what?"

"I'm not sure, maybe there's a village nearby, or maybe someone is playing games."

"Don't you think the sensors would have tripped if someone were close enough to create strange reflections with sound effects?"

Alexis threw open the flap. "There has to be an explanation."

"Yeah, you got your wish. This place knew you were coming."

"Come on, let's go."

"Right now? You want to go out there in the middle of the night with a forest of hungry animals?"

Alexis turned to him and glared. "It's not like we could sleep after what just happened."

James shrugged, grabbed a couple of flashlights, and followed her out.

"What's up with you and the weird stuff, anyway?" James asked.

"What are you talking about, James?"

"Your lab spontaneously creates what might have been a wormhole, we go to Japan and see a weird earthquake that reveals a diamond field, we have an extreme close encounter of the third kind, and now we're seeing ghosts in Belize.

"I assumed you were the weirdness magnet," Alexis said. "Isn't your research in extraterrestrial beings?"

James muttered something under his breath as they walked the perimeter checking the sensors. They found nothing out of the ordinary. Alexis checked her equipment and changed the batteries in her digital recorders before heading back to the tent. Hoping the voices would return, she placed several recorders outside the tent.

"What did you catch on your camera?" James asked.

"Nothing."

"Now what?"

"I'll check the recorders in the morning to see if we caught any voices—or images."

Alexis tried to sleep, but she couldn't stop listening for voices, and she wondered how she could have seen what she had. She tried to reconcile science and evidence-based reasoning with the natural beliefs of her heart. She was always taught that loved ones went to Heaven after death, but tonight she believed differently. If they were in Heaven, how could spirits reside on earth? If ghosts existed, were they once alive? She believed there had to be an explanation.

James had referred to the weird phenomena happening around her, and he didn't even know everything. Perhaps she was attracting these strange things. But why? And how?

Still unable to sleep, Alexis retrieved the crystal from her bag, taking care not to disturb James, who was sleeping soundly. Using the light from her tablet, she started working on translating the inscriptions on the crystal. Alexis kept all of the data and notes that she was taking down about the crystal in an encrypted file, including the inscriptions she had already translated. In an application marked with a star icon, she went over some of the notes to refresh her thoughts.

After two hours, she had found only ten modern languages. The remaining markings would require additional research.

But she had noticed that most of the inscriptions she recognized were closely neighbored to each other geographically. One set of markings had been etched in Austronesian characters. Alexis knew that at least twelve versions of that style were known in the Philippines. A few spaces away, she recognized an Old Eastern Slavic word for *destination*, which started her thinking about the northeast area of Russia. She decided to map them out, hoping it would help her figure out the other symbols, thinking that they might correspond in between one another.

She opened a blank map of the world on her tablet and looked at James, making sure he was asleep before she turned on her portable printer and printed a plain black-and-white blank map of the continents.

With a red pencil, Alexis marked the known areas that corresponded with the inscriptions on the crystal. Alexis recognized one of them as the Kanji symbol for tree, so she marked Japan. Another space was marked with an alpha and omega, so she put a red dot on Greece. Alexis marked ten red dots across the map. They all fell within a path she had seen before. The path was distinct, two red dots passing along the west coast of North America down to one in western South America, before jumping to Europe with three red dots. The path became disconnected when it jumped across to the eastern coast of Australia and up to Japan. If she connected them, she'd have two lines, but it might be a coincidence. She needed more data.

She stared at the ten dots spread across the map. *Path*. The word was everywhere. When she had fainted, the man in white spoke of it. In her dreams the man in white and her cousin spoke of it. The letter from Baba had told her to stay on the path.

Questions swirled through her mind. Was the crystal a map of the path? Had they really seen something earlier that night? What was the connection between Alexis and the man who killed Aunt Sarah? She wished Ben were there.

The sun was beginning to peep over the eastern ridge of the temple, creating a warm glow on Alexis's side of the tent. She waited until the shadows inside the temple retreated and then slipped out of the tent. She wanted to walk through the temple rooms and explore the ritual sites by herself. A ground fog lifted from the dew-covered grass as flashes of sunlight broke through the canopy of tree branches overhead. Alexis walked quietly, taking in the stale smell of the abandoned temple grounds. She tried to imagine how it would have look hundreds of years ago, before the disappearance of the Mayan tribes that worshiped on these very grounds.

Show her ...
... help her ...

The whispers came softly through the air, and Alexis followed the sounds coming from the opening of the temple.

CHAPTER SEVENTY-ONE

SOMEWHERE THE SUN WAS hours from rising, and shadows still ruled the land. Ben stood on the edge of a rough stone shoreline, looking out at the Pacific Ocean. The moon was barely visible, leaving very little reflection on the water.

Azure walked up from behind. "Master. Why did you ask me to come here?"

Ben turned back and pointed to the large statues that looked out into the ocean. "Do you remember when these were put here?"

"Yes. It was before this island broke away." Azure looked west toward a large land mass miles away.

"That was at a time when we greatly outnumbered the planet's humans," Ben said as though he was nostalgic for that period in history.

"Because we turned most of the people away from the light," Azure said with a laugh.

"Yet those were lost by the flood, and it left us outnumbered when the waters receded."

"We outnumber them now," Azure reminded him.

"Not if you count the ones that have died and crossed, because they are almost more than double our numbers."

"Does that mean it's time?"Azure asked.

"We are a mere fable. No one fears our existence."

"I remember a time when we were a true threat," Azure said.

"That is the reason I have asked you to this spot, to serve as a reminder of who we are truly. The people of this planet are not even close to explaining these ancient structures, let alone our existence."

The extant monumental statues seemed to be standing watch, protecting the desolate island. Their expressions were as the stone they were carved from, and their height exceeded that of five men.

"How does it feel?"

Ben turned his head slightly but didn't make eye contact. "How does what feel?"

"Their skin, what does it feel like?"

Ben gazed back at the Pacific. "It has always felt the same, like a dead fish. It has never been any different."

"Until you touched her?"

Ben turned, and his eyes were a perfect blend of blue and green, something Azure had not seen before. He knew it was because of Alexis, and he wasn't going to dig any deeper.

"How would you like me to proceed?" Azure asked.

"Make it be known to all that keeping the balance is key, but I implore them to open the eyes of those who sit on high." Ben's eyes changed to black. "And then we'll see who comes to answer their cries."

Azure nodded and disappeared.

CHAPTER SEVENTY-TWO

A FEW HOURS HAD PASSED since Alexis had entered the courtyard of the Cahal Pech temple. James was now walking with her, taking in the majestically eerie sensations that the ancient structure offered.

"You know, there's alien lore about these sites," James said.

"Of course there is," Alexis replied. "You alien types always think the unexplainable is easily explained with the help of aliens, which are also unexplained. You wind up going around in an unexplained circle."

"Everybody does that—religious fanatics, evolutionists, the list is long."

"That's why I'm not part of an organized group. Too many opinions, not enough facts. But after the other night, I do believe in alien life."

"I would hope so."

Alexis shook her head. "I just can't figure out what other beings would want with this world."

"There are plenty of theories."

"What's yours?" Alexis asked.

"I think they're looking for something."

Alexis laughed, and it echoed through the temple grounds. "Talk about your vague explanations. Of course, they're looking for something. Why else fly millions of light years to risk being caught by us?"

"No, I think they're looking for a specific item," James explained.

"Why would they want a relic from our history? Wait, are you one of those who think ancient cultures gained all their knowledge from aliens?"

"It's not that hard ..."

Alexis stopped. "Shhh."

"What?"

James came into the opening of small alcove in the center of the temple. It was only a couple of feet taller than Alexis, with rounded corners on the ceiling. The sun barely found its way inside, but there was light enough to dimly illuminate the stone walls and reveal the ancient artwork etched there.

"Not all of them are words," Alexis whispered.

"Words? What does that have to do with aliens?"

"No, sorry." Alexis pointed to a character on the wall. "This symbol."

The faded petroglyph was a square approximately ten inches wide. Two inches from the top, a solid horizontal line ran two-thirds of the way across, with a soft wavy line hanging vertically from the end. A faint "Y" staff was holding everything in place within the square.

"I couldn't figure out a lot of the inscriptions on the crystal because they were so detailed, but now this makes sense. It's a landmark. These types of generic symbols are all over the Mayan ruins."

"How many Mayan temples have you visited?" James asked.

"Only this one, but I've read a lot of books about the Maya people and their temples and folklore."

Alexis got out her smart tablet and clicked on a file to bring up the layout of the crystal inscriptions.

"What does this marking have to do with the crystal?" James asked.

Alexis held the tablet in front of James and pointed to the corresponding marking on the temple wall.

"Interesting, but that could be on a lot of cave drawings."

Alexis reached into the inside pocket of her bag and pulled out the crystal. "Despite the simplicity of this one symbol written by an ancient culture, it's a part of this profoundly complex system of inscriptions."

"Do you take that everywhere?"

"I don't want to leave it anywhere. Anyway, all along I have thought the stories of this crystal were just tales my grandmother told to entertain me, and I only kept the crystal for sentimental value. But it seems to be more than a gift shop novelty."

James put out his hand. "Can I see it?"

Alexis handed James the crystal. Squares of prisms danced all over the room and as she let go, his hand seemed to shift a little. Alexis gasped as it fell to the floor. The crystal hit the ground once before James caught it.

"Why did you move?"

"Shhh, what was that?" James was getting up off the ground and looking around the room.

Alexis could hear a low hum echoing off the walls. It sounded familiar. She shut off her tablet. "It sounds like that noise we heard coming from the blue orb in my lab."

"Yeah," James whispered.

"But louder and not as concentrated."

"It does seem to be coming from all directions. Grab your temperature gauge."

"I don't have it. It's in the case next to the tent bag."

"I'll get it," James said before stepping out of the temple to retrieve the gauge.

Alexis sat and closed her eyes, listening, but the echo was fading. Soon, silence was the only sound, and she didn't need a thermometer to feel that the room was getting cooler. A cold breeze brushed her face, and she had the feeling of something or someone weighing on her chest. She opened her eyes and saw Azure standing a few inches from her.

"I am not your subconscious, Alexis, I am real." His voice was sweet and calm.

"Right. So prove it."

"How?"

"Tell me something I wouldn't already know."

"That crystal you hold tightly is very old, and its symbols will guide you to key points on this planet."

"I already figured that out."

"Do you know that it will lead you to knowledge desired by kings?"

"I had a dream about that." Alexis closed her eyes. She wanted him to go away.

"Did your dreams mention the name of the place where you will receive this knowledge?"

"I assume it's the Garden of Eden, since this is supposed to be from the tree of the knowledge of good and evil."

Alexis began to shiver as the cold air enveloped her. Azure was standing as close to her as he could. He had taken a chance by attempting to bring Alexis into his reality, but he needed to dig deeper and find a more personal way into her mind. He leaned in and whispered into her right ear. As he did, his eyes went dark.

"Did your dreams tell you why you were chosen and why the crystal is important to all?"

His voice began to feel different to Alexis. "If you're my subconscious, you wouldn't be able to answer those questions, because they're unknown to me." Alexis opened her eyes to see the change in Azure's position and the darkness in his eyes.

"I will answer one of them now, and the other will come after you do something for me." Azure stepped in front of Alexis. "But I will still answer one of them regardless of your help."

Alexis thought about everything she had seen and been through in her life, especially in the past few months. There wasn't much that frightened her conscious mind, and as far as she knew this wasn't a dream.

"Why me?"

"Alexis, you are one of the many daughters of Eve. It has been foretold that one in your direct lineage would be able to unlock the mysteries to save us all."

"My grandmother spoke of this, but would not all women be daughters of Eve, since she was the supposed first female? What do you mean *save us all*?" Alexis asked.

"Ah, it is very true that all are daughters but also very false. Though Eve was the first human, she was not the only being on this planet that looked similar to you."

"What?" Alexis was still trying to grasp the idea that Azure wasn't her crazy mind manifesting itself.

"There was another who bore offspring. Her name was Lilith, and she mothered a lineage that was never supposed to come out of the Garden of Eden."

"Now I know you're insane." *Or I am.*

Alexis closed her eyes again to block Azure from her view. "If the stories my grandmother told me were true, nowhere did she say or did I read of two women being created for Adam."

"Lilith was not meant for Adam. She was to be the companion of another, but her wickedness changed everything. Her companion was so angry at Adam for lying with the only woman made for him that he encouraged Eve to eat of the fruit. That's why you are here and why you are to solve this."

Alexis stood up and tried to gather her thoughts. "Let me get this straight. You're telling me that the Devil had a girlfriend? And Adam slept with her?"

"The word you use for him is not who he is. That is the childish name given by your ancestors when they told their children lies."

"Okay, he's not a horned beast with hooves. Then what is the truth?"

"I can't tell you everything, for I am bound by certain sacred laws to keep the balance."

"Then why are you here?"

There was a shuffling of feet coming through the temple, and Azure began to fade as he spoke. "This journey you have started will take you many places, and you will find where it all started. It is there that you will be able to save us."

Alexis was thinking of so many things this explained, yet it created more questions. "Wait, are you saying that some humans are mixed with some other beings?" *Why am I talking to a hallucination?*

"Trust that you're lucid. I must leave, but I will return to you soon. Alexis, this is the reason you were chosen."

"Who are you?" Alexis called, but Azure was gone.

James came back carrying a small digital device. "Temperature is normal."

"Right," Alexis said, but she wasn't thinking about the temperature.

"Alexis, what are you looking at?"

"Nothing. I'm just exhausted. It's been a strange week."

"That it has."

"Let's get the equipment and head to the hotel and meet up with Ben."

"Are we coming back tonight?" James asked.

"Only to grab this device. But I'd like to do an audio walkthrough as well. Let's hope those voices come back. But if you want to stay at the hotel, I'll bring Ben."

"I might opt out tonight."

"Why?" Alexis was holding what appeared to be a spool of copper wire with a type of digital monitor screen at both ends.

"Just exhausted."

"As I recall, you didn't have any problems getting back to sleep last night."

"I didn't want to see anything again," he said.

"And I couldn't hear anything over your snoring."

James pointed to the device she was holding. "Does this work?"

"This will be turned on remotely after the sun goes down and the tourists are gone."

"Why didn't you put that out last night?"

"I couldn't. This can't be running with all the other pieces of equipment, the readings would have been wrong. This is an extremely sensitive electromagnetic generator. I brought it to see if it will alter the radar."

"Who's monitoring the radar?"

"My system back at the lab is synced to the satellite directed here, and I run everything from my tablet."

Alexis stepped out into the courtyard of the temple. A lot of light was peeking over the huge stone walls. She walked over and placed the device on the east side of the temple where huge drifts of flowering vines hung.

James held back the vines. "Since that is an emitter of electromagnetic waves, do you think it will draw in more of what we heard last night?"

Alexis bent down and placed the device on the ground. "That's not really its purpose. I'm not an expert on voice phenomena, but it's possible. That's why I'd like to do a walkthrough before I take it back."

"I'm definitely staying at the hotel tonight."

Alexis laughed.

"Hey, what if someone steals this?"

Alexis shook her head. "They would get the biggest shock of their life." She stood up. "Once I set it place, the security mode will put out a small electrical charge if anyone or anything messes with it. It will be safe, trust me."

James was noticeably relieved. "Your trust issues come in handy sometimes."

"You have no idea."

Alexis was considering the possibility that Azure was not a figment of her imagination. She thought about the warnings in her dreams. *A man will lead me off my path. But who? What if it's this guy I keep seeing?*

The warnings in her grandmother's note made it seem as if there would be danger and more traveling ahead. Alexis had so many questions now. *Who is he? Does Baba know all of this? Is this all real?*

Alexis kept her thoughts to herself as they headed back to the hotel. The world outside appeared more confusing, and her perception was beginning to feel like a lie.

CHAPTER SEVENTY-THREE

"SHE WILL BE HERE soon." Azure stood at Ben's in the palm-filled lobby of the hotel. There was no one standing nearby to notice them.

"Azure, how do you know this?" Ben asked.

"Please know that my intentions are good."

"You followed her," Ben said, but there was no anger in his voice.

"I found out what she knows."

Ben glanced at Azure. "I hope this is some experiment you're doing with sarcasm. I would hate to find out she saw you again."

"Ellory and Zavdiel came up with the idea of revealing ourselves to her to help her solve the puzzle. We can have her choose our side when she knows the truth."

Ben's eyes were black.

"Master, I think they have been coming to her through dreams with the same idea."

"What?" Ben snapped a strange look at him. "She was talking to James about her dreams?"

"No. She wasn't near him when ..."

"How close were you to her? You know what, forget the how, just tell me what you know."

"She knew too much about the crystal to have not had some help. She had a dream about where the crystal would lead."

"I wouldn't put it past the Messengers to hide in her dreams. It's the only place I cannot go." Ben stepped into the elevator.

"I could speak with her."

"Why would you need to do that?"

"If we get Alexis to join our side, she can reverse our fate," Azure said.

Ben's eyes were as the depth of a cave at midnight, and his voice a hurricane tearing through Azure. "I don't want her to join us."

Ben realized the energy he was emitting was beginning to pull negative vibes from all around. He softened his tone. "I don't want Alexis joining us, do you understand?"

Azure had only known of Ben being so upset one other time, in the Garden of Eden.

"Master, how ..."

"Azure, I fear the privilege I am about to invest you with. To keep Alexis focused on solving the crystal, we must do everything to stay ahead of the Light, but I can't have her finding out who I am."

"What would you have me do?"

"Follow her, but don't let her see you. There is a reason you are to be hidden in the dark."

Ben slid the keycard into the door lock and then looked back at Azure, stopping him before he could enter the suite. Azure knew he was to go no further with Ben.

"Don't come near her when she is with me."

Azure nodded, and Ben shut the door.

Ben was in the hotel suite when someone knocked on the door. He opened it and saw James was standing there with an armful of equipment. James came in and Ben closed the door.

"Where is Alexis?" Ben asked.

James dropped the equipment on the small dining table and then turned to Ben. "She said she'd be here in a few minutes. She's calling her grandmother, I think."

"I was going to head out and grab something to eat for everyone. I'll try to catch her in the lobby." Ben started toward the door and then stopped and looked at James. "Anything special you'd like?"

"No, anything's fine."

"I will return."

"This room is amazing by the way," James said, looking around. "There is a private pool? Which one is my room?"

There was no answer. James turned around to find himself alone.

CHAPTER SEVENTY-FOUR

ALEXIS STOOD OUTSIDE the hotel with her cell phone to her ear, waiting for her grandmother to come on the line.

Ben, invisible to the human eye, watched and waited. He moved closer to take in Alexis's energy and feel what she felt. She was confused and nervous, yet Ben couldn't understand why she would be in such a state. He knew Alexis had been through a lot of negative things, and her mind was swirling with pieces to a puzzle she barely understood, but even that wouldn't make her look nervous.

"Alexis, my child, are you alone?" Baba's sweet voice carried the same nervousness.

"Yes, why?"

"I know why you are calling, but the phone is not the place to talk about this."

"Talk about what, Baba? Is there something you haven't told me?"

"I presume you're calling about the journal."

"What? No, hold on, what about the journal?"

"Never mind, sweetie, we will talk when you come home," Baba replied.

Alexis didn't want to yell at her grandmother or demand answers about something she wasn't in search of, so she pulled her thoughts back on track.

"Baba, I'm calling about the crystal. Were all those stories you told me about it true?"

There was a long silence.

"Baba, I need to know if I'm losing my mind. I need to know why this crystal you gave me keeps coming up."

"You're not crazy. But what about the crystal?"

"I've had strange dreams about it. So please answer me—was it really handed down like you said?"

"Yes."

"Remind me why you gave it to me and not Aunt Sarah or my mother."

"I knew all those years ago that you would be the one with the mind to figure it out. You absorbed everything I told you. You just need to remember."

"I don't remember you mentioning anything about men in dark suits or a woman created before Eve. Is this all true?"

"Alexis, what men in dark suits?"

Alexis hadn't told her family about the attack in her apartment or what she had seen. "I have experienced some strange things lately, and I've been seeing things in my dreams and when I'm awake."

"Alexis, we shouldn't be talking about this over the phone."

"It doesn't matter, I'm alone."

"I want you to stay safe."

"Baba, is there anything I should know that you haven't told me?"

"When did you see the dark-suited man?"

"I've seen them a few times, but this last time was different."

"I do not understand how you see them."

"They're not like the government type of suited men, more like the vanishing-into-thin-air type. Anytime I've seen them it was in a dream or during a traumatic experience, but recently it's been in open daylight."

"Alexis, have they spoken to you?"

"One of them did directly."

"What did he say?"

"He told me of a women created before Eve."

Alexis was talking about to Azure, and Ben knew exactly how Azure had received this detailed information.

"She was never to be like us," Baba said quietly, her voice barely above a whisper. "Alexis, please be cautious of the dark shadows, they will lie for their own purposes."

"What shadows?"

"Never mind, we will discuss this when you get home."

"I need answers."

Ben's anger had become his weakness, but now Alexis was in the crosshairs of Azure's scheme, and it infuriated him. The wind began to whistle as it swept through where Alexis stood, and buckets of dark clouds spilled across the sky. Ben needed to find Azure, but then ...

"Baba, I need to go. There's a storm coming, and I know Ben will be worried. We will talk about this more, and I want real answers."

"Be careful, child, and remember that chaos will cause you to wander."

"And chaos cannot exist in a mind of order. I know, I love you Baba." Alexis let out a sigh. *This is not the reality I expected.*

Ben found his anchor for peace and decided he could take care of Azure later, because his mission was now greater. The wind stopped, and the dark clouds dissipated as fast as they had gathered. The sun returned to cast its warming light.

Alexis turned around into Ben's arms.

"Good morning, my beautiful angel," he said.

Alexis smiled into his glistening eyes. "Wow, impeccable timing, Benjamin. Are you headed out?"

"I hope so. Are you interested in brunch?"

"Definitely!"

Alexis wasn't hungry, but she didn't want to miss an opportunity to spend time alone with Ben. They started walking to the only nearby restaurant.

The place was simple but welcoming. The walls were stucco, and three were adorned with local art and hanging baskets of exotic plants. The rear of the restaurant had large windows that opened to the outside, and as they waited for the waitress to seat them, Alexis looked through the windows to the brilliance of the bright sun bathing the tropical landscape.

"I thought there was going to be a bad storm there for a second," Ben said.

"Me too. It was weird how fast it blew over." Alexis was still gazing out at the peaceful day.

Ben grabbed her hand as the waitress escorted them to their seat. "You appear distracted."

"I'm really exhausted. I didn't sleep much last night," Alexis said as they were seated on the open patio area.

"Why is that?"

Alexis laughed in disbelief. "As if Japan wasn't crazy enough."

"Are you ready to order?" the waitress asked. She had ginger hair braided to one side and a dusting of freckles across her nose.

"I'll have poached eggs with a side of bacon, and fry jacks, please," Alexis said, fighting the urge to yawn.

Ben placed his order but then called the waitress back. "We'd like our order to go, and please add one of the breakfast specials."

The waitress left, and Ben turned back to Alexis. "Is there something you want to talk about?"

"Maybe later. I want to sleep a couple hours and then go over the stuff we found last night, think about some other theories swimming in my head. But there is one thing."

"Anything you want."

"I hate to ask."

"Ask. Please."

Alexis blushed at his willingness to please her. "Will you lie beside me?"

"Are you still having those dreams?"

"Yes, and I really don't want to have one when I lie down, especially since nothing makes sense right now. The last thing I need is a vivid dream to throw a wrench into the mix."

"Okay."

She looked at Ben thinking she was confusing him. "I would feel more relaxed if you're next to me."

Ben wrapped his hand around hers. "I said anything."

"Why the sudden change?"

"How do you mean?"

"Why did you change your mind about a relationship with me?"

"I promise to tell you everything, but I think we should talk about it once you've rested."

"Promise?"

"I promise."

The two waited for their order and then headed to the suite. Ben carried Alexis's bags as she held on to his arm. She couldn't wait to lie down.

The hallway was festooned with beautiful artwork, but for Alexis it barely registered. She could hardly keep her eyes open. She leaned against the wall with her eyes closed while Ben unlocked door.

"Do you feel okay, Alexis?"

"I'm so tired."

"Let me help you in."

After they entered the room, James came around the corner. "It's about time, I'm starving."

Ben set the bag from the restaurant on the dining table. The suite's kitchen, dining nook, and two of the bedrooms occupied the area near a large sliding glass door that accessed an open space with a small personal pool and exclusive lounging. Directly across from that area was the master bedroom. Ben led Alexis toward the master bedroom.

James picked up a map with red marks. "Hey, Alexis, why were you mapping out the Air Force bases?"

"I didn't." She yawned as she turned around to look at the paper in his hand.

James walked into the lounge area and handed her the page. "That's what it looks like."

She scanned the page. "What makes you think these represent military spots?"

"I'll show you." James pulled out his smart phone and began typing in a search. "These are the U.S. bases around the world."

Alexis compared the map she had made and the one James was showing her. They created the same paths along coastlines and through the same continents.

"These are just points of reference to something I'm working on with the crystal. I first thought it was a unique pattern, which now doesn't seem so unique when I see that. But since you mentioned that, I did notice a similar pattern with the UFO sightings from the other night." Alexis reached into the side of her bag and handed James another map with dots.

"You know I don't believe in coincidence," James said.

"Can we talk after I take a little nap? That way I can think straight and sort facts from conspiracy."

James was glancing from the two maps to his phone. "Yeah, sure, happy napping."

Ben navigated Alexis to a luxurious room of soft white cotton sheets and amber pendant lights. She slipped off her shoes and felt the coolness of the wood floors. A smell of citrus permeated the air.

"I'm going to shower off all this bug spray and dirt from last night before I lie down."

Ben pointed to the teak chaise sitting in the corner of the room. "I'll be right here waiting for you."

"Or you could join me." Suddenly Alexis didn't feel so tired.

Ben nearly tripped over the chaise. "What?"

"Why don't you help me shower?"

Over time, Ben had watched people go through the motions of love and has seen the elegant way people move their bodies together, but never had he wanted to know the feeling for himself—until now. But he had no idea what would happen if he touched Alexis. What if he was the one causing her body to shut down? For so many reasons, he couldn't chance losing her.

"I don't know, I'm not very good at ..."

"Showering?"

"Before that, can we talk? I want to tell you ..."

Alexis stopped him with a kiss. "There will be plenty of time to talk after."

CHAPTER SEVENTY-FIVE

THE MASTER OF ALL that is evil, the one whose heart is tiled with anger and vengeance, was staring at something he was never given the chance to experience. Ben had become disoriented when Alexis took his hand and brought him in closer to her as she undressed near the shower.

"I have never ... Alexis, I'm not sure we should."

"Shh." Alexis began to unbutton his shirt. "We're not going to do anything but take a shower. Besides, I remember when you didn't want to kiss me."

"That was different."

"How?"

Ben looked at Alexis through the steam rising in the bathroom and followed her into the large travertine-covered shower. Warm water sprayed from several directions, keeping their bodies wet.

Alexis had her back pressed against the cool travertine as she pulled Ben's body onto hers. "Relax, I promise not to hurt you."

Ben was losing all sense of direction and couldn't see anyone except the person in front of him. For that moment he was only able to feel the warmth of Alexis's bare skin against his, and nothing else mattered. The water was falling onto his face, and running over the top of Alexis's breasts. He denied his will and gave in to an unfamiliar desire as he wrapped his arms around Alexis and embraced her lips with his own. As his hands slid down to the small of her back, a new energy coursed through Alexis and found its way to Ben, triggering a flood of emotions he had lost long ago. Alexis's mind was in a state of euphoria as Ben kissed her neck while exploring the rest of her body with his hands. The warm water barely slipped between them and

Alexis could feel Ben lifting her from the floor, but she noticed that something was wrong.

Alexis slowly let him go and pulled away. "Ben, are you okay? You're trembling."

Ben didn't realize that what he was feeling inside had manifested outward, causing him to shiver. "Um, I think I'll wait for you out there."

He grabbed a towel from the top shelf of the wicker cabinet to wipe his face, and then he leaned back and kissed Alexis on the cheek. "Everything is fine."

Alexis was peering out around the fogged glass partition. "Will you still lie down with me after I finish showering?"

"Yes, I will go grab us some bottled water while you finish."

He could see her silhouette pressed up against the glass. Her beauty was something he didn't deserve but knew he couldn't be without. Ben took in a deep breath as he got dressed and let out an exhalation before he left the room. He was losing sight of things and needed to regain perspective. Ben needed to find Azure.

CHAPTER SEVENTY-SIX

AT THE CAHAL PECH temple site, Azure was scanning the room where he'd talked with Alexis earlier that morning. He found the symbol she had shown James, which resembled one of the markings on the crystal. Azure rubbed his hand over the surface, trying to understand what it all meant. Like his companions, he'd been given only pieces of the stories that told of the end of the existences he currently knew, but it was clear that Alexis was a key to finding answers.

"Its translation is *the fallen one*," Ben said. He had once again caught Azure by surprise.

"I know." Azure said. "I also know why you're here this time."

"Do you?"

"You're angry with me."

"Anger is only for petty things I can rise above. It's the matter of trust that I cannot avoid overseeing."

"My punishment is deserved, and I take it knowing I was trying to save us," Azure said. "I only went to her in hope of changing things."

Ben walked to the wall where other clay-colored symbols were painted near the etchings. "They were clever to scatter them."

"The symbols? Or the humans?"

"Both."

Ben closed his eyes and lowered his head as he placed his hand on the wall and felt the coolness of the stone.

"This is why it has taken us this long to find the crystal. We cannot take a chance. She must solve it. I can't allow distractions."

"How?"

"I need to see what I am unable to see with my own eyes."

"Master, how will you get Alexis Zen to move forward on the crystal?"

Ben looked up. His eyes were black, but they were filled with sadness instead of rage. "You were one of the few I trusted."

"You can still trust me."

"What assurance do I have?"

"I can get her to choose," Azure said.

"Do you not see how free will has destroyed these humans?" Ben motioned his hand between the two of them. "I won't have it destroying this. And I don't want this for her."

The air turned chill, and the wind picked up and whistled through the caverns. The moisture on the walls reflected stray bits of sunlight that filtered in.

"I must keep my followers within certain guidelines, and I can't accept excuses that would weaken my power. Those who act against the order of darkness, and no others, must be punished. Do you understand?"

"I understand," Azure said. "I deviated from the lines of obedience. I want you to know that I have a sense of what you are feeling."

"What I feel is not the same," Ben snapped.

"Last night, after everyone left the dolerite circle, something happened to me. I entered the center, and it felt strange. There was sorrow and pain, but not as though it were the humans."

"What do you mean?"

"I think I felt my own pain and sorrow. I don't remember what happiness feels like, but I want to, and Alexis Zen is our only chance at being free. I know you have felt something with her, and now you also desire freedom."

Ben couldn't deny his emotions and the unfamiliar feelings he was experiencing with Alexis, but this could not save Azure.

The wind rose up until it screamed through the halls of the temple. A glowing orb began to materialize, but it was different from any Azure had seen, and the cold was more intense than any he'd ever experienced. The light was brighter, with a pale blue glow outlining the edges of the opening. It grew to the height of Azure.

"Where are you sending me? This is not the outer realm."

Ben's eyes were back to a beautiful shade of golden-brown amber.

"Azure, I cannot excuse your actions, because it was not my will, and thus a punishment must take place. Yet I know your intentions were true to the nature of our eternity, and for this I will spare you torment, for now. This portal will lead you to the plane of spiritual darkness."

Azure could hear voices coming through the center of the circle. "I don't understand. Is this not where the human dead reside?"

"Yes, the ones we have control over. And if you are correct, then this is how they are able to enter Alexis's dreams, except they have access through the plane of spiritual light. Do not interact with Messengers, only guide her to solve the crystal as she sleeps."

Azure's relief at escaping the outermost darkness nearly brought tears. "Master, thank you."

"Don't thank me. All that pain and sorrow you spoke of feeling last night at the stone circle, this is where it came from, and it will be multiplied by the billions of lost souls wandering in that dimension. In there, you can't escape those feelings."

Azure knew then he probably wasn't coming back. "I will always serve you."

Azure stepped inside the orb. An instant later it was gone. Ben disappeared right before a tour group made its way in through the tree line.

Alexis had barely stepped out of the bathroom when Ben came back into the suite with two bottles of water. Her eyes were heavy with exhaustion, but she tried to hide behind her smile when she saw Ben.

"Come on." Ben motioned her to the bed and pulled down the sheets so she could climb in.

"What was it you wanted to talk about?"

"It can wait for now, you need to rest."

Alexis wore only a tiny white T-shirt and bikini-cut lace panties. She slipped beneath the covers, and Ben knelt beside her on the bed to kiss her forehead.

"Sweet dreams, my beautiful Alexis."

She was asleep before Ben could pull the blinds shut.

CHAPTER SEVENTY-SEVEN

ALEXIS TOOK IN the freshness of the air, which carried the scent of black orchids and red ginger across the room. She stretched out against the warmth of the sheets. Her eyes opened to an empty chair beside the bed.

Ben's voice came from behind her. "Did you think I wouldn't stay?"

"I wasn't sure." She found solace when her eyes met Ben's.

The pendant lights above her cast a soft golden light onto her cheek and down her neck. Ben leaned over and stroked the side of her face. "Did you sleep well?"

"Perfectly, but I should start the day." Alexis hurried out of bed and grabbed a longer pair of yoga pants and a bra.

Ben sat on the edge of the bed watching her. "No dreams?"

"Um."

"Alexis, are you in a hurry?"

"I really need to make a phone call."

"Okay, I can give you some privacy," Ben offered.

"Thanks, but some fresh air would be good, so I'll just walk outside the hotel."

"Let me walk you to the door."

"Okay."

Alexis and Ben walked to the main suite. James was asleep face down on the couch, wearing only his shorts. Alexis nudged the bottom of his feet.

"Rise and shine!"

He jumped up, practically falling off the couch. "That's not even funny, Alexis."

"Then why am I laughing?"

"Why do I have to get up?"

"We have work to do." She was sorting through the pile of things sitting on the table. "And there is not a lot of time to do it, so can you get over here?"

"Hey, I'm not going back out there. We can pick up your little devices in the morning." James headed over to the table.

"I wasn't planning on going over there until around 4 a.m., you big baby."

"Then what are we doing right now?"

Alexis pulled out her tablet and placed it on the table in front of him. "I'm going to go make a call. Will you start transferring the data from last night and email it to Jason in the tech department on base?"

"Yeah, but why are you not reviewing it?" James asked as she started for the door.

"He is much better at listening to white noise for hours and scanning dark screen footage."

"That would be boring."

"He owes me a favor. I fixed him up with a girl from my old high school." Alexis stopped before she made it to the door.

"You better hope it works out."

"They're married."

"Oh."

Alexis shut the door behind her, leaving Ben and James confused. Ben sat down at the far end of the table. He looked outside to the personal pool. The water reflected sunlight onto the wall of the master suite room, creating a shimmering piece of art.

"What's so scary about Cahal Pech?" Ben asked James.

James was reading the local newspaper while he waited for the data to download. "Everything."

Ben picked up the two maps, the one Alexis had sketched out on the hotel stationary in Hawaii and the one with ten red dots. He glanced at James. "Did she ever say why she made this map?"

"Kind of, but I was certain she was plotting the points of the Air Force bases around the world." James put down the newspaper. "What does it look like to you?"

Ben studied the dots, seeing the distinct path. "I don't have a clue. This is not really my thing."

"Military bases are reportedly common UFO hotspots, but I'm not sure why this map with red dots would follow those places."

"She hasn't finished translating the crystal. This map could change."

"That's true."

Alexis came through the door holding her cell phone to her ear. "What am I looking for specifically?"

She walked past Ben and James and proceeded into her suite.

"Who was she calling?" James asked Ben.

"She didn't say." Ben watched her through the floor-to-ceiling sliding glass door.

Alexis returned holding the black journal her grandmother had sent to her for her birthday. She grabbed her tablet and brought up the crystal inscriptions. The black notebook was turned to the last entry written by her grandmother.

"Okay, I'm looking at it," Alexis said into the phone.

Baba's voice wasn't loud enough for James to hear, but Ben was standing close enough to listen.

"Alexis, do you see anything similar between the pages and the crystal?" Baba asked.

"Yeah, they are both random and chaotic, and they don't make any sense."

"Alexis, I want you to go over each entry and then look at the crystal," Baba said.

"I don't know all the languages in this journal."

"I know you will find a way. Call me next time, but only when you are alone. I love you. Be safe."

"Why when I'm alone? Baba? Baba?" Alexis set her phone down next to her tablet and looked at the two men.

"Problems?" James asked.

"I think my grandmother hung up on me."

Alexis shrugged it off and continued to look at the journal pages.

"Why do you have those out?" Ben inquired about the journal and her tablet with the crystal pictures.

"It seems that they're somehow connected, but instead of answers I get coded replies from my grandmother."

"Maybe she doesn't know the answer," James suggested.

"Oh, she knows, but she told me nothing could be gained by her telling me the answers. I am so tired of not being told the full story."

"I can relate to that," James said under his breath.

"How about I help you?" Ben said.

"Thanks, but I don't want to bore you with all these ancient languages."

"I know a few languages from traveling all my life."

"Languages. I'm an idiot."

She flipped back to the beginning of the black journal, searching the pages.

Ben leaned in. "Languages? Care to elaborate?"

"I can't believe I didn't put it together before." Alexis was skimming over the pages of text and then looking at her smart tablet screen, which showed the crystal's inscriptions. She pointed to the image on her tablet. "Here are the languages or symbols that I know."

"Okay."

"And these are the journal entries that are in the same order sequence."

"It's the map key."

James perked up. "Wait. Did I miss something?"

Alexis pointed. "This symbol is found throughout the Maya architecture, and we found one on the wall when we were at Cahal

Pech. Its corresponding entry in the journal is written in K'iche, which is the Maya language spoken near Guatemala."

"I assumed the Mayans all spoke the same language," James said.

"Not all Americans speak perfect English."

"Point taken."

Alexis grabbed the map that was lying near Ben and penciled a red dot by Guatemala. "There are a few versions, but now that it's been mixed with Spanish over the years, not many are fluent in Mayan."

"Have you translated any of these journal entries?" Ben asked.

She flipped to a page that interested her. "No, but I did see this one on our flight to Hawaii, though it didn't click at the time. This is what some would call a Brythonic language."

"Great Britain? I'm impressed by your knowledge of this."

"Languages are a hobby."

Alexis found the inscription that corresponded to the journal entry, a series of dashes that created a simple pattern of two circles, one inside the other.

Alexis scratched the screen on her tablet. "What is that?"

Ben leaned in. "Is that another part of this, or is that just a smudge on the picture?"

"I'm not sure. I'll be right back."

Alexis went to her room. Ben could see she was comparing the tablet image to the actual crystal. It didn't take long before she came back.

"It's a part of the original, but I don't know how this marking ties to anything in Great Britain."

"What does the journal say?" Ben asked.

"Hold on, let me write this down, because I won't remember all of these words once I start spouting out the translation," Alexis reached over and grabbed a piece of printer paper from the side of the equipment bag.

"Okay. *The mouth of the rivers will lead them away.*" Alexis squinted as she tried to remember the language she learned the summer of her junior year, when she took some courses abroad.

"Each divided with wealth but all brought together by death. Stand inside the bluestone circle to open a hidden gate."

James sprang up out of his seat. "Did you say bluestone?"

"Yeah, I'm sure that's what this means," Alexis said. "Why?"

"Can I see the crystal inscription that's supposed to go with it?"

Alexis handed the tablet to James.

"I knew it," he said

"What is it, schoolboy?" Alexis asked.

James could barely contain himself. "Stonehenge."

"How can you be so certain?" Ben asked.

"Because I've seen this middle part of the marking on one of the stones, and bluestone is an old British term for all the twenty different dolerite-type rocks found at Stonehenge."

Alexis grinned. "Let me guess."

James grinned back. "Yes, it's also a known UFO hotspot."

"I figured as much," Alexis replied.

"I would bet that's the meaning of the two circles on that marking," James said.

"An aerial view." Alexis put a red dot by England.

Ben pointed to the map. "What made you decide to do this?"

"I had a hunch to map out these different locations, thinking I could figure out the ones I didn't know with areas nearby that didn't have red dots."

"It also lines up with the bases and UFOs," James said.

"This theory seems to be working a lot more easily than I thought it would, with it creating two paths across the world."

"Two paths?" Ben looked closer. "Can I see that?"

Alexis handed him the page with all the red dots.

"James, not everything is explained by the government's alien conspiracies."

James laughed. "Which implies that some things can be."

"The only thing explained by UFOs are UFOs," Alexis said. "And even if we saw one, the same questions remain—who are they and why are they here?"

"Didn't you mention there were other things similar to this map?" Ben asked.

Alexis pulled up the Internet on her tablet. "The eyewitness accounts from the other night, they kind of follow these same lines"

Alexis pointed out a handful of UFO sightings that matched up with the red dots on the map. Ben and James read over several of the eyewitness accounts and watched a few of the amateur videos.

Alexis had an idea. "James, you mentioned that there was a website that kept track of sightings."

"Yes, why?"

"Can you pull it up?"

James pulled up the website that served as the world's database for reports of unidentified objects found flying in the sky. The site noted that the lists were reported and verified by separate sources before being placed on the page for viewers. Alexis read over several and noticed a link for a map.

"Pull up the map," Alexis said.

"Do you want 2D or 3D?"

"2D, I want to see it flat."

On the screen, a world map displayed thousands of tiny orange dots representing reported UFO sightings. The dots were spread over the world, but there was a concentration along the path shown on the other two maps.

"Holy crap," Alexis said.

"What?"

"I've seen this before. Can you print that?"

"What have you seen before?" Ben asked.

She started flipping through the pages of the journal. "This path around the world."

"I thought you said there were two paths," James said.

"I did."

"But?"

That's why Baba had me learn this stuff. "There are still two, but somehow they come together to make one. I just have to find the connection."

Ben rubbed the top of her hand. "You don't have to do this alone."

"I appreciate that, but ..."

"What about the languages for the rest of these dots?" Ben continued.

"Probably need to go over them again, now that we know this journal is a piece to this crystal puzzle."

"Once this is figured out, then what?" James asked.

Alexis shrugged. "That's the one question no one will answer when I ask."

"Who could you have possibly asked?" James asked.

"Every childhood story my grandmother told was supposed to prepare me for this, or at least that's what she says. I have asked her what it all means, but she just responds with an allegory that creates more questions. And ..." Alexis paused.

"And what?" James asked.

Alexis looked at Ben and found support in his eyes. "Never mind. It's not important."

"Who else knows about the crystal?" James asked.

"Other than my grandmother, no one." She hesitated. "But recently I've been piecing a lot of this together through my dreams."

"Dreams? Who are you talking to in your sleep?"

"My subconscious creations are helping me work through the confusion. Kind of like talking to myself, but asleep." Alexis would rather sound eccentric than admit the truth about who she was talking to in her dreams.

Earlier, when Alexis had awakened, it became clear to her that her dreams were real and the crystal played an important role in answering her questions. There was nothing specific in her dreams, just a strong feeling that came over her. A feeling that she trusted.

James chuckled. "You know, Alexis, every time I think I have you pegged, you throw me for a loop with a new part of your personality."

"Is that a bad thing?" she asked.

"Not at all. I've enjoyed our trip together."

"Thank you, James, me too."

The day wore on into the soft darkness of dusk, and the three of them worked closely, going over all the entries they could translate, writing everything down on a yellow legal pad. Alexis numbered each journal entry according to its corresponding inscription to ensure it was kept in the original order.

James and Ben had been silently searching out the symbols, looking for familiar cave art or ancient structures. But one of the markings had James stumped.

"Hey, is there any way I could see the crystal?"

"Sure."

When Alexis began to get up, Ben took hold of her hand.

"You should be careful with that. We can't afford to have it break."

James pointed to the screen. "I just want to confirm these lines. I can't tell if there are four or five on this marking."

Ben let go of Alexis's hand, and she walked toward her suite. A blanket of stars was beginning to cover the night sky, and Ben watched, waiting for Alexis to return.

Alexis headed into her suite and opened her luggage. The crystal was secure inside the black velvet bag nestled inside the mess of clothing. She was about to pick it up when she heard a whisper.

"Alexis."

"Ben." She turned to find no one there.

"Alexis."

She could tell the voice was male, but couldn't get a sense of its direction.

"Who are you? Why can't I see you?"

"I am here to warn you."

The voice was becoming more clear, and Alexis began to feel a warmth come over her body.

"Warn me? About what?"

"The one who killed your aunt is close to you, and he will try to take your life as well."

She knew the man responsible for her aunt's death was also dead. But she remembered her vision on the balcony in Hawaii. The man in white spoke to her there, and later in her dream he told her of one who was the cause of all her suffering. Was this the same person?

"Tell me, who?"

"Come to the temple alone tonight, and I will show you."

"Tell me who you are."

Alexis felt a chill run across her arms and knew the voice was gone. She was left with another question lingering in her head. Who sought to harm her? She tried to think of people in her life that she considered close, and no one stood out suspiciously.

She needed to focus on the crystal. She would deal with the mysterious voice that night, in the temple. But she wouldn't go alone.

Alexis came back with the crystal. Both James and Ben's eyes were lit up, but James reached out to take it.

Alexis didn't smile as she put it in his hand. "If you break that, hell will be your penance."

"Interesting choice of words," Ben said.

James made a rough sketch on his notepad of the marking that wasn't clear on the tablet to make it easier to refer to as he searched several online libraries and databases for a match. The marking was a series of vertical lines curving at both ends, with two distinct parallel horizontal crescent lines that slashed through the others. James was finding it hard to describe it as he tried narrowing his search.

Alexis was working on finding the proper translation for the Mayan marking, which was the same one she'd found in the Cahal Pech temple.

"Why is there a red pencil mark on Rapa Nui?" Ben asked, pointing to the small triangular island far west of Chile.

"Because there is a twelve-meter-long panel at Ahu Ra'ai that has very distinct lines that look like the marking I found on the crystal." Alexis reached over and grabbed the smart tablet to show Ben the marking.

Ben examined it. "I've seen these types of lines on a petroglyph in Moab, Utah."

"Yes, but this is the one from Easter Island."

"How do you know for sure?"

"Because of the unique curvature of both vertical and these two parallel lines. I did a report on cave art in college."

James was hovering over the table, trying to see the marking. "Which marking did you say was from Easter Island?"

Alexis pointed. "This one, why?"

James picked up the crystal and turned it over. "I saw another one earlier that I thought was from Easter Island—here, this one."

Alexis studied it. "It does look like rongorongo style, but I don't know what this one means, either."

Ben touched Alexis on the hand, sending a jolt of energy through both of them. "What did the journal entries say about them?"

"I haven't gotten to those pages, because I don't know much Pascuan."

"I know someone at the base who might be able to help," James said. "But you won't like the who part."

Alexis thought for a moment, and then it dawned on her who James was talking about. One of the women in the lab had been working on sonar technology in the Pacific and was well versed in the language of Easter Island. Paige Anderson, one of the women on Level 6 who enjoyed needling Alexis.

"I won't ask Paige for help," Alexis said. "I'll find another way."

"Who are we talking about?" Ben asked.

"Some witch named Paige," Alexis said.

"I could ask her to translate it for me," James suggested. "She won't even know what or who it's for."

Alexis slid her chair back and stood up. "All right. I need a break anyway."

"I'll call her now," James said.

"Do you guys need anything?" she asked James and Ben.

James shook his head while he waited for Paige to answer the phone.

"Would you like some company?" Ben asked.

"I'd love your company," Alexis said.

CHAPTER SEVENTY-EIGHT

BEN TOOK HER HAND and led her outside to the patio and private pool. A warm breeze brushed Alexis's face and scattered the moon's reflection on the pool's gently rippling surface.

"Sit down with me," Ben said. He took off his sandals and sat down on the side of the pool.

Alexis sat close enough to wrap her left foot around his down in the cool water. They were silent for a moment, taking in the warm night air and listening to someone playing a guitar nearby. Alexis was happy.

Ben took her hand. "Alexis?"

She felt her heart begin to race. "Yes?"

"Do you believe our fates are predetermined?"

"You mean where we will end up when this life is over?"

"Yes."

"That would be pointless. Why even live if you already know you're doomed or vice versa. Why do you ask?"

Ben gazed at the infinite starscape above them. "I was curious. We've never talked about things of that nature."

Alexis lay her head on his shoulder. "What are your thoughts on predestination?"

Ben didn't know how to answer the question. "All I know at this very moment is where I want to be."

"And where is that?"

Ben pressed his forehead against hers. "I want to be with you, but ..."

Alexis kissed him before he could say anything else.

CHAPTER SEVENTY-NINE

HUNDREDS OF MILES NORTH of Belize, in a small suburb of Dayton, Ohio, sat Paige Anderson. She was at her cluttered desk diligently translating the two small pages of text James had emailed her moments ago. As she typed the email in response, seven men watched from the darkness. Cezar and six others watched her finish the last line of the second page.

Paige sat back in her chair. "Done."

Cezar leaned over and whispered something into her subconscious.

A few seconds later her eyes seemed to focus on her surroundings, and Paige scratched her head. *Why am I at my desk? And what did I just send?* She had no recollection of what she had just worked on.

I need a cigarette. Paige had never smoked nor desired it before that moment. Outside the house, Cezar and the other six watched.

"Smoking?" one of the men said to Cezar. "You could have had her do anything, but you picked smoking?"

Cezar continued to watch. "You are right, Desion, but she still has to drive somewhere to fulfill this urge, and I'm pretty sure that glass she has been refilling isn't sparkling grape juice."

"She could kill someone." Desion didn't sound pleased. "We are not to change their fate, it will shift the balance."

"All their fates have been decided, and they will all eventually die. Why does it matter if it is sooner rather than later?" Cezar asked.

"I know you could sense her lonely melancholy, why add more?" Desion replied. "You have risked her life for your own."

"I didn't make her so depressed that she drank all that wine. That was you."

"I didn't make her do anything, you know that. She chose this path of misery when she ..." Desion saw the point Cezar was making and became silent.

Inside the house, Paige was searching for her car keys. Cezar peered at her from outside. "We have never made them do anything they did not already want to do. But some are weaker than others, making them easier to push."

"We are not to cause harm, that power is reserved for those of pure blackness."

"Maybe that's who I want to be," Cezar said. He turned around and saw that he was alone.

CHAPTER EIGHTY

BEN AND ALEXIS WERE a few feet away from the pool, lying together on a plush outdoor sofa upholstered in vivid-red canvas. Three banana trees between the pool area and the suite screened them from view.

Alexis looked up at Ben. "What did you want to tell me earlier?"

"I want to be with you."

"But?" Alexis could already hear an excuse coming.

Ben ran his fingers through her hair. "It's just that you don't know me well enough to decide to be with me."

"We have plenty of time to get to know each other."

"Yes, but there are things you should know."

Alexis moved her body closer and gazed into his eyes. "Do you want to be with me?"

"Yes."

"Are you going to hurt me?"

"No, I don't plan to. I just want you to know ... more about my past." Ben wanted to be completely honest about who he truly was, but he knew it would be too much for Alexis right now.

"When we get back to Ohio you can tell me anything you want, but right now let's forget either of our pasts," Alexis said.

"Okay."

Alexis put her head on his shoulder. "Besides, you next to me has been the source of peace during all this."

Ben could feel her breath against his neck. "Speaking of that, you shouldn't have to do this alone. I know you had another dream."

Alexis wanted to share everything, but the tingling in her body was drawing her lips closer to Ben's. She took a chance by slowly putting her bottom lip to his and then waited to feel his lips come all the way to hers. His strong hands were soft as they brushed the back of her neck, pulling her closer. She brought her upper body up off the cushion and straddled Ben's lap. Alexis stopped kissing him when she began to feel dizzy.

Ben got up. "Alexis?"

She opened her eyes to see the stars above were streaks of light and the sound of the guitar was like a muffled tuba.

"Concentrate on my voice and stay with me," Ben said.

"I'm fine, I need complex carbs, that's all."

Ben let out a breath. "Sorry, I thought ... never mind. I will get the menu and have them bring us some food."

James was yelling out to Alexis from the dining area. "Paige must have worked on it right away. I'll email a copy to you."

"Okay, I'll check it later."

"Where do you want this?" James was standing in the door looking down at his hand. "I didn't send her ... oh, crap, no!"

At that instant Ben, who was looking back at Alexis, collided with James, who was holding the quartz crystal. Alexis let out a gasp when she saw it rotate into the air. Alexis's heart raced as she pictured it shattering into a million pieces on the cement patio. James tried to grab it as the crystal spiraled down, but he wasn't close enough. Ben scrambled to get up after being knocked back by James. Alexis dove off the chaise lounge scraping her knees on the hard ground and realizing she was still inches from catching it. Alexis squeezed her eyes shut, then put her head down, awaiting the dreaded sound of the quartz hitting the ground and breaking into unrecognizable pieces. But the sound wasn't what she expected.

Alexis heard a high-pitched echoing in her head as the crystal pinged. It pinged only once. There was no crashing or shattering. She didn't hear anything but ringing as the ping echoed around her. Alexis began to open her eyes when she didn't hear Ben's voice.

Suspended two feet off the ground, the crystal was emitting a pale glow. Alexis got up and moved closer to see how it was even possible. The light was like a translucent flame as it radiated from a bright orange coming from within the crystal.

"James, how is this possible?"

When there was no response, Alexis looked around for James and Ben. The light was extremely bright and blocked her view, so she moved around and saw James completely still and motionless. She didn't see Ben anywhere. Alexis examined James and checked everything in the room, trying to figure out what was happening. Nothing was moving. There was no wind and no sound. Only Alexis.

She knelt down to get a better perspective and reached her hand out to feel the light. The rays changed to a translucent cerulean as they shot through her fingers, casting beautiful lines of brightness onto her cheeks. Alexis took in a deep breath before she took the crystal from where it was suspended.

A strong gust of wind came in from the left and swept across the patio, putting everything back into motion. James was standing right where he'd been when everything was frozen in time. But now Ben appeared to be standing to her right. Alexis didn't understand why she hadn't seen him there before. She looked at the crystal in her hand. It was undamaged but no longer glowing.

Ben was concerned. During the period when Alexis was walking in the suspension of time, he'd been unable to see her or feel her. When the crystal pinged, Ben was blinded and could only see darkness and feel eternal despair. For those seconds, it wasn't the darkness that frightened him nor overwhelming dread that saddened him—it was the thought of not seeing Alexis.

Ben put his arms around her. "Alexis, are you all right?"

"Tell me you saw that," she whispered.

The wind continued to pick up, and a strange cloud cover moved overhead, blotting out the stars. For the first time, Ben was unsure of what might happen next, but he knew he needed to get Alexis away from where they stood.

Ben took her hand. "It looks like we're going to get that tropical storm from the west coast. We should take cover."

James shouted his agreement over the howling winds tearing through the palm trees.

Alexis was silent. She was beginning to put the pieces together. Ben brought her into the main suite and sat her on the couch. Once they were inside, they watched the changing weather through the large sliding glass door. Right before Ben pulled the blinds across it, Alexis noticed ice forming around its edges.

"This storm is coming out of nowhere," James said. He was standing far away from the glass.

"I don't think it's a storm," Alexis said softly while she looked at the crystal.

"What else could it be?" James asked.

She turned to him. "Where have you heard that humming before?"

He shook his head and shrugged. "No idea."

Alexis moved to where he was and showed him the crystal in her hand. "Do you remember where this was the day you found it?"

"Yeah, it was on the floor of your lab."

"Do you remember what else happened that day?"

James looked stricken. "The orb. You think that's what's happening out there?"

"Makes perfect sense. Something that powerful needs energy. "

"What are you guys talking about?" Ben asked.

"Heat is that energy, and the magnetic field is being altered."

Alexis didn't have time to explain everything to Ben, so she answered James's question first. "I know how the orb was created." She held up the crystal. "This created a frequency and a vibration."

"How can you be so sure, that could have been ..."

"Look outside, James. Look at the ice forming on the windows. These are the similarities I showed you in those security camera videos. That was no CAS freezer. That guy was sucked into one of these."

James started toward the patio.

Ben stood in front of Alexis. "I don't think we should go out there. That storm sounds intense."

James didn't listen. He walked past Ben, and Alexis followed behind him. Ben put his arms around her. "Please don't go out there."

"I want to see this."

James opened the sliding glass door to find a large oscillating ball of blue electricity with a black orb center only a few feet from him. Frigid air swept into the room and rushed across Alexis's face. Ben pulled her behind him. She could see from the distance that this orb was bigger than the one they'd found in her lab.

"It's huge," Alexis murmured, not believing what she was seeing.

The orb stretched from the ground to above the roof of the suite, and the diameter of the dark center opening was almost four feet.

Alexis noticed James clenching the panels of glass door trying to view the orb. "James what's happening?"

"It's like a vacuum!" Fear came through his voice, and Alexis saw the dismay in his eyes as he slipped off the threshold.

"Get away from the door," Alexis shouted. She tried to pull away from Ben, but he pulled her back.

"Alexis, stay here."

"James!" Alexis could see him struggling to stay in the doorway.

The arctic air painted the walls with crystals of ice, and Alexis could see her breath as she tried to move toward James to help him.

James looked at her, fear written on his face. "Alexis, stay back."

Alexis turned to Ben, tears streaming down her cheeks. "Please, we have to help him."

"I can't lose you," Ben said. He gathered her in his arms and held her tight, feeling her sadness. He knew the greater loss if James was sucked into the orb. "Stay here, Alexis!"

Ben positioned Alexis behind him and cautiously made his way to James. He had no control over this portal and wasn't sure where it led. James was barely able to hold on to the doorframe with one hand as the orb opening moved closer. It drew James's legs into the center. The ice formations began to move across the window to his fingers, and the excruciating cold was no longer bearable. The doorframe slipped from his grasp.

Ben caught James's forearm and braced himself against the interior wall, trying to pull him in. The force of the portal was so powerful that Ben was only stopping him from going any further, but he couldn't bring him back inside. Ben could barely hold on and knew the portal wouldn't close until someone was taken to the other side, or the one who controlled it commanded it to close. Ben shut his eyes to channel all of his power and pulled with all his strength. There came a scream right before Ben pulled one last time.

"No!" James cried out, and Ben felt his body release from the vacuum of the portal.

Ben opened his eyes. He saw James sprawled across his legs and let out a sigh of relief. The portal was gone, and the air was warming up. The ice crystals disappeared from the window, and the humming sound ebbed away. But there was a sense of sorrow nearby. James was alive and breathing, so why was he so sad?

Ben looked behind him where he had left Alexis standing and then back at James with a darkness forming in his eyes. "Where is Alexis?"

James looked up with bloodshot eyes and tears streaming. "She's gone. She tried to pull me inside."

Ben couldn't move. He realized the scream he had heard was Alexis's. James kept repeating she was gone. And Ben disappeared.

CHAPTER EIGHTY-ONE

ATOP A BEAUTIFUL GREEN hillside that overlooked the city, several family members, friends, and coworkers gathered together to show their love and support one another after a terrible loss. Eyes welled over with tears, and hearts were filled with sorrow, but understanding eluded their minds.

James stood in the back among many others, trying to hide his pain. He surveyed the crowd of people dressed in black, searching for Ben, but didn't find him. James felt guilty over the death of Alexis and could only imagine what Ben was going through.

A faint recording of "I Need Thee Every Hour" finished playing, and a member of the local church branch stepped up to the front to welcome everyone to the service.

"Today we come in mourning for the loss of someone taken from us too soon, but we find peace knowing she is in the care of our Father in Heaven. Alexis's grandmother requested that we read something written several years ago by Alexis." The man unfolded a sheet of paper and began to read.

Throughout our lives we will search for peace that calms the world around us.

We will search for answers to things we are incapable of understanding.

Our hopes of fruition will strengthen our faith in all things, but it's not until death that we realize that only the peace from within our own hearts will calm the world around us.

Knowing that the answers will not lead any closer to understanding, but the understanding of what we already know will guide us to a great state of mind.

From the beginning, man has always needed answers, and yet I end this no closer than that day. But my faith is stronger in all that is true, and my heart is full of all that is right.

There was silence as the man folded the paper and placed it in the inside pocket of his suit jacket. He took off his glasses and wiped his eyes.

"Alexis knew early in life to find her peace with God and seek out the goodness in all things. The family has asked that we come to this same peace and find strength with each other to get through this difficult time."

Everyone paid their respects to Alexis's parents and grandparents before they left the cemetery. James was asked to stay behind, so he waited by the black granite headstone with angel wings carved above Alexis's name. The headstone had a large arrangement of daisies beneath the words,

Alexis Faith Zen

Beloved Daughter Whose Path Has Continued On Through Into The Light

James stared at the words and couldn't stop thinking about how Alexis died by saving him. He hoped that she had truly found the light.

"James."

He turned to see a small elderly woman standing by herself. "Yes ma'am."

"I know that Alexis didn't die skydiving over the ocean," Baba said calmly. "She hated to fly, but the how is not important. Please tell me she took the crystal and journal with her."

"I'm not sure what you mean."

"They weren't with her belongings, and since you never found her body, I thought maybe she had them with her."

James tried to recall everything that happened. "I don't know where they are. I am so sorry."

"Never mind. I will ask him." Baba gestured toward the man standing in a military uniform next to a black SUV.

James put his arm over her shoulder. "Mrs. Prollofsky, I will find out what happened to those things. Please, you have been through a lot, you should be with your family."

"Thank you for your kindness. Alexis always spoke nicely of you, and I know you cared for her." Baba headed in the opposite direction and left with the rest of Alexis's family.

James pivoted in the direction of his car, but stopped when he saw someone in a black suit lingering at the bottom of the hill by the tree line. He walked down the hill toward the tall maple trees. The man didn't budge or acknowledge James.

"Why didn't you come up there to pay your respects?" James asked.

"She isn't there, so why pay respects to a piece of rock?" Ben's eyes were dark with the loss of Alexis, but hidden by his sunglasses.

"Ben, she is gone. You saw that thing. We have no idea where it came from or even how to recreate it." A tear rolled down his cheek. "I should have let go. She'd still be here."

"Yes, you should have," Ben said.

"I have lived with that thought every second since it happened," James said fiercely. He started to walk to his car when he remembered something. He tossed a cream-colored envelope to Ben. "Someone wanted me to give this to you when you showed up."

The wax seal on the back was embossed with the same insignia on Ben's business cards, and the front was addressed to *Benjamin Asael*.

"James, who gave this to you?" Ben asked.

"I didn't get to see the woman's face. She was gone by the time I turned around. Who knew you would be here?"

Ben broke the seal and pulled out a rectangular slip of paper. He read the words over and over again.

James turned back. "You know what, Ben ..."

Ben was gone. James looked around, but Ben was nowhere to be found. James was about to leave again when he saw the slip of paper and envelope lying on the ground. He picked the paper up and read it.

Death can only be taken through a door that is opened by one key.

Exhausted by what your eyes may see and torn by the fear living in your heart.

Vibrance radiates through the crystal gate where only the angels can stay.

In the beginning, thirteen pieces did a tree bear, but the one below will set her free.

Love can only be conquered through sacrificing everything.

With love,

Lilith

James smiled as he reached into his pocket to grab his cell phone. He dialed a number and waited for someone to answer. Right as he slipped the paper into his pocket and began walking up the hill to his car, someone answered on the other end. But they only listened as James spoke.

"Hey, it's me. I was right about there being twelve other crystals, and I think I know how we can find the missing ones."

EPILOGUE

ALEXIS LAY HELPLESSLY on the ground with her eyes tightly closed. She didn't want to see what death had brought her, and she feared to see where the blackness had taken her through. Nevertheless, Alexis couldn't stop her ears from listening to the sounds.

Where am I?

It sounded like water trickling across rocks, and grass bending in front of her—but how was that possible?

Are those voices?

"Alexis, will you come with us?" A calming whisper came into her mind, and Alexis didn't want to open her eyes to see the gates of Heaven or Hell, so she stayed quiet and still.

"Alexis, you can open your eyes." It was a different voice, one that sounded like a bass drum vibrating deep inside her.

"I wasn't ready to die. I didn't want to leave. I want to go back." Alexis was sobbing.

"You are not dead, sweet child," the woman said.

"What?"

Alexis slowly opened her eyes and peered through her arms as she lay on the ground. She was in a patch of flowing jade grass surrounded by tall auburn trees and lavender clematis that stretched up toward a sapphire sky filled with clouds. It was like a painting of new colors sparkling across an amazing canvas. Alexis got up off the ground to see the two she had been speaking with and found she was giving audience to several people dressed in white.

"Please explain how I am not dead?" Alexis asked the woman standing closest to her.

"It would be better if we showed you." The woman offered a hand to Alexis to guide her along the way.

Alexis walked with the group of twelve men and women through the forest, taking in wonderfully amazing hues. The sounds were like a perfectly tuned symphony, and the breeze was soft as it brushed across her body. She didn't feel like she was dead, but then she had nothing to compare it to. The stone path led them to a cottage that sat along a glistening creek.

Alexis turned to the woman beside her. "Where is this?"

"As I said, it would be better to show you." The woman, who was beautiful, looked to be in her twenties but carried herself with the grace and wisdom of someone much older.

The cottage didn't seem like much from the outside. It was small, with only three windows across the front. When Alexis walked inside, everything changed. It was a vast open space with windowless white walls and marble floors outlined with an elaborate molding. In the center of the room was a large antique table with no chairs. A crystal chandelier hung in the center of the room casting purple and green prisms onto the table. Alexis moved closer to the table and saw several maps spread out on it.

One of the men standing directly behind Alexis asked, "What do see?"

"A bunch of random maps," Alexis said.

"Look closer," he said.

Alexis gazed at the pages before her on the table. At first, they appeared to be maps of the world, but she realized that the geography was all wrong on most of them. All but one looked like nothing she had ever seen. Alexis scrutinized them, trying to make sense of why the other maps didn't look like the world she knew. Something caught her attention. It was the writing. Alexis had seen it before.

"What language is this?"

"This is the tongue of the first," the man with the deep voice said.

Alexis looked down at her hand, which was still holding tight to the crystal. Her memory was foggy, but each map had the same strange writing that matched something she remembered, one of the inscriptions on the crystal—the first inscription—and the first journal entry.

"What are these maps of?" Alexis asked while she continued to examine the pages. She pulled a page from the mix. "Hold on, why do you have this here? It's not a map."

"Which question would you like answered?" asked a tall man standing off in the distance.

Alexis thought about it and said, "Let's start with where I am."

A hum of whispering arose from the others. She glanced around to see that the number of people in white had more than tripled.

"You are in the realm of the Messenger of the Light, or Angels, as you on the other side call us." The man stepped closer to the table. "And that is a map."

"What kind of map? I have seen this before."

He pointed to one of the nine circular areas on the page Alexis was holding. "You are here, right now."

"How did I get here?" Her voice was trembling.

The man pointed to her hand.

"The crystal?"

"You passed through one of the crystal gates."

Alexis was visibly shaking with the overwhelming thought of where she stood, and she had no reason to question what the man had told her. She remembered what happened right before the orb appeared.

"Don't worry, you have plenty of time to ask us whatever you would like to know," said the woman who had helped Alexis through the forest earlier.

"Plenty of time? How long do I have to stay here?" Alexis asked. Everyone turned to the man across the table from Alexis.

"I'm sorry, but you are here until he saves you," the man said.

"He who?" There was a long pause, and Alexis could feel everyone looking at her.

"He is the one who is to blame for so much pain and despair in your life, and the one who has ensured the taste of pain and suffering to all others."

"That could be any man," Alexis pointed out.

The soft-spoken woman put her hand on Alexis's shoulder and spoke in a firm tone. "This one has specifically sought to destroy you."

Alexis turned and looked at her. "Who?"

"I'm sorry," the man said. "But that question we are not allowed to answer."

"Why would he want to save me if he has only wanted to destroy me?" Alexis asked.

"We wondered about that as well—until now."

"How can he save me if no one knows I'm here?"

The man disappeared into the white walls as did everyone around her, leaving her alone with a whole new emptiness.

Alexis Zen's Map

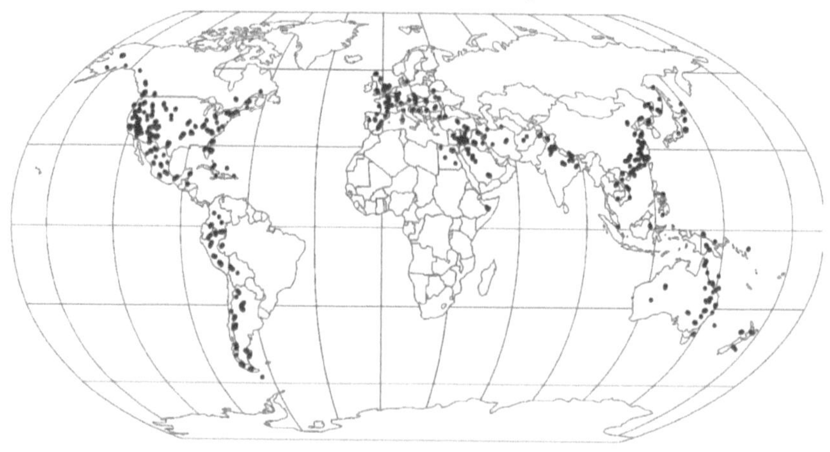

U.S. Military Bases

Areas of UFO Sightings

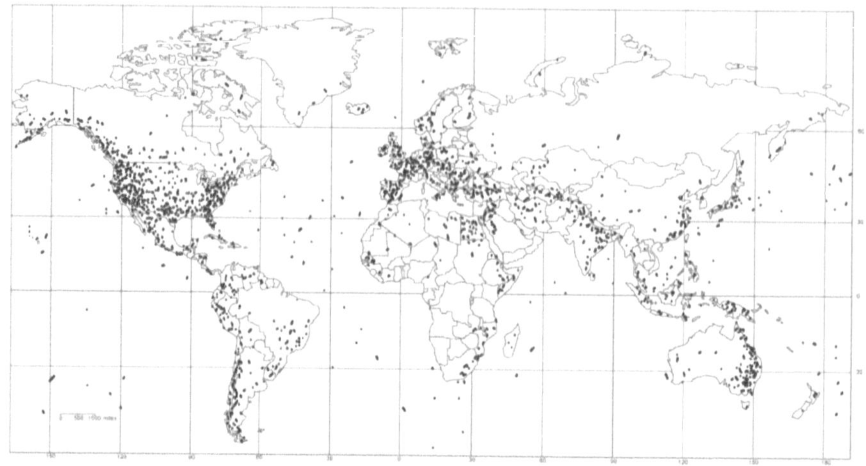

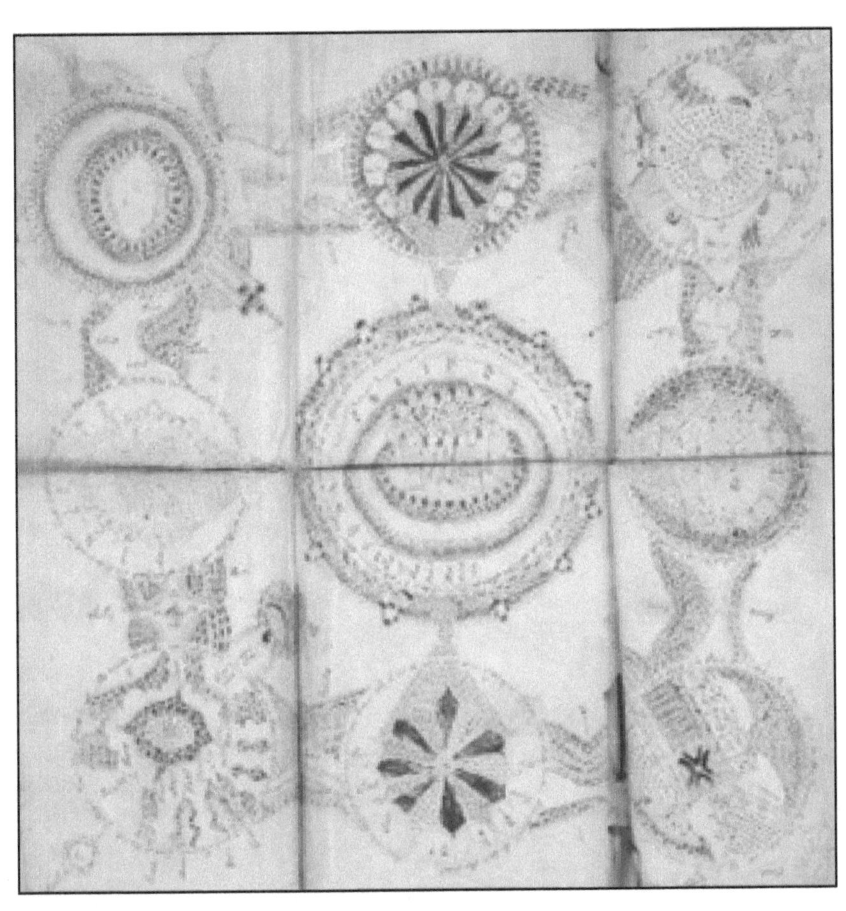

www.ingramcontent.com/pod-product-compliance
Lightning Source LLC
Chambersburg PA
CBHW030421310726
48979CB00009B/1558/J

9781936307340